Books
shed by Ballantine Books
yright © 1990 by Loren D. Estleman and Martin H.
enberg

rights reserved under International and Pan-American
yright Conventions. Published in the United States by
antine Books, a division of Random House, Inc., New
k, and simultaneously in Canada by Random House of
ada Limited, Toronto.

rary of Congress Catalog Card Number 90-90296

BN 0-8041-0555-3

anufactured in the United States of America

rst Edition: November 1990

Step into the world of shadows and secrets, perps and cops, wiseguys and gumshoes, with the top writers of the genre!

# P.I. FILES

Fourteen criminal cases together for the first time!

D1115715

# P.I. FILES

Edited by
Loren D. Estle1
and
Martin H. Green

IVY BOOKS • NEW YORK

# CONTENTS

# ACKNOWLEDGMENTS

"Fedoras and Flourishes: The State of the Private-Eye Art" by Loren D. Estleman—Copyright © 1990 by Loren D. Estleman.

"By the Dawn's Early Light" by Lawrence Block—Copyright © 1984 by Lawrence Block. Reprinted by permission of the author.

"On the Prod" by L.J. Washburn—Copyright © 1987 by L.J. Washburn. Reprinted by permission of the author.

"Death of an Iron Maiden" by Wayne D. Dundee—Copyright © 1985 by HB Enterprises. Reprinted by permission of the author.

"Skin Deep" by Sara Paretsky—Copyright © 1987 by Sara Paretsky. Reprinted by permission of the author.

"Sherlocks" by Al Sarrantonio—Copyright © 1982 by Al Sarrantonio. Reprinted by permission of the author.

"The Crooked Way" by Loren D. Estleman—Copyright © 1988 by Loren D. Estleman. Reprinted by permission of the author.

"She Didn't Come Home" by Sue Grafton—Copyright © 1986 by Sue Grafton. Reprinted by permission of the author.

"Turn Away" by Edward Gorman—Copyright © 1987 by Edward Gorman. Reprinted by permission of the author.

"A Shot in the Arm" by Richard Deming—Copyright © 1948 by Richard Deming. Reprinted by permission of the agents for the author's Estate, the Scott Meredith Literary Agency, Inc., 845 Third Avenue, New York, NY 10022.

"Eighty Million Dead" by Michael Collins—Copyright © 1984 by Michael Collins. Reprinted by permission of the author.

"The Heat is Killing Me!" by Fletcher Flora—Copyright © 1953 by Fletcher Flora. Reprinted by permission of the agents for the author's Estate, the Scott Meredith Literary Agency, Inc., 845 Third Avenue, New York, NY 10022.

"Ride the Lightning" by John Lutz—Copyright © 1984 by Davis Publications, Inc. Reprinted by permission of the author.

"Down this Mean Street" by Robert Twohy—Copyright © 1980 by Davis Publications, Inc. Reprinted by permission of the author.

"The Forever Trip" by Rob Kantner—Copyright © 1985 by Davis Publications, Inc. Reprinted by permission of the author.

# Loren D. Estleman

# FEDORAS AND FLOURISHES: THE STATE OF THE PRIVATE-EYE ART

IT'S BEEN SAID THAT IN TWO HUNDRED YEARS, AMERICAN letters have produced only two authentically homegrown literary types: the cowboy and the hard-boiled private eye. How fitting, then, that this anthology should include both Lucas Hallam, L. J. Washburn's gunslinger-turned-private-eye in the "new" West of early Hollywood, and Matt Scudder, Lawrence Block's quintessential big-city gumshoe of post-Prohibition America. The stories featuring these characters, along with the twelve others that comprise this volume, represent the best of the new breed and the old, from the unjustly neglected Richard Deming and Fletcher Flora to Sue Grafton and Sara Paretsky, women currently engaged in revolutionizing an area of writing once dominated by men.

Like all healthy forms, the private-eye story is a genre in flux. Thanks to certain literary refinements contributed by the legendary Raymond Chandler, Ross Macdonald, and John D. MacDonald, as well as quantum leaps forward in social consciousness as exemplified herein by Michael Collins (the amorality of the assassin), Rob Kantner and Ed Gorman (the nightmare of lingering death by ordinary causes), and Paretsky ("the subcutaneous racism of wealth"—the author's words, commenting on "Skin Deep"), the very term "hard-boiled" has become an anachronism. The quick fists and impertinent attitude of old have given way to a new sensitivity and a controlled rage against cosmic injustices light-years removed from the gangsters and corrupt cops of the pulps.

1

And yet the pulp tradition survives. Unadulterated in the brittle period narratives of Flora's Danny Clive and Deming's Manville Moon (who, like Collins' Dan Fortune, is no less a hero for the loss of a limb), and celebrated in Wayne D. Dundee's "Death of an Iron Maiden," the intrinsically American values of the lone rebel are the constant that sets the genre apart.

(Ironic humor, too, is alive and thriving. Check out Robert Twohy's "Down This Mean Street" and its unique setting.)

If we accept Washburn's Hallam as the dawn of the private eye, then it's appropriate we include the twilight. "Sherlocks" presents Al Sarrantonio's Phil Matheson in a John Henry–like contest with a detecting machine in a future that seems much closer now than it did when the story first appeared in the now-defunct *Spiderweb* magazine eight years ago.

The detectives' names ring like the roll at an American Round Table: Ben Perkins. Kinsey Millhone. Amos Walker. Joe Hannibal. Dan Fortune. Flog O'Flanahan. Manville Moon. Danny Clive. Matt Scudder. Parnell. Lucas Hallam. Phil Matheson. Alo Nudger. Could these monickers have originated anywhere but on the frontier? (V.I. Warshawski is an exception; yet it would be at home on the back of a Chicago Bear's jersey, notwithstanding the undisputed femaleness of the name's owner.)

But enough of this regionalism. These stories speak in the universal language of adventure and require neither illustration nor exposition. They are the state of the private-eye art, and the best news is that most of these authors are still performing.

# Lawrence Block

# BY THE DAWN'S EARLY LIGHT

A LL THIS HAPPENED A LONG TIME AGO.

Abe Beame was living in Gracie Mansion, though even he seemed to have trouble believing he was really the mayor of the city of New York. Ali was in his prime, and the Knicks still had a year or so left in Bradley and DeBusschere. I was still drinking in those days, of course, and at the time it seemed to be doing more for me than it was doing to me.

I had already left my wife and kids, my home in Syosset and the N.Y.P.D. I was living in the hotel on West 57th Street where I still live, and I was doing most of my drinking around the corner in Jimmy Armstrong's saloon. Billie was the nighttime bartender. A Filipino youth named Dennis was behind the stick most days.

And Tommy Tillary was one of the regulars.

He was big, probably six-two, full in the chest, big in the belly too. He rarely showed up in a suit but always wore a jacket and tie, usually a navy or Burgundy blazer with gray flannel slacks or white duck pants in warmer weather. He had a loud voice that boomed from his barrel chest and a big, clean-shaven face that was innocent around the pouting mouth and knowing around the eyes. He was somewhere in his late forties and he drank a lot of top-shelf Scotch. Chivas, as I remember it, but it could have been Johnnie Black. Whatever it was, his face was beginning to show it, with patches of permanent flush at the cheekbones and a tracery of broken capillaries across the bridge of the nose.

We were saloon friends. We didn't speak every time we ran into

3

each other, but at the least we always acknowledged each other with a nod or a wave. He told a lot of dialect jokes and told them reasonably well, and I laughed at my share of them. Sometimes I was in a mood to reminisce about my days on the force, and when my stories were funny, his laugh was as loud as anyone's.

Sometimes he showed up alone, sometimes with male friends. About a third of the time he was in the company of a short and curvy blonde named Carolyn. "Carolyn from the Caro-line" was the way he occasionally introduced her, and she did have a faint Southern accent that became more pronounced as the drink got to her.

Then one morning I picked up the *Daily News* and read that burglars had broken into a house on Colonial Road, in the Bay Ridge section of Brooklyn. They had stabbed to death the only occupant present, one Margaret Tillary. Her husband, Thomas J. Tillary, a salesman, was not at home at the time.

I hadn't known Tommy was a salesman or that he'd had a wife. He did wear a wide yellow-gold band on the appropriate finger, and it was clear that he wasn't married to Carolyn from the Caroline, and it now looked as though he was a widower. I felt vaguely sorry for him, vaguely sorry for the wife I'd never even known of, but that was the extent of it. I drank enough back then to avoid feeling any emotion very strongly.

And then, two or three nights later, I walked into Armstrong's and there was Carolyn. She didn't appear to be waiting for him or anyone else, nor did she look as though she'd just breezed in a few minutes ago. She had a stool by herself at the bar and she was drinking something dark from a lowball glass.

I took a seat a few stools down from her. I ordered two double shots of bourbon, drank one, and poured the other into the black coffee Billie brought me. I was sipping the coffee when a voice with a Piedmont softness said, "I forget your name."

I looked up.

"I believe we were introduced," she said, "but I don't recall your name."

"It's Matt," I said, "and you're right, Tommy introduced us. You're Carolyn."

"Carolyn Cheatham. Have you seen him?"

"Tommy? Not since it happened."

"Neither have I. Were you-all at the funeral?"

"No. When was it?"

"This afternoon. Neither was I. There. Whyn't you come sit next to me so's I don't have to shout. Please?"

She was drinking a sweet almond liqueur that she took on the rocks. It tastes like dessert, but it's as strong as whiskey.

"He told me not to come," she said. "To the funeral. He said it was a matter of respect for the dead." She picked up her glass and stared into it. I've never known what people hope to see there, though it's a gesture I've performed often enough myself.

"Respect," she said. "What's he care about respect? I would have just been part of the office crowd; we both work at Tannahill; far as anyone there knows, we're just friends. And all we ever were is friends, you know."

"Whatever you say."

"Oh, *shit*," she said. "I don't mean I wasn't fucking him, for the Lord's sake. I mean it was just laughs and good times. He was married and he went home to Momma every night and that was jes' fine, because who in her right mind'd want Tommy Tillary around by the dawn's early light? Christ in the foothills, did I spill this or drink it?"

We agreed she was drinking them a little too fast. It was this fancy New York sweet-drink shit, she maintained, not like the bourbon she'd grown up on. You knew where you stood with bourbon.

I told her I was a bourbon drinker myself, and it pleased her to learn this. Alliances have been forged on thinner bonds than that, and ours served to propel us out of Armstrong's, with a stop down the block for a fifth of Maker's Mark—her choice—and a four-block walk to her apartment. There were exposed brick walls, I remember, and candles stuck in straw-wrapped bottles, and several travel posters from Sabena, the Belgian airline.

We did what grownups do when they find themselves alone together. We drank our fair share of the Maker's Mark and went to bed. She made a lot of enthusiastic noises and more than a few skillful moves, and afterward she cried some.

A little later, she dropped off to sleep. I was tired myself, but I put on my clothes and sent myself home. Because who in her right mind'd want Matt Scudder around by the dawn's early light?

Over the next couple of days, I wondered every time I entered Armstrong's if I'd run into her, and each time I was more relieved than disappointed when I didn't. I didn't encounter Tommy, either, and that too was a relief and in no sense disappointing.

Then one morning I picked up the *News* and read that they'd arrested a pair of young Hispanics from Sunset Park for the Tillary burglary and homicide. The paper ran the usual photo—two skinny kids, their hair unruly, one of them trying to hide his face from the camera, the other smirking defiantly, and each of them handcuffed to a broad-shouldered, grim-faced Irishman in a suit. You didn't need the careful caption to tell the good guys from the bad guys.

Sometime in the middle of the afternoon I went over to Armstrong's for a hamburger and drank a beer with it. The phone behind the bar rang, and Dennis put down the glass he was wiping and answered it. "He was here a minute ago," he said. "I'll see if he stepped out." He covered the mouthpiece with his hand and looked quizzically at me. "Are you still here?" he asked. "Or did you slip away while my attention was diverted?"

"Who wants to know?"

"Tommy Tillary."

You never know what a woman will decide to tell a man or how a man will react to it. I didn't want to find out, but I was better off learning over the phone than face to face. I nodded and took the phone from Dennis.

I said, "Matt Scudder, Tommy. I was sorry to hear about your wife."

"Thanks, Matt. Jesus, it feels like it happened a year ago. It was what, a week?"

"At least they got the bastards."

There was a pause. Then he said, "Jesus. You haven't seen a paper, huh?"

"That's where I read about it. Two Spanish kids."

"You didn't happen to see this afternoon's *Post*."

"No. Why, what happened? They turn out to be clean?"

"The two spics? Clean? Shit, they're about as clean as the men's room in the Times Square subway station. The cops hit their place and found stuff from my house everywhere they looked. Jewelry they had descriptions of, a stereo that I gave them the serial number, everything. Monogrammed shit. I mean, that's how clean they were, for Christ's sake."

"So?"

"They admitted the burglary but not the murder."

"That's common, Tommy."

"Lemme finish, huh? They admitted the burglary, but according to them it was a put-up job. According to them, I hired them to hit my place. They could keep whatever they got and I'd have everything out and arranged for them, and in return I got to clean up on the insurance by overreporting the loss.''

"What did the loss amount to?"

"Shit, *I* don't know. There were twice as many things turned up in their apartment as I ever listed when I made out a report. There's things I missed a few days after I filed the report and others I didn't know were gone until the cops found them. You don't notice everything right away, at least I didn't, and on top of it, how could I think straight with Peg dead? You know?''

"It hardly sounds like an insurance setup."

"No, of course it wasn't. How the hell could it be? All I had was a standard home-owner's policy. It covered maybe a third of what I lost. According to them, the place was empty when they hit it. Peg was out.''

"And?"

"And I set them up. They hit the place, they carted everything away, and I came home with Peg and stabbed her six, eight times, whatever it was, and left her there so it'd look like it happened in a burglary.''

"How could the burglars testify that you stabbed your wife?"

"They couldn't. All they said was they didn't and she wasn't home when they were there, and that I hired them to do the burglary. The cops pieced the rest together.''

"What did they do, take you downtown?"

"No. They came over to the house, it was early, I don't know what time. It was the first I knew that the spics were arrested, let alone that they were trying to do a job on me. They just wanted to talk, the cops, and at first I talked to them, and then I started to get the drift of what they were trying to put onto me. So I said I wasn't saying anything more without my lawyer present, and I called him, and he left half his breakfast on the table and came over in a hurry, and he wouldn't let me say a word.''

"And the cops didn't take you in or book you?"

"No."

"Did they buy your story?"

"No way. I didn't really tell 'em a story, because Kaplan wouldn't let me say anything. They didn't drag me in, because they don't have a case yet, but Kaplan says they're gonna be building one if they can. They told me not to leave town. You believe it? My wife's dead, the *Post* headline says, 'QUIZ HUSBAND IN BURGLARY MURDER,' and what the hell do they think I'm gonna do? Am I going fishing for fucking trout in Montana? 'Don't leave town.' You see this shit on television, you think nobody in real life talks this way. Maybe television's where they get it from.''

I waited for him to tell me what he wanted from me. I didn't have long to wait.

"Why I called," he said, "is Kaplan wants to hire a detective. He figured maybe these guys talked around the neighborhood, maybe they bragged to their friends, maybe there's a way to prove they did the killing. He says the cops won't concentrate on that end if they're too busy nailing the lid shut on me."

I explained that I didn't have any official standing, that I had no license and filed no reports.

"That's OK," he insisted, "I told Kaplan what I want is somebody I can trust, somebody who'll do the job for me. I don't think they're gonna have any kind of a case at all, Matt, but the longer this drags on, the worse it is for me. I want it cleared up, I want it in the papers that these Spanish assholes did it all and I had nothing to do with anything. You name a fair fee and I'll pay it, me to you, and it can be cash in your hand if you don't like checks. What do you say?"

He wanted somebody he could trust. Had Carolyn from the Caroline told him how trustworthy I was?

What did I say? I said yes.

I met Tommy Tillary and his lawyer in Drew Kaplan's office on Court Street, a few blocks from Brooklyn's Borough Hall. There was a Syrian restaurant next door and, at the corner, a grocery store specializing in Middle Eastern imports stood next to an antique shop overflowing with stripped-oak furniture and brass lamps and bedsteads. Kaplan's office ran to wood paneling and leather chairs and oak file cabinets. His name and the names of two partners were painted on the frosted-glass door in old-fashioned gold-and-black lettering. Kaplan himself looked conservatively up-to-date, with a three-piece striped suit that was better cut than mine. Tommy wore his burgundy blazer and gray flannel trousers and loafers. Strain showed at the corners of his blue eyes and around his mouth. His complexion was off too.

"All we want you to do," Kaplan said, "is find a key in one of their pants pockets, Herrera's or Cruz's, and trace it to a locker in Penn Station, and in the locker there's a foot-long knife with their prints and her blood on it."

"Is that what it's going to take?"

He smiled. "It wouldn't hurt. No, actually, we're not in such bad shape. They got some shaky testimony from a pair of Latins who've been in and out of trouble since they got weaned to Tropicana. They got what looks to them like a good motive on Tommy's part."

"Which is?"

I was looking at Tommy when I asked. His eyes slipped away from mine. Kaplan said, "A marital triangle, a case of the shorts and strong money motive. Margaret Tillary inherited a little over a quarter of a million dollars six or eight months ago. An aunt left a million two, and it got cut up four ways. What they don't bother to notice is he loved his wife, and how many husbands cheat? What is it they say—ninety percent cheat and ten percent lie?"

"That's good odds."

"One of the killers, Angel Herrera, did some odd jobs at the Tillary house last March or April. Spring cleaning; he hauled stuff out of the basement and attic, a little donkeywork. According to Herrera, that's how Tommy knew him to contact him about the burglary. According to common sense, that's how Herrera and his buddy Cruz knew the house and what was in it and how to gain access."

"The case against Tommy sounds pretty thin."

"It is," Kaplan said. "The thing is, you go to court with something like this and you lose even if you win. For the rest of your life, everybody remembers you stood trial for murdering your wife, never mind that you won an acquittal.

"Besides," he said, "you never know which way a jury's going to jump. Tommy's alibi is he was with another lady at the time of the burglary. The woman's a colleague; they could see it as completely aboveboard, but who says they're going to? What they sometimes do, they decide they don't believe the alibi because it's his girlfriend lying for him, and at the same time they label him a scumbag for screwing around while his wife's getting killed."

"You keep it up," Tommy said, "I'll find myself guilty, the way you make it sound."

"Plus he's hard to get a sympathetic jury for. He's a big, handsome guy, a sharp dresser, and you'd love him in a gin joint, but how much do you love him in a courtroom? He's a securities salesman, he's beautiful on the phone, and that means every clown who ever lost a hundred dollars on a stock tip or bought magazines over the phone is going to walk into the courtroom with a hard-on for him. I'm telling you, I want to stay the hell *out* of court. I'll *win* in court, I know that, or the worst that'll happen is I'll win on appeal, but who needs it? This is a case that shouldn't be in the first place, and I'd love to clear it up before they even go so far as presenting a bill to the grand jury.''

"So from me you want—''

"Whatever you can find, Matt. Whatever discredits Cruz and Herrera. I don't know what's there to be found, but you were a cop and now you're private, and you can get down in the streets and nose around.''

I nodded. I could do that. "One thing," I said. "Wouldn't you be better off with a Spanish-speaking detective? I know enough to buy a beer in a bodega, but I'm a long way from fluent.''

Kaplan shook his head. "A personal relationship's worth more than a dime's worth of *'Me llamo Matteo y ¿como está usted?'* ''

"That's the truth," Tommy Tillary said. "Matt, I know I can count on you.''

I wanted to tell him all he could count on was his fingers. I didn't really see what I could expect to uncover that wouldn't turn up in a regular police investigation. But I'd spent enough time carrying a shield to know not to push away money when somebody wants to give it to you. I felt comfortable taking a fee. The man was inheriting a quarter of a million, plus whatever insurance his wife had carried. If he was willing to spread some of it around, I was willing to take it.

So I went to Sunset Park and spent some time in the streets and some more time in the bars. Sunset Park is in Brooklyn, of course, on the borough's western edge, above Bay Ridge and south and west of Greenwood Cemetery. These days, there's a lot of brownstoning going on there, with young urban professionals renovating the old houses and gentrifying the neighborhood. Back then, the upwardly mobile young had not yet discovered Sunset Park, and the area was a mix of Latins and Scandinavians, most of the former Puerto Ricans, most of the latter Norwegians. The balance was gradually shifting from Europe to the islands, from light to dark, but this was a process that had been going on for ages and there was nothing hurried about it.

I talked to Herrera's landlord and Cruz's former employer and one of his recent girlfriends. I drank beer in bars and the back rooms of bodegas. I went to the local station house, I read the sheets on both of the burglars and drank coffee with the cops and picked up some of the stuff that doesn't get on the yellow sheets.

I found out that Miguelito Cruz had once killed a man in a tavern brawl over a woman. There were no charges pressed; a dozen witnesses reported that the dead man had gone after Cruz first with a broken bottle. Cruz had most likely been carrying the knife, but several witnesses insisted it had been tossed to him by an anonymous benefactor, and there hadn't been enough evidence to make a case of weapons possession, let alone homicide.

I learned that Herrera had three children living with their mother in Puerto Rico. He was divorced, but wouldn't marry his current girlfriend because he regarded himself as still married to his ex-wife in the eyes of God. He sent money to his children when he had any to send.

I learned other things. They didn't seem terribly consequential then and they've faded from memory altogether by now, but I wrote them down in my pocket notebook as I learned them, and every day or so I duly reported my findings to Drew Kaplan. He always seemed pleased with what I told him.

I invariably managed to stop at Armstrong's before I called it a night. One night she was there, Carolyn Cheatham, drinking bourbon this time, her face frozen with stubborn old pain. It took her a blink or two to recognize me. Then tears started to form in the corners of her eyes, and she used the back of one hand to wipe them away.

I didn't approach her until she beckoned. She patted the stool beside hers and I eased myself into it. I had coffee with bourbon in it and bought a refill for her. She was pretty drunk already, but that's never been enough reason to turn down a drink.

She talked about Tommy. He was being nice to her, she said. Calling up, sending flowers. But he wouldn't see her, because it wouldn't look right, not for a new widower, not for a man who'd been publicly accused of murder.

"He sends me flowers with no card enclosed," she said. "He calls me from pay phones. The son of a bitch."

Billie called me aside. "I didn't want to put her out," he said, "a nice woman like that, shit-faced as she is. But I thought I was gonna have to. You'll see she gets home?"

I said I would.

I got her out of there, and a cab came along and saved us the walk. At her place, I took the keys from her and unlocked the door.

She half sat, half sprawled on the couch. I had to use the bathroom, and when I came back, her eyes were closed and she was snoring lightly.

I got her coat and shoes off, put her to bed, loosened her clothing and covered her with a blanket. I was tired from all that and sat down on the couch for a minute, and I almost dozed off myself. Then I snapped awake and let myself out.

I went back to Sunset Park the next day. I learned that Cruz had been in trouble as a youth. With a gang of neighborhood kids, he used to go into the city and cruise Greenwich Village, looking for homosexuals to beat up. He'd had a dread of homosexuality, probably flowing as it generally does out of a fear of a part of himself, and he stifled that dread by fag bashing.

"He still doan' like them," a woman told me. She had glossy black hair and opaque eyes, and she was letting me pay for her rum and orange juice. "He's pretty, you know, an' they come on to him, an' he doan' like it."

I called that item in, along with a few others equally earth-shaking. I bought myself a steak dinner at The Slate over on Tenth Avenue, then finished up at Armstrong's, not drinking very hard, just coasting along on bourbon and coffee.

Twice, the phone rang for me. Once, it was Tommy Tillary, telling me how much he appreciated what I was doing for him. It seemed to me that all I was doing was taking his money, but he had me believing that my loyalty and invaluable assistance were all he had to cling to.

The second call was from Carolyn. More praise. I was a gentleman, she assured me, and a hell of a fellow all around. And I should forget that she'd been bad-mouthing Tommy. Everything was going to be fine with them.

I took the next day off. I think I went to a movie, and it may have been *The Sting*, with Newman and Redford achieving vengeance through swindling.

The day after that, I did another tour of duty over in Brooklyn. And the day after that, I picked up the *News* first thing in the morning. The headline was nonspecific, something like "KILL SUSPECT HANGS SELF IN CELL," but I knew it was my case before I turned to the story on page three.

Miguelito Cruz had torn his clothing into strips, knotted the strips together, stood his iron bedstead on its side, climbed onto it, looped his homemade rope around an overhead pipe and jumped off the upended bedstead and into the next world.

That evening's six o'clock TV news had the rest of the story. Informed of his friend's death, Angel Herrera had recanted his original story and admitted that he and Cruz had conceived and executed the Tillary burglary on their own. It had been Miguelito who had stabbed the Tillary woman when she walked in on them. He'd picked up a kitchen knife while Herrera watched in horror. Miguelito always had a short temper, Herrera said, but they were friends, even cousins, and they had hatched their story to protect Miguelito. But now that he was dead, Herrera could admit what had really happened.

I was in Armstrong's that night, which was not remarkable. I had it in mind to get drunk, though I could not have told you why, and that *was* remarkable, if not unheard of. I got drunk a lot those days, but I rarely set out with that intention. I just wanted to feel a little better, a little more mellow, and somewhere along the way I'd wind up waxed.

I wasn't drinking particularly hard or fast, but I was working at it, and then somewhere around ten or eleven the door opened and I knew who it was before I turned around. Tommy Tillary, well dressed and freshly barbered, making his first appearance in Jimmy's place since his wife was killed.

"Hey, look who's here!" he called out and grinned that big grin. People rushed over to shake his hand. Billie was behind the stick, and he'd no sooner set one up on the house for our hero than Tommy insisted on buying a round for the bar. It was an expensive gesture—there must have been thirty or forty people in there—but I don't think he cared if there were three hundred or four hundred.

I stayed where I was, letting the others mob him, but he worked his way over to me and got an arm around my shoulders. "This is the man," he announced. "Best fucking detective ever wore out a pair of shoes. This man's money," he told Billie, "is no good at all tonight. He can't buy a drink; he can't buy a cup of coffee; if you went and put in pay toilets since I was last here, he can't use his own dime."

"The john's still free," Billie said, "but don't give the boss any ideas."

"Oh, don't tell me he didn't already think of it," Tommy said. "Matt, my boy. I love you. I was in a tight spot, I didn't want to, walk out of my house, and you came through for me."

What the hell had I done? I hadn't hanged Miguelito Cruz or coaxed a confession out of Angel Herrera. I hadn't even set eyes on either man. But he was buying the drinks, and I had a thirst, so who was I to argue?

I don't know how long we stayed there. Curiously, my drinking slowed down even as Tommy's picked up speed. Carolyn, I noticed, was not present, nor did her name find its way into the conversation. I wondered if she would walk in—it was, after all, her neighborhood bar, and she was apt to drop in on her own. I wondered what would happen if she did.

I guess there were a lot of things I wondered about, and perhaps that's what put the brakes on my own drinking. I didn't want any gaps in my memory, any gray patches in my awareness.

After a while, Tommy was hustling me out of Armstrong's. "This is celebration time," he told me. "We don't want to sit in one place till we grow roots. We want to bop a little."

He had a car, and I just went along with him without paying too much attention to exactly where we were. We went to a noisy Greek club on the East Side, I think, where the waiters looked like Mob hit men. We went to a couple of trendy singles joints. We wound up somewhere in the Village, in a dark, beery cave.

It was quiet there, and conversation was possible, and I found myself asking him what I'd done that was so praiseworthy. One man had killed himself and another had confessed, and where was my role in either incident?

"The stuff you came up with," he said.

"What stuff? I should have brought back fingernail parings, you could have had someone work voodoo on them."

"About Cruz and the fairies."

"He was up for murder. He didn't kill himself because he was afraid they'd get him for fag bashing when he was a juvenile offender."

Tommy took a sip of Scotch. He said, "Couple of days ago, huge black guy comes up to Cruz in the chow line. 'Wait'll you get up to Green Haven,' he tells him. 'Every blood there's gonna have you for a girlfriend. Doctor gonna have to cut you a brand-new asshole, time you get outa there.' "

I didn't say anything.

"Kaplan," he said. "Drew talked to somebody who talked to somebody, and that did it. Cruz took a good look at the idea of playin' drop the soap for half the jigs in captivity, and the next thing you know, the murderous little bastard was dancing on air. And good riddance to him.''

I couldn't seem to catch my breath. I worked on it while Tommy went to the bar for another round. I hadn't touched the drink in front of me, but I let him buy for both of us.

When he got back, I said, "Herrera."

"Changed his story. Made a full confession."

"And pinned the killing on Cruz."

"Why not? Cruz wasn't around to complain. Who knows which one of 'em did it, and for that matter, who cares? The thing is, you gave us the lever."

"For Cruz," I said. "To get him to kill himself."

"And for Herrera. Those kids of his in Santurce. Drew spoke to Herrera's lawyer, and Herrera's lawyer spoke to Herrera, and the message was, 'Look, you're going up for burglary whatever you do, and probably for murder; but if you tell the right story, you'll draw shorter time, and on top of that, that nice Mr. Tillary's gonna let bygones be bygones and every month there's a nice check for your wife and kiddies back in Puerto Rico.' ''

At the bar, a couple of old men were reliving the Louis-Schmeling fight, the second one, where Louis punished the German champion. One of the old fellows was throwing roundhouse punches in the air, demonstrating.

I said, "Who killed your wife?"

"One or the other of them. If I had to bet, I'd say Cruz. He had those little beady eyes; you looked at him up close and you got that he was a killer.''

"When did you look at him up close?"

"When they came and cleaned the house, the basement and the attic. Not when they came and cleaned me out; that was the second time.''

He smiled, but I kept looking at him until the smile lost its certainty. "That was Herrera who helped around the house," I said. "You never met Cruz."

"Cruz came along, gave him a hand."

"You never mentioned that before."

"Oh, sure I did, Matt. What difference does it make, anyway?"

"Who killed her, Tommy?"

"Hey, let it alone, huh?"

"Answer the question."

"I already answered it."

"You killed her, didn't you?"

"What are you, crazy? Cruz killed her and Herrera swore to it, isn't that enough for you?"

"Tell me you didn't kill her."

"I didn't kill her."

"Tell me again."

"I didn't fucking kill her. What's the matter with you?"

"I don't believe you."

"Oh, Jesus," he said. He closed his eyes, put his head in his hands. He sighed and looked up and said, "You know, it's a funny thing with me. Over the telephone, I'm the best salesman you could ever imagine. I swear I could sell sand to the Arabs, I could sell ice in the winter, but face to face I'm no good at all. Why do you figure that is?"

"You tell me."

"I don't know. I used to think it was my face, the eyes and the mouth; I don't know. It's easy over the phone. I'm talking to a stranger, I don't know who he is or what he looks like, and he's not lookin' at me, and it's a cinch. Face to face, especially with someone I know, it's a different story." He looked at me. "If we were doin' this over the phone, you'd buy the whole thing."

"It's possible."

"It's fucking certain. Word for word, you'd buy the package. Suppose I was to tell you I did kill her, Matt. You couldn't prove anything. Look, the both of us walked in there, the place was a mess from the burglary, we got in an argument, tempers flared, something happened."

"You set up the burglary. You planned the whole thing, just the way Cruz and Herrera accused you of doing. And now you wriggled out of it."

"And you helped me—don't forget that part of it."

"I won't."

"And I wouldn't have gone away for it anyway, Matt. Not a chance. I'da beat it in court, only this way I don't have to go to court. Look, this is just the booze talkin', and we can forget it in the morning, right? I didn't kill her, you didn't accuse me, we're still buddies, everything's fine. Right?"

Blackouts are never there when you want them. I woke up the next day and remembered all of it, and I found myself wishing I didn't. He'd killed his wife and he was getting away with it. And I'd helped him. I'd taken his money, and in return I'd shown him how to set one man up for suicide and another into making a false confession.

And what was I going to do about it?

I couldn't think of a thing. Any story I carried to the police would be speedily denied by Tommy and his lawyer, and all I had was the thinnest of hearsay evidence, my own client's own words when he and I both had a skinful of booze. I went over it for a few days, looking for ways to shake something loose, and there was nothing. I could maybe interest a newspaper reporter, maybe get Tommy some press coverage that wouldn't make him happy, but why? And to what purpose?

I rankled. But I would just have a couple of drinks, and then it wouldn't rankle so much.

Angel Herrera pleaded guilty to burglary, and in return, the Brooklyn D.A.'s office dropped all homicide charges. He went Upstate to serve five to ten.

And then I got a call in the middle of the night. I'd been sleeping a couple of hours, but the phone woke me and I groped for it. It took me a minute to recognize the voice on the other end.

It was Carolyn Cheatham.

"I had to call you," she said, "on account of you're a bourbon man and a gentleman. I owed it to you to call you."

"What's the matter?"

"He ditched me," she said, "and he got me fired out of Tannahill and Company so he won't have to look at me around the office. Once he didn't need me to back up his story, he let go of me, and do you know he did it over the phone?"

"Carolyn—"

"It's all in the note," she said. "I'm leaving a note."

"Look, don't do anything yet," I said. I was out of bed, fumbling for my clothes. "I'll be right over. We'll talk about it."

"You can't stop me, Matt."

"I won't try to stop you. We'll talk first, and then you can do anything you want."

The phone clicked in my ear.

I threw my clothes on, rushed over there, hoping it would be pills, something that took its time. I broke a small pane of glass in the downstairs door and let myself in, then used an old credit card to slip the bolt of her spring lock.

The room smelled of cordite. She was on the couch she'd passed out on the last time I saw her. The gun was still in her hand, limp at her side, and there was a black-rimmed hole in her temple.

There was a note, too. An empty bottle of Maker's Mark stood on the coffee table, an empty glass beside it. The booze showed in her handwriting and in the sullen phrasing of the suicide note.

I read the note. I stood there for a few minutes, not for very long, and then I got a dish towel from the Pullman kitchen and wiped the bottle and the glass. I took another matching glass, rinsed it out and wiped it, and put it in the drainboard of the sink.

I stuffed the note in my pocket. I took the gun from her fingers, checked routinely for a pulse, then wrapped a sofa pillow around the gun to muffle its report. I fired one round into her chest, another into her open mouth.

I dropped the gun into a pocket and left.

They found the gun in Tommy Tillary's house, stuffed between the cushions of the living-room sofa, clean of prints inside and out. Ballistics got a perfect match. I'd aimed for soft tissue with the round shot into her chest, because bullets can fragment on impact with bone. That was one reason I'd fired the extra shots. The other was to rule out the possibility of suicide.

After the story made the papers, I picked up the phone and called Drew Kaplan. "I don't understand it," I said. "He was free and clear; why the hell did he kill the girl?"

"Ask him yourself," Kaplan said. He did not sound happy. "You want my opinion, he's a lunatic. I honestly didn't think he was. I figured maybe he killed his wife, maybe he didn't. Not my job to try him. But I didn't figure he was a homicidal maniac."

"It's certain he killed the girl?"

"Not much question. The gun's pretty strong evidence. Talk about finding somebody with the smoking pistol in his hand, here it was in Tommy's couch. The idiot."

"Funny he kept it."

"Maybe he had other people he wanted to shoot. Go figure a crazy man. No, the gun's evidence, and there was a phone tip—a man called in the shooting, reported a man running out of there and gave a description that fitted Tommy pretty well. Even had him wearing that red blazer he wears, tacky thing makes him look like an usher at the Paramount."

"It sounds tough to square."

"Well, somebody else'll have to try to do it," Kaplan said. "I told him I can't defend him this time. What it amounts to, I wash my hands of him.''

I thought of that when I read that Angel Herrera got out just the other day. He served all ten years because he was as good at getting into trouble inside the walls as he'd been on the outside.

Somebody killed Tommy Tillary with a homemade knife after he'd served two years and three months of a manslaughter stretch. I wondered at the time if that was Herrera getting even, and I don't suppose I'll ever know. Maybe the checks stopped going to Santurce and Herrera took it the wrong way. Or maybe Tommy said the wrong thing to somebody else and said it face to face instead of over the phone.

I don't think I'd do it that way now. I don't drink anymore, and the impulse to play God seems to have evaporated with the booze.

But then, a lot of things have changed. Billie left Armstrong's not long after that, left New York too; the last I heard he was off drink himself, living in Sausalito and making candles. I ran into Dennis the other day in a bookstore on lower Fifth Avenue full of odd volumes on yoga and spiritualism and holistic healing. And Armstrong's is scheduled to close the end of next month. The lease is up for renewal, and I suppose the next you know, the old joint'll be another Korean fruit market.

I still light a candle now and then for Carolyn Cheatham and Miguelito Cruz. Not often. Just every once in a while.

# L. J. Washburn

# ON THE PROD

THE KID WAS ON THE PROD. HALLAM COULD SEE THAT AS SOON as the boy stepped through the door of the Waterhole.

About nineteen or twenty, Hallam guessed, with sandy hair, broad shoulders, and a tight-jawed look on his face. His clothes were cheap and rumpled, probably from a long bus or train ride, and he clutched a cloth cap tightly in his left fist. He couldn't have been more than a few days off the farm back in Iowa or Nebraska or some such place.

The boy paused just inside the door of the speakeasy and let his eyes adjust to the dimness. When his gaze hit Hallam, a fresh determination came over him and he strode across the room. Hallam watched him come and wondered what the hell *this* was all about.

"You're Lucas Hallam?"

The words came out flat and hard as the boy stopped beside the table. He paid no attention to the other three men seated there.

They were a formidable-looking bunch. Hallam had been sharing a drink with Jack Montgomery, Neal Hart, and the youngster known only as Pecos. All four of them were still in costume from that day's shooting, and they would have looked more at home in a saloon in Dodge or Abilene or Tombstone forty years earlier, rather than in a speakeasy in downtown Hollywood. All the boys from Gower Gulch came to the Waterhole, though, when the day's ridin' jobs were done. It was the closest thing to the life they had once known, the closest thing to home.

Hallam wore boots and buckskins, and his battered old hat was

on the table in front of him. The big Colt holstered at his right hip
was loaded with blanks at the moment, but it was no prop. Neither
was the Bowie knife that rode his left hip. But the kid didn't look
dangerous, just mad and a little uncertain of himself, so Hallam
sat easy.

"Happens I am," he answered after a long moment. "What
business is it of yours, boy?"

"My name is Jamie Brinke. I'm looking for my brother, and
I'm told you know him."

Hallam picked up the rest of his drink, tossed it off. If this had
to do with Joe Brinke, chances were there would be trouble after
all. There usually was.

"I know him," he said. "Don't reckon I could tell you where
to find him tonight, though."

For the first time, the boy looked at Hallam's companions, then
said, "Could we talk in private?"

"These here are my friends. Anything you got to say to me, you
can say in front of 'em."

Jamie Brinke's expression grew more sullen. "Joe made you
sound like a real lobo wolf. Don't look like much to me."

The young man to Hallam's right started to rise, his hot blood
showing. Hallam put a big hand on his arm to stop him. "Hold on
there, Pecos," he said softly. "Boy's got a right to his opinions."

"And I got a right not to like 'em," Pecos growled.

Hallam stood up and jerked his head at a vacant table in another
corner of the big room. "Maybe we'd best go over there and talk
after all." He turned away and stalked across the room without
looking back to see if Jamie Brinke was following.

He was. As Hallam dropped into a chair, automatically taking
the one that would put his back against the wall, Jamie sat down
across the table from him.

"I've gotta find Joe," he said. "It's real important. Sorry if I
hurt your feelings over there. It's just that you don't look like a
famous gunfighter."

Hallam shook his head. "Don't go pinnin' that name on me,
boy. All the famous gunfighters are dead."

"Don't look like a private eye, either," Jamie objected.

Hallam sighed. "Got any more statements you want to make, or
do we get on with this business 'bout your brother?"

Jamie ducked his head, chewed his lip for a moment, then
blurted, "Dammit! I always say the wrong thing. I guess I'm just
a stupid farmboy, Mr. Hallam—"

"No call for that," Hallam quietly told him. "Los Angeles is a mighty big town. I got a mite rattled myself, the first time I rode in. Now you just settle down and tell me why it's so important you get in touch with your brother."

Jamie nodded, took a deep breath. "Well . . . it's our pa. He's sick, and he wants to see Joe again before he . . . before he . . ." His face twisting with emotion, Jamie broke off for a moment, then went on hurriedly, "Ma's been gone a couple years now. I thought Joe would come back home then, but he didn't. And now with Pa sick, I just thought I'd come out here and find Joe. I know he'll go back with me now."

Hallam didn't say anything. He sat and tried to find the words to tell this boy not to get his hopes up.

But how do you tell a kid that his big brother is a cold, no-good, half-crazy bastard?

It had been about three years since Hallam had started hearing stories about Joe Brinke. At first Brinke had been on the wrong side of the law, running rum in down the coast from Mexico. Word had it that he was for hire, too, for any kind of illegal job as long as the money was right. He had done some work for a bail bondsman and had eventually gotten his P.I. ticket, though Hallam figured he had had to grease a few palms along the way. There were several unsolved killings that seemed to have Joe Brinke's name on them. Supposedly, the things Brinke had endured over in Europe during the War had hardened him to death and suffering and left him little better than a vicious animal. He and Hallam had crossed paths uneventfully a few times, being in the same line of work, but Hallam had always watched his back around Brinke, just from instinct.

He didn't believe for a minute that Brinke would pay any attention to his brother's plea to come home. Hallam didn't think there was that much human feeling left in the man. But he might be wrong, and he sensed that there was a mighty upset boy beneath the tough show Jamie tried to put on.

"You got an address for your brother?" he asked.

Jamie nodded. "Joe don't live there anymore, though. Landlady said he moved out about six months ago. She didn't have no idea where he is now."

"Who put you on my trail?"

"Mr. Messner, the fella Joe used to work for. He said you might know how to get hold of him."

Hallam nodded. He had done a few jobs for the same bondsman who had employed Brinke, Kenneth Messner. It had been a while, though, since he had talked to either Messner or Joe Brinke.

Seeing Hallam's hesitation, Jamie dug inside his coat and started to say, "If it's money, I guess I can hire you—"

"Put it away, boy," Hallam snapped, letting his annoyance show through for the first time. "I'll do what I can to help you, and you don't need to be payin' me."

"It wouldn't have been much," Jamie said as he took his hand back out, "but it'd'a been worth it to find Joe."

"Well . . ." Hallam stood up, settled the big hat on his head, lifted a hand in farewell to his friends across the room. He wasn't sure he was doing the right thing by going along with what Jamie Brinke wanted, but he had been a kid once, too. A long time ago, to be sure, but Hallam remembered.

They left the Waterhole together.

Hallam knew where most of the speaks in town were even though the Waterhole was about the only place where he did any drinking. He and Jamie spent over an hour going from one to the next. The bartenders all knew Hallam, and they didn't mind telling him that they hadn't seen Joe Brinke lately and didn't know where to find him now.

"Don't get discouraged, boy," Hallam said as they drove away from their eighth stop in Hallam's flivver. "Lots of places to drink in this town. Somebody's bound to have seen your brother."

Jamie was clearly torn between concern over finding his brother and awe and excitement at being surrounded by the lights and bustle of the big city. Their route took them within a couple of blocks of a mob behind police barricades. A maze of spotlight beams crosshatched the night sky. Jamie pointed at the uproar and exclaimed, "What's that?"

"Movie premiere," Hallam told him. "De Mille's got a new picture openin' up. Lots of folks show up to see and be seen."

"Cecil B. De Mille?"

"Yep."

"He's a real famous picture-man, ain't he?"

" 'Spose so. Some folks think so."

Jamie glanced over at Hallam. "Sounds like you don't."

Hallam spat out the open window beside him. "He don't know sic 'em about cowboys, I'll tell you that much. Man ought to

respect the folks he works with. De Mille's goin' to get some good
men killed some day. Already killed some good horses makin'
'em do damn-fool stunts.''

Jamie was silent for a moment, then said, "How'd you wind up
in the movies anyway, Mr. Hallam? A man who's done the things
you have, I mean."

Hallam grinned. "Hell, boy, the money's good. And I get to
work with fellers like the ones back there at the Waterhole. You
don't find them ol' boys just everywhere. It's better than workin'
in some broke-down Bill show, that's for sure."

"What about being a detective, though?"

"Guess being in the Pinkertons got that in my blood. But I take
the cases I want to, and I do picture work when I want to, and if
I feel like taking a drive out to the desert and rememberin' old
times, I do that. Not a bad life for an old feller like me."

The car was quiet again after that, but Jamie seemed a little
more impressed with Hallam now.

Another half hour went by, and they had stopped at three more
speakeasies before their luck changed. The bartender in a red-lit
dive called Lucifer's Lagoon had talked to Brinke earlier in the
evening.

"Couldn't tell you where he's staying now, though," the man
said. "He just comes in here for a drink now and then. He
wouldn't be home tonight anyway."

"Why's that?" Hallam prodded. He had bought a drink for
himself and left his change on the bar. Now he casually nudged a
dollar bill a little closer to the bartender.

The bill disappeared as the man swiped his bar rag across the
mahogany. "He was working. Said something about going on a
job up in the hills."

"He say whereabouts in the hills?"

The bartender shrugged. "Wouldn't know for sure. You might
try up behind the Hollywoodland sign."

Hallam knew the area. The hills up there were pretty sparsely
settled. The main feature was the big sign that a land speculator
had put up to advertise a housing development below. Some shady
dealings went on around there, and Hallam wasn't surprised that
one of Joe Brinke's cases might take him up into the hills.

Hallam left his drink unfinished, thanked the bartender, and
took Jamie in tow. When they were back in the flivver, Jamie
asked, "Do you think we'll find Joe now, Mr. Hallam?"

"Got a chance, anyway. Time'll tell, boy."

He pointed the nose of the car toward Hollywoodland.

Traffic was still heavy, but then it never slowed down much until well after midnight. For a town where the main industry was moviemaking with its early-morning calls, folks sure didn't sleep much.

Hallam had little to say on the drive. The wide, palm-lined boulevards turned into narrower blacktop roads that snaked through the canyons and led onto the heights. There were a few houses up here, but they were well off the road and far apart. Lights were spread out in a broad blanket below, but darkness had closed in on the car. The weak beams of the headlights only made the blackness more intense.

"Do you have any idea where to look?" Jamie asked. Now that they were away from the bright lights, his worry about his brother had resurfaced again.

"Not for sure," Hallam said. "Only so many roads up here, though, and I know most of 'em. We'll just drive around for a spell, see what we see."

For a while all they saw was the road, the scrubby bushes pressing in from the side, and an occasional rabbit darting through the lights. Hallam's route twisted and turned until Jamie was hopelessly confused. Hallam knew where he was, though, knew how to get back out.

Then the headlight beams bounced back off the chrome of a parked car.

Hallam hit the brakes gently and eased the flivver to a stop. The parked car was a nondescript roadster, but he thought it was familiar. Seemed like he had seen Joe Brinke driving a car like it.

"Is that Joe's car, Mr. Hallam?" Jamie asked. He was sitting forward in the seat, young face intense.

"I think it might be," Hallam said. "You just stay put. I'll take a look around."

Hallam eased out of the car and walked toward the other one. He had left his headlights on and the glow from them threw a long shadow at his feet. As far as he could tell, the parked car was empty. Something about the situation sent a tickle of warning along his spine, and he wished he had slipped live cartridges into his Colt, rather than the blanks from the movie set. If trouble came, he'd just have to make do with the Bowie.

He stopped beside the roadster and bent his big frame to peer in through the window. As he had thought, the vehicle was deserted. Carefully Hallam opened the driver's door and reached inside to check something. Yep, this was Brinke's car, all right; Hallam's fingers found the specially made pocket under the seat where Brinke usually kept a pistol. The gun was gone now, and Hallam wondered what that meant.

Feeling Jamie's eyes on him, Hallam went back to the flivver. He stooped and spoke through the open window. "It's your brother's car, all right. But there's no sign of—"

A woman's scream shattered the stillness of the night.

Hallam jerked upright, his hand flashing to his gun. Then he grunted, yanked open the car door, and snapped, "Box o' shells in the car pocket. Get 'em, boy!"

Jamie looked stunned, but Hallam's harsh command spurred him to action. He grabbed the shells from the glove compartment and passed them to Hallam.

The scream wasn't repeated, but Hallam's keen ears had picked up the general direction during the few seconds it had lasted. He swung in that direction and called back over his shoulder, "Stay in the car!"

He didn't wait to see whether or not Jamie did as he was told.

Hallam ran through the night, his stiff right leg slowing him down some. As he felt the aches and pain, memories of the gunfights and brawls that had caused them flashed through his mind. Souvenirs of wild times . . .

And it looked like tonight might be added to the list.

Without thinking about it, he dumped the blanks and jammed fresh shells into the Colt's cylinder. He suddenly heard running footsteps off to his right and veered in that direction, pushing his way through the thick brush, thankful that he was wearing tough buckskins. The ground was sloping up now under his feet. He kept climbing the hill, the Colt ready in his hand.

He broke out into a clearing. There was enough moonlight for him to see another man burst into the open across from him. The man turned, reached behind him, and pulled a girl out of the brush. Neither of them noticed Hallam until the big man roared, "Hold it, you two!"

They froze and stared across the clearing at Hallam, seeing a tall, broad-shouldered man in boots, buckskins, and hat who was pointing a heavy Dragoon Colt at them.

They must have thought they had lost their minds.

The scene lasted only a moment. Then another man popped out of the brush, to Hallam's left this time. Hallam turned that way and saw the dim flicker of moonlight on steel.

He dove forward as gun blasts boomed and muzzle flashes split the darkness.

Even as he landed on the hard ground, slugs zipping over his head, Hallam's finger was tightening on the trigger. The Colt roared and bucked in his hand, and he saw the second man throw himself to the side to dodge the fire. Hallam rolled, trying to get to cover himself, and caught a glimpse of the fleeing couple disappearing back into the undergrowth.

Hallam found a little clump of rocks and settled himself behind them as best he could. The other man had faded back into the brush, too, so all Hallam could do was wait. It would be a fool play to try to move now. He would just have to wait out the other fella. Wasn't the first time he'd been in a spot like this, but it could still get powerful hard on the nerves.

A ways off, probably on the other side of the hill, car doors slammed and an engine kicked over. Hallam grimaced in the darkness. Probably the first man and the girl making their getaway in a car they had stashed. He wondered if the man had been Joe Brinke—the light in the clearing hadn't been good enough to determine identities—then decided it probably wasn't. Brinke's car was parked on this side of the hill.

Other than that, Hallam didn't have one damn idea what was going on here.

He decided to take a chance. "Brinke!" he called. "That you out there, Joe Brinke? This's Lucas Hallam! No call for us to be shootin' at each other!"

A pebble rolled, close at hand, just to his left.

Hallam whirled, saw a shadow coming at him, kicked out just in time. His boot heel sank into the man's stomach and sent him spinning away. Hallam was up and after him in a second, cracking the Colt across the man's wrist and making his drop his pistol. Hallam brought his left around, felt the satisfying jar up his arm as fist met jaw and knocked the man sprawling.

Then Hallam was standing over him, the Colt lined on his forehead, the click of the hammer being drawn back unnaturally loud in the sudden stillness.

"Just take it easy, Brinke," Hallam said, a little out of breath. "You know what this horse pistol'll do to your head if I pull the trigger."

Brinke looked up at him with a killing glare and said, "You goddamn idiot cowboy! You know what you did, Hallam? You just let a kidnapper get away, you stupid bastard!"

Hallam's eyes narrowed in surprise at Brinke's bitter words. He had walked into something bigger than he had thought here, but he still didn't intend to let Brinke take any more shots at him. He stepped back a pace and gestured with the muzzle of the Colt. "Get up," he grated. "We can hash that out later. Right now we're goin' back down to your car. Your brother's probably worried sick about you after all that shootin'."

"Jamie's here?" Brinke sounded only vaguely interested as he climbed to his feet under Hallam's watchful eye. "What the hell does he want?"

"Wants to see you. I'll let him tell you the rest of it."

Hallam collected the gun he had knocked out of Brinke's hand; then the two of them walked down the hill, Hallam ready and perfectly willing to put a slug in Brinke's leg if he tried anything. Brinke cooperated, though, and in a few minutes they emerged from the brush onto the road. Jamie was waiting in Hallam's car, but when he saw them coming he leaped out and ran toward them.

"Joe!" he cried. "Are you all right, Joe? I heard the shooting—"

"What do you want, kid?" Brinke cut in. His voice was icy.

"I came out to find you, Joe. It's Pa. He's real sick, and he wants to see you. Can you come back home with me, Joe?"

"Too busy. I've got a case . . . if your cowboy friend here hasn't totally ruined it."

Jamie glanced at Hallam, saw the gun in his hand. Anger and confusion played over his face. "What are you doing, Mr. Hallam?" he demanded.

"Just keepin' your brother from killin' me," Hallam answered. He holstered the Colt, though, feeling that the violence was over . . . at least for the moment.

In the harsh yellow glare of the headlights, Joe Brinke's taut, flat-planed face was set in emotionless lines as he growled, "Go home, kid. I've got no time for you or Pa."

Jamie stared at his brother, unable to believe the heartless words he had just heard. Looking at him, Hallam felt like knocking Brinke down again. He was sure it would feel mighty good. . . .

Brinke turned away from Jamie, dismissing the boy. He said to Hallam, "I've got to go explain to my client how this job got botched. I want you along so I can show him who's to blame."

"Suits me just fine," Hallam told him. "Like to know more about this business, anyway."

Brinke held out his hand. "My gun."

Hallam had stuck the pistol behind his belt. He took it out now, unloaded it, and handed back gun and cartridges separately. He ignored the sneer on Brinke's face.

Jamie caught at his brother's arm. "What about me?" he asked. "What do I do now?"

"First thing, get your damn hands off me! Then go home, like I told you."

Hallam said, "Come along with me, boy. After we go see your brother's client, I'll take you to the train station."

"All right," Jamie said numbly. He stood there and watched while Brinke got into the roadster and started the engine. Then Hallam touched his shoulder.

"Let's go," Hallam said.

As they drove down out of the hills, Hallam right behind Brinke, Hallam thought about skipping the meeting with Brinke's client and taking Jamie directly to the station. But he kept coming back to Brinke's angry accusation. If he was responsible for a kidnapper getting away, he wanted to know the details of it. This whole thing didn't sit well with him.

Something was wrong, damn wrong.

There was a lot of money and power in this room, symbolized by the thick carpet, plush chairs, and massive mahogany desk. The three men who glowered at Hallam and Brinke were used to wielding that power. Hallam knew all three and didn't particularly like any of them.

Arthur Norton was one of the studio's top executives and occupied the chair behind the big desk. His hair, what was left of it, was iron gray. He held a pencil in blunt fingers and tapped it annoyingly on the desk top, but no one complained. Leaning against the desk, one hip perched on the corner, was Kurt Prescott, a tall man with dark curly hair. He was wearing a tuxedo, which told Hallam that he had been called to this meeting from the party following De Mille's premiere. As an up-and-coming director, Prescott couldn't afford to miss such a party. Hallam had worked for him on some two-reelers, before Prescott graduated to features, and thought he was a competent picture-maker.

The third man, Leonard Yates, stood in the background and watched while the other two did most of the talking. He was the mildest-looking of the three, with sandy hair and watery blue eyes behind rimless glasses, but Hallam knew that many people in town were afraid to cross him. They had good reason to be. He was the most influential agent in Hollywood, and his word could help make a career . . . or break one.

"I hope you know what you've done, Hallam," Norton snapped. "Elysse Millay is going to be one of our biggest stars. At least she will be if that maniac doesn't hurt her!"

"Said I was sorry," Hallam rumbled. "I'll help get her back, if that's what you want."

"The hell you will!" Brinke snarled. "The studio hired *me* to handle the ransom payoff and bring the girl back."

"Perhaps that was a mistake," Prescott put in.

Brinke took a step forward, his face contorting in rage, then stopped himself with a visible effort. Prescott hadn't moved from his casual pose, but Hallam thought he saw a flicker of fear in the director's eyes.

"There's no need for violence, gentlemen," Leonard Yates said. "The harm has already been done."

Brinke reached inside his shirt and pulled out a paper-wrapped packet. "At least you've still got your fifty grand," he said as he tossed it on Norton's desk. "Too bad you probably won't get another chance to spend it."

"We don't know that," Norton said. "The kidnapper may call again."

"And if he does," Prescott added, "I think we should let Mr. Hallam handle the transaction." Afraid or not, the director seemed determined to speak his mind.

"I don't mind helpin'," Hallam said. "But it wasn't Brinke's fault. He might've caught up with them two if I hadn't come along."

"The kidnapper had already panicked and started running, taking Elysse with him." Norton picked up the pace of the tapping pencil. "No doubt because of something Brinke did to scare him."

"I didn't do anything!" Brinke objected hotly. "I followed orders. The guy just spooked, that's all."

Hallam could accept that. He had been filled in on the background, had seen the ransom note, and had come to the conclusion that Elysse Millay's kidnapper was an extremely lucky amateur. The man had walked into Miss Millay's Hollywood apartment in broad daylight and taken her out through a lobby full of people. The actress had evidently been too frightened to make any kind of outcry. Then he had called the studio and told Norton to expect a ransom note with the directions for the payoff. The note had demanded fifty thousand dollars and had given specific instructions about delivery. Brinke had been hired to handle that delivery, but then the kidnapper had run for some reason.

And that was when Hallam came in.

"What happened up there doesn't really matter," Leonard Yates said quietly. "The only thing we're concerned with is Elysse's safe return. I'm sure the poor girl is terrified."

"We have a lot of plans for her. She's going to be a big, big star when *Passion Flower* comes out." Norton rubbed a weary hand over his eyes.

"It's my best picture yet," Prescott said. "Elysse is marvelous in it. She's going to outshine Swanson and Pickford and all the rest. Mark my words."

Hallam said, "Sounds like quite an epic. But gettin' the gal back safe is more important, ain't it?"

"Of course," Yates replied. "Consider yourself hired, Mr. Hallam."

Brinke tensed and was about to explode again in protest.

The shrill ring of the phone on Norton's desk made everyone in the room freeze.

Then Norton snatched up the phone and barked, "Yes?" His drawn face became even more tense as he waited and listened.

"Yes," he finally said. "We've been waiting to hear from you. Listen, I don't know what happened, but I assure you, all we want is Miss Millay's safe return. . . . Yes . . . Yes, I understand. No tricks. Of course. You have my word on it."

There were beads of sweat on the movie executive's brow.

"All right," he said, then cradled the phone. He looked up at the anxious circle of faces around the desk. "We've been very lucky, gentlemen. The kidnapper still wants to deal."

"He tell you why he spooked earlier?" Hallam asked.

"No, he said nothing about that. He just told me that the site for the payoff has been changed. He wants the money brought out to the ranch house on our location lot." Norton glanced at Hallam. "I'm sure you're familiar with the place."

A grin tugged at Hallam's wide mouth. "Made a few pictures there."

"Anything else, Arthur?" Prescott asked.

"Yes. The price has gone up." Norton grimaced. "He wants seventy-five thousand now."

Yates took a deep breath, then said slowly, "We can put our hands on an extra twenty-five. Elysse is worth it."

The other two nodded in agreement. "Well, Mr. Hallam," Norton said, "will you be ready to go as soon as we have the money for you?"

"I'll be ready," Hallam said.

"Wait just a goddamned minute!" Brinke objected. "This is my case. I'm not being cut out of it!"

"You *are* out of it," Norton said coldly. "Now leave the studio, or I'll call the police."

Hallam saw the fires in Brinke's eyes, the way the man stood, and knew they were real close to trouble—blood trouble. He let his hand fall on the butt of the Colt and said softly, "Don't do it, Brinke."

Brinke's eyes flashed from Hallam to the three movie men then back again. Abruptly his lip curled, and he spat a couple of vile names at them; but then he turned on his heel and stalked out of the room.

Hallam went to the door as Brinke stormed out through the anteroom where they had left Jamie to wait for them. Jamie watched his brother's disappearing back but didn't try to go after him. Instead, he turned and said, "What now, Mr. Hallam?"

"Don't have time to take you to the station after all," Hallam told him. "Got a chore I've got to do. We'll get you a cab, though."

"Couldn't I come with you?"

Hallam smiled. "Don't reckon that'd be a good idea. You go on back home, son. Your pa needs you now."

"What about Joe?"

"Was I you . . . I'd say I never found him. . . ."

Norton brushed past him in the doorway. "Come along, Hallam," he snapped. "We'll get the rest of that money for you."

Hesitantly Jamie said, " 'Scuse me, sir, but while I was waitin' I noticed a bunch of men outside. Some of 'em had cameras, and they were all yellin'."

"Dammit!" Prescott and Yates had followed Norton out of the meeting room, and the exclamation came from the director. "Reporters! If the press has gotten hold of this kidnapping, they'll turn it into a three-ring circus! We'd better get Hallam out the back way."

"I agree," Yates said. "We can't take any chances, not now. Not with Elysse's life at stake."

Hallam had to go along with that.

Besides, he would have rather faced the Wild Bunch again than a bunch of story-hungry reporters.


Hallam had lost track of the times he had been out to the ranch. He had worked for all of the studios at one time or another, from Poverty Row to the big boys, and knew all the location shooting areas. This one was about fifteen miles from town and had a lot of rugged country on it. Just the kind of nice isolated place a kidnapper might choose for an exchange.

He had bid a quick good-bye to Jamie Brinke after arranging to have the boy picked up at the studio and taken to the train station. Jamie said he had enough money for his ticket back home, but Hallam had told him to take a little extra. Never could tell when a man might run a little short, he explained. Jamie had gripped his hand hard, and then Hallam was gone, hustled away by Norton, Prescott, and Yates. They had handed him the package of money, fatter now that the extra twenty-five thousand had been added. Hallam hadn't asked where they were able to lay their hands on that much money after ten o'clock at night. With their business being so scandal-prone, some of the studios had taken to keeping emergency funds on hand.

Now, as he drove through the warm night, Hallam's thoughts were divided between Jamie Brinke and this kidnapping business. Joe Brinke's callous treatment of his brother was just one more black mark on the man's record. Wasn't really any of his affair, though, Hallam decided. It didn't pay a man to mix into any kind of family troubles.

The kidnapping was something else; that was more in his line of work. But he had still been surprised at being handed the job. Much as he hated to agree with Brinke about anything, he was partly to blame for the first exchange attempt going wrong.

He had a chance to make up for that now, though. If he could only shake the feeling that he had been lied to somewhere along the way . . .

Hallam left his headlights on and didn't try to be the least bit unobtrusive as he drove onto the ranch. He headed straight for the old homestead that was used for ranch house scenes. Instinct told him he was being watched. He hoped so.

He came to a stop in front of the house, killed the flivver's engine, and climbed out. The money was tucked inside his fringed buckskin shirt. He reached up and patted the bulge, and again he had the sensation of being watched.

He stood still for a long moment, listening, letting his senses work. A faint creak came to his ears, and he knew it was a floorboard. He was ready when the screen door of the house flew open and a lantern threw a harsh yellow glare in his eyes.

Hallam stood stock-still and let the man with the lantern study him. He had picked up a rifle, too, since the skirmish in the hills. Hallam could see the barrel of it poking into the light.

"Who the hell are you, old-timer?"

The voice was nervous. Hallam was careful to stay still as he answered, "Lucas Hallam. I've got the money from the studio."

A quick intake of breath from the porch. "Let me see it."

Hallam slowly reached inside his shirt and pulled out the packet.

"Toss it up here."

Hallam shook his head. "Not till I see the girl."

"I could just shoot you and take it."

Hallam grinned. "Then shoot straight, son. Happen you don't put me down right off, I'll have time to throw a little lead myself."

The man was silent for a moment. Hallam was aware of movement just inside the door of the house, and then the kidnapper growled, "All right, get out here."

The girl came out of the house and into the circle of light. Her expensive frock was now torn and dirty, and her blond hair, once carefully styled, was in disarray. She looked more exhausted than frightened.

Hallam studied her for a few seconds, then rumbled, "You all right, girl?"

She nodded wearily. "I'm fine. I just want to go home."

Hallam weighed the money packet in his big hand then lightly tossed it toward the porch. The thought of going for his gun while the kidnapper's eyes followed the money had occurred to him, but he didn't do it. He was willing to play it straight as long as the other fella did.

The lantern shifted; the barrel of the rifle dipped. The man was going for the money—

The crack of a shot and the crash of the lantern sounded together.

Closest cover was the porch. Hallam went for it as another shot boomed in the night. The man on the porch gasped. The rifle clattered to the ground.

"Hank!" the girl screamed.

Then Hallam wrapped an arm around each of them and drove on through the open door as more slugs thudded into the walls of the house. All three of them sprawled on the bare floor in the darkness.

The girl was struggling; the man was limp and his shirt was wet, sticky. Hallam got a hand on the girl's shoulder and put some weight on her.

"Dammit, settle down! I'm on your side. I'm not with whoever's doin' that shootin'!"

The girl stopped fighting but only because a bubbling moan from the man made her stiffen and start crying. "Hank . . ." she whispered.

Hallam let go of her and came up in a crouch. In the dim moonlight that filtered in from outside, he saw her scuttle across the floor and throw herself on the man. That brought another groan of pain. Hallam felt sorry for him, but there was nothing he could do, not as long as they were pinned down like this. Bullets were still hitting the walls, screaming through the open door and windows.

Hallam spotted a table shoved into one corner of the room. He went to it, hauled it closer to the two figures on the floor, turned it on its side. It was better than nothing.

He hunkered down behind he table and said harshly, "All right, Miss Millay, tell it quick."

She turned to look at him, her face a pale splotch in the shadows. "He's hurt!"

"And he'll likely die happen we don't get out of here right quick. The truth now: this was no kidnappin', was it?"

"Of course not!" Elysse Millay sobbed. "Hank and I are . . . friends. He agreed to help me out when this came up."

"You needed money, that it? Way your bosses talked about you, you could've just asked for it."

"No! No, it wasn't the money. He's going to bleed to death—"

"Publicity, then," Hallam cut in.

"Yes, yes! What else do you want out of me? It was all Kurt Prescott's idea. My name would be in all the papers, he said. He said everybody would want to come see *Passion Flower*, to see the beautiful brave girl who got kidnapped. The bastard!"

Hallam put his hand on Hank's chest. The man was still bleeding heavily, and his breathing was irregular. Hallam had heard that sound before. He didn't like it, not one little bit.

"What happened earlier tonight?"

"That man, the one who was supposed to deliver the money, he was crazy! He tried to kill Hank. I think he would have killed me, too. Surely Prescott let him in on it. He had to know the whole thing was a gag! Why would he try to kill us?"

"Maybe he wanted the money for himself. Maybe he just felt like it," Hallam said softly. "But whatever the reason, I figure that's him out there takin' pot shots at us."

"Oh, Lord, what are we going to do?"

Hallam knew the answer to that one, but he didn't like it.

"Reckon I've got to go out there," he said.

Suddenly he became aware that the shots had stopped. He thought he heard something else, though.

There was another car coming.

Colt in hand, Hallam went to the window and looked cautiously out. He saw the headlights of the approaching vehicle on the trail that ran through the trees. It came to a stop behind Hallam's old flivver, and he could tell that it was a low-slung roadster. The driver left the motor running and got out.

"Brinke?" The call was low-pitched, barely carrying to the house. But Hallam recognized the voice anyway, just like he recognized the tall, lean figure.

It was the director of *Passion Flower*, Kurt Prescott.

A grin creased Hallam's leathery face. Looked like there was some double-crossin' going on tonight.

"Get out of here, you damn fool!" Joe Brinke called from the trees. He was too late.

Hallam's Colt roared and bucked, and the slug kicked up dirt between Prescott's feet.

"Hold it right there, Prescott!" Hallam called. "Be still or I'll drop you."

Prescott didn't move except to start sweating. "Hallam? Is that you, Hallam? By God, man, what are you doing?"

"Call off your dog, Prescott," Hallam said. "Game's over. You and Brinke lost. Miss Millay and the money are both safe with me, and they're goin' back to the studio."

Frightened though he was, Prescott couldn't keep anger from seeping into his voice. "I don't know what the hell you're talking about—"

"Nice show you and Brinke put on back there," Hallam said. "I reckon you were both tryin' to cover yourselves after the first murder attempt went sour."

"Murder!" Elysse Millay gasped from behind him.

"Yes, ma'am," Hallam said to her, his words loud enough that Prescott and Brinke could still hear. "That phony kidnappin' might've been good publicity, but it was even better as an excuse to get back at you and your friend. That Mr. Prescott likes being known as a ladies' man. Guess he didn't take kindly to bein' turned down."

Hallam was guessing on that part, but the way Prescott's face contorted told him that he had hit close to home.

And if a picture with a kidnapped star would do good business, one with a dead one might do even better. Hallam remembered seeing the stuffed corpse of a famous gunfighter and bounty hunter on exhibition in a traveling medicine show. Nope, you couldn't go wrong banking on the morbidity of the paying customers.

"You're crazy, Hallam!" Prescott shouted. "Elysse, if you're in there, come on out, darling. I promise no one will hurt you."

"Hank's hurt!" she cried in reply. "You've got to help us, Kurt!"

Hallam saw the brief, furtive smile on Prescott's face. "Of course I'll help you—"

"Don't listen to him, girl," Hallam warned.

"Come on out, darling," Prescott urged.

Now he was ready to play the hero, Hallam saw. Had to give the man credit for trying to seize the opportunity. He still thought he had a chance to get Elysse Millay.

"No!" Brinke's voice came from the woods. "I'm doing the job I was paid to do. Get out of here, Prescott! Now!"

Prescott half turned, and his hand went furtively under his coat. "Forget it, Brinke. Our deal's off—"

And then he was snatching a pistol out, turning, raising the gun. He fired twice toward the trees, then tried to duck to one side as Brinke fired back.

He staggered, grunted, folded up in the middle. He sat down clutching his stomach and then swayed over onto his side.

Hallam was out the window in a rolling dive as soon as he saw Brinke's muzzle flashes. He lit down shooting. Slugs chewed the ground around him as he rolled toward the cars. He came up, ducked between them, and froze, sights lined on the shadowy figure that was Joe Brinke.

There was a click. Brinke's hammer fell on an empty shell . . . just as Hallam, after counting shots, had gambled his life that it would.

"Got a couple left, Joe," Hallam said. "Wouldn't mind usin' 'em, either."

A mirthless chuckle came from the gloom. Carefully Brinke emerged into the glow cast by the lights of Prescott's roadster. His gun was in his hand. He dropped it to the dirt, a cold smile on his face.

"You wouldn't shoot an unarmed man," he said.

"You're not a man," Hallam said. "You're a mad dog, let run loose too long."

"What the hell are you talking about? What did I do?"

"Killed a couple of men, for starters.

"A kidnapper and a would-be killer." Brinke gestured at Prescott's body. "There's your villain. He planned the whole thing. He wanted the girl and her boyfriend dead right from the start. I could have handled it, too, but he got nervous after you stuck your nose in. Thought it would look better if he fired me and hired you. That way I could work behind the scenes. He was afraid Norton and Yates would eventually figure out he was manipulating them. Hell, he even got them to pay my salary for doing his dirty work. That ransom money's mine."

"You're admittin' your part in it, though."

"Admitting, hell." He nodded toward the house, where loud racking sobs told Hallam that Hank had died. Brinke went on, "The girl's too broken up to know what's happening. As for the rest, this conversation never took place. As far as the cops are concerned, I just did a public service by knocking off a kidnapper and the guy who hired him. If you say different, then it's your word against mine. No proof, Hallam, not a bit. It'll just look like I pulled your fat out of the fire and you got jealous."

"I really ought to shoot you," Hallam breathed.

"You won't. Your stupid cowboy code of honor won't let you."

Hallam stood for a long moment looking at the sneer of contempt on Brinke's face. Then he sighed heavily and let down the hammer of the Colt. "You're right," he said as he slid the big pistol back in its holster.

"Damn fool."

Brinke's hand was a blur as he went for the hideout gun Hallam knew he carried at the small of his back.

A flicker of steel, a thump—

Brinke stepped back, his draw unfinished, and looked down in surprise at the bone handle of the Bowie knife that protruded from his chest. He stared at it for at least five seconds, then pitched forward on his face.

"That's a chore been needin' done for a long time," Hallam said to the night. Too bad the man named Hank had had to die, too, just for going along with what he thought was a publicity stunt to help the girl.

A lot of people would be asking questions about tonight, Hallam knew, from the cops on down to Jamie Brinke. He'd tell them the only thing he knew to tell them—the truth. What happened from then on out wasn't up to him.

Hallam reached through the open window of Prescott's car, killed the engine that had been purring all along.

Then he went into the house to collect the girl.

# Wayne D. Dundee

# DEATH OF AN
# IRON MAIDEN

Lita Perry's office at the Mid-City Health Club was, like the woman herself, compact, neat, stripped of frills. The only things in evidence that weren't strictly necessary to the business of running the club were the trophies lining a shelf behind her desk and the dozen or so framed photographs hanging on the walls. The latter, on examination, proved to be shots of Ms. Perry posing in competition for various female bodybuilding contests. I made the inevitable comparison but found it difficult to connect the rippling, glistening figure in any of the photos to the trim, tanned young woman who sat behind the desk wearing a crisp white blouse and no-nonsense skirt.

"A lot of people do that," she said tersely.

"Do what?" I asked.

"Sit there and compare me to those pictures. I sometimes feel as if they expect me to strip down and strike a pose to prove myself."

"Sorry," I said, embarrassed because I hadn't realized I was being so obvious. "Meant no offense."

She shook her head, tossing the loose dark curls that framed her face. It was a pretty enough face the way it was and with some makeup and a more carefully attended hairdo and a less dour expression it might have been beautiful. "No," she said, "I'm the one who's sorry. I was being overly sensitive. The way things have been going lately, it doesn't take much to set me off."

"You said on the phone that you were having some trouble you

40

wanted me to look into. I gather it's something more serious than people upsetting you by comparing you to your photos?''

''Of course it is. How much do you know about the sport of women's bodybuilding, Mr. Hannibal?''

I shrugged. ''Not a great deal. It's still a relatively new thing, but seems to have caught on in a big way. Judging from the trophies, I'd say you've done pretty well at it.''

''When I was active in it, yes, I did quite well. But I retired from competition just over a year ago. The monetary rewards were never that great, and after a while all the training and traveling didn't seem worth it anymore. When I had an opportunity to settle down and open this club and earn a steady income, well, I grabbed it. Now, however, I'm planning a comeback of sorts. You see, I'm entered in the Miss Ni-Bod Contest that's scheduled to be held here in Rockford next month.''

''Miss what?''

''Miss Northern Illinois Body—Miss Ni-Bod, for short. It's one of the first major competitions of its kind to be held anywhere in the Rockford area and a sure bet to receive plenty of media coverage. If I do well in it, you can imagine what a boost the publicity would give my business here.''

''Does your business need a boost?''

''Doesn't everyone's?'' She made a face. ''But there's more to it than that. The club does okay, we turn a decent profit. Only most of my customers are bored housewives or secretaries who just want to firm up their fannies a little for hubby or boyfriend. And I'm certainly not saying there's anything wrong with that. God love 'em, they're the ones who keep clubs like this going all across the country. When I retired from competition, however, I hadn't planned on keeping away from things entirely. I'd hoped to attract some women who were serious bodybuilders to my club. At the risk of sounding corny, I considered myself one of the pioneers of the sport. With my knowledge and experience, I feel I have a great deal to offer anyone going into it now. All I need is the chance to prove it.''

''That's very interesting, Ms. Perry, but—''

''Don't do that. Please. Don't call me 'Ms.' Perry. I hate that title. Whenever I hear anyone use it, it sounds as if there's a mosquito loose in the room. Make it Miss or, better yet, just Lita.''

''All right, Mis . . . uh, Lita. Your desire to be a trainer of champions and all that is very interesting, but when do we get to why you need a private detective?''

She regarded me for several moments without saying anything. Her right hand rested on the desktop in front of her and its fingers drummed a thoughtful tattoo. The hand was smooth and unlined and the fingernails shone with a clear polish. But the movement of the fingers caused the muscles in her forearm to ripple like waves on wind-whipped water, and I was reminded that this little lady could probably crack walnuts in the crook of that very arm.

"Someone doesn't want me to win the Miss Ni-Bod Contest," she stated flatly.

I nodded. "Doesn't seem surprising. I would imagine that's the hope of every girl who's entered against you."

"But this someone is taking steps to made damn *sure* I don't win."

"What kind of steps? You mean threats?"

"No, nothing quite so crude. He's being considerably more psychological about it, trying to mess up my mind, wreck my concentration. You see, concentration and discipline during this phase of the training—especially for me, coming back from a year's layoff—is extremely crucial. If I don't have it, if I'm distracted too much, I won't have a snowball's chance when I step out on that contest stage."

"You'll have to be a little less vague. Exactly what's been done against you?"

She made a gesture with her hand. "Name it. Sabotage of equipment here at the club, mysterious plumbing and electrical problems at my home, everything short of sugar in the gas tank of my car. Half a dozen different incidents over the past couple weeks, each one very costly and time consuming and distracting. He's doing quite a thorough job."

"You keep saying 'he.' Are you just speaking figuratively, or do you have an idea who's behind it?"

"Oh, I have an idea who's behind it all right, and a pretty damn god one—Derek Humboldt, my former trainer."

"The Derek Humboldt of Humboldt's Gym?"

"The same."

"Why?"

"Because he never forgave me for retiring from competition and quitting him. He said I left him holding the dirty end of the stick, that he'd put all that work into me and then I threw it away. On top of that, I went into business against him. *He'd* put in all the work, mind you—what the hell did he think *I* was doing all that time!? Anyway, now that I'm entered in the Miss Ni-Bod and there's a better than even chance I'll bet out his current girl, well, apparently his ego just can't handle it.''

"You seem pretty sure of winning."

"One of the things Derek taught me was self-confidence. I haven't forgotten it. Like I said, I've got the experience. That alone gives me the edge over most of the girls I'll be up against.''

"Have you confronted Humboldt in any way?"

"Yes. I lost my cool one time after we found some cables cut on one of the Universal weight machines. I called him on the phone. He laughed at me and said I was letting my imagination run away with me. Then he turned nasty and threatened to sue me for slander if I made any more accusations that I couldn't back up.''

"So you haven't gone to the police?''

"No. But not because of Derek's threat. I have other reasons for not wanting to bring the police into this. Reasons you'd probably find a little silly.''

I grinned. ''When it comes right down to it, most of the reasons people have for not going to the cops are a little silly. But that's what keeps guys like me in business.''

She made another gesture, using both hands this time. ''It's just that I *don't* have any real proof against Derek, exactly as he pointed out. And even if I did . . . well, I'd still be a little reluctant to sic the police on him. After all, I do own him a great deal. He took me as a skinny kid with no goal in life and taught me discipline and self-confidence—all the things I've been talking about—and showed me I could make something of myself. I guess what I'm saying is that I feel some sort of warped loyalty to him.''

"Under the circumstances, I'd think that would wear thin in a hurry.''

"I just want the harassment stopped, that's all. What's done is done. I just want to be able to concentrate on my training so I can win the Miss Ni-Bod and hopefully attract a following that will be interest in serious bodybuilding under my guidance.''

"So you want me to determine for sure if Humboldt's the one behind your trouble and then make him back off. Is that it?''

She nodded. ''Can you do it?''

I nodded back. ''Sounds like something I could handle. Let's find out.''

When I emerged from the Mid-City Health Club, a light, powdery snow was falling. The February sky was heavy with low-hanging, slate gray clouds that obliterated the afternoon sun and threatened to spill plenty more of the white stuff before they were through.

I walked a few steps away from the front door and paused, still under the protection of the building's awning. I took out a cigarette and wasted no time in firing up. About a third of the way through my meeting with Lita Perry I had started to reach for the pack but, considering the surroundings, it hadn't seemed very appropriate. So I'd held off, even though by the time the meeting was ended I was feeling the nudges of a full-fledged nicotine fit.

I sucked the smoke deep now, held it in an extra long time, then blew it out into the crisp air. It tasted and felt fine. Luckily, not enough of the health-conscious atmosphere had rubbed off to spoil my enjoyment of a good smoke.

Behind me, the club doors opened again and a somewhat dumpy, brown-haired woman exited, struggling slightly with an oversized gym bag. I watched her make her way across the parking lot, stepping carefully on the patches of ice and packed old snow that were being made newly slick by the fresh stuff. She crossed to the bus stop shelter on the far side of the lot where she unceremoniously dumped the gym bag at her feet and produced a pack of smokes of her own. I grinned. She extracted one of those slim brown cigarillos, set fire to it, and took an extra long drag just as I had done.

"Attagirl," I said under my breath. "Don't let 'em brainwash you."

I piled into my old Mustang, its vinyl seat stiff and icy cold through the thin fabric of my slacks, backed it out of its slot, then threaded it carefully through the busy parking lot. Even this late in the winter, there were plenty of idiots around who acted like they had never driven on snow and ice before. When I was ready to turn out onto State Street, I had to wait for a city bus that came hissing to a stop alongside the shelter. I saw my fellow smoker hoist up her bag and get ready to board. She took a final drag on her cigarillo, gripping it somewhat mannishly between her thumb and forefinger, then flipped it under the bus's tires and went up the boarding steps. After she was out of sight, I felt as if I should have waved goodbye.

It was three on the nose when I ducked back out of the snow and into the dim warmth of The Bomb Shelter, the bar where I do most of my serious drinking. This afternoon's visit, however, happened to be more or less in the line of duty.

The Bomber himself, all six-and-a-half feet and three-hundred-plus pounds of him, was behind the bar. "Hey, Joe," he rumbled when he saw me. "Looking for a good place to get snowed in?"

If you're an avid enough sports fan, the name Bomber Brannigan might be familiar to you. He was a pretty decent heavyweight in his prime, the high point of his career being the night he went the distance with a pre-champion Sonny Liston, back when the big ugly bear was building his reputation as being indestructible. Bomber lost the decision, but those who were there say he gave a mighty good account of himself, and if he hadn't chipped a bone in his knockout right hand in the ninth round—while he was dealing Liston the worst of it—he might very well have snapped the bear's unbeaten string far ahead of a certain loud-mouthed kid from Louisville. It was that troublesome right that made him quit the prizefight ring and enter the more colorful and lucrative sport of pro wrestling. He was a force to be reckoned with in the wrestling game for a dozen and a half years, retiring finally to settle here in Rockford and open The Bomb Shelter. It was at that point that our paths crossed, and even though he's somewhat past fifty, scarred and grizzled and almost a hundred pounds over his prime fighting weight, I'd still rather have him backing me in a physical confrontation than anyone else I know.

I climbed onto my usual bar stool and said, "I need some information and a shot and a beer. Not necessarily in that order."

The Bomber nodded. "Got two out of three for sure."

When I had a Bud and some bourbon in front of me, I said, "Derek Humboldt, Humboldt's Gym up in Loves Park. Know him?"

"Sure. I know him."

Because of his background, The Bomber still spends a fair amount of time in and around area gyms, keeping an eye on the local talent. His rear end may be wider than his shoulders these days, but he can still outlift and out-armwrestle ninety-nine percent of the bronze prettyboys who challenge him. The remaining one percent are draws; I've never yet heard of anyone flat out beating him.

"Up until about a year ago," I went on, "this Humboldt was training and apparently managing a female bodybuilder named Lita Perry."

"Ah, yes, lovely Lita. One of the original iron maidens. You know, of course, that Humboldt was more than just her trainer and manager?"

"What do you mean?"

He spread his hands. "Come on, Joe. Lita Perry is a very foxy-looking lady. If you don't mind your chicks having biceps bigger than Charlie Atlas, that is. All that training and traveling time spent together . . . well, it's understandable if ol' Derek took more than a coach/athlete interest in her. They had a very hot romance going."

So. There was an interesting little sidelight I hadn't figured on. I'm used to being lied to in my line of work, of course, frequently by my own clients; and, up to a point, I could understand Lita not wanting to air this bit of dirty laundry. But it could have a bearing on the case, damn it, and it made me sore that she hadn't seen fit to tell me about it. When I next talked to her, tentatively sometime tomorrow, I'd have to make sure she wasn't holding out any more choice little tidbits. In the meantime, I laid out the rest of what she had told me for The Bomber. When I was through, I said, "Well? Humboldt the type who could do something like that?"

He made a thoughtful face. "Hard to say, Joe. When it comes to women, guys can do some pretty screwy things. If Derek is the one behind Lita's harassment, though, I'd say it's more an act of jealousy than of malice."

"Why jealousy? You mean she left him for another guy?"

"No. Matter of fact, you could say it was the other way around. The way I heard it, she quit him because he wouldn't divorce his wife and turn their affair into something more respectable. And you want to know something else? After all this time, I still don't think they're over each other."

The call came at half past seven the next morning. I'd already punched the snooze alarm for the second time and was concentrating mightily on catching those few extra z's. I'm not the type who bounds eagerly and cheerfully out of bed to face the new day. I grabbed the bedside phone in mid-ring and growled a none-too-pleasant "Yeah?" into it.

It was a female voice on the other end of the line, soft and uncertain. "Mr. . . . Hannibal?"

I swallowed some of my annoyance. This voice didn't sound as if it needed me barking back at it. "Yeah, this's Hannibal," I said.

"This is Betty . . . Betty Carpenter. I work for Lita Perry. That is, I . . . we met yesterday at the health club."

I remembered her. A petite, shapely black girl with incredible almond eyes. "Sure, Betty. What's up?"

"I'm calling from the club now. . . . I thought you should know, there's been . . . Oh, it's awful Mr. Hannibal—Lita's dead!"

Outside, the snow was still falling, harder now, bigger, wetter flakes but fortunately with no wind to speak of. I left my southside apartment and drove angrily—recklessly, considering the conditions. After my talk with The Bomber yesterday, it seemed too late in the day to do much else on the Perry case and the beer was tasting especially good, so I'd stayed right there and held down my barstool until well after dark. Then home, a raid on the refrigerator, and to bed. Now I wondered if I'd gotten off my ass and done something—anything—would Lita Perry still be alive?

The parking lot of the shopping center where Mid-City Health Club was located was comparatively empty this early, the other businesses that it served not opening until the more standard hour of nine. Lita had explained to me that she opened at six to accommodate several professional women who preferred to get their exercising out of the way before their workday began.

There was a slew of official vehicles, several with flashing red-and-blue lights, clustered near the entrance to the club. I parked on the edge of the pack and trudged hurriedly through the deepening snow. The two uniforms stationed outside the door knew me and knew I was expected. They let me by with nothing more than a couple curt nods.

Inside, the lobby was crowded with people, mostly men, melted snow glistening on their collars and caps. Betty was there, looking tiny and frightened, her almond eyes even wider than I remembered. She fought bravely to hold back her tears when she saw me, but couldn't manage it. I went over and put an arm around her. She leaned gratefully against me. We were barely acquaintances, but mine was probably the friendliest face she'd seen all morning. In addition to that, we both sensed we were the only ones in the room feeling any emotion over what had happened to Lita.

When I had Betty calmed down somewhat, I told one of the fresh-faced young cops to take her somewhere where she could lie—or at least sit—down. Then I stamped the last of the snow off my boots and walked in to where the body was. My client's body.

She was in the free-weight room, lying on her back in a position to do bench presses. A handful of county coroner's men were huddled around her, concealing her from the waist up. But I could see both ends of a barbell poking out past their white-coated rumps and it was wincingly obvious what had happened. The bar wasn't up on the support hooks where it belonged when not in use, but down a couple feet lower and tilted in an odd way. It wouldn't be a pretty sight.

Lieutenant of Detectives Ed Terry stood nearby, motionless except for his eyes. He watched me for a minute, then sauntered over. Terry is a short, broad, balding fireplug of a man with a permanently sour expression and thick black eyebrows that leap and wriggle above his eyes when he gets excited, like two wooly caterpillars doing a mating dance. He's a cop clear to the bone, and a damn good one. We'd butted heads a few times back when I first turned private then had settled into a state of coexistence that gradually led to grudging respect for each other. But I wouldn't expect him ever to admit it.

He said, "The Carpenter girl arrived to open the club this morning and found her like that. Not a pleasant thing to see before breakfast."

"This is no accident," I said tightly. "No matter what it looks like, it's no accident."

Terry craned his neck to look up at me, one of the wooly caterpillars cocking with interest. "What makes you say that?" he wanted to know.

I gave it to him, told him why Lita Perry had hired me the previous day, about the harassment, and even named the one she suspected was behind it. "But you know all that," I concluded. "Betty Carpenter would have told you as much. You allowed her to call me because you wanted me here to get my side of it. So now you've got it. What's your next move?"

"You still haven't told me why this couldn't just be an accident."

"Because it's too much of a goddamn coincidence, that's why. It stinks, and you know it. Don't try to jerk me around, Ed. That's my client laying dead over there, and I'm not in a real swell mood."

As if on cue, one of the coroner's men stepped aside at that point and I suddenly had my first full view of Lita Perry in death. Her head was turned to one side with the weighted chrome bar angled across her left temple, imbedded slightly where it had crushed her skull and facial bones. I couldn't see her eyes but her mouth was spread in a ghastly grin, the perfect teeth outlined in dried blood.

I could feel Terry watching me. I walked over and jabbed a thumb to indicate the weight discs on one end of the bar. "How much weight is on here?" I said.

The coroner's men stopped doing what they were doing.

Terry frowned. "What difference does it make?"

I leaned closer to examine the weights, not touching anything, did some quick mental addition. "Over a hundred and fifty pounds," I announced, straightening back up. "There's a solid indication right there that this wasn't an accident."

"The woman was a professional bodybuilder who ran this club. Lifting heavy weights is what she did, Joe. The Carpenter girl said she'd been staying nights after the club closed to do her training. So she was here along, the bar slipped somehow, fell on her and killed her."

I shook my head. "No good. It's too much weight, don't you see? I'm not saying she *couldn't* lift that much, I'm saying she *wouldn't* have been working with that much under the circumstances. Sure she stayed nights and trained, she mentioned about that yesterday. But any weight training she did alone would have consisted of a high number of reps with only a moderate amount of weight. She was a pro, she knew better than to fool around with this much weight by herself, without a spotter."

"So what are you saying? Somebody else dropped the bar on her while she was lying there, for crying out loud?"

"It could have happened that way, it could have happened a dozen different ways. I don't know the how of it. Not yet anyway. I just know it wasn't an accident. That's all I'm trying to get across."

The lieutenant gave an exasperated sigh. "I know, I know. You've been singing that same song ever since you walked in here."

The deputy coroner, a mousy little guy named Steinmertz, cleared his throat. "If you gentlemen would please take your . . . ah, discussion somewhere else? We'd like to finish our examination so Ms. Perry's remains can be—"

"*Miss* Perry," I said quickly.

Steinmertz looked puzzled. "I beg your pardon?"

I said, "Call her Miss—not Ms. She hated that title."

He adjusted his glasses and thrust out his chin stubbornly. "I'm sorry, but it's a long-standing departmental policy that all females we come in contact with be referred to as—"

I shoved my face close to his. "And it's my policy, four eyes, that if you call her 'Ms.' again I'll make you a whole lot sorrier."

"Take it easy, Joe," Terry said, stepping between us.

"Nuts to taking it easy," I shot back. "You seem to be handling that part of it okay. Are you going to stand around all morning watching these clowns play 'Quincy' or are you going after Humboldt?" I waited a bet. "Or do I have to do it myself?"

Terry's mouth pulled into a hard, tight line. In a chilled voice, he said, "I think you'd better back off, mister. It just so happens I've already had Derek Humboldt placed under surveillance. *If* we decide we have a murder case here, my boys will be in a position to bring him in on a moment's notice. In the meantime, I suggest you extract your foot from your mouth and follow me into the other room so these gentlemen can be left alone to finish doing their job."

We buried Lita Perry two days later, on a Saturday morning. It had finally stopped snowing and the temperature was on the rise. The cemetery was covered with wet gray slush. Lita had no close relatives that anyone knew so the turnout for the graveside service was depressingly small.

Betty Carpenter was there, standing with a group of women I assumed to be health club regulars. I stood by myself. I guess the preacher said some good words but I don't remember what they were. When he was done, I turned and headed toward my car. Out of the corner of my eye I saw the cemetery groundsmen moving up, getting ready to perform the final part of the ritual, the part we like to think about least.

"Joe?"

Betty Carpenter materialized at my side and put a hand on my arm. I stopped walking.

"I don't mean to pry," she said, "but I . . . Well, I just want to say something. I hope you're not blaming yourself in any way for what happened to Lita. I mean, you were only on the job a few hours and none of us—least of all Lita—thought there was any real danger behind the things that were happening."

"Sure," I said. "Thanks, kid."

"Darn it, you are feeling guilty, aren't you?"

I looked at the ground. "I don't know. I keep asking myself if I should be. Maybe that's the same thing."

She stared down at the ground with me for a while. "A couple of times after we'd closed up and everybody else was gone," she said, "Lita asked me to stay for a while and keep her company, you know, while she did her workout. But I always had something else to do. Real important stuff like washing my hair or laundry or some stupid movie on TV I didn't want to miss. So she quit asking me. Now I find myself wondering if I'd stayed one of those other times if maybe she would have asked me to keep her company on the night she was killed and . . . Well, I guess what I'm saying is that we can all find something to feel guilty about if we try hard enough."

I didn't know what to say to that and apparently Betty Carpenter didn't know what else to say to me either. After a minute, she leaned up to give me a quick kiss on the cheek, then turned and hurried toward where the group of women stood waiting for her.

I had someone waiting for me, too. Ed Terry stood leaning against the side of my Mustang, hands jammed into the pockets of a rumpled overcoat, expression sour as usual. He withdrew a pack of cigarettes and shook one out for me. I took it, leaned into the light he offered.

After I'd exhaled some smoke, he said, "We took Derek Humboldt into custody yesterday afternoon."

I nodded. "I heard."

"You had it pegged pretty damn close that morning at the health club. The autopsy turned up particles of black paint in one of the head wounds, and the lab boys matched it to the paint on the weight discs from the set Lita Perry was working with. So we had to ask ourselves if the chrome bar fell on her the way it first looked, where did the black paint come from? Careful examination of the individual weight discs produced one with traces of human blood on it—the same type as Ms. Perry's. The way we saw it then was that somebody had brained her with the weight, laid her out on the bench, dropped the bar on her in an attempt to make it look like an accident. The clincher came when we were able to lift a set of prints from the bloody weight and match them to Humboldt."

"He confess to anything?"

"Not yet. But he will. Even his alibi stinks. His wife was out of town on an overnight trip, and he claims he was home alone watching a basketball game on TV."

I smoked my cigarette and tried not to listen to the sound of the backhoe starting to fill Lita's grave.

Terry cleared his throat. "I, uh, guess I came to say thanks. I'd like to think we still would have put it all together. But without you pushing . . . well, maybe we could have overlooked something.''

"Just nail the bastard," I told him. "Nail him good."

I spent that afternoon trying to drink away the memory of—and guilt over?— a dead client. When I caught myself trying to pick a fight in the third bar in a row, I decided I wasn't fit for public consumption and went home.

I switched on the TV from force of habit and flopped into my easy chair with an open six-pack on the floor beside me. The evening news was in progress on one of the local channels, and the subject being covered, like a recurring bad dream, was the arrest of Derek Humboldt for Lita's murder. I swore out loud and started up out of the chair to change the channel.

A pre-recorded videotape was showing an attractive middle-aged woman coming down the front steps of the county courthouse, flanked by two bland-looking men who had the air of attorneys about them. The announcer identified the woman as Maggie Humboldt, wife of the accused killer. The camera followed her and her two companions as they eeled through the gaggle of reporters, muttering "no comment" to shouted questions, and made their way to a waiting car parked at the curb. While one of the men held a door for her, Mrs. Humboldt paused momentarily and raised a cigarette to her lips. It was one of those slim brown cigarillos, and she held it somewhat mannishly between her thumb and forefinger. She took a hard final drag and then flipped it into the street, under the car's rear tire, before ducking into the back seat.

I froze with my hand on the selector knob.

When I turned away from the set, I was stone cold sober.

The grandfather clock in the hallway bonged ten o'clock. I sat in the dark and waited.

I'd heard her car pull into the driveway a couple minutes ago and now I heard the rattle of keys in the front door. She came in, began flipping on wall switches. I slitted my eyes to soften the glare as lights blinked on around me. She entered the living room, purse slung over her shoulder, with purposeful strides. Halfway in she spotted me, stopped short, gulped a quick intake of air.

She was indeed a handsome woman. TV hadn't done her justice at all. Tall and full-bodied, with a generous mouth and smoldering dark eyes. Long caramel-colored hair cascaded down from beneath a stylish, broad-brimmed hat.

"Welcome home, Maggie," I said to her.

"How did you get in here?" she gasped.

"It wasn't hard," I replied. "You have a fine home here, you really ought to protect it with better locks."

She seemed to regain her composure in record time. "I know you," she said. "You're the detective, the one who's caused so much trouble for my husband."

I chuckled. "Oh, you're good, Maggie. You're real good. *I'm* the cause of your husband's trouble?"

"It was your accusations, based on what that insane Perry woman told you, that made him a prime suspect to the police."

"But it was his own fingerprints that put him behind bars, lady."

She didn't know what to say to that, so she decided to get angry. "What are you doing in my house!?" she demanded.

"I just dropped by to tell you that it didn't work."

"I don't know what you're talking about. What didn't work?"

"Your little scheme for revenge, Maggie. You came close. Damn close. It was a simple little thing like the way you hold your cigarette and then flip it away after you've taken the final drag that gave you away. I saw you do it for the first time outside Lita Perry's health club the day she hired me. Of course you were rigged up to look like a frumpy housewife then. But when I saw you do the same thing this evening on the television news—when you were you—I started to put everything together."

"You're crazy. You're not making any sense."

"It's all right there," I said, pointing to the oversized gym bag that I'd laid out on the couch. "That's what I came looking for. I found it tucked away in a corner of the basement, I'm sure you know which one. Inside are the bulky clothes and dark wig you wore whenever you went for your workout at the Mid-City Health Club. Lita must have met you a few times during the years she trained under your husband but it wasn't likely you two came into contact very often, especially after she and Derek started their affair. So it only took a simple disguise to keep her from recognizing you."

"I don't have to listen to any more of this. I'm calling the police."

"Go ahead," I said. "Save me the trouble."

She didn't move, of course. She just looked at me as if I were something she'd found stuck to the bottom of her shoe.

"Exactly when did you find out about the affair between Lita and your husband and decide you were going to get even with them?'' I wanted to know.

She wouldn't answer me.

''It must have been pretty tricky getting a key to the health club long enough to have it duplicated,'' I went on. ''I figure you must have taken it from Lita's desk one day when you were ostensibly there for a workout, left long enough to have it copied, then returned and replaced the original before anyone noticed it was missing. After that, of course, it was easy for you to slip in at night after the club was closed and start doing costly damage to the equipment. And while you had Lita's key ring you decided to have a duplicate made of her house key as well, enabling you to harass her on more than one front. Considering the bitterness with which they parted and their business rivalry, not to mention the upcoming Miss Ni-Bod Contest, you knew Lita would blame your husband for the harassment. You planned on killing her all along, didn't you? That was her punishment. And Derek's was being framed for her murder. An intricate, custom-fitted frame designed by you right down to staging a phony trip out of town so he'd be alone and have no alibi for the night she was killed.''

Those smoldering eyes had turned ice cold. ''You're so smart,'' she said contemptuously. ''If I'm the one behind it all, as you imply, how did I get Derek's fingerprints on the weight that supposedly killed the Perry tramp?''

''Simple. All barbell weights tend to look pretty much alike. You merely switched a weight disc from Lita's club with one from your husband's gym. After you were sure he'd handled the bogus weight often enough to leave his fingerprints all over it, you switched back. And when you slipped into the Mid-City on the night of the murder, while Lita was there alone, you made sure that it was the weight you used to bash in her brains. Then you staged the phony accident that you knew the police would eventually see through. You don't look as if you can lift a hundred-and-fifty-plus pounds but I guess that much hate and anger can produce a pretty amazing adrenaline rush, can't it? Tell me, did it give you some extra amount of satisfaction to drop that barbell on her after you'd already killed her?''

She pulled the silvery little automatic from her purse with surprising deftness and speed. It was a small-calibre weapon, but the unwavering eye of its muzzle looked as deep and dark and deadly as the mouth of a cannon. Some belittle the effectiveness of a small-calibre gun, but I know better. I habitually carry one as an emergency piece, a two-shot .22 Magnum derringer clipped inside my right boot (where it was doing me a fat lot of good at the moment!), and it's saved my bacon more than once. A lighter slug doesn't carry the punch to a non-vital area, of course, but aimed accurately one can kill you just as dead as an artillery shell.

I cursed myself silently. I hadn't figured on a gun. Damn it to hell, I just hadn't figured on her having a gun!

"You've deduced yourself right into an early grave, Mr. Hotshot Detective," Maggie Humboldt snarled.

"That's the trouble with murder," I replied, sitting very still in the chair. "It keeps growing, like cancer. You kill once, then you have to kill again to cover up the first one, and on and on. It never seems to end."

She smiled coldly. "We all have our crosses to bear, don't we?"

"If shooting is your style, why didn't you just put a bullet in Lita and your husband?"

"That was my first intent. That's why I bought this little gem and learned how to use it. But then it struck me: Why should I allow myself to end up in jail on top of what they'd already done to me? Even though their romance had supposedly burnt itself out, I couldn't just let them get away with it, don't you see? That's when I devised my grand scheme. It was beautiful. And I still intend to make it work, damn you."

I shook my head. "There's nothing beautiful about what you've done. You're sick."

"Shut up! You don't know what they put me through. Look at me. I'm an attractive, passionate woman. Why would any man find it necessary to seek satisfaction somewhere else? An iron maiden, Derek called her. He tried to say it with contempt after they'd split up. But I could see in his eyes that he still cared for her, that he wanted her back. Why!? Why did he desire *me* less than a . . . a musclebound *freak!?*"

She was working herself up, psyching herself into pulling the trigger, and in her wild-eyed state it wasn't gong to take much more. I figured I had only a matter of seconds. Twisting suddenly in the chair, I reached out, swept the lamp from the end table, hurled it in her direction. She made the amateur's mistake of being diverted by the tossed object and fired at it instead of me. The lamp exploded in mid-air, raining shards of glass and china down on the carpet. By the time she started to swing the gun back to me, I was up out of the chair and had covered the distance between us.

I threw myself against her, reaching for her gun hand. My momentum carried us both to the floor. The little automatic flew from her grasp and went skidding away. I landed partially on top of her but she still had enough starch left to begin clawing and punching at me while she spat vile curses.

Looking down at her, her face distorted in rage, my mind flashed to another woman's distorted face that I had recently gazed down upon—Lita Perry, her head crushed under the weight of a barbell. I had no qualms whatsoever about what I did next. I drew back my fist and hit Maggie Humboldt as hard as I've ever hit anyone in my life. The blow knocked her colder than her own murderous heart.

I got slowly to my feet, walked over to the telephone, and with hands that were starting to shake I dialed Ed Terry's number at police headquarters.

# Sara Paretsky

# SKIN DEEP

## 1

THE WARNING BELL CLANGS ANGRILY AND THE SUBMARINE
dives sharply. Everyone to battle stations. The Nazis pursuing
closely, the bell keeps up its insistent clamor, loud, urgent, filling
my head. My hands are wet: I can't remember what my job is in
this cramped, tiny boat. If only someone would turn off the alarm
bell. I fumble with some switches, pick up an intercom. The noise
mercifully stops.

"Vic! Vic, is that you?"

"What?"

"I know it's late. I'm sorry to call so late, but I just got home
from work. It's Sal, Sal Barthele."

"Oh, Sal. Sure." I looked at the orange clock readout. It was
four-thirty. Sal owns the Golden Glow, a bar in the south Loop I
patronize.

"It's my sister, Vic. They've arrested her. She didn't do it. I
know she didn't do it."

"Of course not, Sal—Didn't do what?"

"They're trying to frame her. Maybe the manager . . . I don't
know."

I swung my legs over the side of the bed. "Where are you?"

She was at her mother's house, 95th and Vincennes. Her sister
had been arrested three hours earlier. They needed a lawyer, a good
lawyer. And they needed a detective, a good detective. Whatever
my fee was, she wanted me to know they could pay my fee.

57

"I'm sure you can pay the fee, but I don't know what you want me to do," I said as patiently as I could.

"She—they think she murdered that man. She didn't even know him. She was just giving him a facial. And he dies on her."

"Sal, give me your mother's address. I'll be there in forty minutes."

The little house on Vincennes was filled with neighbors and relatives murmuring encouragement to Mrs. Barthele. Sal is very black, and statuesque. Close to six feet tall, with a majestic carriage, she can break up a crowd in her bar with a look and a gesture. Mrs. Barthele was slight, frail, and light-skinned. It was hard to picture her as Sal's mother.

Sal dispersed the gathering with characteristic firmness, telling the group that I was here to save Evangeline and that I needed to see her mother alone.

Mrs. Barthele sniffed over every sentence. "Why did they do that to my baby?" she demanded of me. "You know the police, you know their ways. Why did they come and take my baby, who never did a wrong thing in her life?"

As a white woman, I could be expected to understand the machinations of the white man's law. And to share responsibility for it. After more of this meandering, Sal took the narrative firmly in hand.

Evangeline worked at La Cygnette, a high-prestige beauty salon on North Michigan. In addition to providing facials and their own brand-name cosmetics at an exorbitant cost, they massaged the bodies and feet of their wealthy clients, stuffed them into steam cabinets, ran them through a Bataan-inspired exercise routine, and fed them herbal teas. Signor Giuseppe would style their hair for an additional charge.

Evangeline gave facials. The previous day she had one client booked after lunch, a Mr. Darnell.

"Men go there a lot?" I interrupted.

Sal made a face. "That's what I asked Evangeline. I guess it's part of being a Yuppie—go spend a lot of money getting cream rubbed into your face."

Anyway, Darnell was to have had his hair styled before his facial, but the hairdresser fell behind schedule and asked Evangeline to do the guy's face first.

Sal struggled to describe how a La Cygnette facial worked—neither of us had ever checked out her sister's job. You sit in something like a dentist's chair, lean back, relax—you're naked from the waist up, lying under a big down comforter. The facial expert—cosmetician was Evangeline's official title—puts cream on your hands and sticks them into little electrically heated mitts, so your hands are out of commission if you need to protect yourself. Then she puts stuff on your face, covers your eyes with heavy pads, and goes away for twenty minutes while the face goo sinks into your hidden pores.

Apparently while this Darnell lay back deeply relaxed, someone had rubbed some kind of poison into his skin. "When Evangeline came back in to clean his face, he was sick—heaving, throwing up, it was awful. She screamed for help and started trying to clean his face—it was terrible, he kept vomiting on her. They took him to the hospital, but he died around ten tonight.

"They came to get Baby at midnight—you've got to help her, V. I.—even if the guy tried something on her, she never did a thing like that—she'd haul off and slug him, maybe, but rubbing poison into his face? You go help her."

## 2

Evangeline Barthele was a younger, darker edition of her mother. At most times, she probably had Sal's energy—sparks of it flared now and then during our talk—but a night in the holding cells had worn her down.

I brought a clean suit and makeup for her: justice may be blind but her administrators aren't. We talked while she changed.

"This Darnell—you sure of the name?—had he ever been to the salon before?"

She shook her head. "I never saw him. And I don't think the other girls knew him either. You know, if a client's a good tipper or a bad one they'll comment on it, be glad or whatever that he's come in. Nobody said anything about this man."

"Where did he live?"

She shook her head. "I never talked to the guy, V. I."

"What about the PestFree?" I'd read the arrest report and talked briefly to an old friend in the M.E.'s office. To keep roaches and other vermin out of their posh Michigan Avenue offices, La Cygnette used a potent product containing a wonder chemical called chorpyrifos. My informant had been awestruck—"Only an operation that didn't know shit about chemicals would leave chorpyrifos lying around. It's got a toxicity rating of five—it gets you through the skin—you only need a couple of tablespoons to kill a big man if you know where to put it.''

Whoever killed Darnell had either known a lot of chemistry or been lucky—into his nostrils and mouth, with some rubbed into the face for good measure; the pesticide had made him convulsive so quickly that even if he knew who killed him he'd have been unable to talk, or even reason.

Evangeline said she knew where the poison was kept—everyone who worked there knew, knew it was lethal and not to touch it, but it was easy to get at. Just in a little supply room that wasn't kept locked.

"So why you? They have to have more of a reason than just that you were there."

She shrugged bitterly. "I'm the only black professional at La Cygnette—the other blacks working there sweep rooms and haul trash. I'm trying hard not to be paranoid, but I gotta wonder."

She insisted Darnell hadn't made a pass at her or done anything to provoke an attack—she hadn't hurt the guy. As for anyone else who might have had opportunity, salon employees were always passing through the halls, going in and out of the little cubicles where they treated clients—she'd seen any number of people, all with legitimate business in the halls, but she hadn't seen anyone emerging from the room where Darnell was sitting.

When we finally got to bond court later that morning, I tried to argue circumstantial evidence—any of La Cygnette's fifty or so employees could have committed the crime, since all had access and no one had motive. The prosecutor hit me with a very unpleasant surprise: the police had uncovered evidence linking my client to the dead man. He was a furniture buyer from Kansas City who came to Chicago six times a year, and the doorman and the maids at his hotel had identified Evangeline without any trouble as the woman who accompanied him on his visits.

Bail was denied. I had a furious talk with Evangeline in one of the interrogation rooms before she went back to the holding cells.

"Why the hell didn't you tell me? I walked into the courtroom and got blindsided."

"They're lying," she insisted.

"Three people identified you. If you don't start with the truth right now, you're going to have to find a new lawyer and a new detective. Your mother may not understand, but for sure Sal will."

"You can't tell my mother. You can't tell Sal!"

"I'm going to have to give them some reason for dropping your case, and knowing Sal it's going to have to be the truth."

For the first time she looked really upset. "You're my lawyer. You should believe my story before you believe a bunch of strangers you never saw before."

"I'm telling you, Evangeline, I'm going to drop your case. I can't represent you when I know you're lying. If you killed Darnell we can work out a defense. Or if you didn't kill him and knew him we can work something out, and I can try to find the real killer. But when I know you've been seen with the guy any number of times, I can't go into court telling people you never met him before."

Tears appeared on the ends of her lashes. "The whole reason I didn't say anything was so Mama wouldn't know. If I tell you the truth, you've got to promise me you aren't running back to Vincennes Avenue talking to her."

I agreed. Whatever the story was, I couldn't believe Mrs. Barthele hadn't heard hundreds like it before. But we each make our own separate peace with our mothers.

Evangeline met Darnell at a party two years earlier. She liked him, he liked her—not the romance of the century, but they enjoyed spending time together. She'd gone on a two-week trip to Europe with him last year, telling her mother she was going with a girlfriend.

"First of all, she has very strict morals. No sex outside marriage. I'm thirty, mind you, but that doesn't count with her. Second, he's white, and she'd murder me. She really would. I think that's why I never fell in love with him—if we wanted to get married I'd never be able to explain it to Mama."

This latest trip to Chicago, Darnell thought it would be fun to see what Evangeline did for a living, so he booked an appointment at La Cygnette. She hadn't told anyone there she knew him. And when she found him sick and dying she'd panicked and lied.

"And if you tell my mother this, V. I.—I'll put a curse on you. My father was from Haiti, and he knew a lot of good ones."

"I won't tell your mother. But unless they nuked Lebanon this morning or murdered the mayor, you're going to get a lot of lines in the paper. It's bound to be in print."

She wept at that, wringing her hands. So after watching her go off with the sheriff's deputies, I called Murray Ryerson at the *Herald-Star* to plead with him not to put Evangeline's liaison in the paper. "If you do she'll wither your testicles. Honest."

"I don't know, Vic. You know the *Sun-Times* is bound to have some kind of screamer headline like DEAD MAN FOUND IN FACE-LICKING SEX ORGY. I can't sit on a story like this when all the other papers are running it."

I knew he was right, so I didn't push my case very hard.

He surprised me by saying, "Tell you what: you find the real killer before my deadline for tomorrow's morning edition and I'll keep your client's personal life out of it. The sex scoop came in too late for today's paper. The *Trib* prints on our schedule and they don't have it, and the *Sun-Times* runs older, slower presses, so they have to print earlier."

I reckoned I had about eighteen hours. Sherlock Holmes had solved tougher problems in less time.

### 3

Roland Darnell had been the chief buyer of living-room furnishings for Alexander Dumas, a high-class Kansas City department store. He used to own his own furniture store in the nearby town of Lawrence, but lost both it and his wife when he was arrested for drug smuggling ten years earlier. Because of some confusion about his guilt—he claimed his partner, who disappeared the night he was arrested, was really responsible—he'd only served two years. When he got out, he moved to Kansas City to start a new life.

I learned this much from my friends at the Chicago police. At least, my acquaintances. I wondered how much of the story Evangeline had known. Or her mother. If her mother didn't want her child having a white lover, how about a white ex-con, ex- (presumably) drug-smuggling lover?

I sat biting my knuckles for a minute. It was eleven now. Say they started printing the morning edition at two the next morning, I'd have to have my story by one at the latest. I could follow one line, and one line only—I couldn't afford to speculate about Mrs. Barthele—and anyway, doing so would only get me killed. By Sal. So I looked up the area code for Lawrence, Kansas, and found their daily newspaper.

The *Lawrence Daily Journal-World* had set up a special number for handling press inquiries. A friendly woman with a strong drawl told me Darnell's age (forty-four); place of birth (Eudora, Kansas); ex-wife's name (Ronna Perkins); and ex-partner's name (John Crenshaw). Ronna Perkins was living elsewhere in the country and the *Journal-World* was protecting her privacy. John Crenshaw had disappeared when the police arrested Darnell.

Crenshaw had done an army stint in Southeast Asia in the late sixties. Since much of the bamboo furniture the store specialized in came from the Far East, some people speculated that Crenshaw had set up the smuggling route when he was out there in the service. Especially since Kansas City immigration officials discovered heroin in the hollow tubes making up chair backs. If Darnell knew anything about smuggling, he had never revealed it.

"That's all we know here, honey. Of course, you could come on down and try to talk to some people. And we can wire you photos if you want."

I thanked her politely—my paper didn't run too many photographs. Or even have wire equipment to accept them. A pity—I could have used a look at Crenshaw and Ronna Perkins.

La Cygnette was on an upper floor of one of the new marble skyscrapers at the top end of the Magnificent Mile. Tall, white doors opened onto a hushed waiting room reminiscent of a high-class funeral parlor. the undertaker, a middle-aged, highly made-up woman seated at a table that was supposed to be French provincial, smiled at me condescendingly.

"What can we do for you?"

"I'd like to see Angela Carlson. I'm a detective."

She looked nervously at two clients seated in a far corner. I lowered my voice. "I've come about the murder."

"But—but they made an arrest."

I smiled enigmatically. At least I hoped it looked enigmatic. "The police never close the door on all options until after the trial." If she knew anything about the police she'd know that was a lie—once they've made an arrest you have to get a presidential order to get them to look at new evidence.

The undertaker nodded nervously and called Angela Carlson in a whisper on the house phone. Evangeline had given me the names of the key players at La Cygnette; Carlson was the manager.

She met me in the doorway leading from the reception area into the main body of the salon. We walked on thick, silver pile through a white maze with little doors opening onto it. Every now and then we'd pass a white-coated attendant who gave the manager a subdued hello. When we went by a door with a police order slapped to it, Carlson winced nervously.

"When can we take that off? Everybody's on edge, and that sealed door doesn't help. Our bookings are down as it is."

"I'm not on the evidence team, Ms. Carlson. You'll have to ask the lieutenant in charge when they've got what they need."

I poked into a neighboring cubicle. It contained a large white dentist's chair and a tray covered with crimson pots and bottles, all with the cutaway swans that were the salon's trademark. While the manager fidgeted angrily I looked into a tiny closet where clients changed—it held a tiny sink and a few coat hangers.

Finally she burst out, "Didn't your people get enough of this yesterday? Don't you read your own reports?"

"I like to form my own impressions, Ms. Carlson. Sorry to have taken your time, but the sooner we get everything cleared up, the faster your customers will forget this ugly episode."

She sighed audibly and led me on angry heels to her office, although the thick carpet took the intended ferocity out of her stride. The office was another of the small treatment rooms with a desk and a menacing phone console. Photographs of a youthful Mme. de Leon, founder of La Cygnette, covered the walls.

Ms. Carlson looked through a stack of pink phone messages. "I have an incredibly busy schedule, Officer. So if you could get to the point . . ."

"I want to talk to everyone with whom Darnell had an appointment yesterday. Also the receptionist on duty. And before I do that I want to see their personnel files."

"Really! All these people were interviewed yesterday." Her eyes narrowed suddenly. "Are you really with the police? You're not, are you? You're a reporter. I want you out of here now. Or I'll call the real police."

I took my license photostat from my wallet. "I'm a detective. That's what I told your receptionist. I've been retained by the Barthele family. Ms. Barthele is not the murderer, and I want to find out who the real culprit is as fast as possible."

She didn't bother to look at the license. "I can barely tolerate answering police questions. I'm certainly not letting some snoop for hire take up my time. The police have made an arrest on extremely good evidence. I suppose you think you can drum up a fee by getting Evangeline's family excited about her innocence, but you'll have to look elsewhere for your money."

I tried an appeal to her compassionate side, using half-forgotten arguments from my court appearances as a public defender. (Outstanding employee, widowed mother, sole support, intense family pride, no prior arrests, no motive.) No sale.

"Ms. Carlson, you the owner or the manager here?"

"Why do you want to know?"

"Just curious about your stake in the success of the place and your responsibility for decisions. It's like this: you've got a lot of foreigners working here. The immigration people will want to come by and check out their papers.

"You've got lots and lots of tiny little rooms. Are they sprinklered? Do you have emergency exits? The fire department can make a decision on that.

"And how come your only black professional employee was just arrested and you're not moving an inch to help her out? There are lots of lawyers around who'd be glad to look at a discrimination suit against La Cygnette.

"Now if we could clear up Evangeline's involvement fast, we could avoid having all these regulatory people trampling around upsetting your staff and customers. How about it?"

She sat in indecisive rage for several minutes: how much authority did I have, really? Could I offset the munificent fees the salon and the building owners paid to various public officials just to avoid such investigations? Should she call headquarters for instruction? Or her lawyer? She finally decided that even if I didn't have a lot of power I could be enough of a nuisance to affect business. Her expression compounded of rage and defeat, she gave me the files I wanted.

Darnell had been scheduled with a masseuse, the hair expert Signor Giuseppe, and with Evangeline. I read their personnel files, along with that of the receptionist who had welcomed him to La Cygnette, to see if any of them might have hailed from Kansas City or had any unusual traits, such as an arrest record for heroin smuggling. The files were very sparse. Signor Giuseppe Fruttero hailed from Milan. He had no next-of-kin to be notified in the event of an accident. Not even a good friend. Bruna, the masseuse, was Lithuanian, unmarried, living with her mother. Other than the fact that the receptionist had been born as Jean Evans in Hammond but referred to herself as Monique from New Orleans, I saw no evidence of any kind of cover-up.

Angela Carlson denied knowing either Ronna Perkins or John Crenshaw or having any employees by either of those names. She had never been near Lawrence herself. She grew up in Evansville, Indiana, came to Chicago to be a model in 1978, couldn't cut it, and got into the beauty business. Angrily she gave me the names of her parents in Evansville and summoned the receptionist.

Monique was clearly close to sixty, much too old to be Roland Darnell's ex-wife. Nor had she heard of Ronna or Crenshaw.

"How many people knew that Darnell was going to be in the salon yesterday?"

"Nobody knew." She laughed nervously. "I mean, of course *I* knew—I made the appointment with him. And Signor Giuseppe knew when I gave him his schedule yesterday. And Bruna, the masseuse, of course, and Evangeline."

"Well, who else could have seen their schedules?"

She thought frantically, her heavily mascaraed eyes rolling in agitation. With another nervous giggle she finally said, "I suppose anyone could have known. I mean, the other cosmeticians and the makeup artists all come out for their appointments at the same time. I mean, if anyone was curious they could have looked at the other people's lists."

Carlson was frowning. So was I. "I'm trying to find a woman who'd be forty now, who doesn't talk much about her past. She's been divorced, and she won't have been in the business long. Any candidates?"

Carlson did another mental search then went to the file cabinets. Her mood was shifting from anger to curiosity, and she flipped through the files quickly, pulling five in the end.

"How long has Signor Giuseppe been here?"

"When we opened our Chicago branch in 1980 he came to us from Miranda's—I guess he'd been there for two years. He says he came to the States from Milan in 1970."

"He a citizen? Has he got a green card?"

"Oh, yes. His papers are in good shape. We are very careful about that at La Cygnette." My earlier remark about the immigration department had clearly stung. "And now I really need to get back to my own business. You can look at those files in one of the consulting rooms—Monique, find one that won't be used today."

It didn't take me long to scan the five files, all uninformative. Before returning them to Monique I wandered on through the back of the salon. In the rear a small staircase led to an upper story. At the top was another narrow hall lined with small offices and storerooms. A large mirrored room at the back filled with hanging plants and bright lights housed Signor Giuseppe. A dark-haired man with a pointed beard and a bright smile, he was ministering gaily to a thin, middle-aged woman, talking and laughing while he deftly teased her hair into loose curls.

He looked at me in the mirror when I entered. "You are here for the hair, Signora? You have the appointment?"

*"No, Signor Giuseppe. Sono qui perchè la sua fama se è sparsa di fronte a lei. Milano è una bella città, non è vero?"*

He stopped his work for a moment and held up a deprecating hand. "Signora, it is my policy to speak only English in my adopted country."

*"Una vera stupida e ignorante usanza io direi."* I beamed sympathetically and sat down on a high stool next to an empty customer chair. There were seats for two clients. Since Signor Giuseppe reigned alone, I pictured him spinning at high speed between customers, snipping here, pinning there.

"Signora, if you do not have the appointment, will you please leave? Signora Dotson here, she does not prefer the audience."

"Sorry, Mrs. Dotson," I said to the lady's chin. "I'm a detective. I need to talk to Signor Giuseppe, but I'll wait."

I strolled back down the hall and entertained myself by going into one of the storerooms and opening little pots of La Cygnette creams and rubbing them into my skin. I looked in a mirror and could already see an improvement. If I got Evangeline sprung maybe she'd treat me to a facial.

Signor Giuseppe appeared with a plastically groomed Mrs. Dotson. He had shed his barber's costume and was dressed for the street. I followed them down the stairs. When we got to the bottom I said, "In case you're thinking of going back to Milan— or even to Kansas—I have a few questions."

Mrs. Dotson clung to the hairdresser, ready to protect him.

"I need to speak to him alone, Mrs. Dotson. I have to talk to him about bamboo."

"I'll get Miss Carlson, Signor Giuseppe," his guardian offered.

"No, no, Signora. I will deal with this crazed woman myself. A million thanks. *Grazie, grazie.*"

"Remember, no Italian in your adopted America," I reminded him nastily.

Mrs. Dotson looked at us uncertainly.

"I think you should get Ms. Carlson," I said. "Also a police escort. Fast."

She made up her mind to do something, whether to get help or flee I wasn't sure, but she scurried down the corridor. As soon as she had disappeared, he took me by the arm and led me into one of the consulting rooms.

"Now, who are you and what is this?" His accent had improved substantially.

"I'm V. I. Warshawski. Roland Darnell told me you were quite an expert on fitting drugs into bamboo furniture."

I wasn't quite prepared for the speed of his attack. His hands were around my throat. He was squeezing and spots began dancing in front of me. I didn't try to fight his arms, just kicked sharply at his shin, following with a knee to his stomach. The pressure at my neck eased. I turned in a half circle and jammed my left elbow into his rib cage. He let go.

I backed to the door, keeping my arms up in front of my face and backed into Angela Carlson.

"What on earth are you doing with Signor Giuseppe?" she asked.

"Talking to him about furniture." I was out of breath. "Get the police and don't let him leave the salon."

A small crowd of white-coated cosmeticians had come to the door of the tiny treatment room. I said to them, "This isn't Giuseppe Fruttero. It's John Crenshaw. If you don't believe me, try speaking Italian to him—he doesn't understand it. He's probably never been to Milan. But he's certainly been to Thailand, and he knows an awful lot about heroin."

## 4

Sal handed me the bottle of Black Label. "It's yours, Vic. Kill it tonight or save it for some other time. How did you know he was Roland Darnell's ex-partner?"

"I didn't. At least not when I went to La Cygnette. I just knew it had to be someone in the salon who killed him, and it was most likely someone who knew him in Kansas. And that meant either Darnell's ex-wife or his partner. And Giuseppe was the only man on the professional staff. And then I saw he didn't know Italian—after praising Milan and telling him he was stupid in the same tone of voice and getting no response it made me wonder."

"We owe you a lot, Vic. The police would have never dug down to find that. You gotta thank the lady, Mama."

Mrs. Barthele grudgingly gave me her thin hand. "But how come those police said Evangeline knew that Darnell man? My baby wouldn't know some convict, some drug smuggler."

"He wasn't a drug smuggler, Mama. It was his partner. The police have proved all that now. Roland Darnell never did anything wrong." Evangeline, chic in red with long earrings that bounced as she spoke, made the point hotly.

Sal gave her sister a measuring look. "All I can say, Evangeline, is it's a good thing you never had to put your hand on a Bible in court about Mr. Darnell."

I hastily poured a drink and changed the subject.

# Al Sarrantonio

# SHERLOCKS

THE HOTEL ROOM SMELLED LIKE ROSEWATER. IT WAS TWELVE foot by twelve foot square, with a few sticks of cheap furniture stuck in the corners, green wall-to-wall carpeting that curled up as it reached the walls, a rumpled bed with an open suitcase on it and one small, dirty window that gave a good view of the metallic wall on the hotel a few yards away next door. A man lay on the carpeting in the center of the room. He was long and lean, with thinning blond hair and a youthful face with a lot of angles in it. There was a startled expression in his eyes, which were open wide. He lay on his stomach, with his head to one side, and there was a very large kitchen knife with a plastic handle standing straight up out of his back.

Lieutenant Henry Virgil, a small man who looked as much like a weasel as any creature that was not in fact a weasel possibly could, was circling the corpse nervously as his assistant Buckers bent over it. Virgil's black pebbly eyes stabbed this way and that, out through the doorway, daring anyone who stood out there, myself included, to enter the room.

I looked at the two old-line cops who were with me in the hall, waiting to photograph and bag the body, and they looked at me, and the three of us had the same look of resigned disgust on our faces.

Inside the room, Virgil said, "Well?" to Buckers, who then lifted the slim black tentacles of his sherlock from the body and checked the readout on the flat box strapped to his shoulder that the tentacles led into. "The light's still green, sir," he said in a small voice. He was a large, square man, but was scared to death of Virgil. "It's still collecting." Virgil nodded briskly, and Buckers bent over the body again. Four other technicians, clean shaven and efficient as whisk brooms, were minutely combing every inch of the walls, floor, ceiling and furniture with their own machines.

I stood watching until I became uncomfortable, and then I shifted my weight against the doorjamb and said, in as pleasant a voice as I could, "The guy's dead, Virgil. Can't you go back to your computer room and let these poor fellows out here do their dirty work?"

Virgil seemed to leap across the room at me. "That's it, Matheson," he said. "I agreed to let you up here on the condition that you didn't open your mouth."

He took me by the arm and pulled me toward the elevator. I didn't resist. I gave appealing looks to the cops in the hallway, but there was nothing they could do.

"I'd like to squeeze your arm right off," Virgil said. I tried to talk reasonably but he cut me off. "I don't want you bothering my people. Just because someone was stupid enough to hire you to look into this murder doesn't mean you can follow my crew around like a gawker with a bag of peanuts. I don't care how many old friends you have on the force. I want you to stay away from me." His anger subsided a bit as the elevator doors opened. I stepped into the car without saying anything. The doors were closing when Virgil stopped them with his hand. He shook his head in mock sadness and said, "I really feel sorry for you, Matheson. Why don't you stop playing detective and get yourself a job?"

He let the doors close.

He wasn't so far from the truth. I hadn't had a solid investigative job—even a wife-cheating assignment—in six months, and ever since the sherlocks had become commercially available two years before, my caseload had been down about sixty percent. Most of the big agencies were using the machines now, and almost all the younger PIs were using the things, coupled with a databank service. I was starting to feel old.

That morning, though, I'd suddenly found myself involved with a murder case when I'd got up to find a note pinned to the pillow next to my head and an open window where whoever had pinned it had entered and exited. The note had read:

$2,000 HAS BEEN CREDITED TO YOUR ACCOUNT. FIND OUT WHO MURDERED VINDEBEER AT THE SEDGEWICK HOTEL.

There hadn't been any signature, but after checking with the bank and finding that the money had indeed been deposited, I'd decided there was nothing to do but put on some clothes and go down to the Sedgewick. There I'd found Virgil and his sherlockers, and a dead body, presumably named Vindebeer. And that's where I stood now.

It was getting dark by the time I reached home. I had a little haven in the middle of all the high-rise metal spires on 212th Street, because about seventy-five years ago, when all the forty-floor monsters were springing up everywhere, a gray-haired old lady named Mrs. Cornelius had refused to sell her two-floor Victorian. They built right up to the border of her eighth-of-an-acre plot, but she ignored them. I'd bought the place from her daughter about ten years ago and blessed Mrs. Cornelius every time I stepped through the gate.

I blessed her now, but when I stepped through, I noticed that the front door was wide open. No one was inside, but I found a folded note attached to my easy chair in the den. This one read:

GO TO NORTH DOCKS TOMORROW AT 2:30 P.M. AND STAND BY
EAST TOWER ELEVATOR.

This one was also unsigned. I didn't really like the game with the notes, but there didn't seem to be anything to do about it at the moment. So I ate dinner, read a Perry Mason for a couple of hours, then went to bed.

In the morning I went down to the North Manhattan police station to see Jack Rutgers. I poked my head into the computer terminal as I walked by and saw that Lt. Virgil was pacing around nervously, shouting instructions to Buckers and his other assistants, leaping from panel to panel and adjusting dials and reading meters. When he saw me he growled, so I hurried past.

Rutgers was a nearly bald man in his middle fifties. He wore an open vest, sweated a lot, and had a round, thoughtful face. He wore round spectacles which he was always taking off and cleaning with his handkerchief. He was the only old-timer left who had any control at all over Virgil. He had been pretty friendly to me over the years. His office was cluttered with plants; when I walked in, he told me to move a couple aside and find a place to sit.

"I'm glad you're here, Phil," he said. He took off his spectacles. "I'd like to bat some ideas back and forth with you."

"I'm working on the Vindebeer case," I said.

His eyebrows went up. "You know his name? Did Virgil tell you?"

"I don't think Virgil has thought of looking in the guy's wallet yet. Someone left me a note with the name on it, though." I told him about my anonymous client. "The only thing I was able to figure out from the short time I was at the hotel yesterday was that his fellow hadn't been here very long since he hadn't even bothered to unpack. Is there anything you can add to that?"

"Phil," he sighed, polishing his glasses, "you know damn well that the sherlock boys only tell me what I pull out of them. They just about run things here now. When I retire they will run things. I was able to find out that this Vindebeer boy was from Norway, though. He'd been in the country only six days, and spent very little time in the hotel. He'd been out looking for a job—he was some sort of technician. A couple of nights he went to a bar called The Norseman on 204th Street. We got all this from the doorman at the hotel who'd talked to him a couple of times. Seems he'd been kind of lonely. There were no fingerprints in the hotel room except for his own. No one suspicious was seen entering or leaving the hotel before or after the murder; nobody heard anything. One of the sherlocks found a brown hair that didn't belong to the victim. That's all there is now; Virgil says he's still running olfactory tests on a kind of rosewater scent the sherlocks detected." He paused. "You have no idea who broke into your place and left the notes?"

"Nope." I got up to leave, slowly, because I knew Rutgers didn't want me to go yet. He was rubbing his spectacles thoughtfully and I sat down again. I knew what was coming since we'd been through it before.

"Plants need watering, Jack," I said. "Look a bit dried out."

He stopped polishing, pointed his spectacles at me and said, in a confidential sort of way. "You know, twenty years ago you and I would have hated each other's guts—in a respectful kind of way. The police captain and the sharp young detective, eyeball to eyeball." He shook his head. "I know it was never really like that, Phil, but still, the way it was was better than this. They think they can solve every crime with little sensors, data banks and electric eyes. Well, I don't think they work as well as men do."

"I don't either," I said. "But apparently the things work. And somebody above you thinks they're worth the investment. I may be old-fashioned, Jack, and I know I'll never use one of those things. But if someone else wants to use them that's fine with me. I'll still rely on my own wits, even if I go down trying.''

"Yeah,'' he said, and then he was silent, cleaning his glasses. "Keep in touch, Phil.''

"I will. Thanks for the information.'' And this time, when I got up, I left.

The docks of north New York City are nestled in a basin by Inwood. The Hudson River used to flow by there before it was diverted inland into New Jersey, through and behind the cliffs. Don't ask me why the Hudson River was chopped up like a birthday cake and put back together somewhere else, because I don't really know. It was some sort of public works project, and the money was there, so it got done. I think there's an amusement park in Jersey on the banks where the river goes by now.

When the river was drained at Inwood, natural walls were left against the river banks, and the empty basin that was formed was coated with quickly constructed transport offices and launching docks and turned into a cargo port. The place looked nice in the beginning; thirty years later the better facilities in Philadelphia and Virginia had most of the shuttle cargo business and the Inwood docking area was pretty much a ghost port. Now a lot of it was abandoned, and the other parts were used by fly-by-night transporters. The surrounding neighborhood wasn't too nice, either.

I took the creaky east-end elevator down to basin level, staring up at the launch gantry and empty, dilapidated control towers. When the car finally wheezed to a halt at the bottom I threw the rusting metal caging back and stepped out.

A long block of shabby structures—abandoned travel offices, mostly—lay in front of me. The block stretched straight as an arrow to the west end of the docks, and I could make out the creaky framework of the other elevator from where I stood.

I checked my watch and noted that it was now two-thirty. Fifteen minutes went by. No one used the elevator or came down the shabby lane to meet me. After a half hour my feet got tired; twenty minutes later I decided to give up. As I turned around to get back on the elevator I heard a shuffling noise behind me and then everything turned black.

Even though I don't use a sherlock, I do make certain concessions to modern technology. There was a piece of equipment which I wore that probably saved my head from being split open.

It's a thin membrane of ultra-high-impact plastic which fits skin tight at the base of my skull and up around my ears. I can't feel it when it's there, and unless you look close it can't be seen. A friend of mine had sent it to me; one just like it had saved his head a couple of times from the poundings of annoyed husbands.

The impact of the blow knocked me down. I was staggering to my feet when everything suddenly went dark gray and I dropped out cold. Someone had used gas on me—and I wasn't wearing a nose filter.

I awoke in a small room. There was a tiny light bulb on the ceiling directly over my head that threw off sour light that hurt my eyes. There weren't any windows. When I tried to get up I discovered that my arms were tied to the bottom of the bed I was lying on.

Someone came and stood over me, cutting off the sour light. It was a young girl, with long, straggly brown hair and a small chin and a grim, set mouth. Not very pretty. She held her hair back with one hand and leaned over me.

"You're not groggy?" Her voice was throaty, hard-edged.

"A little," I said. "Would you mind telling me what's going on?"

She straightened up, and I saw what looked like a smirk on her face. "I think we'd better have this out now."

I just looked at her.

"I'll make this concise," she went on. "If you don't leave my father alone, I'll do anything I have to to stop you. You have no business with us."

"I'm sorry," I said, "but I really don't know what you're talking about. If you'll—"

"I've warned you," she said, and then she uncovered something in her hand, moving it close to my face, and the next thing I knew I was waking up in front of the east-end elevator.

I made my way back home. There weren't any notes waiting for me there. An hour later I had just settled into a warm bath when Jack Rutgers called to tell me that another young technician from Norway had been murdered.

This victim had lived in one of the nicer parts of town, a swanky apartment building in the lower 90s. The front of the place was sealed tight and operated by a voice-print activated computer that wouldn't let me in. There were no police outside, but I finally was able to get in when an elderly, wide-eyed couple, who had obviously just heard about the murder, left the building. Once inside I merely followed the line of uniformed policemen who had been dropped like peas along the route to the victim's apartment.

When I walked into the living room I found Buckers and Virgil bent over a woman on the couch. She'd been stabbed in the chest. Buckers was tracing the outline of her body with the tentacles attached to his sherlock; a few more men were crawling here and there, little black boxes in hand.

I got the woman's name, Ingri Hoffman, from one of the cops standing outside. After waiting around for a while I discovered that that was about all they knew. I stayed out of Virgil's way. I thought I smelled a hint of rosewater, but I couldn't be sure.

I stood watching the sherlocks at work for a few minutes. I can't help it, I just don't like the little black boxes. They have retracting tentacles, electronic eyes, olfactory filters and audio sensors; they collect data, sniff out criminal odors, study fingerprints, footprints, breathprints, collect bits of clothing and skin and strands of hair, beep, whiz, talk to each other, correlate information with a central data bank. And though the courts were still tied up in knots over whether the evidence presented via a sherlock was admissable, it seemed that after eight long years they were slowly coming around to favor the little machines.

The last image I had in my eyes as I turned to leave was of Ingri Hoffman on the couch; and Buckers, bright and eager as a puppy, sliding the slender cold tentacles of his sherlock over her dead body.

The Norseman Inn was what I would call a gimmick bar. It was small, dark and congenial, and everything in it was made of different-sized pieces of wood. The beer mugs and wine goblets were wooden, the tables were square slabs of wood, the bar itself was half a tree, sliced lengthwise and resting on huge wooden blocks. There were horned helmets and carved spears on the wall behind the bar, and though there was piped-in music, it was set low enough so that people could talk. Things were very carefully engineered: you could see and hear only the people in your immediate vicinity. There were a lot of young working girls.

I pulled a heavy wooden stool up close to the bar and motioned for a bartender to stay after he'd poured a beer for me. I asked him if he knew Helmut Vindebeer.

He thought for a moment, then shook his head and frowned. He was built like a Viking, of course, and the frown he made through his beard when I repeated the name told me he didn't know Vindebeer by name. I described the technician to him and his memory seemed to warm a little.

"I remember him," he said, the Viking persona dissolving into a Brooklyn accent. "He was in here three, maybe four nights in a row. That was about it. He looked like he belonged in the place, very Norwegian-looking, very naive-looking too. I guess he came in because of the name, thought he'd meet a lot of Scandinavians, who knows. I felt a little sorry for him, the guy really looked lost. But I remember that the first time he came in it didn't take him long to meet a few people—there were one, maybe two people I remember him latching onto. As a matter of fact, they *were* Scandinavians. Wait here a minute."

He went to the other end of the bar, looking out over the crowd. He served a couple of customers down there, then came back.

"I think I found the two he was talking to: a guy and a girl. They're sitting at a table along the wall in the back. She's got a blue-and-white striped dress on, pretty good-looking. The guy has short black hair. Okay?" He smiled his Viking smile through the beard.

I thanked him and took my beer to the back room, threading my way through a lot of wooden tables and chairs.

The guy and the girl both had nice smiles, and they were sitting together on one side of a booth. They responded to Vindebeer's name when I asked if they knew him. The guy asked me to sit down on the other side of the table and I did so. His name was William Anderson—when he talked he sounded Scandinavian. So did the girl.

It turned out that they had met both Vindebeer and each other the first night Vindebeer had come into the bar. Vindebeer had been very shy, but friendly, and his accent had drawn them to him. Then Anderson told me that there had been another girl who had attached herself to their little group that night also.

"She was very animated, very bright," he said. He then went on to describe the girl I had seen dead an hour before.

They'd known about Vindebeer's death, but when I told them that the girl was dead too they got a little upset.

"I don't understand," the girl, Helga, said after a few moments. She looked a bit older than she dressed, and she now held Anderson's hand tightly. "They both looked so happy. We were all so happy that first night. All of us had been alone, and then we all met at once."

I asked her if they'd gotten together with Vindebeer or the girl again.

"Yes," she said. "We met a couple of nights later, and once again the night after that. Helmut was very happy that last night because Ingri was going to get him a job."

"She was trying to get him a job," William corrected. "She worked for a research scientist, a well-known man, as his assistant, and was trying to get Helmut a job with his project. They were both technicians."

Neither could remember the scientist's name. I took a sip of my beer, which was now flat. "Did anything strange happen that night you were together? Did you meet anyone else?"

They both shook their heads.

"Did they say anything about the job Helmut was trying to get?"

"Not much," Anderson answered. "Just that this scientist needed another assistant. They mostly talked about how strange this scientist and his daughter were."

"Strange?"

The girl spoke up. "Ingri told us some very funny stories about the things these two people had done, how they were always complaining about being bothered, that people wouldn't leave them alone."

She looked down at her drink, and I looked down at mine. There was silence for a few minutes.

"Do you think someone would try to hurt William or me?" the girl said.

"I'm not sure, but I don't think so," I said. "Can I get you two another drink?"

"No, thank you," Anderson said. "I think we'll be leaving soon. Actually, we came here tonight to see if Ingri might come."

"I see," I said. "Well, is there anything else you can remember? Anything at all?"

There was another silence, this one longer. Then Helga said, and she was almost crying. "Only . . . that they looked very happy together. I thought they looked very happy."

On the way out I met Buckers coming in, who gave me a nasty look and passed on. Virgil was close behind him. I stepped in front of him so he couldn't avoid me.

"What's new, Lieutenant?" I said.

He scowled and made a motion to walk around me, then stopped. "I told you to stay out of this, Matheson."

"You know I've been hired to look into it."

"By who—the Man in the Moon?" He gave a short laugh. "You don't even know who your client is."

"Would you like to bet I get to the bottom of this before your sherlocks do?" I knew I was putting my foot in my mouth, but couldn't help it.

"You're on," he said. "Fifty bucks?"

"Fifty bucks it is, Lieutenant. See you around."

He walked toward the bar, shaking his head.

I took a long walk home, and when I got there there was another note from my anonymous employer waiting for me. This one was taped to the refrigerator door and read:

GO BACK TO NORTH DOCKS AT 9:00 TOMORROW MORNING.

I rolled it into a ball and threw it away. It was just about midnight. I grabbed a flashlight, made sure my neck guard was in place, put in my nose filters and left for the North Docks.

To say the least, the docks were dark. I took the west-end elevator down, thinking it might be in better running order than the other one and make less noise, but if anything it groaned even louder. When I got to the bottom I could barely make out where I was, but flicking the beam of my flash this way and that soon told me what I already knew—that I was at the opposite end of the street bordered with travel offices that ran to the east end. I began to slowly make my way up one side of the street, pausing at each closed building with my flash off, trying to detect the least sound or possibly a flicker of light coming from inside.

When I'd gone about halfway up the block I thought I heard something close behind me, a footstep or a shifting in the dark. I stopped but nothing followed it; but as I turned to go on someone rushed out at me from the darkened doorway I'd just passed and grabbed at me from behind.

I felt a little jab in the side and was down and out in about four seconds.

When I woke up there was one hell of a sore spot on my left side where a needle had been pushed in crookedly. I was trussed up again in the room with the sour yellow light.

"Your doing this twice to me is quite embarrassing," I said. The girl was standing off to one side, her back to me. It looked like she was going through my billfold.

"Keep quiet." She turned around, and I saw that she held a sherlock in her hand. She replaced my billfold in my breast pocket and then moved the sherlock slowly over my body.

"Where did you get that thing?" I asked.

She ignored my question. "You're a detective?"

I nodded.

"You're not who I thought you were," she said evenly. "Who sent you to look for my father and me?"

"I don't know, to tell you the truth." I told her about the notes to see what kind of reaction I'd get.

She finished with the sherlock and put it on a table behind her. I said, "Is your father here now?"

"If he was anywhere near here you'd be dead."

She stood still for a moment, just staring at me, and then she left the room. When she came back she leaned over me.

I smelled rosewater, and my heart almost stopped.

She grabbed at something on a table against the wall. I was sure it was a knife, long-bladed and plastic handled; but after the split second it took my eyes to tell my brain what it was seeing I realized that it was a hypodermic. She plugged it savagely into my arm, and I quickly went under. When I swam up I found myself once again at the base of the elevator.

The next morning I called on Jack Rutgers to see if anyone had come up with anything on Ingri Hoffman.

"As a matter of fact," he said, "Virgil did come up with something. There was a partial print on the knife handle this time, and also another strand of long brown hair, which was found on the rug near the body. The olfactory tests also showed a correlation on a type of perfume detected at the scene of the first murder. It's a kind of rosewater, from Scandinavia."

"Has anyone been able to find out who she was working for?"

"No. And we may have some trouble finding out because it now looks as though the girl was in the country illegally; Vindebeer wasn't but that doesn't help because he hadn't really started working for this fellow yet."

I told him about my two visits to the North Docks, and he listened in silence, polishing his glasses with his handkerchief.

"You went there last night alone?"

I smiled sheepishly. "Sure it was stupid. But even though this girl's father is the scientist who hired Vindebeer and Ingri Hoffman, everything still doesn't fit. The girl may be the killer, but then again maybe she's not. And I still don't know who hired me, or why.''

He sighed. ''Well, looks like I can send some men out to the docks to flush the two of them out; at least we know the general area they're hiding from where you got ambushed last night. Why don't you sit tight for a little while, and I'll give you a call later.''

''Sure,'' I said. ''Sounds fair enough. And Jack.''

His face had a probing look.

''Give those plants some water. They're starting to wilt.''

He hesitated. ''Right,'' he said.

I spent the rest of the day going through the last few days' junk mail and thinking. No matter how I twisted things around, everything always pointed back to whoever was leaving me those notes. There was a connection somewhere that I didn't have. And if the girl was the cat she seemed to be and eluded Rutgers's men, and if the note-man didn't reveal himself, the whole thing could stay very confused indeed.

As I was putting a late dinner on Rutgers called. He had nothing to tell me on the girl and her father, but it seemed that Virgil wanted to talk to me, and that there might be the possibility of trading some information. I figured what the heck and headed downtown.

Halfway there I remembered I'd left the two front burners of the stove on and rather than burn my house down I turned back.

The front door had been opened, and as I reached the front porch the scent of rosewater hit my nostrils.

I edged the door all the way open and reached around to the umbrella stand where I kept a heavy stick. It was pretty dark inside. I raised the stick in front of me and slipped inside.

I took two steps, then heard two sounds at once. There was a girl's scream from one side of the living room, and at the same time a lamp fell over as someone rushed at me from the other side. I could barely see but I could tell that it was a man and that he had an upraised hand with something in it. He ran into me and the hand swung down at my chest but I knocked it out of the way. He scrambled to his feet and pulled at the front door and ran out. Whatever he'd been holding fell to the porch behind him.

I lay breathing heavily for a moment. Suddenly someone turned on the hall light overhead. I was momentarily blinded, but I pushed my way to my feet and threw my arms out defensively, blinking fiercely. After a few seconds I was able to see that the girl with the light brown eyes stood before me.

I told her to stay away from me while I shut the front door and then walked over to my writing desk and took out a gun from the bottom drawer. There was a folded note taped to the desk and I pulled it off. I waved the gun at the girl, sat down in a chair and told her to sit down in one opposite me.

She did as she was told—she was shaking like a leaf and looked dazed—and then I asked her what she was doing in my house.

"I . . . came here to bring you to my father," she managed to get out.

"Wasn't that your father who just tried to kill me?"

She shook her head no.

I ignored her for a minute and pulled open the note, which read:

YOU MUST RETURN TO NORTH DOCKS AND LOCATE SCIENTIST AND DAUGHTER. 10:30 TONIGHT. CASE DEPENDS ON IT. 2000 MORE DOLLARS IN YOUR ACCOUNT.

"Hell," I said, and showed the note to the girl. "Do you know who wrote this?"

She was really shook up for some reason but when she saw the look on my face and the way I held the gun she managed to open her mouth. "No."

"What's your name?"

"I . . . thought you knew. My name is Angela Beberger. My father is Edward Beberger."

"Edward Beberger?" I said, startled. Edward Beberger was the inventor of the sherlocks.

The girl began to talk, in a kind of stupor. "I came here because my father wants to see you. He thinks you can be trusted."

"What about the man who was here?"

"He was here when I came. He's the man who's been after my father and me all this time. He made me tell him where my father is. . . ."

It all came into focus. I went to the front door and opened it, and there on the front porch was a pump sprayer, the kind you use to water plants. It was filled with rosewater. I showed it to Angela Beberger.

"He was spraying that all over when I came in. I only had three bottles. Two of them were stolen. They belonged to my mother when she was alive. She brought them from Norway—"

"Is your father alone now?" I asked.

"Yes."

I made a phone call to Virgil and then turned back to the girl. "Take me to him," I said.

When we got to the North Docks the floodlights were on and Virgil was waiting with his men.

"He's up on one of the rocket gantrys," he said to me. "I wish I could kick you out of here and handle this myself, but he's got Edward Beberger with him, and he says he'll kill him if we don't let you go up."

I looked up into the bright lights and could just make out two figures perched on a gantry arm that swung out high above us. I told Angela Beberger to stay with Virgil and took a step toward the gantry. I stopped and turned back to Virgil.

"How close were you to finding out what was going on?"

It was an effort for him to tell me. "We thought for sure it was the girl, here. I owe you some money, Matheson."

I turned back to the gantry. I took the service steps up the side one by one, in silence.

"Hello, Jack," I said as I reached the top. He was on a small platform suspended between two girders about twenty feet away from me.

Below the platform was a drop of about a hundred meters. It was windy up there, and the floodlights gave everything a stark, black-and-white appearance.

Beberger was propped up against a steel canister with a plastic-handled knife in his chest. He looked dead.

Rutgers sat down on the platform with his feet dangling over the edge and began to polish his spectacles. "I had hoped it would take a lot longer for us to reach this point," he said calmly. "Things didn't go the way I planned, Phil."

"If you hadn't dropped that rosewater at my house tonight it might have taken me quite a while to figure things out."

"But the girl had decided to trust you. That was another thing I hadn't counted on. I thought I had the two of them too scared to trust God himself. That's why I had to get to Beberger tonight."

"How long had you been harassing them?"

"A couple of months," he continued in a matter-of-fact tone. "It was easy. I started with anonymous phone calls; after a while I showed up at their place and said the police had received a threat against them. I picked up the rosewater, a few strands of hair, a kitchen knife with fingerprints on it—enough to throw the sherlocks off for a while. After I killed Vindebeer they didn't know what to think; it was obvious I was involved and since I was a cop who could they turn to? I kept up the phone calls. Then they disappeared. I knew they were hiding down here at the docks somewhere, but I couldn't find them. That girl was smart. That's when I started leaving you notes.''

"To get me to flush out Beberger for you?"

"That was part of it. The girl knew my face, but I thought that if she got a chance to get ahold of someone else who was possibly involved, I could track the two of them down. She was so careful, though; even though I found out where they were hiding, she moved her father right after getting rid of you. That's why I wanted you to go back, to give me another shot. But there was more to it than that, Phil.'' His voice rose a bit, and took on a bit of an hysterical edge. "You see, the whole idea was for you to come in cold and figure things out before the sherlocks did. The whole idea was for you to beat that damned machine.''

"Like Paul Bunyan?"

"Yes.''

"That's why you killed Vindebeer and Ingri Hoffman?''

"No!'' He looked straight at me. "I killed the two of them because Beberger was expanding his research.''

I gave a puzzled look.

"Come on, Phil! Don't you read the papers? He wasn't content with developing the god-damned black box Virgil is fondling down there. He was assembling a new research team to perfect the sherlocks; and eventually he was going to develop a centralized data bank that would replace almost all of the detective force in the city. *Ninety-five percent.* Most of the remaining personnel would be data computer experts, with only rudimentary police training. In one fell swoop, no more detectives. A way of life wiped out in a generation.''

I was silent while he rubbed at his glasses. Then I said, "What now, Jack?"

He put his spectacles down on the platform and looked at me with his tired eyes. "I don't know, Phil. I suppose we could end this like an Alfred Hitchcock film with the two of us grappling on this little platform. Or I could sit here and start to weep like the crazy person I must be and let you lead me down to a squad car and a straitjacket.'' He paused. "I've been confused for a long time, Phil, and this whole thing ended too soon. But I guess you'll be the hero after.'' He sighed heavily, pointing at Beberger. "I didn't kill him. He's only unconscious; there's no knife blade in the handle. Anyway,'' he smiled weakly, ''there are other people carrying on the same type of research he's doing, so I guess it wouldn't have made much of a difference. Give me a hand down, will you?''

He took a step toward me with his hand out. I don't think it was the wind or that he slipped or that he didn't have his glasses on, but after one step he stumbled and fell from the platform soundlessly, hitting the concrete below hard. I looked down at his crumpled body then at his spectacles lying on the platform. I picked up the spectacles and put them in my pocket.

Beberger was alive, as Rutgers had said, and when he came to I helped him down the steps of the gantry into the waiting arms of his daughter. I then waited solemnly as Virgil counted out five crisp ten-dollar bills into my hand. He wasn't happy about it.

''You know,'' he said, watching as Jack Rutgers's body was bagged and carried off, ''I still can't believe a cop like that could do something like this. I knew he was a relic, but I didn't know he was a stupid relic.''

I almost hit him then, but he quickly went on, seeing the look in my eyes. ''Don't get me wrong, Matheson. I respected that guy. I knew he was like the old dog who can't learn new tricks, and I had every intention of forcing him out when I could, but, after all, we were all after the same thing, right? We just have different ways of doing it now, right?''

''Sure, Virgil. Whatever you say.''

He seemed to want more, some kind of reassurance that what he was doing was worthwhile, but I left him to his little black boxes then: already a couple of his lab technicians were crawling up the gantry like sterile spiders to let their machines sniff what there was to be sniffed.

When I got up to street level and stepped out of the elevator I almost hailed a taxi, feeling the fifty dollars in my pocket already trying to leap out, but at the last moment I kept my hailing arm down and began to walk.

With the fifty dollars I renewed my investigator's license.

# Loren D. Estleman

# THE CROOKED WAY

YOU COULDN'T MISS THE INDIAN IF YOU'D WANTED TO. HE was sitting all alone in a corner booth, which was probably his idea, but he hadn't much choice because there was barely enough room in it for him. He had shoulders going into the next country and a head the size of a basketball, and he was holding a beer mug that looked like a shot glass between his calloused palms. As I approached the booth he looked up at me—not very far up—through slits in a face made up of bunched ovals with a nose like the corner of a building. His skin was the color of old brick.

"Mr. Frechette?" I asked.

"Amos Walker?"

I said I was. Coming from him my name sounded like two stones dropping into deep water. He made no move to shake hands, but he inclined his head a fraction of an inch and I borrowed a chair from a nearby table and joined him. He had on a blue shirt buttoned to the neck, and his hair, parted on one side and plastered down, was blue-black without a trace of gray. Nevertheless he was about fifty.

"Charlie Stoat says you track like an Osage," he said. "I hope you're better than that. I couldn't track a train."

"How is Charlie? I haven't seen him since that insurance thing."

"Going under. The construction boom went bust in Houston just when he was expanding his operation."

"What's that do to yours?" He'd told me over the telephone he was in construction.

"Nothing worth mentioning. I've been running on a shoestring for years. You can't break a poor man."

I signaled the bartender for a beer and he brought one over. It was a workingman's hangout across the street from the Ford plant in Highland Park. The shift wasn't due to change for an hour and we had the place to ourselves. "You said your daughter ran away," I said, when the bartender had left. "What makes you think she's in Detroit?"

He drank off half his beer and belched dramatically. "When does client privilege start?"

"It never stops."

I watched him make up his mind. Indians aren't nearly as hard to read as they appear in books. He picked up a folded newspaper from the seat beside him and spread it out on the table facing me. It was yesterday's *Houston Chronicle*, with a banner:

BOYD MANHUNT MOVES NORTHEAST
Bandit's Van Found Abandoned in Detroit

I had read a related wire story in that morning's *Detroit Free Press*. Following the unassisted shotgun robberies of two savings-and-loan offices near Houston, concerned citizens had reported seeing twenty-two-year-old Virgil Boyd in Mexico and Oklahoma, but his green van with Texas plates had turned up in a city lot five minutes from where we were sitting. As of that morning, Detroit Police Headquarters was paved with Feds and sun-crinkled out-of-state cops chewing toothpicks.

I refolded the paper and gave it back. "Your daughter's taken up with Boyd?"

"They were high school sweethearts," Frechette said. "That was before Texas Federal foreclosed on his family's ranch and his father shot himself. She disappeared from home after the first robbery. I guess that makes her an accomplice to the second."

"Legally speaking," I agreed, "if she's with him and it's her idea. A smart DA would knock it down to harboring if she turned herself in. She'd probably get probation."

"She wouldn't do that. She's got some crazy idea she's in love with Boyd."

"I'm surprised I haven't heard about her."

"No one knows. I didn't report her missing. If I had, the police

would have put two and two together and there'd be a warrant out
for her as well."

I swallowed some beer. "I don't know what you think I can do
that the cops and the FBI can't."

"I know where she is."

I waited. He rotated his mug. "My sister lives in Southgate. We
don't speak. She has a white mother, not like me, and she takes
after her in looks. She's ashamed of being half Osage. First chance
she had, she married a white man and got out of Oklahoma. That
was before I left for Texas, where nobody knows about her.
Anyway she got a big settlement in her divorce."

"You think Boyd and your daughter will go to her for a getaway stake?"

"They won't get it from me, and he didn't take enough out of
Texas Federal to keep a dog alive. Why else would they come
here?"

"So if you know where they're headed, what do you need me
for?"

"Because I'm being followed and you're not."

The bartender came around to offer Frechette a refill. The big
Indian shook his head and he went away.

"Cops?" I said.

"One cop. J. P. Ahearn."

He spaced out the name as if spelling a blasphemy. I said I'd
never heard of him.

"He'd be surprised. He's a commander with the Texas State
Police, but he thinks he's the last of the Texas Rangers. He wants
Boyd bad. The man's a bloodhound. He doesn't know about my
sister, but he did his homework and found out about Suzie and that
she's gone, not that he could get me to admit she isn't away
visiting friends. I didn't see him on the plane from Houston. I
spotted him in the airport here when I was getting my luggage."

"Is he alone?"

"He wouldn't share credit with Jesus for saving a sinner." He
drained his mug. "When you find Suzie I want you to set up a
meeting. Maybe I can talk sense into her."

"How old is she?"

"Nineteen."

"Good luck."

"Tell me about it. My old man fell off a girder in Tulsa when
I was sixteen. Then I was fifty. Well, maybe one meeting can't

make up for all the years of not talking after my wife died, but I can't let her throw her life away for not trying.''

"I can't promise Boyd won't sit in on it.''

"I like Virgil. Some of us cheered when he took on those bloodsuckers. He'd have gotten away with a lot more from that second job if he'd shot this stubborn cashier they had, but he didn't. He wouldn't hurt a horse or a man.''

"That's not the way the cops are playing it. If I find him and don't report it I'll go down as an accomplice. At the very least I'll lose my license.''

"All I ask is that you call me before you call the police.'' He gave me a high-school graduation picture of a pretty brunette he said was Suzie. She looked more Asian than American Indian. Then he pulled a checkbook out of his hip pocket and made out a check to me for fifteen hundred dollars.

"Too much,'' I said.

"You haven't met J. P. Ahearn yet. My sister's name is Harriett Lord.'' He gave me an address on Eureka. "I'm at the Holiday Inn down the street, room 716.''

He called for another beer then and I left. Again he didn't offer his hand. I'd driven three blocks from the place when I spotted the tail.

The guy knew what he was doing. In a late-model tan Buick he gave me a full block and didn't try to close up until we hit Woodward, where traffic was heavier. I finally lost him in the grand circle downtown, which confused him just as it does most people from the greater planet Earth. The Indians who settled Detroit were being farsighted when they named it the Crooked Way. From there I took Lafayette to I–75 and headed downriver.

Harriett Lord lived in a tall white frame house with blue shutters and a large lawn fenced by cedars that someone had bullied into cone shape. I parked in the driveway, but before leaving the car I got out the unlicensed Luger I keep in a pocket under the dash and stuck it in my pants, buttoning my coat over it. When you're meeting someone they tell you wouldn't hurt a horse or a man, arm yourself.

The bell was answered by a tall woman around forty, dressed in a khaki shirt and corduroy slacks and sandals. She had high cheekbones and slightly olive coloring that looked more like sun than heritage and her short hair was frosted, further reducing the Indian effect. When she confirmed that she was Harriet Lord I gave her a card and said I was working for her brother.

Her face shut down. "I don't have a brother. I have a half-brother, Howard Frechette. If that's who you're working for, tell him I'm unavailable." She started to close the door.

"It's about your niece Suzie. And Virgil Boyd."

"I thought it would be."

I looked at the door and got out a cigarette and lit it. I was about to knock again when the door opened six inches and she stuck her face through the gap. "You're not with the police?"

"We tolerate each other on the good days, but that's it."

She glanced down. Her blue mascara gave her eyelids a translucent look. Then she opened the door the rest of the way and stepped aside. I entered a living room done all in beige and white and sat in a chair upholstered in eggshell chintz. I was glad I'd had my suit cleaned.

"How'd you know about Suzie and Boyd?" I used a big glass ashtray on the Lucite coffee table.

"They were here last night." I said nothing. She sat on the beige sofa with her knees together. "I recognized him before I did her. I haven't seen her since she was four, but I take a Texas paper and I've seen his picture. They wanted money. I thought at first I was being robbed."

"Did you give it to them?"

"Aid a fugitive? Family responsibility doesn't cover that even if I felt any. I left home because I got sick of hearing about our proud heritage. Howard wore his Indianness like a suit of armor, and all the time he resented me because I could pass for white. He accused me of being ashamed of my ancestry because I didn't wear my hair in braids and hang turquoise all over me."

"He isn't like that now."

"Maybe he's mellowed. Not toward me, though, I bet. Now his daughter comes here asking for money so she and her desperado boyfriend can go on running. I showed them the door."

"I'm surprised Boyd went."

"He tried to get tough, but he's not very big and he wasn't armed. He took a step toward me and I took two steps toward him and he grabbed Suzie and left. Some Jesse James."

"I heard his shotgun was found in the van. I thought he'd have something else."

"If he did, he didn't have it last night. I'd have noticed, just as I notice you have one."

I unbuttoned my coat and resettled the Luger. I was getting a different picture of "Mad Dog" Boyd from the one the press was painting. "The cops would call not reporting an incident like that being an accessory," I said, squashing out my butt.

"Just because I don't want anything to do with Howard doesn't mean I want to see my niece shot up by a SWAT team."

"I don't suppose they said where they were going."

"You're a good supposer."

I got up. "How did Suzie look?"

"Like an Indian."

I thanked her and went out.

I had a customer in my waiting room. A small angular party crowding sixty wearing a tight gray three-button suit, steel-rimmed glasses and a tan snap-brim hat squared over the frames. His crisp gray hair was cut close around large ears that stuck out, and he had a long sharp jaw with a sour mouth slashing straight across. He stood up when I entered. "Walker?" It was one of those bitter pioneer voices.

"Depends on who you are," I said.

"I'm the man who ought to arrest you for obstructing justice."

"I'll guess. J. P. Ahearn."

"*Commander* Ahearn."

"You're about four feet short of what I had pictured."

"You've heard of me." His chest came out a little.

"Who hasn't?" I unlocked the inner office door. He marched in, slung a look around and took possession of the customer's chair. I sat down behind the desk and reached for a cigarette without asking permission. He glared at me through his spectacles.

"What you did downtown today constitutes fleeing and eluding."

"In Texas, maybe. In Michigan there has to be a warrant out first. What you did constitutes harassment in this state."

"I don't have official status here. I can follow anybody for any reason or none at all."

"Is this what you folks call a Mexican standoff?"

"I don't approve of smoking," he snapped.

"Neither do I, but some of it always leaks out of my lungs." I blew at the ceiling and got rid of the match. "Why don't let's stop circling each other and get down to why you're here?"

"I want to know what you and the Indian talked about."

"I'd show you, but we don't need the rain."

He bared a perfect set of dentures, turning his face into a skull. "I ran your plate with the Detroit Police. I have their complete cooperation in this investigation. The Indian hired you to take money to Boyd to get him and his little Osage slut to Canada. You delivered it after you left the bar and lost me. That's aiding and abetting and accessory after the fact of armed robbery. Maybe I can't prove it, but I can make a call and tank you for forty-eight hours on suspicion."

"Eleven."

He covered up his store-boughts. "What?"

"That's eleven times I've been threatened with jail," I said. "Three of those times I wound up there. My license has been swiped at fourteen times, actually taken away once. Bodily harm—you don't count bodily harm. I'm still here, six feet something and one hundred eighty pounds of incorruptible PI with a will of iron and a skull to match. You hard guys come and go like phases of the moon."

"Don't twist my tail, son. I don't always rattle before I bite."

"What's got you so hot on Boyd?"

You could have cut yourself on his jaw. "My daddy helped run Parker and Barrow to ground in '34. *His* daddy fought Geronimo and chased John Wesley Hardin out of Texas. My son's a Dallas city patrolman, and so far I don't have a story to hand him that's a blister on any of those. I'm retiring next year."

"Last I heard Austin was offering twenty thousand for Boyd's arrest and conviction."

"Texas Federal has matched it. Alive *or* dead. Naturally, as a duly sworn officer of the law I can't collect. But you being a private citizen—"

"What's the split?"

"Fifty-fifty."

"No good."

"Do you know what the pension is for a retired state police commander in Texas? A man needs a nest egg."

"I meant it's too generous. You know as well as I do those rewards are never paid. You just didn't know I knew."

He sprang out of his chair. There was no special animosity in his move; that would be the way he always got up.

"Boyd won't get out of this country even if you did give him money," he snapped. "He'll never get past the border guards."

"So go back home."

"Boyd's *mine.*"

The last word ricocheted. I said, "Talk is he felt he had a good reason to stick up those savings-and-loans. The company was responsible for his father's suicide."

"If he's got the brains God gave a mad dog he'll turn himself in to me before he gets shot down in the street or kills someone and winds up getting the needle in Huntsville. And his squaw right along with him." He took a shabby wallet out of his coat and gave me a card. "That's my number at the Houston post. They'll route your call here. If you're so concerned for Boyd you'll tell me where he is before the locals gun him down."

"Better you than some stranger, that it?"

"Just keep on twisting, son. I ain't in the pasture yet."

After he left, making as much noise in his two-inch cowboy heels as a cruiserweight, I called Barry Stackpole at the Detroit *News*.

"Guy I'm after is wanted for Robbery, Armed," I said, once the small talk was put away. "He ditched his gun and then his stake didn't come through and now he'll have to cowboy a job for case dough. Where would he deal a weapon if he didn't know anybody in town?"

"Emma Chaney."

"Ma? I thought she'd be dead by now."

"She can't die. The Detroit cops are third in line behind Interpol and Customs for her scalp and they won't let her until they've had their crack." He sounded pleased, which he probably was. Barry made his living writing about crime, and when it prospered he did, too.

"How can I reach her?"

"Are you suggesting I'd know where she is and not tell the authorities? Got a pencil?"

I tried the number as soon as he was off the line. On the ninth ring, I got someone with a smoker's wheeze. "Uh-huh."

"The name's Walker," I said. "Barry Stackpole gave me this number."

The voice told me not to go away and hung up. Five minutes later the telephone rang.

"Barry says you're okay. What do you want?"

"Just talk. It isn't cheap like they say."

After a moment the voice gave me directions. I hung up not knowing if it was male or female.

\*     \*     \*

It belonged to Ma Chaney, who greeted me at the door of her house in rural Macomb County wearing a red Japanese kimono with green parrots all over it. The kimono could have covered a Toyota. She was a five-by-five chunk with marcelled orange hair and round black eyes embedded in her face like nail heads in soft wax. A cigarette teetered on her lower lip. I followed her into a parlor full of flowered chairs and sofas and pregnant lamps with fringed shades. A long strip of pimply blond youth in overalls and no shirt took his brogans off the coffee table and stood up when she barked at him. He gaped at me, chewing gum with his mouth open.

"Mr. Walker, Leo," Ma wheezed. "Leo knew my Wilbur in Ypsi. He's like another son to me."

Ma Chaney had one son in the criminal ward at the Forensic Psychiatry Center in Ypsilanti and another on Florida's Death Row. The FBI was looking for the youngest in connection with an armored car robbery in Kansas City. The whole brood had come up from Kentucky when Old Man Chaney got a job on the line at River Rouge and stayed on after he was killed in a propane tank explosion. Now Ma, the daughter of a Hawkins County gunsmith, made her living off the domestic weapons market.

"You said talk ain't cheap," she said, when she was sitting in a big overstuffed rocker. "How cheap ain't it?"

I perched on the edge of a hard upright with doilies on the arms. Leo remained standing, scratching himself. "Depends on whether we talk about Virgil Boyd," I said.

"What if we don't?"

"Then I won't take up any more of your time."

"What if we do?"

"I'll double what he's paying."

She coughed. The cigarette bobbed. "I got a business to run. I go around scratching at *re*wards I won't have no customers."

"Does that mean Boyd's a customer?"

"Now, why'd that Texas boy want to come to Ma? He can deal hisself a shotgun at any K mart."

"He can't show his face in the legal places and being new in town he doesn't know the illegal ones. But he wouldn't have to ask around too much to come up with your name. You're less selective than most."

"You don't have to pussyfoot around old Ma. I don't get a lot of second-timers on account of I talk for money. My boy Earl in Florida needs a new lawyer. But I only talk after, not before. I start setting up customers I won't get no first-timers."

"I'm not even interested in Boyd. It's his girlfriend I want to talk to. Suzie Frechette."

"Don't know her." She rocked back and forth. "What color's your money?"

Before leaving Detroit I'd cashed Howard Frechette's check. I laid fifteen hundred dollars on the coffee table in twenties and fifties. Leo straightened up a little to look at the bills. Ma resumed rocking. "It ain't enough."

"How much is enough?"

"If I was to talk to a fella named Boyd, and if I was to agree to sell him a brand-new Ithaca pump shotgun and a P-38 still in the box, I wouldn't sell them for less than twenny-five hunnert. Double twenny-five hunnert is five thousand."

"Fifteen hundred now. Thirty-five hundred when I see the girl."

"I don't guarantee no girl."

"Boyd then. If he's come this far with her he won't leave her behind."

She went on rocking. "They's a white barn a mile north on this road. If I was to meet a fella named Boyd, there's where I might do it. I might pick eleven o'clock."

"Tonight?"

"I might pick tonight. If it don't rain."

I got up. She stopped rocking.

"Come alone," she said. "Ma won't."

On the way back to town I filled up at a corner station and used the pay telephone to call Howard Frechette's room at the Holiday Inn. When he started asking questions I gave him the number and told him to call back from a booth outside the motel.

"Ahearn's an anachronism," he said ten minutes later. "I doubt he taps phones."

"Maybe not, but motel operators have big ears."

"Did you talk to Suzie?"

"Minor setback," I said. "Your sister gave her and Boyd the boot and no money."

"Tight bitch."

"I know where they'll be tonight, though. There's an old auto court on Van Dyke between 21 and 22 Mile in Macomb County, the Log Cabin Inn. Looks like it sounds." I was staring at it across the road. "Midnight. Better give yourself an hour."

He repeated the information.

"I'm going to have to tap you for thirty-five hundred dollars," I said. "The education cost."

"I can manage it. Is that where they're headed?"

"I hope so. I haven't asked them yet."

I got to my bank just before closing and cleaned out my savings and all but eight dollars in my checking account. I hoped Frechette was good for it. After that I ate dinner in a restaurant and went to see a movie about a one-man army. I wondered if he was available.


The barn was just visible from the road, a moonlit square at the end of a pair of ruts cut through weeds two feet high. It was a chill night in early spring and I had on a light coat and the heater running. I entered a dip that cut off my view of the barn, then bucked up over a ridge and had to stand the Chevy on its nose when the lamps fell on a telephone pole lying across the path. A second later the passenger's door opened and Leo got in.

He had on a mackinaw over his overalls and a plaid cap. His right hand was wrapped around a large-bore revolver and he kept it on me, held tight to his stomach, while he felt under my coat and came up with the Luger. "Drive." He pocketed it.

I swung around the end of the pole and braked in front of the barn, where Ma was standing with a Coleman lantern. She was wearing a man's felt hat and a corduroy coat with sleeves that came down to her fingers. She signaled a cranking motion and I rolled down the window.

"Well, park it around back," she said. "I got to think for you, too?"

I did that and Leo and I walked back. He handed Ma the Luger and she looked at it and put it in her pocket. She raised the lantern then and swung it from side to side twice.

We waited a few minutes, then were joined by six feet and two hundred and fifty pounds of red-bearded young man in faded denim jacket and jeans carrying a rifle with an infrared scope. He had come from the direction of the road.

"Anybody following, Mason?" asked Ma.

He shook his head, and I stared at him in the lantern light. He had small black eyes like Ma's with no shine in them. This would be Mace Chaney, for whom the FBI was combing the western states for the Kansas armored car robbery.

"Go on in and warm yourself," Ma said. "We got some time."

He opened the barn door and went inside. It had just closed when two headlamps appeared down the road. We watched them

approach and slow for a turn onto the path. Ma, lighting a cigarette off the lantern, grunted.

"Early. Young folks all got watches and they can't tell time."

Leo trotted out to intercept the car. A door slammed. After a
pause the lamps swung around the fallen telephone pole and came
up to the barn, washing us all in white. The driver killed the lamps
and engine and got out. He was a small man in his early twenties
with short brown hair and stubble on his face. His flannel shirt and
khaki pants were both in need of cleaning. He had scant eyebrows
that were almost invisible in that light, giving him a perennially
surprised look. I'd seen that look in Frechette's *Houston Chronicle* and in both Detroit papers.

"Who's he?" He was looking at me.

I had a story for that, but Ma piped up. "You ain't paying to ask
no questions. Got the money?"

"Not all of it. A thousand's all Suzie could get from the
sharks."

"The deal's two thousand."

"Keep the P-38. The shotgun's all I need."

Ma had told me twenty-five hundred; but I was barely listening
to the conversation. Leo had gotten out on the passenger side,
pulling with him the girl in the photograph in my pocket. Suzie
Frechette had done up her black hair in braids, and she'd lost
weight, but her dark eyes and coloring were unmistakable. With
that hairstyle and in a man's work shirt and jeans and boots with
western heels she looked more like an Indian than she did in her
picture.

Leo opened the door and we went inside. The barn hadn't been
used for its original purpose for some time, but the smell of moldy
hay would remain as long as it stood. It was lit by a bare bulb
swinging from a frayed cord and heated by a barrel stove in a
corner. Stacks of cardboard cartons reached almost to the rafters,
below which Mace Chaney sat with his legs dangling over the
edge of the empty loft, the rifle across his knees.

Ma reached into an open carton and lifted out a pump shotgun
with the barrel cut back to the slide. Boyd stepped forward to take
it. She swung the muzzle on him. "Show me some paper."

He hesitated then drew a thick fold of bills from his shirt pocket
and laid it on a stack of cartons. Then she moved to cover me.
Boyd watched me add thirty-five hundred to the pile.

"What's *he* buying?"

Ma said, "You."

"Cop!" He lunged for the shotgun. Leo's revolver came out.
Mace drew a bead on Boyd from the loft. He relaxed.

I was looking at Suzie. "I'm a private detective hired by your
father. He wants to talk to you."

"He's here?" She touched Boyd's arm.

He tensed. "It's a damn cop trick!"

"You're smarter than that," I said. "You had to be, to pull
those two jobs and make your way here with every cop between
here and Texas looking for you. If I were one, would I be alone?"

"Do your jabbering outside." Ma reversed ends on the shotgun
for Boyd to take. He did so and worked the slide.

"Where's the shells?"

"That's your headache. I don't keep ammo in this firetrap."

That was a lie or some of those cartons wouldn't be labeled C-4
EXPLOSIVES. But you don't sell loaded guns to strangers.

Suzie said, "Virgil, you never load them anyway."

"Shut up."

"Your father's on his way," I said. "Ten minutes, that's all he
wants."

"Come on." Boyd took her wrist.

"Stay put."

This was a new voice. Everyone looked at Leo, standing in
front of the door with his gun still out.

"Leo, *what* in the *hell*—"

"Ma, the Luger."

She shut her mouth and took my gun out of her right coat pocket
and put it on the carton with the money. Then she backed away.

"Throw 'er down, Mace." He covered the man in the loft, who
froze in the act of raising the rifle. They were like that for a
moment.

"Mason," Ma said.

His shoulders slumped. He snapped on the safety and dropped
the rifle eight feet to the earthen floor.

"You, too, Mr. Forty Thousand Dollar *Re*ward," Leo said.
"Even empty guns give me the jumps."

Boyd cast the shotgun onto the stack of cartons with a violent
gesture.

"That's nice. I cut that money in half if I got to put a hole in
you."

"That reward talk's just PR," I said. "Even if you get Boyd to the cops they'll probably arrest you, too, for dealing in unlicensed firearms.''

''Like hell. I'm through getting bossed around by fat old ladies. Let's go, Mr. *Re*ward.''

''No!'' screamed Suzie.

An explosion slapped the walls. Leo's brows went up, his jaw dropping to expose the wad of pink gum in his mouth. He looked down at the spreading stain on the bib of his overalls and fell down on top of his gun. He kicked once.

Ma was standing with a hand in her left coat pocket. A finger of smoking metal poked out of a charred hole. ''Dadgum it, Leo,'' she said, ''this coat belonged to my Calvin, rest his soul.''

I was standing in front of the Log Cabin Inn's deserted office when Frechette swung a rented Ford into the broken paved driveway. He unfolded himself from the seat and loomed over me.

''I don't think anyone followed me,'' he said. ''I took a couple of wrong turns to make sure.''

''There won't be any interruptions then. The place has been closed a long time.''

I led him to one of the log bungalows in back. Boyd's Plymouth, stolen from the same lot where he'd left the van, was parked alongside it facing out. We knocked before entering.

All of the furniture had been removed except a metal bedstead with sagging springs. The lantern we had borrowed from Ma Chaney hung hissing from one post. Suzie was standing next to it. ''Papa.'' She didn't move. Boyd came out of the bathroom with the shotgun. The Indian took root.

''Man said you had money for us,'' Boyd said.

''It was the only way I could get him to bring Suzie here,'' I told Frechette.

''I won't pay to have my daughter killed in a shootout.''

''Lying bastard!'' Boyd swung the shotgun my way. Frechette backhanded him, knocking him back into the bathroom. I stepped forward and tore the shotgun from Boyd's weakened grip.

''Empty,'' I said. ''But it makes a good club.''

Suzie had come forward when Boyd fell. Frechette stopped her with an arm like a railroad gate. ''Take Dillinger for a walk while I talk to my daughter,'' he said to me.

I stuck out a hand, but Boyd slapped it aside and got up. His right eye was swelling shut. He looked at the Indian towering a foot over him, then at Suzie, who said, "It's all right. I'll talk to him."

We went out. A porch ran the length of the bungalow. I leaned the shotgun against the wall and trusted my weight to the railing. "I hear you got a raw deal from Texas Federal."

"My old man did." He stood with his hands rammed deep in his pockets, watching the pair through the window. "He asked for a two-month extension on his mortgage payment, just till he brought in his crop. Everyone gets extensions. Except when Texas Federal wants to sell the ranch to a developer. He met the 'dozers with a shotgun. Then he used it on himself."

"That why you use one?"

"I can't kill a jackrabbit. It used to burn up my old man."

"You'd be out in three years if you turned yourself in."

"To you, right? Let you collect that reward." He was still looking through the window. Inside, father and daughter were gesturing at each other frantically.

"I didn't say to me. You're big enough to walk into a police station by yourself."

"You don't know Texas Federal. They'd hire their own prosecutor, see I got life, make an example. I'll die first."

"Probably, the rate you're going."

He whirled on me. The parked Plymouth caught his eye. "Just who the hell are you? And why'd you—" He jerked his chin toward the car.

I got out J. P. Ahearn's card and gave it to him. His face lost color.

"You work for that headhunter?"

"Not in this life. But in a little while I'm going to call that number from the telephone in that gas station across the road."

He lunged for the door. I was closer and got in his way. "I don't know how you got this far with a head that hot," I said. "For once in your young life listen. You might get to like it."

He listened.

"This is Commander Ahearn! I know you're in there, Boyd. I got a dozen men here and if you don't come out we'll shoot up the place!"

Neither of us had heard them coming, and with the moon behind a cloud the thin, bitter voice might have come from anywhere. This time Boyd won the race to the door. He had the reflexes of a deer.

"Kill the light!" I barked to Frechette. "Ahearn beat me to it. He must have followed you after all."

We were in darkness suddenly. Boyd and Suzie had their arms around each other. "We're cornered," he said. "Why didn't that old lady have shells for that gun?"

"We just have to move faster, that's all. Keep him talking. Give me a hand with this window." The last was for Frechette, who came over and worked his big fingers under the swollen frame.

"There's a woman in here!" Boyd shouted.

"Come on out and no one gets hurt!" Ahearn sounded wired. The window gave with a squawking wrench.

"One minute, Boyd. Then we start blasting!"

I hoped it was enough. I slipped out over the sill.


"The car! Get it!"

The Plymouth engine turned over twice in the cold before starting. The car rolled forward and began picking up speed down the incline toward the road. Just then the moon came out, illuminating the man behind the wheel, and the night came apart like mountain ice breaking up, cracking and splitting with the staccato rap of handgun fire and the deeper boom of riot guns. Orange flame scorched the darkness. Slugs whacked the car's sheet metal and shattered the windshield. Then a red glow started to spread inside the vehicle and fists of yellow flame battered out the rest of the windows with a *whump* that shook the ground. The car rolled for a few more yards while the shooters, standing now and visible in the light of the blaze, went on pouring lead into it until it came to a stop against a road sign. The flame towered twenty feet above the crackling wreckage.

I approached Ahearn, standing in the overgrown grass with his shotgun dangling, watching the car burn. He jumped a little when I spoke. His glasses glowed orange.

"He made a dash, just like you wanted."

"If you think I wanted this, you don't know me," he said.

"Save it for the Six O'Clock News."

"What the hell are you doing here, anyway?"

"Friend of the family. Can I take the Frechettes home, or do you want to eat them here?"

He cradled the shotgun. "We'll just go inside together."

We found Suzie sobbing in her father's arms. The Indian glared at Ahearn. "Get the hell out of here."

"He was a desperate man," Ahearn said. "You're lucky the girl's alive."

"I said get out or I'll ram that shotgun down your throat."

He got out. Through the window I watched him rejoin his men. There were five, not a dozen as he'd claimed. Later I learned that three of them were off-duty Detroit cops and he'd hired the other two from a private security firm.

I waited until the fire engines came and Ahearn was busy talking to the firefighters, then went out the window again and crossed to the next bungalow, set farther back where the light of the flames didn't reach. I knocked twice and paused and knocked again. Boyd opened the door a crack.

"I'm taking Suzie and her father back to Frechette's motel for looks. Think you can lie low here until we come back in the morning for the rental car?"

"What if they search the cabins?"

"For what? You're dead. By the time they find out that's Leo in the car, if they ever do, you and Suzie will be in Canada. Customs won't be looking for a dead bandit. Give everyone a year or so to forget what you look like and then you can come back. Not to Texas, though, and not under the name Virgil Boyd."

"Lucky the gas tank blew."

"I've never had enough luck to trust to it. That's why I put a box of C-4 in Leo's lap. Ma figured it was a small enough donation to keep her clear of a charge of felony murder."

"I thought you were some kind of corpse freak." He still had the surprised look. "You could've been killed starting that car. Why'd you do it?"

"The world's not as complicated as it looks," I said. "There's always a good and a bad side. I saw Ahearn's."

"You ever need anything," he said.

"If you do things right I won't be able to find you when I do." I shook his hand and returned to the other bungalow.

A week later, after J. P. Ahearn's narrow, jug-eared features had made the cover of *People*, I received an envelope from Houston containing a bonus check for a thousand dollars signed by Howard Frechette. He'd repaid the thirty-five hundred I'd given Ma before going home. That was the last I heard from any of them. I used the money to settle some old bills and had some work done on my car so I could continue to ply my trade along the Crooked Way.

# Sue Grafton

# SHE DIDN'T COME HOME

SEPTEMBER IN SANTA TERESA. I'VE NEVER KNOWN ANYONE yet who doesn't suffer a certain restlessness when autumn rolls around. It's the season of new school clothes, fresh notebooks, and finely sharpened pencils without any teeth marks in the wood. We're all eight years old again and anything is possible. The new year should never begin on January 1. It begins in the fall and continues as long as our saddle oxfords remain unscuffed and our lunch boxes have no dents.

My name is Kinsey Millhone. I'm female, thirty-two, twice divorced, "doing business" as Kinsey Millhone Investigations in a little town ninety-five miles north of Los Angeles. Mine isn't a walk-in trade like a beauty salon. Most of my clients find themselves in a bind and then seek my services, hoping I can offer a solution for a mere thirty bucks an hour, plus expenses. Robert Ackerman's message was waiting on my answering machine that Monday morning at nine when I got in.

"Hello. My name is Robert Ackerman and I wonder if you could give me a call. My wife is missing and I'm worried sick. I was hoping you could help me out." In the background, I could hear whiney children, my favorite kind. He repeated his name and gave me a telephone number. I made a pot of coffee before I called him back.

A little person answered the phone. There was a murmured, child-size hello and then I heard a lot of heavy breathing close to the mouthpiece.

"Hi," I said, "can I speak to your daddy?"

"Yes." Long silence.

"Today?" I added.

The receiver was clunked down on a tabletop and I could hear the clatter of footsteps in a room that sounded as if it didn't have any carpeting. In due course, Robert Ackerman picked up the phone.

"Lucy?"

"It's Kinsey Millhone, Mr. Ackerman. I just got your message on my answering machine. Can you tell me what's going on?"

"Oh, wow, yeah. . . ."

He was interrupted by a piercing shriek that sounded like one of those policeman's whistles you use to discourage obscene phone callers. I didn't jerk back quite in time. "Shit, that hurt."

I listened patiently while he dealt with the errant child.

"Sorry," he said when he came back on the line. "Look, is there any way you could come out to the house? I've got my hands full and I just can't get away."

I took his address and brief directions, then headed out to my car.

Robert and the missing Mrs. Ackerman lived in a housing tract that looked like it was built in the forties before anyone ever dreamed up the notion of family rooms, country kitchens, and his 'n' her solar spas. What we had here was a basic drywall box; cramped living room with a dining L, a kitchen and one bathroom sandwiched between two nine-by-twelve-foot bedrooms. When Robert answered the door I could just about see the whole place at a glance. The only thing the builders had been lavish with was the hardwood floors, which, in this case, was unfortunate. Little children had banged and scraped these floors and had brought in some kind of foot grit that I sensed before I even asked to step inside.

Robert, though harried, had a boyish appeal; a man in his early thirties perhaps, lean and handsome, with dark eyes and dark hair that came to a pixie point in the middle of his forehead. He was wearing chinos and a plain white T-shirt. He had a baby, maybe eight months old, propped on his hip like a grocery bag. Another child clung to his right leg, while a third rode his tricycle at various walls and doorways, making quite loud sounds with his mouth.

"Hi, come on in," Robert said. "We can talk out in the back-yard while the kids play." His smile was sweet.

I followed him through the tiny disorganized house and out to the backyard, where he set the baby down in a sandpile framed with two-by-fours. The second child held onto Robert's belt loops and stuck a thumb in its mouth, staring at me while the tricycle child tried to ride off the edge of the porch. I'm not fond of children. I'm really not. Especially the kind who wear hard brown shoes. Like dogs, these infants sensed my distaste and kept their distance, eyeing me with a mixture of rancor and disdain.

The backyard was scruffy, fenced in, and littered with the fifty-pound sacks the sand had come in. Robert gave the children homemade-style cookies out of a cardboard box and shooed them away. In fifteen minutes the sugar would probably turn them into lunatics. I gave my watch a quick glance, hoping to be gone by then.

"You want a lawn chair?"

"No, this is fine," I said and settled on the grass. There wasn't a lawn chair in sight, but the offer was nice anyway.

He perched on the edge of the sandbox and ran a distracted hand across his head. "God, I'm sorry everything is such a mess, but Lucy hasn't been here for two days. She didn't come home from work on Friday and I've been a wreck ever since."

"I take it you notified the police."

"Sure. Friday night. She never showed up at the baby-sitter's house to pick the kids up. I finally got a call here at seven asking where she was. I figured she'd just stopped off at the grocery store or something, so I went ahead and picked 'em up and brought 'em home. By ten o'clock, when I hadn't heard from her, I knew something was wrong. I called her boss at home and he said as far as he knew she'd left work at five as usual, so that's when I called the police."

"You filed a missing persons report?"

"I can do that today. With an adult, you have to wait seventy-two hours, and even then, there's not much they can do."

"What else did they suggest?"

"The usual stuff, I guess. I mean, I called everyone we know. I talked to her mom in Bakersfield and this friend of hers at work. Nobody has any idea where she is. I'm scared something's happened to her."

"You've checked with hospitals in the area, I take it."

"Sure. That's the first thing I did."

"Did she give you any indication that anything was wrong?"

"Not a word."

"Was she depressed or behaving oddly?"

"Well, she was kind of restless the past couple of months. She always seemed to get excited around this time of year. She said it reminded her of her old elementary-school days." He shrugged. "I hated mine."

"But she's never disappeared like this before."

"Oh, heck no. I just mentioned her mood because you asked. I don't think it amounted to anything."

"Does she have any problems with alcohol or drugs?"

"Lucy isn't really like that," he said. "She's petite and kind of quiet. A homebody, I guess you'd say."

"What about your relationship? Do the two of you get along okay?"

"As far as I'm concerned, we do. I mean, once in a while we get into it, but never anything serious."

"What are your disagreements about?"

He smiled ruefully. "Money, mostly. With three kids, we never seem to have enough. I mean, I'm crazy about big families, but it's tough financially. I always wanted four or five, but she says three is plenty, especially with the oldest not in school yet. We fight about that some . . . having more kids."

"You both work?"

"We have to. Just to make ends meet. She has a job in an escrow company downtown, and I work for the phone company."

"Doing what?"

"Installer," he said.

"Has there been any hint of someone else in her life?"

He sighed, plucking at the grass between his feet. "In a way, I wish I could say yes. I'd like to think maybe she just got fed up or something and checked into a motel for the weekend. Something like that."

"But you don't think she did."

"Unh-uh, and I'm going crazy with anxiety. Somebody's got to find out where she is."

"Mr. Ackerman. . . ."

"You can call me Rob," he said.

Clients always say that. I mean, unless their names are something else.

"Rob," I said, "the police are truly your best bet in a situation like this. I'm just one person. They've got a vast machinery they can put to work and it won't cost you a cent."

"You charge a lot, huh?"

"Thirty bucks an hour plus expenses."

He thought about that for a moment, then gave me a searching look. "Could you maybe put in ten hours? I got three hundred bucks we were saving for a trip to the San Diego Zoo."

I pretended to think about it, but the truth was, I knew I couldn't say no to that boyish face. Anyway, the kids were starting to whine and I wanted to get out of there. I waived the retainer and said I'd send him an itemized bill when the ten hours were up. I figured I could put a contract in the mail and reduce my contact with the short persons who were crowding around him now, begging for more sweets. I asked for a recent photograph of Lucy, but all he could come up with was a two-year-old snapshot of her with the two older kids. She looked beleaguered even then, and that was before the third baby came along. I thought about quiet little Lucy Ackerman whose three strapping sons had legs the size of my arms. If I were she, I knew where I'd be. Long gone.

Lucy Ackerman was employed as an escrow officer for a small company on State Street not far from my office. It was a modest establishment of white walls, rust-and-brown-plaid furniture with burnt orange carpeting. There were Gauguin reproductions all around and a live plant on every desk. I introduced myself first to the office manager, a Mrs. Merriman, who was in her sixties, had tall hair, and wore lace-up boots with stiletto heels. She looked like a woman who'd trade all her pension monies for a head-to-toe body tuck.

I said, "Robert Ackerman has asked me to see if I can locate his wife."

"Well, the poor man. I heard about that," she said with her mouth. Her eyes said, "Fat chance!"

"Do you have any idea where she might be?"

"I think you'd better talk to Mr. Sotherland." She had turned all prim and officious, but my guess was she knew something and was dying to be asked. I intended to accommodate her as soon as I'd talked to him. The protocol in small offices, I've found, is ironclad.

Gavin Sotherland got up from his swivel desk and stretched a big hand across the desk to shake mine. The other member of the office force, Barbara Hemdahl, the bookkeeper, got up from her chair simultaneously and excused herself. Mr. Sotherland watched her depart and then motioned me into the same seat. I sank into leather still hot from Barbara Hemdahl's backside, a curiously intimate effect. I made a mental note to find out what she knew, and then I looked, with interest, at the company vice president. I picked up all these names and job titles because his was cast in stand-up bronze letters on his desk, and the two women both had white plastic name tags affixed to their breasts, like nurses. As nearly as I could tell, there were only four of them in the office, including Lucy Ackerman, and I couldn't understand how they could fail to identify each other on sight. Maybe all the badges were for clients who couldn't be trusted to tell one from the other without the proper IDs.

Gavin Sotherland was large, an ex-jock to all appearances, maybe forty-five years old, with a heavy head of blond hair thinning slightly at the crown. He had a slight paunch, a slight stoop to his shoulders, and a grip that was damp with sweat. He had his coat off, and his once-starched white shirt was limp and wrinkled, his beige gabardine pants heavily creased across the lap. Altogether, he looked like a man who'd just crossed a continent by rail. Still, I was forced to credit him with good looks, even if he had let himself go to seed.

"Nice to meet you, Miss Millhone. I'm so glad you're here." His voice was deep and rumbling, with confidence-inspiring undertones. On the other hand, I didn't like the look in his eyes. He could have been a con man, for all I knew. "I understand Mrs. Ackerman never got home Friday night," he said.

"That's what I'm told," I replied. "Can you tell me anything about her day here?"

He studied me briefly. "Well, now, I'm going to have to be honest with you. Our bookkeeper has come across some discrepancies in the accounts. It looks like Lucy Ackerman has just walked off with half a million dollars entrusted to us."

"How'd she manage that?"

I was picturing Lucy Ackerman, free of those truck-busting kids, lying on a beach in Rio, slurping some kind of rum drink out of a coconut.

Mr. Sotherland looked pained. "In the most straightforward manner imaginable," he said. "It looks like she opened a new bank account at a branch in Montebello and deposited ten checks that should have gone into other accounts. Last Friday, she withdrew over five hundred thousand dollars in cash, claiming we were closing out a big real estate deal. We found the passbook in her bottom drawer." He tossed the booklet across the desk to me and I picked it up. The word *VOID* had been punched into the pages in a series of holes. A quick glance showed ten deposits at intervals dating back over the past three months and a zero balance as of last Friday's date.

"Didn't anybody else double-check this stuff?"

"We'd just undergone our annual audit in June. Everything was fine. We trusted this woman implicitly and had every reason to."

"You discovered the loss this morning?"

"Yes, ma'am, but I'll admit I was suspicious Friday night when Robert Ackerman called me at home. It was completely unlike that woman to disappear without a word. She's worked here eight years, and she's been punctual and conscientious since the day she walked in."

"Well, punctual at any rate," I said. "Have you notified the police?"

"I was just about to do that. I'll have to alert the Department of Corporations too. God, I can't believe she did this to us. I'll be fired. They'll probably shut this entire office down."

"Would you mind if I had a quick look around?"

"To what end?"

"There's always a chance we can figure out where she went. If we move fast enough, maybe we can catch her before she gets away with it."

"Well, I doubt that," he said. "The last anybody saw her was Friday afternoon. That's two full days. She could be anywhere by now."

"Mr. Sotherland, her husband has already authorized three hundred dollars' worth of my time. Why not take advantage of it?"

He stared at me. "Won't the police object?"

"Probably. But I don't intend to get in anybody's way, and whatever I find out, I'll turn over to them. They may not be able to get a fraud detective out here until late morning anyway. If I get a line on her, it'll make you look good to the company *and* to the cops."

He gave a sigh of resignation and waved his hand. "Hell, I don't care. Do what you want."

When I left his office, he was putting the call through to the police department.

I sat briefly at Lucy's desk, which was neat and well organized. Her drawers contained the usual office supplies; no personal items at all. There was a calendar on her desktop, one of those loose-leaf affairs with a page for each day. I checked back through the past couple of months. The only personal notation was for an appointment at the Women's Health Center August 2 and a second visit last Friday afternoon. It must have been a busy day for Lucy, what with a doctor's appointment and ripping off her company for half a million bucks. I made a note of the address she'd penciled in at the time of her first visit. The other two women in the office were keeping an eye on me, I noticed, though both pretended to be occupied with paperwork.

When I finished my search, I got up and crossed the room to Mrs. Merriman's desk. "Is there any way I can make a copy of the passbook for that account Mrs. Ackerman opened?"

"Well, yes, if Mr. Sotherland approves," she said.

"I'm also wondering where she kept her coat and purse during the day."

"In the back. We each have a locker in the storage room."

"I'd like to take a look at that too."

I waited patiently while she cleared both matters with her boss, and then I accompanied her to the rear. There was a door that opened onto the parking lot. To the left of it was a small restroom and, on the right, there was a storage room that housed four connecting upright metal lockers, the copy machine, and numerous shelves neatly stacked with office supplies. Each shoulder-high locker was marked with a name. Lucy Ackerman's was still securely padlocked. There was something about the blank look of that locker that seemed ominous somehow. I looked at the lock, fairly itching to have a crack at it with my little set of key picks, but I didn't want to push my luck with the cops on the way.

"I'd like for someone to let me know what's in that locker when it's finally opened," I remarked while Mrs. Merriman ran off the copy of the passbook pages for me.

"This, too," I said, handling her a carbon of the withdrawal slip Lucy'd been required to sign in receipt of the cash. It had been folded and tucked into the back of the booklet. "You have any theories about where she went?"

Mrs. Merriman's mouth pursed piously, as though she were debating with herself about how much she might say.

"I wouldn't want to be accused of talking out of school," she ventured.

"Mrs. Merriman, it does look like a crime's been committed," I suggested. "The police are going to ask you the same thing when they get here."

"Oh. Well, in that case, I suppose it's all right. I mean, I don't have the faintest idea where she is, but I do think she's been acting oddly the past few months.''

"Like what?"

"She seemed secretive. Smug. Like she knew something the rest of us didn't know about."

"That certainly turned out to be the case," I said.

"Oh, I didn't mean it was related to that," she said hesitantly. "I think she was having an affair."

That got my attention. "An affair? With whom?"

She paused for a moment, touching at one of the hairpins that supported her ornate hairdo. She allowed her gaze to stray back toward Mr. Sotherland's office. I turned and looked in that direction too.

"Really?" I said. "No wonder he was in a sweat," I thought.

"I couldn't swear to it," she murmured, "but his marriage has been rocky for years, and I gather she hasn't been that happy herself. She has those beastly little boys, you know, and a husband who seems determined to spawn more. She and Mr. Sotherland . . . Gavie, she calls him . . . have . . . well, I'm sure they've been together. Whether it's connected to this matter of the missing money, I wouldn't presume to guess." Having said as much, she was suddenly uneasy. "You won't repeat what I've said to the police, I hope."

"Absolutely not," I said. "Unless they ask, of course."

"Oh. Of course."

"By the way, is there a company travel agent?"

"Right next door," she replied.

I had a brief chat with the bookkeeper, who added nothing to the general picture of Lucy Ackerman's last few days at work. I retrieved my VW from the parking lot and headed over to the health center eight blocks away, wondering what Lucy had been up to. I was guessing birth control and probably the permanent sort. If she were having an affair (and determined not to get pregnant again in any event), it would seem logical, but I hadn't any idea how to verify the fact. Medical personnel are notoriously stingy with information like that.

I parked in front of the clinic and grabbed my clipboard from the backseat. I have a supply of all-purpose forms for occasions like this. They look like a cross between a job application and an insurance claim. I filled one out now in Lucy's name and forged her signature at the bottom where it said "authorization to release information." As a model, I used the Xerox copy of the with-drawal slip she'd tucked in her passbook. I'll admit my methods would be considered unorthodox, nay illegal, in the eyes of law-enforcement officers everywhere, but I reasoned that the information I was seeking would never actually be used in court, and therefore it couldn't matter *that* much how it was obtained.

I went into the clinic, noting gratefully the near-empty waiting room. I approached the counter and took out my wallet with my California Fidelity ID. I do occasional insurance investigations for CF in exchange for office space. They once made the mistake of issuing me a company identification card with my picture right on it that I've been flashing around quite shamelessly ever since.

I had a choice of three female clerks and, after a brief assess-ment, I made eye contact with the oldest of them. In places like this, the younger employees usually have no authority at all and are, thus, impossible to con. People without authority will often simply stand there, reciting the rules like mynah birds. Having no power, they also seem to take a vicious satisfaction in forcing others to comply.

The woman approached the counter on her side, looking at me expectantly. I showed her my CF ID and made the form on the clipboard conspicuous, as though I had nothing to hide.

"Hi. My name is Kinsey Millhone," I said. "I wonder if you can give me some help. Your name is what?"

She seemed wary of the request, as though her name had mag-ical powers that might be taken from her by force. "Lillian Vin-cent," she said reluctantly. "What sort of help did you need?"

"Lucy Ackerman has applied for some insurance benefits and we need verification of the claim. You'll want a copy of the release form for your files, of course."

I passed the forged paper to her and then busied myself with my clipboard as though it were all perfectly matter-of-fact.

She was instantly alert. "What is this?"

I gave her a look. "Oh, sorry. She's applying for maternity leave, and we need her due date."

"Maternity leave?"

"Isn't she a patient here?"

Lillian Vincent looked at me. "Just a moment," she said, and moved away from the desk with the form in hand. She went to a file cabinet and extracted a chart, returning to the counter. She pushed it over to me. "The woman has had a tubal ligation," she said, her manner crisp.

I blinked, smiling slightly as though she were making a joke. "There must be some mistake."

"Lucy Ackerman must have made it, then, if she thinks she can pull this off." She opened the chart. "She was just in here Friday for a final checkup and a medical release. She's sterile."

I looked at the chart. Sure enough, that's what it said. I raised my eyebrows and then shook my head slightly. "God. Well. I guess I better have a copy of that."

"I should think so," the woman said and ran one off for me on the desktop dry copier. She placed it on the counter and watched as I tucked it onto my clipboard.

She said, "I don't know how they think they can get away with it."

"People love to cheat," I replied.

It was nearly noon by the time I got back to the travel agency next door to the place where Lucy Ackerman had worked. It didn't take any time at all to unearth the reservations she'd made two weeks before. Buenos Aires, first class on Pan Am. For one. She'd picked up the ticket Friday afternoon just before the agency closed for the weekend.

The travel agent rested his elbows on the counter and looked at me with interest, hoping to hear all the gory details, I'm sure. "I heard about that business next door," he said. He was young, maybe twenty-four, with a pug nose, auburn hair, and a gap between his teeth. He'd make the perfect costar on a wholesome family TV show.

"How'd she pay for the tickets?"

"Cash," he said. "I mean, who'd have thunk?"

"Did she say anything in particular at the time?"

"Not really. She seemed jazzed and we joked some about Montezuma's revenge and stuff like that. I knew she was married and I was asking her all about who was keeping the kids and what her old man was going to do while she was gone. God, I never in a million *years* guessed she was pulling off a scam like that, you know?"

"Did you ask why she was going to Argentina by herself?"

"Well, yeah, and she said it was a surprise." He shrugged. "It didn't really make sense, but she was laughing like a kid, and I thought I just didn't get the joke."

I asked for a copy of the itinerary, such as it was. She had paid for a round-trip ticket, but there were no reservations coming back. Maybe she intended to cash in the return ticket once she got down there. I tucked the travel docs onto my clipboard along with the copy of her medical forms. Something about this whole deal had begun to chafe, but I couldn't figure out quite why.

"Thanks for your help," I said, heading toward the door.

"No problem. I guess the other guy didn't get it either," he remarked.

I paused, mid-stride, turning back. "Get what?"

"The joke. I heard 'em next door and they were fighting like cats and dogs. He was pissed."

"Really," I said. I stared at him. "What time was this?"

"Five-fifteen. Something like that. They were closed and so were we, but Dad wanted me to stick around for a while until the cleaning crew got here. He owns this place, which is how I got in the business myself. These new guys were starting, and he wanted me to make sure they understood what to do."

"Are you going to be here for a while?"

"Sure."

"Good. The police may want to hear about this."

I went back into the escrow office with mental alarm bells clanging away like crazy. Both Barbara Hemdahl and Mrs. Merriman had opted to eat lunch in. Or maybe the cops had ordered them to stay where they were. The bookkeeper sat at her desk with a sandwich, apple, and a carton of milk neatly arranged in front of her, while Mrs. Merriman picked at something in a plastic container she must have brought in from a fast-food place.

"How's it going?" I asked.

Barbara Hemdahl spoke up from her side of the room. "The detectives went off for a search warrant so they can get in all the lockers back there, collecting evidence."

"Only one of 'em is locked," I pointed out.

She shrugged. "I guess they can't even peek without the paperwork."

Mrs. Merriman spoke up then, her expression tinged with guilt. "Actually, they asked the rest of us if we'd open our lockers voluntarily, so of course we did."

Mrs. Merriman and Barbara Hemdahl exchanged a look.

"And?"

Mrs. Merriman colored slightly. "There was an overnight case in Mr. Sotherland's locker, and I guess the things in it were hers."

"Is it still back there?"

"Well, yes, but they left a uniformed officer on guard so nobody'd walk off with it. They've got everything spread out on the
copy machine."

I went through the rear of the office, peering into the storage
room. I knew the guy on duty and he didn't object to my doing a
visual survey of the items, as long as I didn't touch anything. The
overnight case had been packed with all the personal belongings
women like to keep on hand in case the rest of the luggage gets
sent to Mexicali by mistake. I spotted a toothbrush, slippers, a
filmy nightie, prescription drugs, hairbrush, extra eyeglasses in a
case. Tucked under a change of underwear, I spotted a round
plastic container, slightly convex, about the size of a compact.

Gavin Sotherland was still sitting at his desk when I stopped by
his office. His skin tone was gray and his shirt was hanging out,
big rings of sweat under each arm. He was smoking a cigarette
with the air of a man who's quit the habit and has taken it up again
under duress. A second uniformed officer was standing just inside
the door to my right.

I leaned against the frame, but Gavin scarcely looked up.

I said, "You knew what she was doing, but you thought she'd
take you with her when she left."

His smile was bitter. "Life is full of surprises," he said.

I was going to have to tell Robert Ackerman what I'd discovered, and I dreaded it. As a stalling maneuver, just to demonstrate
what a good girl I was, I drove over to the police station first and
dropped off the data I'd collected, filling them in on the theory I'd
come up with. They didn't exactly pin a medal on me, but they
weren't as pissed off as I thought they'd be, given the number of
civil codes I'd violated in the process. They were even moderately
courteous, which is unusual in their treatment of me. Unfortu-
nately, none of it took that long, and before I knew it, I was
standing at the Ackermans' front door again.

I rang the bell and waited, bad jokes running through my head.
Well, there's good news and bad news, Robert. The good news is
we've wrapped it up with hours to spare so you won't have to pay
me the full three hundred dollars we agreed to. The bad news is your
wife's a thief, she's probably dead, and we're just getting out a
warrant now, because we think we know where the body's stashed.

The door opened and Robert was standing there with a finger to
his lips. "The kids are down for their naps," he whispered.

I nodded elaborately, pantomiming my understanding, as though the silence he'd imposed required this special behavior on my part.

He motioned me in and together we tiptoed through the house and out to the backyard, where we continued to talk in low tones. I wasn't sure which bedroom the little rugrats slept in, and I didn't want to be responsible for waking them.

Half a day of playing papa to the boys had left Robert looking disheveled and sorely in need of relief.

"I didn't expect you back this soon," he whispered.

I found myself whispering too, feeling anxious at the sense of secrecy. It reminded me of grade school somehow; the smell of autumn hanging in the air, the two of us perched on the edge of the sandbox like little kids, conspiring. I didn't want to break his heart, but what was I to do?

"I think we've got it wrapped up," I said.

He looked at me for a moment, apparently guessing from my expression that the news wasn't good. "Is she okay?"

"We don't think so," I said. And then I told him what I'd learned, starting with the embezzlement and the relationship with Gavin, taking it right through to the quarrel the travel agent had heard. Robert was way ahead of me.

"She's dead, isn't she?"

"We don't know it for a fact, but we suspect as much."

He nodded, tears welling up. He wrapped his arms around his knees and propped his chin on his fists. He looked so young, I wanted to reach out and touch him. "She was really having an affair?" he asked plaintively.

"You must have suspected as much," I said. "You said she was restless and excited for months. Didn't that give you a clue?"

He shrugged one shoulder, using the sleeve on his T-shirt to dash at the tears trickling down his cheeks. "I don't know," he said. "I guess."

"And then you stopped by the office Friday afternoon and found her getting ready to leave the country. That's when you killed her, isn't it?"

He froze, staring at me. At first, I thought he'd deny it, but maybe he realized there wasn't any point. He nodded mutely.

"And then you hired me to make it look good, right?"

He made a kind of squeaking sound in the back of his throat and sobbed once, his voice reduced to a whisper again. "She shouldn't have done it . . . betrayed us like that. We loved her so much. . . ."

"Have you got the money here?"

He nodded, looking miserable. "I wasn't going to pay your fee out of that," he said incongruously. "We really did have a little fund so we could go to San Diego one day."

"I'm sorry things didn't work out," I said.

"I didn't do so bad, though, did I? I mean, I could have gotten away with it, don't you think?"

I'd been talking about the trip to the zoo. He thought I was referring to his murdering his wife. Talk about poor communication. God.

"Well, you nearly pulled it off," I said. Shit, I was sitting there trying to make the guy *feel* good.

He looked at me piteously, eyes red and flooded, his mouth trembling. "But where did I slip up? What did I do wrong?"

"You put her diaphragm in the overnight case you packed. You thought you'd shift suspicion onto Gavin Sotherland, but you didn't realize she'd had her tubes tied."

A momentary rage flashed through his eyes and then flickered out. I suspected that her voluntary sterilization was more insulting to him than the affair with her boss.

"Jesus, I don't know what she saw in him," he breathed. "He was such a pig."

"Well," I said, "if it's any comfort to you, she wasn't going to take *him* with her, either. She just wanted freedom, you know?"

He pulled out a handkerchief and blew his nose, trying to compose himself. He mopped his eyes, shivering with tension. "How can you prove it, though, without a body? Do you know where she is?"

"I think we do," I said softly. "The sandbox, Robert. Right under us."

He seemed to shrink. "Oh, God," he whispered. "Oh, God, don't turn me in. I'll give you the money. I don't give a damn. Just let me stay here with my kids. The little guys need me. I did it for them. I swear I did. You don't have to tell the cops, do you?"

I shook my head and opened my shirt collar, showing him the mike. "I don't have to tell a soul. I'm wired for sound," I said, and then I looked over toward the side yard.

For once, I was glad to see Lieutenant Dolan amble into view.

# Edward Gorman

# TURN AWAY

ON THURSDAY SHE WAS THERE AGAIN. (THIS WAS ON A SOAP opera he'd picked up by accident looking for a western movie to watch since he was all caught up on his work.) Parnell had seen her Monday but not Tuesday then not Wednesday either. But Thursday she was there again. He didn't know her name, hell it didn't matter, she was just this maybe twenty-two twenty-three year old who looked a lot like a nurse from Enid, Oklahoma he'd dated a couple times (Les Elgart had been playing the Loop) six seven months after returning from WWII.

Now this young look-alike was on a soap opera and he was watching.

A frigging soap opera.

He was getting all dazzled up by her, just as he had on Monday, when the knock came sharp and three times, almost like a code.

He wasn't wearing the slippers he'd gotten recently at K mart so he had to find them, and he was drinking straight from a quart of Hamms so he had to put it down. When you were the manager of an apartment building, even one as marginal as The Alma, you had to go to the door with at least a little "decorousness," the word Sgt. Meister, his boss, had always used back in Parnell's cop days.

It was 11:23 A.M. and most of the Alma's tenants were at work. Except for the ADC mothers who had plenty of work of their own kind what with some of the assholes down at Social Services (Parnell had once gone down there with the Jamaican woman in 201 and threatened to punch out the little bastard who was holding up her check), not to mention the sheer simple burden of knowing the sweet innocent little child you loved was someday going to end up just as blown-out and bitter and useless as you yourself.

He went to the door, shuffling in his new slippers which he'd bought two sizes too big because of his bunions.

The guy who stood there was no resident of the Alma. Not with his razor-cut black hair and his three-piece banker's suit and the kind of melancholy in his pale blue eyes that was almost sweet and not at all violent. He had a fancy mustache spoiled by the fact that his pink lips were a woman's.

"Mr. Parnell?"

Parnell nodded.

The man, who was maybe thirty-five, put out a hand. Parnell took it, all the while thinking of the soap opera behind him and the girl who looked like the one from Enid, Oklahoma. (Occasionally he bought whack-off magazines but the girls either looked too easy or too arrogant so he always had to close his eyes anyway and think of somebody he'd known in the past.) He wanted to see her, fuck this guy. Saturday he would be 61 and about all he had to look forward to was a phone call from his kid up the Oregon coast. His kid, who, God rest her soul, was his mother's son and not Parnell's, always ran a stopwatch while they talked so as to save on the phone bill. Hi Dad Happy Birthday and It's Been Really Nice Talking To You. I-Love-You-Bye.

"What can I do for you?" Parnell said. Then as he stood there watching the traffic go up and down Cortland Boulevard in baking July sunlight, Parnell realized that the guy was somehow familiar to him.

The guy said, "You know my father."

"Jesus H. Christ—"

"—Bud Garrett—"

"—Bud. I'll be god damned." He'd already shaken the kid's hand and he couldn't do that again so he kind of patted him on the shoulder and said, "Come on in."

"I'm Richard Garrett."

"I'm glad to meet you, Richard."

He took the guy inside. Richard looked around at the odds and ends of furniture that didn't match and at all the pictures of dead people and immediately put a smile on his face as if he just couldn't remember when he'd been so enchanted with a place before, which meant of course that he saw the place for the dump Parnell knew it to be.

"How about a beer?" Parnell said, hoping he had something besides the generic stuff he'd bought at the 7-11 a few nights ago.

"I'm fine, thanks."

Richard sat on the edge of the couch with the air of somebody waiting for his flight to be announced. He was all ready to jump up. He kept his eyes downcast and he kept fiddling with his wedding ring. Parnell watched him. Sometimes it turned out that way. Richard's old man had been on the force with Parnell. They'd been best friends. Garrett, Sr. was a big man, six three and fleshy but strong, a brawler and occasionally a mean one when the hootch didn't settle in him quite right. But his son . . . Sometimes it turned out that way. He was manly enough, Parnell supposed, but there was an air of being trapped in himself, of petulance, that put Parnell off.

Three or four minutes of silence went by. The soap opera ended with Parnell getting another glance of the young lady. Then a "CBS Newsbreak" came on. Then some commercials. Richard didn't seem to notice that neither of them had said anything for a long time. Sunlight made bars through the venetian blinds. The refrigerator thrummed. Upstairs but distantly a kid bawled.

Parnell didn't realize it at first, not until Richard sniffed, that Bud Garrett's son was either crying or doing something damn close to it.

"Hey, Richard, what's the problem?" Parnell said, making sure to keep his voice soft.

"My, my Dad."

"Is something wrong?"

"Yes."

"What?"

Richard looked up with his pale blue eyes. "He's dying."

"Jesus."

Richard cleared his throat. "It's how he's dying that's so bad."

"Cancer?"

Richard said, "Yes. Liver. He's dying by inches."

"Shit."

Richard nodded. Then he fell once more into his own thoughts. Parnell let him stay there awhile, thinking about Bud Garrett. Bud had left the force on a whim that all the cops said would fail. He started a rent-a-car business with a small inheritance he'd come into. That was twenty years ago. Now Bud Garrett lived up in Woodland Hills and drove the big Mercedes and went to Europe once a year. For a time Bud and Parnell had tried to remain friends but beer and champagne didn't mix. When the Mrs. had died Bud had sent a lavish display of flowers to the funeral and a note that Parnell knew to be sincere but they hadn't had any real contact in years.

"Shit," Parnell said again.

Richard looked up, shaking his head as if trying to escape the aftereffects of drugs. "I want to hire you."

"Hire me? As what?"

"You're a personal investigator aren't you?"

"Not anymore. I mean I kept my ticket—it doesn't cost that much to renew it—but hell I haven't had a job in five years." He waved a beefy hand around the apartment. "I manage these apartments."

From inside his blue pin-striped suit Richard took a sleek wallet. He quickly counted out five one hundred dollar bills and put them on the blond coffee table next to the stack of Luke Short paperbacks. "I really want you to help me."

"Help you do what?"

"Kill my father."

Now Parnell shook his head. "Jesus, kid, are you nuts or what?"

Richard stood up. "Are you busy right now?"

Parnell looked around the room again. "I guess not."

"Then why don't you come with me?"

"Where?"


When the elevator doors opened to let them out on the sixth floor of the hospital, Parnell said, "I want to be sure you understand me."

He took Richard by the sleeve and held him and stared into his pale blue eyes. "You know why I'm coming here, right?"

"Right."

"I'm coming to see your father because we're old friends. Because I cared about him a great deal and because I still do. But that's the only reason."

"Right."

Parnell frowned. "You still think I'm going to help you, don't you?"

"I just want you to see him."

On the way to Bud Garrett's room they passed an especially

good-looking nurse. Parnell felt guilty about recognizing her beauty. His old friend was dying just down the hall and here Parnell was worrying about some nurse.

Parnell went around the corner of the door. The room was dark. It smelled sweet from flowers and fetid from flesh literally rotting.

Then he looked at the frail yellow man in the bed. Even in the shadows you could see his skin was yellow.

"I'll be damned," the man said.

It was like watching a skeleton talk by some trick of magic.

Parnell went over and tried to smile his ass off but all he could muster was just a little one. He wanted to cry until he collapsed. You sonofabitch, Parnell thought, enraged. He just wasn't sure who he was enraged with. Death or God or himself—or maybe even Bud himself for reminding Parnell of just how terrible and scary it could get near the end.

"I'll be damned," Bud Garrett said again.

He put out his hand and Parnell took it. Held it for a long time.

"He's a good boy, isn't he?" Garrett said, nodding to Richard.

"He sure is."

"I had to raise him after his mother died. I did a good job, if I say so myself."

"A damn good job, Bud."

This was a big private room that more resembled a hotel suite. There was a divan and a console tv and a dry bar. There was a Picasso lithograph and a walk-in closet and a deck to walk out on. There was a double-sized water bed with enough controls to drive a space ship and a big stereo and a bookcase filled with hardcovers. Most people Parnell knew dreamed of living in such a place. Bud Garrett was dying in it.

"He told you," Garrett said.

"What?" Parnell spun around to face Richard, knowing suddenly the worst truth of all.

"He told you."

"Jesus, Bud, you sent him, didn't you?"

"Yes. Yes, I did."

"Why?"

Parnell looked at Garrett again. How could somebody who used to have a weight problem and who could throw around the toughest drunk the barrio ever produced get to be like this. Nearly every time he talked he winced. And all the time he smelled. Bad.

"I sent for you because none of us is perfect," Bud said.

"I don't understand."

"He's afraid."

"Richard?"

"Yes."

"I don't blame him. I'd be afraid too." Parnell paused and stared at Bud. "You asked him to kill you, didn't you?"

"Yes. It's his responsibility to do it."

Richard stepped up to his father's bedside and said, "I agree with that, Mr. Parnell. It is my responsibility. I just need a little help is all."

"Doing what?"

"If I buy cyanide, it will eventually be traced to me and I'll be tried for murder. If you buy it, nobody will ever connect you with my father."

Parnell shook his head. "That's bullshit. That isn't what you want me for. There are a million ways you could get cyanide without having it traced back."

Bud Garrett said, "I told him about you. I told him you could help give him strength."

"I don't agree with any of this, Bud. You should die when it's your time to die. I'm a Catholic."

Bud laughed hoarsely. "So am I, you asshole." He coughed and said, "The pain's bad. I'm beyond any help they can give me. But it could go on for a long time." Then, just as his son had an hour ago, Bud Garrett began crying almost imperceptibly. "I'm scared, Parnell. I don't know what's on the other side but it can't be any worse than this." He reached out his hand and for a long time Parnell just stared at it but then he touched it.

"Jesus," Parnell said. "It's pretty fucking confusing, Bud."

"It's my life. I'm sane, I'm sober. I should be able to decide, shouldn't I?"

But all Parnell could say was, "It's pretty fucking confusing, Bud. It's pretty fucking confusing."

Richard took Parnell out to dinner that night. It was a nice place. The table cloths were starchy white and the waiters all wore shiny shoes. Candles glowed inside red glass.

They'd had four drinks apiece, during which Richard told Parnell about his two sons (six and eight respectively) and about the perils and rewards of the rent-a-car business and about how much he liked windsurfing even though he really wasn't much good at it.

Just after the arrival of the fourth drink, Richard took something from his pocket and laid it on the table.

It was a cold capsule.

"You know how the Tylenol Killer in Chicago operated?" Richard asked.

Parnell nodded.

"Same thing," Richard said. "I took the cyanide and put it in a capsule."

"Christ. I don't know about it."

"You're scared too, aren't you?"

"Yeah, I am."

Richard sipped his whiskey-and-soda. With his regimental striped tie he might have been sitting in a country club. "May I ask you something?"

"Maybe."

"Do you believe in God?"

"Sure."

"Then if you believe in God, you must believe in goodness, correct?"

Parnell frowned. "I'm not much of an intellectual, Richard."

"But if you believe in God, you must believe in goodness, right?"

"Right."

"Do you think what's happening to my father is good?"

"Of course I don't."

"Then you must also believe that God isn't doing this to him—right?"

"Right."

Richard held up the capsule. Stared at it. "All I want you to do is give me a ride to the hospital. Then just wait in the car down in the parking lot."

"I won't do it."

Richard signaled for another round.

"I won't god damn do it," Parnell said.

By the time they left the restaurant Richard was too drunk to drive. Parnell got behind the wheel of the new Audi. "Why don't you tell me where you live? I'll take you home and take a cab from there."

"I want to go to the hospital."

"No way, Richard."

Richard slammed his fist against the dashboard. "You fucking owe him that, man!" he screamed.

Parnell was shocked, and a bit impressed, with Richard's violent side. If nothing else, he saw how much Richard loved his old man.

"Richard, listen."

Richard sat in a heap against the opposite door. His tears were dry ones, choking ones. "Don't give me any of your speeches." He wiped snot from his nose on his sleeve. "My Dad always told me what a tough guy Parnell was." He turned to Parnell, anger in him again. "Well, I'm not tough, Parnell, and so I need to borrow some of your toughness so I can get that man out of his pain and grant him his one last fucking wish. DO YOU GOD DAMN UNDERSTAND ME?"

He smashed his fist on the dashboard again.

Parnell turned on the ignition and drove them away.

When they reached the hospital, Parnell found a parking spot and pulled in. The mercury vapor lights made him feel as though he were on Mars. Bugs smashed against the windshield.

"I'll wait here for you," Parnell said.

Richard looked over at him. "You won't call the cops?"

"No."

"And you won't come up and try to stop me?"

"No."

Richard studied Parnell's face. "Why did you change your mind?"

"Because I'm like him."

"Like my father?"

"Yeah. A coward. I wouldn't want the pain either. I'd be just as afraid."

All Richard said, and this he barely whispered, was "Thanks."

While he sat there Parnell listened to country western music and then a serious political call-in show and then a call-in show where a lady talked about Venusians who wanted to pork her and then some salsa music and then a religious minister who sounded like Foghorn Leghorn in the old Warner Brothers cartoons.

By then Richard came back.

He got in the car and slammed the door shut and said, completely sober now, "Let's go."

Parnell got out of there.

They went ten long blocks before Parnell said, "You didn't do it, did you?"

Richard got hysterical. "You sonofabitch! You sonofabitch!"

Parnell had to pull the car over to the curb. He hit Richard once, a fast clean right hand, not enough to make him unconscious but enough to calm him down.

"You didn't do it, did you?"

"He's my father, Parnell. I don't know what to do. I love him so much I don't want to see him suffer. But I love him so much I don't want to see him die, either."

Parnell let the kid sob. He thought of his old friend Bud Garrett and what a good god damn fun buddy he'd been and then he started crying, too.

When Parnell came down Richard was behind the steering wheel.

Parnell got in the car and looked around at the empty parking lot and said, "Drive."

"Any place especially?"

"Out along the East River road. Your old man and I used to fish off that little bridge there."

Richard drove them. From inside his sportcoat Parnell took the pint of Jim Beam.

When they got to the bridge Parnell said, "Give me five minutes alone then you can come over, ok?"

Richard was starting to sob again.

Parnell got out of the car and went over to the bridge. In the hot night you could hear the hydroelectric dam half a mile downstream and smell the fish and feel the mosquitoes feasting their way through the evening.

He thought of what Bud Garrett had said, "Put it in some whiskey for me, will you?"

So Parnell had obliged.

He stood now on the bridge looking up at the yellow circle of moon thinking about dead people, his wife and many of his WWII friends, the rookie cop who'd died of a sudden tumor, his wife with her rosary-wrapped hands. Hell, there was probably even a chance that nurse from Enid, Oklahoma was dead.

"What do you think's on the other side?" Bud Garrett had asked just half an hour ago. He'd almost sounded excited. As if he were a farm kid about to ship out with the Merchant Marines.

"I don't know," Parnell had said.

"It scare you, Parnell?"

"Yeah," Parnell had said. "Yeah it does."

Then Bud Garrett had laughed. "Don't tell the kid that. I always told him nothin' scared you."

got me was a curdling look through her thick glasses,
ook the key and wrapped it in her handkerchief.

ing to my own room, I stared at the walls and thought
next move in the campaign to keep Vivian from dope.
ccepting the job I had realized that once Vivian's treat-
ached the stage where she was allowed out of the house,
d be impossible to keep the girl in sight constantly for six
. She probably would spend most of her time trying to
me and would only have to be lucky once. I had reasoned
y only chance of success was to let her run, tail her to her
of drug and eliminate the source.

at afternoon, her first outside the house since the treatment
d, Vivian obligingly but unknowingly had led me to private
tive Joseph Alamado, who maintained his office in a ram-
kle building on Second Street. Now, my problem was how to
he goods on Joe and shove him behind bars while I was
dicapped by not being able to leave Vivian. I still hadn't
ed the problem when I fell asleep.

When I awoke at eight, I shaved and dressed, then tapped on my
ompetent charge's door. When there was no answer, I tapped
in, waited a minute, then unlocked the door and walked in.
I thought she was sleeping until I caught the faint purplish cast
her features and saw that her eyes were wide open. For a
oment I stood looking down at her, feeling a dull rage mount
ithin me and mix with self-recrimination. Drawing back the
overs, I lifted one thin arm and found the fresh needle puncture
ust above the wrist. Vivian had had her last shot in the arm, and
hadn't been morphine. It hadn't been self-administered either,
ecause the syringe was missing.

I tried to tell myself there had been no intimation of danger to
Vivian's life, and even if there had been, keeping her in a locked
and barred room was ample protection, but I couldn't sell myself
the alibi. For this was the second murder, and after the first, I
should have been on guard. Half-heartedly I told myself Vivian's
mother had been murdered before I took this job, that her killing
had apparently been done by a motiveless maniac, that I hadn't
been retained either to solve Mrs. Banner's murder or prevent
Vivian's, but any way I looked at it, the situation boiled down to
one point: I had let a client get murdered right under my nose. And
the fact that I thought I could guess the murderer, or at least the
instigator, was little consolation to either Vivian or me.

\*     \*     \*

Richard came up the bridge after a time. At first he stood maybe
a hundred feet away from Parnell. He leaned his elbows on the
concrete and looked out at the water and the moon. Parnell
watched him, knowing it was all Richard, or anybody, could do.

Look out at the water and the moon and think about dead people
and how you yourself would soon enough be dead.

Richard turned to Parnell then and said, his tears gone completely now, sounding for the first time like Parnell's sort of man,
"You know, Parnell, my father was right. You're a brave sonofabitch. You really are."

Parnell knew it was important for Richard to believe that—that
there were actually people in the world who didn't fear things the
way most people did—so Parnell didn't answer him at all.

He just took his pint out and had himself a swig and looked
some more at the moon and the water.

# Richard Deming

# A SHOT IN THE ARM

How I became legally responsible for an adult incompetent was primarily a matter of economics. For if anyone at all, in the two months prior to Mrs. Quentin Rand's request for my services, had offered me three meals a day to walk his dog or shadow his wife, I'd have steered clear of Vivian Banner as though she had scabies.

But right at a time when food prices were climbing, the demand for private investigators—or at least the one named Manville Moon—dropped to zero. And having a mouth the size of two to feed, I require lots of energy-building food, even when I'm doing nothing to expend the energy.

So, much as I disliked the job, for a month I had lived at the oversized home of Mrs. Quentin Rand as twenty-four-hour-a-day watchdog over her niece, Vivian Banner, and prospects were good that the month would stretch to seven.

Just to make everything cozy, a court had committed Vivian to my care, and she couldn't legally even take a bath unless I gave the O.K. Days she was allowed to move about as she wanted, within the limits of my field of view, but nights I kept her in the locked and barred bedroom between my own room and Mrs. Rand's.

One key had been made for each of Vivian's three doors, and there were no extras. The one to the hall door and to the connecting door between my room and Vivian's were in my possession,

but Mrs. Rand had the key to the door be
her niece's.

Vivian might not have cheered if I
wouldn't have cried either. My job was to
morphine until the doctor decided she was
Vivian liked morphine almost as much as
night she disliked me more intensely than us
Yoder's permission I had allowed her out of t
time, and her attempt to run away and shoot
had been singularly unsuccessful.

When I knocked on her door at dinner ti
through the panel: "Who is it?"

"Moon," I said.

"Go away," she said crossly.

"Time for dinner."

"I don't want any."

I shrugged and went downstairs alone to the ble
dinner with Vivian's angular aunt. The dinner wa
atmosphere was clammy. Mrs. Rand let me build
concerning my social status. I was an employee,
and she obviously would have preferred that I eat in
Nor was it politeness which prevented her from su
but only the certain knowledge that I would tell her to
head in the kitchen sink. With her continual peeri
through the distorting lenses of ribboned nose glasses,
checking my use of the proper fork, Mrs. Rand was n
spiring mealtime companion. Immediately after the la
course, I grunted an apology, went up to my room and
on the connecting door.

"I don't want to talk to you," Vivian called loudly.

Mildly irked, I moved out into the hall and tried her front
I found it locked and continued on to Mrs. Rand's room. I
Mrs. Rand was still downstairs because I had just left her th
but I knocked in order to prove I was a gentleman, pushed o
the door and entered. The connecting door to Vivian's room
locked as tightly as the others.

As I started back out into the hall, I noticed a key lying on Mr
Rand's dresser. Picking it up, I saw it was the key to Vivian'
door.

Back downstairs, I gave the key to Mrs. Rand and said: "You
left this on your dresser again. That makes twice."

The door to Mrs. Rand's room stood slightly ajar. I pushed it open, saw the key was in the lock and walked over to the bed, where Vivian's aunt still lay sleeping. I stood over her long enough to decide from the even rise and fall of her covers that she was all right, then went to the open window. A light gardener's ladder leaned against the side of the house immediately beneath the window.

Returning to the bed, I shook Mrs. Rand awake. She looked up without surprise, and I was startled by my first glimpse of her eyes unprotected by their heavy eyeglasses. Weak and watery and red-ringed, they gave her an appearance of meek frustration, entirely counter to their imperious, haughty glint when magnified.

Apparently conscious of my surprise, she shielded her eyes from the light with the back of one hand and said: "Hand me my glasses from the dresser, if you please."

I found the ribboned, thick-lensed spectacles and gave them to her. When she had them adjusted to her nose, she sat up, pulled the sheet protectively across her shoulders and asked: "What's the matter?"

"You left the key on your dresser again," I said. "Somebody borrowed it."

"Has Vivian run away?"

"She's dead," I said bluntly.

Behind their thick lenses, her eyes widened.

"How . . . What happened?"

"Murder. You'd better get up and phone the police. I have to see a man."

She stared at me as though she had never seen me before. "Where—where are you going?"

"To pick up a guy. Tell the cops to put out a call for Joseph Alamado, a private dick with an office on Second Street. I'm going after him, but he may have holed up. If I find him, I'll bring him back here and turn him over to the cops. Got the name?"

"Alamado. Joseph Alamado." Her eyes were wide and frightened. "Did he kill Vivian?"

"Probably. If he didn't, he knows who did. He's the peddler who supplied Vivian's drugs, and yesterday she threatened to turn him over to the police." I added thoughtfully: "It was probably a hired job. Don't believe Joe has the guts for murder himself. If I thought he had any guts, I'd have squashed him yesterday and Vivian would still be alive." I pondered this idea for a moment then said impatiently: "But I didn't squash him, and post mortem strategy can't bring Vivian back to life. I want to use Harry and the Packard.''

"All right,'' she said. "I'll phone Harry to bring it around front." She reached for her bedside phone.

I said: "I have to get some things from my room. Tell Harry to honk when he's ready.''

She had the phone to her ear and was pressing the inter-house switch when I pulled her door closed behind me.

Back in my room, I slipped off my suit coat, strapped on my shoulder holster and put the coat back on. From my bag I took a pair of handcuffs and stuffed them in my hip pocket. Then I went down to the kitchen, found Nellie, the housekeeper, pouring herself a cup of coffee and had a cup myself while waiting for Harry to honk.

## CHAPTER TWO

### Discreet and Incorruptible

The first time I saw Vivian Banner, six weeks before her death, I was impressed by her beauty. And since few beautiful women call at my apartment, which for reasons of economy doubles as an office, I racked my brain for a method of keeping her for cocktails and politely sending her aunt home as soon as the aunt got around to stating her business.

In a tone of quiet innocence, which suited her soft skin, delicate features and large-irised eyes, Vivian said: "What aunt is trying to say, without shocking you, is that I'm a drug addict.''

I quickly adjusted my thinking and examined the girl again. Her hair was as smooth and golden as the first time I looked, her figure as soft and her complexion as clear. But now I noticed pinched lines at the edges of her nostrils and a faint redness of the eyelids. The large irises I had admired took on a different significance, too. They were large because the pupils had contracted to points.

I said inanely: "I'm out of dope, but I can offer you a cocktail.''

Too often my humor convulses no one but myself. Neither woman died laughing.

Mrs. Quentin Rand said coldly: "My lawyer recommended you, Mr. Moon. Alexander Carson.''

"Alex?'' I said, surprised. Alex Carson once remarked that his highest social ambition was to be seen at my funeral.

"He said you were both discreet and incorruptible.''

"Alex said that?" I asked, even more surprised.

Vivian Banner's soft voice put in: "He also described you as insulting, flippant and uncouth."

I relaxed. "That sounds more like Alex." I had once insultingly refused his bribe to commit perjury, flippantly gathered up the seat of his pants and uncouthly tossed him downstairs.

Mrs. Rand said: "As my niece so abruptly put it, she has been unfortunate enough to contract the morphine habit." Through ribboned glasses with thick, distorting lenses, she frowned at Vivian exactly like my sixth-grade teacher used to frown when I failed to do my homework.

Mrs. Quentin Rand was tall and spare and faintly disapproving of social inferiors like myself. From hearsay and the society news section, I knew a little about her. Her husband was one of the broker suicides of 1929, but something must have been salvaged from the crash, because Mrs. Rand maintained an expensive home complete with servants, and more than once her chauffeur-driven Packard had passed streetcars on which I happened to be riding.

"We want Vivian cured of the habit," Mrs. Rand said.

"Who's 'we'?"

She raised her eyebrows. "The whole family. Myself, Vivian's parents—she's my brother's step-daughter—and of course, Vivian herself wants to be cured."

I said: "You must have gotten the wrong address. I'm not a doctor. I'm a private detective. Aren't there sanitariums for that kind of treatment?"

"I've flunked out of the three best in the country," Vivian said. "They rate me incurable." She flashed a mocking smile but deep in her eyes was a quivering fright. She fished a cigarette from her purse and her hand shook when she put it into her mouth.

Mrs. Rand said: "Dr. James Yoder is now treating Vivian. Her parents have placed her completely in my charge until the cure is effected, and I've had a room prepared at my home. I have also engaged three private nurses. Under the treatment Dr. Yoder has outlined, Vivian must stay in bed for two weeks, be confined to home for another two, and then constantly watched for six months, making the whole treatment run for seven months."

I asked: "Where do I come in?"

"You're to stay with or near Vivian from the time treatment starts until she's cured."

I blinked. "For seven months?"

Mrs. Rand nodded.

"What am I supposed to do?"

Mrs. Rand drew her lips into a prim line. "I know nothing about drug habits, but Dr. Yoder says an addict will use every subterfuge to get drugs while a treatment is being attempted. Right now Vivian wants nothing so much as to be free of the habit. But once the cure starts, she'll try bribery, she'll attempt to sneak out at night, she'll try literally anything she can think of to get more morphine. It will be your job to make sure she doesn't get it. That's where previous treatments have failed and Dr. Yoder believes if we can actually keep her from drugs for six months after the initial treatment, the cure will be permanent."

I thought over the proposition before I said anything. Then I said: "Seven months of my time will run into money."

Mrs. Rand waved that aside. "Expense is not a consideration."

"My fee is twenty-five dollars a day, plus expenses."

Mrs. Rand's straight back straightened even more. "Twenty-five dollars! The nurses I engaged charge only nine!"

I shrugged. "Then hire another nurse."

Vivian said: "After all, Aunt Grace, Dad will be paying for it."

Mrs. Rand gave in, though not graciously. "I suppose we have no choice. But twenty-five dollars! Everywhere you turn, you meet inflation." She looked me over distastefully. "When will you be available?"

I shrugged again. "Maybe tomorrow. Maybe never. Depends on my talk with Dr. Yoder."

"Dr. Yoder? What has he to do with it? We've agreed to your exorbitant fee, and you're engaged."

"Listen, lady," I said, "I'm not for sale like a pound of sausage, and I won't starve next week if I turn you down." I neglected to mention I would starve the week after. "I'll tell you tomorrow if I want the job."

She didn't like it, but there was nothing she could do. She fumed a bit, and talked down to me as though I were one of the hired help, but in the end she left Dr. Yoder's address and her own telephone number, and departed with her niece.

I came out of the war with only a leg and a half instead of the usual quota of two legs. The cork, aluminum and leather substitute, which the Veterans' Administration furnished to replace the missing portion, is as useful and comfortable as science has yet been able to devise, but it is neither as useful nor comfortable as the original right leg.

I started a blister on the stump by walking the six blocks to Dr. Yoder's office, and arrived in a sour mood. Having a false leg has restricted my physical activity very little except when I rub a blister, and then it sometimes leaves me a cripple for as long as two weeks.

Dr. James Yoder was a general practitioner of the type commonly called a "society doctor," which meant his oversized fees were not necessary a criterion of his training and ability. He was in his sixties—stocky, bland and courteous—with an affability which would have made him a pleasant barroom companion, but which failed to inspire my confidence in his professional ability.

"Normally wouldn't discuss a patient's condition with a layman," the doctor said. "But since Mrs. Rand informs me you're to act as some kind of guardian or watchdog over Miss Banner during her treatment, suppose that makes you sort of a colleague."

He showed his teeth in a confidential smile. "Actually, I don't hold much hope for a cure. Nearly as I can determine, Miss Banner's been a morphine habituée since she was twenty, and she's twenty-four now. Claims she takes but one injection a day, but I suspect she uses at least three, and possibly four or five." He frowned slightly and pulled at his lower lip. "Trouble with morphine is it acts on that part of the brain controlling moral tendencies. Habituées are always such infernal liars, even when there's no point in it. Especially dreamers."

"What's a dreamer?" I asked.

"An addict who takes enough drug to throw himself into a dream state. Morphine affects different people differently, you see. Some get all pepped up and don't act any different from you or me, except they're more full of energy. Others pass into a drowsy state and imagine all sorts of things. Have dreams something like opium dreams. Morphine's an alkaloid of opium, you see. All morphine habituées are liars, but dreamers are the worst, and Miss Banner sometimes drugs herself into a coma, lasting hours. Awfully hard to treat a patient who won't tell the truth, you know."

He looked at me for sympathy and I nodded my head. Encouraged, he went on.

"Actually, I think the place for the girl is a locked ward in a sanitarium. Told the family so, but Mrs. Rand has this room fixed up, and insists on home treatment. Says they've tried sanitariums." He snorted. "The girl's been in three as a voluntary patient. Damn-fool family refused to commit her, and all she had to do was walk out." He shrugged. "But it's their money, and if I don't treat her, someone else will."

He glanced at me slyly, as one confederate to another in on a soft touch. I kept my face expressionless.

"Then the treatment's a phony?"

"Oh, no," he protested quickly. "If Miss Banner were actually kept from morphine for several months, she'd probably be cured. But how you going to keep it away from her?" He glowered at me from beneath down-drawn brows. "Judas, man, you don't know what a morphine addict without drugs is like. Twenty-four hours a day she'll have only one thing on her mind . . . Morphine. She'll do anything for it. And I mean literally anything. She'll lie, bribe, steal. She may even try to kill you. If you block all that, she'll try ducking out of your sight. And you can't possibly keep her in sight for six months."

I said: "Why not?"

He looked exasperated. "You going to accompany her to the shower bath? You going to sleep in the same room?" One fist pounded softly on his desk. "Watch the door and she'll be out the window. Watch the window and she'll be out the door."

I stood up. "You take care of your end, Doc, and I'll take care of mine. She won't get any dope."

He said skeptically: "Think not?" Then he shrugged. "All we can do is try. After all, if I don't treat her, they'll just go to another doctor, and if you don't take the case, they'll just hire another private detective. Might as well be us getting the fees."

"Sure," I said. "But just for the record, I'm intending to earn mine."

As a matter of course, the Rand home had been built on Lindell Boulevard, for of all streets in the city, only Lindell was as socially distinguished as the name "Rand." A pleasant but oversized structure of rose granite, it somewhat resembled a public library. Wide lawns kept the neighboring houses on either side a sedate two hundred feet away, which, in a city, is isolation.

A dour-faced housekeeper pushing seventy answered my ring and examined me with eyes bitter at the world.

I said: "What's the matter? Boy friend jilt you?"

She said: "What you want?"

"Mrs. Rand. And a kind smile."

She muttered: "At that face, who could smile?" and stepped aside. "You must be that detective. She said you was ugly, but she missed it by half."

I'm not sensitive about my face. The one I was born with wasn't too bad, but in my early youth, before I learned to duck, a set of brass knuckles gave me a drooping eyelid and a bent nose. Still, I don't think I'm repellent. A maudlin woman once told me I resembled a battered Saint Bernard.

I followed the old woman into a drawing room, where a tea party seemed to be in progress. On the surface it was an innocuous tea party. Only weeks later, when little bits of evidence began to fall into place, did I understand I had viewed the prologue to the first murder, and even contributed to its necessity without realizing it.

Mrs. Rand, a saucer expertly held in her left hand, glanced up as we stopped in the doorway, and thick-lensed glasses, behind which her eyes were magnified out of proportion, glinted as she dismissed the housekeeper with a cold nod of annoyance.

On a sofa next to Mrs. Rand's chair sat a plump woman and a tall, gaunt man who was a male version of Mrs. Rand. Relaxed in an easy chair which seemed to have been specially built for him, with the crook of a heavy cane lying in his lap, was a giant fat man whose quantities of excess flesh could only be described as oozing. His head was a melon, smooth and white and benevolent, and as hairless as the sole of my foot. He was gesturing with a sugared cookie while he discoursed on the subject of ants. I learned that red ants had a much more efficiently organized civilization than humans before Mrs. Rand cut him off by introducing me around.

"These are Vivian's mother and step-father, Mr. Moon," she said, indicating the couple on the sofa. "My brother, Claude Banner, and my sister-in-law, Martha." To the man she said: "Claude, this is Mr. Manville Moon, the private detective I told you about."

I shook hands with Claude Banner and murmured something polite to his wife.

"And this is Mr. Sheridan," Mrs. Rand said, indicating the obese giant. "Norman Sheridan, the entomologist, you know."

Her tone suggested that of course I had heard of Norman Sheridan.

"Oh, yes," I said, never having heard of him, and having only a vague notion that entomology somehow concerned bugs.

His hand gobbled up mine as though I had thrust it into a bucket of dough. I got mine back as quickly as I could.

"Will you have some tea?" Mrs. Rand asked.

I said: "No, thanks."

"Tea is a ritual in this house," she said with a curious air of defensiveness, as though she thought I might not approve. "I think it a shame most Americans have let the custom lapse."

"Delightful custom," rumbled Norman Sheridan, heaving his bulk forward to reach another sugared cookie.

I found myself a chair and prepared to wait patiently for Sheridan to leave so that Vivian's parents, Mrs. Rand and I could discuss our highly private business. But apparently Mrs. Rand kept no secrets from her fat friend.

"Dr. Yoder phoned that you were coming," she said. "When can you start?"

I glanced at Sheridan and hiked my eyebrows.

"You may speak freely before Mr. Sheridan. Norman is one of my oldest friends, and he knows all about Vivian. He spends nearly as much time here as I do."

"A case of unrequited love," Norman explained. "The drone hovering about the queen bee." His gelatinous body shook at his own jest.

I said: "I can start as soon as we agree on terms."

Mrs. Rand drew in her chin and examined me suspiciously. "We have agreed on terms."

"I don't mean financial. I mean concerning my responsibility and authority. Particularly my authority."

"What do you mean by that?"

I said: "Dr. Yoder tells me your niece is pretty far gone. Possibly incurable. He seems to think keeping her from dope for six months after she's allowed out of the house will be a difficult job. If I'm to keep her from it, I want absolute authority over her actions. I want her declared legally incompetent and committed to my care for a period of seven months."

Claude Banner said: "That's ridiculous. Vivian's not incompetent."

"Of course not. You're just hiring a doctor, three nurses and a private detective because she gets lonesome."

He turned a faint red. "My step-daughter is a capable and intelligent young woman, Mr. Moon. I regard her condition as a disease, just as though she had diabetes or heart trouble, and I'll thank you not to refer to her as though she were some kind of moron.''

"Stop kidding yourself," I said. "Vivian's a dope addict and has no more right to exercise her own judgment than a two-year-old. Maybe I didn't make myself clear, so I'll put it in the form of an ultimatum. We'll do things exactly the way I want them done, or you can hire another watchdog.''

Banner said: "In that case, we won't need you.''

"I'll decide that.''

It was the first time Vivian's mother had spoken, and although her voice was quiet, an underlying chord of decisiveness ran through it.

All eyes swiveled toward her. I was surprised at the immediate attention she drew, for she had not impressed me as an imposing personality. Mrs. Banner swept her gaze around the circle in a gesture of what almost seemed defiance, then turned to me.

"Do I understand you want to be appointed Vivian's guardian, Mr. Moon?''

"Her committee," I said. "Guardianship applies only to minors, and they call you a committee instead of a guardian when your charge is an adult incompetent. Amounts to the same thing.''

"Why do you think this necessary?''

I explained why bluntly. "First, I don't want well-meaning interference from you people. Second, I make it a point to finish what I start. Once I take the case, I've no intention of letting anyone fire me. And you can't fire me if a court commits Vivian to my care.''

Mrs. Rand said: "That would involve administration of her funds.''

"So what? You've checked me so thoroughly, you probably know which cheek I shave first in the morning. Think I'd steal your niece's money?''

Mrs. Banner said: "I think we'd better do as Mr. Moon wishes.''

Mrs. Rand's thick glasses glinted as she peered estimatingly at her sister-in-law. Then, with an expression which seemed to ask, "What else can we do?" she said to her brother: "Alex Carson told me I'd find Mr. Moon stubborn, blunt and—ah—tyrannical. But he also recommended him as scrupulously honest and the only person he knew who might accomplish what Dr. Yoder says is necessary. It rather looks like we won't get along with Mr. Moon, but we can't get along without him either."

"Alex Carson is your lawyer, isn't he?" Mrs. Banner asked. "Yes."

"Have him make the necessary arrangements then." Her tone made it almost an order, and again I was surprised, because she didn't look like an imperious person. She turned to me. "I'm sure that between you and Dr. Yoder Vivian will be in excellent hands. You do think this treatment will work, don't you?"

I shrugged. "Possibly. Dr. Yoder told me he advised you people to commit her to a sanitarium and leave her there till she's well, but you prefer home treatment. If Vivian were my daughter, I'd follow the doctor's advice. Of course you might not be able to keep it quiet, but I assume your primary objective is to get Vivian well."

Mrs. Banner glanced sharply at her husband. "You didn't tell me this, Claude."

Banner raised an appeasing hand. "Now, dear, don't get upset. It seems to me Grace has things well organized, and I see no reason to have Vivian committed if we can accomplish the same end without danger of publicity. If this doesn't work, we'll talk about another sanitarium."

His wife continued to look at him coldly without saying anything, until his face turned a faint red. Fumbling out a gold pocket watch, he dropped his eyes to it, looked surprised and rose.

"My plane leaves in an hour and I have to stop at home for my bag. Guess I'll have to borrow your car, Grace."

"Certainly, Claude," Mrs. Rand said. She rose from her chair and pulled a cord hanging against the wall.

Claude Banner said something about getting their coats and disappeared into the hall. As he passed through the door, the ancient housekeeper entered.

Mrs. Rand said: "Send Harry in, will you, Nellie?"

Nellie nodded grumpily, turned around and left.

Banner returned wearing a light topcoat and carrying a short fur jacket, which he held while his wife slipped into it.

"Pleasant to have met you, Mr. Moon," Mrs. Banner said, and held out her hand.

I returned the compliment, wondering again at her previous flash of decisiveness. She looked like the average housewife, plump and goodnatured and inclined to consider her husband the head of the house.

A quiet voice from the doorway said: "You wanted me, madam?"

I glanced that way and there in a neat chauffeur's uniform stood Harry Gusset. My last sight of Harry was when he stood before a judge receiving a two-year sentence for extortion, largely as a result of my testimony. He had been standing on crutches, which was also my fault, since he had broken a leg trying to prevent me from arresting him.

He saw me the same moment I saw him, and he literally seemed to wilt.

Mrs. Rand said: "What's the matter, Harry?"

I don't believe in hounding ex-convicts who try to go straight. Harry's uniform indicated he was trying to make an honest living, and I had no intention of spoiling his chance. Keeping my face expressionless, I gave him a wink.

Straightening his back, he looked sickly at Mrs. Rand and said: "Nothing's the matter, madam."

She peered at him through her glasses. "You look frightened to death."

I said: "He bumped his elbow on the door coming in."

For a moment Harry stared at me blankly. Then he got it. "Yes. The crazy bone. I'll be all right in a minute."

"Oh," said Mrs. Rand, losing interest. "Is the car out front?"

"Yes, ma'am."

"Good. Drive Mr. and Mrs. Banner home and then take Mr. Banner to the airport."

Claude Banner shook my hand and said: "Glad I met you, Moon. Won't see you for about a week because I'm flying south on business tonight. In the meantime Grace can go ahead with incompetency proceedings and I'll sign any necessary papers when I get back."

Norman Sheridan, who had sat beamingly silent for a long time, gripped his cane handle with both fists and heaved his huge body from its chair. "I'd better run along too, Grace. May I hitch a ride, Claude?"

Banner indicated that he could, and Sheridan, his cane ornamentally hooked over a fat forearm, now that it had served what seemed to be its sole function—helping him erect—lumbered out.

In the doorway, Mrs. Banner smiled back at me over her shoulder.

I never saw her again.

## CHAPTER THREE

### No Body at All

"Where's Vivian?" I asked Mrs. Rand. "In her room?"

She shook her head. "Beauty appointment."

"Then I'd like to look at this room you've prepared."

Mrs. Rand led me upstairs and down a hall to the right wing of the house. The room was an ordinary bedroom with private bath and with doors connecting it to other bedrooms on either side. The only "preparations" consisted of three-quarter-inch steel bars at the two bedroom windows and across the bath windows.

"Dr. Yoder says the initial treatment may leave Vivian temporarily irrational," Mrs. Rand said, indicating the bars. "Of course, it's unlikely she'll become so irrational as to attempt suicide, but we're taking no chances.

"That's my bedroom," she said, pointing to the right connecting door. "Yours is the other. I'm sorry you won't have a private bath, but there's a general bath down the hall."

"I'll live," I said.

I examined the locks of the hall door and of the connecting doors into Mrs. Rand's and my bedrooms.

"I want special locks put on all these," I said. "Locks making it impossible to open the door from either side without a key. And have only one key made for each lock."

She raised her eyebrows. "Do you think that really necessary?"

"Yes."

She frowned and said in a prim voice: "Very well. Anything else?"

"Not at the moment. You can start incompetency proceedings immediately. Tell Alex he can reach me at my flat."

Alex phoned me the following afternoon.

"Take about two weeks to put everything through," he said. "But I don't contemplate any hitches. Explained the whole situation to Judge Crawford this morning, and he'll go along if we get proper medical statements and so forth. Yoder will take care of the medical end, and it makes things less complicated that Vivian herself is making no fight."

"She isn't?"

"Think the idea intrigues her. Being ordered around by a Saint Bernard. That's what she calls you."

"I've been called that before," I said. "Bribed any witnesses lately?"

"Aw, don't you ever forget?"

"No," I said.

The following week I spent mainly on my back, listening to my bank account dwindle and allowing my stump blister to heal. It was past the danger of re-irritation when I had a caller.

Lieutenant Hannegan, neat and dapper in his perennial blue serge suit, and looking exactly like a cop in plain clothes, brought an invitation from Inspector Warren Day.

"For what, he didn't say," Hannegan told me. "All I know is he wants you."

Since it was only eleven o'clock in the morning, he had caught me in bed. He waited passively while I shaved and dressed, then drove me over to headquarters.

Several people sat around in the chief of homicide's office. Aside from Warren Day were Mrs. Rand, Vivian, Claude Banner, Norman Sheridan and Harry Gusset. Banner seemed worried, Vivian seemed upset, but the rest looked only puzzled.

Inspector Warren Day ducked his skinny bald head to peer at me over his glasses and said with heavy irony: "Sorry to disturb your rest, Manny. I know it's tiring to lean against a bar every night."

"Always glad to come down and solve any cases you can't handle," I said courteously.

Fishing through his littered ash tray, Day found a cigar butt which satisfied him, stuck it in his mouth without lighting it and leaned back in his chair to view the assemblage.

"I called you people together because you were the last to see Mrs. Banner."

The others waited quietly for him to proceed, but I broke in: "Wait a minute. What's happened to Mrs. Banner?"

Day swiveled his head to peer at me coldly. "She's missing. Hasn't been seen since Mrs. Rand's car dropped her at her home a week ago."

I asked Mrs. Rand: "The day I was at your house?"

She nodded and Claude Banner said: "Harry ran us home and I stopped in just long enough to pick up my bag. Norman was with us, if you remember, and the last any of us saw of her, she was waving from the porch. Harry dropped Norman at his house, and then ran me to the airport. When I got back last night, the house was locked, the fire out and Martha had simply disappeared. I inquired everywhere I could think of and learned no one had seen her since the day I left, so I reported it to the police.''

"She's only missing?" I asked Day.

He moved his skinny head up and down, watching me suspiciously.

"When'd you take over the missing persons bureau?"

"Now listen here, Moon," the inspector started to say.

"She's dead," I said flatly.

Everyone but Claude Banner looked at me, startled. Banner wet his lips and looked at Warren Day. He didn't seem particularly upset. Vivian's mouth drew into a thin line.

"You speak when you're spoken to!" Day exploded. "I'm directing this investigation!"

"Sure. And you're chief of homicide. I don't know what you're pulling, but you wouldn't be interested unless you had a body."

Vivian said: "It's true. My mother's dead." She began to sob quietly.

"Hannegan!" Day shouted at his right-hand man, nearly blasting him over, since he stood only a foot from the inspector's desk. "Clear everybody out but Moon! Keep 'em outside till I call for 'em."

Hannegan shooed the startled group from the office, and Warren Day glared at me furiously. "Why can't you keep your big mouth shut?"

Relaxing in a chair next to his desk, I reached into his cigar humidor, but jerked back empty fingers when he snapped down the lid.

"If you'd take me in on your plans, I wouldn't blow them up," I said reasonably. "How was I supposed to know you had secrets?"

"I didn't want that bunch to know what's going on till I had their stories," Day growled. Dropping his dead cigar in the ash tray, he fished out another butt. "What were you doing at Mrs. Rand's house?"

"Just a social call."

He glared at me over his glasses. "Don't want to cooperate, eh?"

"Sure I do. Soon as you tell me what's going on."

Day chewed his cigar while he examined me with distaste. "All right, Manny," he said finally. "I know if I gave you the rubber hose, I'd get nothing, so I'll save time for both of us. I'll bring you up to date, if you'll unload what you know to me."

·"Fine," I said, and managed to snake out one of his cigars without losing a finger.

"The body showed up at Bakersville, ten miles down the river, about an hour before Banner reported his wife missing. She had a bullet in her and had been dead about a week. We called Banner in late last night to identify the body and told him to keep his mouth shut until we released the news ourselves. He's the only one who knew she was dead."

"Why the secrecy?"

"Wanted to see their reactions. Got to start somewhere, and there's not a sign of a clue."

"How about the bullet?"

"Hit a bone. .45 caliber, but the lab can't tell us whether it came from a gun or a pea-shooter."

I asked: "Think Banner himself did it?"

Day snorted. "Mrs. Rand's chauffeur and that fat guy, Sheridan, both saw Mrs. Banner wave goodbye. After that Banner wasn't out of the chauffeur's sight till he boarded a plane for Mexico City."

"Maybe he flew back again."

Day shook his head. "We had the airlines check passenger lists for that. Just to make sure, we're also making a check-up by Mexico City police, but I think Banner's clear. He makes regular trips to Mexico City every month. Operates an importing business and does all the buying himself. Says he always stays at the same hotel, so it should be easy enough for the Mexico City police to verify his alibi."

He didn't seem inclined to pass on anything else, so I asked: "That the whole story?"

"Yeah. Now what were you doing at Mrs. Rand's place?"

"Just a social call," I said, snaking another cigar from the ash tray.


In spite of her aunt's and step-father's arguments that Vivian's treatment be postponed until she got over the shock of her mother's death, Vivian insisted on going ahead with the original arrangements. Her insistence was fanatical rather than merely determined, for she was obviously terrified at the agony she thought she would go through. As the day of the court session drew near, she developed an air of numb fascination resembling that of an early Christian preparing to throw herself in the flames in pursuit of an ideal. I saw her only twice, and both times she was drugged to the eyebrows.

The murder remained a mystery, at least to me. What progress the homicide department was making, I didn't know, since Warren Day stopped speaking to me after our last session together. And since I was engaged by Mrs. Rand only to keep Vivian away from morphine, and not to solve incidental murders, I made no attempt to check up.

Now that it's all over, and I can look back at the complete picture in all its details, I can see I might have saved Vivian's life if I had done something about her mother's murder. Even if I had merely thought about it seriously, I might have drawn some significance from the casual happenings during the tea party where I met Vivian's mother. Not enough to solve the case, probably, but perhaps enough to stir an awareness of danger to Vivian and place me on guard.

It bothers me still when I think about it, but actually I had no reason to concern myself. In the first place no one asked me to do anything about Mrs. Banner, and I get in enough trouble sticking my nose where I'm hired to stick it, without prying into murders for free. In the second place no one in the family, including Vivian, who was so completely obsessed by her approaching ordeal that she hadn't even time for grief, so much as mentioned the matter. And just because you're a private investigator, you don't tactlessly choose a murdered relative as a conversational subject when you talk to people, unless somebody pays you to pry.

When I thought about it at all, it was to idly wonder if it had been a lunatic murder, one of those tough ones where a nut with no motive except desire to kill picks a victim he never saw before. Those happen, you know, and happen frequently. And the killer is rarely caught until he butchers two or three.

In any event, I left the investigation of Mrs. Banner's murder to the homicide squad and continued to spend most of my time on my back waiting for Judge Crawford to get around to convening court in order to consider the competency of the murdered woman's daughter. The days dragged by one by one and my bank account shrank to zero, and I started a charge account at my favorite restaurant.

But even Judgment Day will arrive if you wait long enough, and nine days after my conversation with Inspector Day, Judge Crawford held a closed session in his chambers. When Alex Carson, Mrs. Rand, Vivian and I left the courtroom together, I bore a document naming me the temporary committee of Miss Vivian Banner, aged 24, declared legally incompetent by court order. The document emphasized in several places that my appointment was temporary, and named a date seven months away at which time the court would again consider evidence of my charge's competence and take such additional action it deemed appropriate.

Mrs. Rand also carried a document, one carefully prepared by Alex Carson and to which my witnessed signature was affixed. In it I declared that I had been employed by the family for the sole purpose of preventing Vivian Banner from obtaining or taking drugs during the next seven months, that by general family agreement I had been chosen as the proper temporary committee for that purpose only, that I had no interest nor claim in Miss Banner's estate and, in the event of her death, I waived all rights of inheritance and/or administration of her estate.

Alex, in spite of his recommendation that I was "scrupulously honest," was taking no chances.

All four of us squeezed into the rear seat of Mrs. Rand's Packard. I offered to sit with Harry, but Mrs. Rand chilled the suggestion as though it were improper. Alex Carson and I drew small folding seats and rode backward, facing the two women.

During the ride to Mrs. Rand's home Alex tried to make light conversation. He looked every inch the distinguished barrister as he sat erect but easily on the uncomfortable, drop-down seat, his gaunt, intelligent features carefully holding a poised smile. Narrow, snow-white sideburns which merged into dark, gray-flecked hair added to the effect of mature integrity. "What an honest looking guy," I thought, feeling to see if I still had my wallet.

Mrs. Rand answered Carson's conversational attempts with monosyllables, and Vivian and I made no attempt to answer at all.

Once Vivian said to me: "How does it feel to be a father, Daddy?"

I scowled at her, expecting to meet a mocking expression. Her lips smiled, but in her eyes was an almost incredible fright. I let my scowl fade into an encouraging grin.

Dr. Yoder was waiting for us in the drawing room when we arrived at the Rand home. With him was a middle-aged nurse in a starched uniform. Dr. Yoder rose from his chair.

"Good afternoon," he said affably in all-inclusive greeting. He introduced the nurse as Miss Livingston, then said to Vivian: "Ready to become a patient?"

"Today? Are we going to start today?"

She looked from one to another of us, and I could see a pulse begin to beat in her throat. Nobody said anything.

"I mean, it's been such a trying day already . . ." Her voice trailed off and she gave a nervous laugh. "Whatever you think best, Doctor. It's just that I didn't expect to start today."

Mrs. Rand said: "I asked Doctor Yoder to be here when we returned from court. There's no point in delay."

The doctor made his voice patronizingly hearty. "Sooner you get to bed, young lady, sooner we'll have you up. Go on upstairs and Miss Livingston will be up in a minute."

Vivian summoned a ghastly smile and left the room without a word. Dr. Yoder immediately dropped his jolly manner and turned professional.

"Nurse has her orders," he said to Mrs. Rand. "Be relieved by a night nurse at eleven. You understand, of course, the nurse is in complete charge of morphine when I'm not here. Please give her any help she needs." He glanced at me. "Afraid not much for you to do next two weeks, Moon."

I asked: "What's this treatment involve?"

He drew down his brows in fair imitation of Lionel Barrymore in a Dr. Gillespie role. "We gradually withdraw the drug. Otherwise too great a shock, you see. Same time we administer cathartics and use hyoscine as an antidote. End of two weeks, hope to shut off medical treatment and let her system rebuild itself. That's when your main problem starts. Meantime, wish you'd stay close by to help the nurse, case Miss Banner becomes violent. Don't anticipate that, but always a possibility."

I said: "I've already moved in. I'll be sleeping in the room right next to her."

"Fine," he said. "Fine arrangement. Be handy if nurse needs you."

I turned to Mrs. Rand. "You have those locks installed?"

"Yes," she said, rummaging in her purse and producing three keys. "They're numbered one, two and three. One is the connecting door to your room, two the hall door and three the key to my bedroom."

I said: "Keep yours," took the other two and handed the hall key to Miss Livingston. "You can pass this on to the other nurses as they change shift. There are no extras, so don't lose it."

Accepting the key, she started from the room, but I stopped her. "When Vivian's ready for bed, have her put on a robe and come back downstairs," I told her.

By the time the nurse returned with Vivian, Dr. Yoder and Alex had gone, Mrs. Rand had disappeared into the rear of the house, and I was alone in the drawing room. Vivian wore a flowered wrap-around housecoat over green nylon pajamas. Clenched fists were thrust into the housecoat pockets.

I went over to her, took her wrists and gently pulled her hands from her pockets. She raised them palm upward and looked at me questioningly.

Smiling at her, I thrust my own hands into the pockets. One held a lace handkerchief and the other was empty.

"Any pajama pockets?" I asked.

She shook her head. "What are you doing? Searching me?"

I said: "You catch on quick. Wait right here," and went right on up to her room.

I wasted fifteen minutes going over every inch of the bathroom and bedroom before I finally found it under a hat in a hat-box on the closet's rear shelf. It was a compact little outfit neatly assembled in a small tin box; an alcohol lamp of the type found in toy chemistry sets, a small test tube, two teaspoons, a bottle of innocent-looking pills and an hypodermic syringe with several extra needles.

Returning to the drawing room, I handed the box to Miss Livingston. "Better turn this over to Dr. Yoder."

Vivian's eyes burned at me with sudden anger. "What right have you to search my room?" she demanded in a high voice.

I said: "We fathers make our own rules. Go on up to bed."

Except for one or two incidents, the next two weeks was a period of utter boredom for me. I had literally nothing to do but sit in my room and wait for the nurse to call me if Vivian grew violent, which she never did. She grew irritable, and her complexion turned muddy and oily from constant sweating. Her eyes reddened and streamed gallons of water, her fingers twitched and occasionally she sobbed with pain in her body joints, and she lost weight until her cheeks were gaunt. But she kept her mind.

To me she seemed pretty sick, but Dr. Yoder seemed pleased with her progress. He stopped by every day, examined Vivian, boomed a few hearty jests and went away with an air of satisfaction.

Norman Sheridan came every day too, asked if Vivian were well enough to have visitors, and nodded understandingly when the nurse informed him she was not. Whereupon he would retire to the drawing room with Mrs. Rand, drink a cup of tea and devour a prodigious amount of sugared cookies.

The first incident to break the boredom was when Nellie, the ancient housekeeper, let Vivian out of her room. She only got as far as her aunt's bedroom, because I discovered it almost at once. When no answer came to my rap on Vivian's door, I unlocked it, found the room empty and the door to Mrs. Rand's room open.

When she heard me enter, Vivian slammed shut the bureau drawer she was rifling, turned her back to the bureau and crouched like a cornered animal, her red-ringed eyes spitting hate at me and her lips pulled back from her teeth.

"What are you looking for, Vivian?" I asked gently.

"A handkerchief." Her voice was a sullen whine.

"I'll have the nurse bring you one. Better get back to bed."

Mrs. Rand's key lay on her dressing table. I picked it up, looked at it, laid it down again and left it there. After seeing Vivian safely relocked in her room, I went downstairs to give Mrs. Rand a verbal blast.

"But I know nothing about it," Vivian's aunt protested. "The key was on my dresser."

"It's still on the dresser," I said. "You simply left the door unlocked."

"I most certainly did not," Mrs. Rand denied. "I tried it very carefully before I came downstairs."

We questioned the servants then, and Nellie readily admitted her guilt. "Can't clean Miss Vivian's room less I open the door, can I?" she asked belligerently. "Can't walk through no closed door."

"You have the nurse let you in and out," I said. "If Vivian gets out again, I'll skin you alive."

She sniffed disdainfully. "Bigger fellers than you tried that and got set on their haunches."

"And you keep that key in your possession," I told Mrs. Rand. "Don't leave it lying on your dresser again."

The second incident occurred not more than an hour later, when Alex Carson made his single visit during Vivian's illness. It was his sole visit because I afterward told him if he stuck his nose inside the house again, I'd break it off even with his face.

I was in the back yard when he called. Every afternoon I spent a half hour there getting some fresh air in my lungs while Mrs. Rand took over my watch. When I came back into the house Mrs. Morgan, the 7:00 A.M. to 3:00 P.M. nurse, met me with fire in her eyes.

"A man named Carson was here and got into Miss Banner's room," she announced indignantly.

"He was?" I asked, mildly irked, but not particularly disturbed.

"Come look at our patient."

I followed her indignant back up the stairs to Vivian's room. Thrusting her key into the door, Mrs. Morgan flung it open and dramatically pointed to the patient, who sat upright in bed talking to Mrs. Rand, who was seated in a bedside chair.

Vivian's complexion was no longer muddy, and there was even a touch of color in her cheeks. Her eyes were still red-ringed, but they were clear and waterless, and the pupils were contracted to points.

She waved at me gaily. "Hello, Daddy."

"Take her in my room," I told Mrs. Morgan. "Search her while you've got her there. If she won't let you, call me."

Vivian docilely allowed herself to be led through the connecting door. Mrs. Rand watched silently while I went over every inch of the bedroom, bathroom and closet.

"What are you looking for?" she asked, when I finally gave up.

I ignored her question. "How did Carson get in here?"

"I let him in. Vivian asked to see him. Why?"

"Were you here all the time?"

"No. Vivian asked to see him alone. Why are you asking this?"

"Because your niece is doped to the heels. Starting right now all visitors will be referred to me. No one uses your key but yourself."

She put her nose in the air and tried to curdle me through her distorting eyeglasses. "Alex Carson wouldn't give Vivian morphine. The whole idea's ridiculous."

"Did you give it to her?"

"Of course not!"

"That leaves Alex," I said.

Mrs. Morgan brought Vivian back into the room and shook her head before I could ask if her search had turned up any drug on Vivian. I told her to throw her patient back in bed and went downstairs to phone.

After twenty minutes of trying, I finally caught Alex at home. To put it conservatively, by that time I was mad.

"Alex," I said, "I knew you were a shyster, but I didn't know you peddled dope."

"What are you talking about?" he asked. I told him my plans for his nose and hung up.

## CHAPTER FOUR

### Human Again

The second two weeks were more interesting, because I had something to do. Vivian was allowed up now, though she still spent much of her time in bed. When she was up she moped around the house dispiritedly, spending most of her time yawning and incessantly smoking cigarettes, and the rest of it trying to sneak out without my catching her. Once she tried violence and put a long scratch on my cheek, but the next meal she had to eat from the mantel. After that she kept her distance.

The nurses had been discharged at the end of the second week, and I now carried both the key to the door between my room and Vivian's and the key to Vivian's hall door. Mrs. Rand still had the third.

I let Vivian pick her own bedtime, but each night when she retired, I carefully locked her in and left her there until she pounded on the connecting door the next morning. Mrs. Rand had instructions to ignore pounding on her door.

By the end of the fourth week Vivian began to look human again. She was thin and extremely nervous and she tired easily, but her complexion began to freshen and her eyes to clear. Dr. Yoder decided she was well enough to leave the house.

"Now your real job begins," he told me. "Amazing success you've had so far. Be nice if you can keep it up." He looked at me, not very hopefully.

"I'll keep it up," I said.

Up till then Vivian shrank from any contacts because of embarrassment at her appearance. Even after she was allowed up, she returned to her room when Norman Sheridan made his daily call, or when any other visitor arrived. But now she blossomed forth all at once.

At Vivian's request I ordered a beauty operator and a dressmaker, both of my own choosing, to report to the Rand home at nine the next morning. They spent three hours together locked in Vivian's room, and when at noon the rap on my door to let them out came, Vivian was again a beautiful woman.

The green knit suit she wore had been subtly altered to compensate for a loss of twelve pounds, changing her thinness to a willowy slenderness. And expert make-up had converted gaunt hollows to interesting high cheek bones. She wasn't the same woman who had visited my apartment nearly seven weeks before, but she was just as beautiful a woman.

"I want to go out to lunch," she informed me imperiously.

I let her have a wolf whistle. "We'll look like beauty and the beast."

For the first time since she had gotten up, she smiled at me, proving that even though she doesn't like you, no woman can resist a compliment.

Norman Sheridan and Mrs. Rand were together in the drawing room when Vivian and I entered. Sheridan heaved his soft bulk erect and let a smile of delight slowly spread across his round face.

"Well, well," he said. "The cocoon has opened and the butterfly emergeth."

"My dear," said Mrs. Rand. "You look stunning."

Being realistic about my own beauty, I deduced they were speaking to Vivian and not to me, so I kept my mouth shut. A flush of pleasure added even more loveliness to Vivian's face.

"We're going out to lunch," she told Mrs. Rand.

"How nice," Vivian's aunt said. She looked at me quietly. "Do be careful of her."

Vivian frowned slightly. "I won't run away, Aunt Grace."

"I didn't mean that," Mrs. Rand protested. "But you're still weak, my dear. Don't overdo it."

Mrs. Rand loaned us the Packard, complete with its sullen chauffeur, Harry. Harry had been avoiding me ever since I moved into the house, probably in deference to our onetime unfriendly relationship. As far as I was concerned, he had served his time and bygones were bygones, so I winked at him in the rear-view mirror as we settled back in our seat. But instead of looking reassured, his face turned pale and he clashed the gears in starting.

Vivian chose the Jefferson to dine, and lunch was pleasant except for a heightened and false vivaciousness on the part of my companion. From across the room it probably looked as though she hung on my every word and replied with delightful banter, but behind her tightly fixed smile her mind was turned inward on her own thoughts. Half the time my remarks got no answer at all, and the rest of the time the answers bore little relation to the questions. Our conversation sounded like a Marx Brothers' script.

A choice example was when she brought up the subject of her

mother's death. I had just remarked that the waitress was slow with our coffee.

"Do you think the police have forgotten about it?" she asked musingly.

"Our coffee?" I said, puzzled.

"It's been over a month now."

"About ten minutes," I said. "It just seems long . . ." I stopped because her blank eyes told me she was a thousand miles away.

"Vivian," I said.

"I don't believe the police are doing a thing. But I'll bet you could solve the case, if you put your mind to it." She smiled brightly at me. "Now that I'm well and really don't need you any more, I think I'll hire you to find my mother's murderer."

"Vivian."

"So much time has passed, you really should start right now. Right after lunch. You can take Harry and I'll take a taxi home."

"Vivian."

I got her attention, and also that of the tables on all four sides of us. "No," I said more softly.

She smiled at me weakly, once again back in the present. Then her smile brightened and she rose. "Excuse me a moment."

Pushing back my chair, I dropped a ten-dollar bill on the table in case we weren't coming back, and said: "I'll go with you."

One eyebrow quirked up in amusement, she shrugged and started across the floor. I followed her across the dining room, through the hotel lobby to a door reading, "Women." She grinned at me quizzically and pushed through the door.

Long ago I had decided that once Vivian was allowed out of the house, it would be impossible to keep her in sight for six months. The only possible way to keep her from morphine was to give her some rope, locate her sources of drug and eliminate the sources.

So instead of foolishly waiting outside the women's room, I ducked out the hotel's side door, loped to the alley and got the windows of the room under observation. I arrived just in time to see her drop lightly to the ground.

When she turned my way, I pulled back my head and faded into the cigar store located at the alley corner. Through the display window glass I saw her stop in front of the store, look in all directions and enter one of the line of cabs parked at the curb.

As soon as she settled back in its interior, I was out of the cigar store and into the taxi immediately behind hers.

"Keep the guy pulling out in sight," I told the cabbie. "But don't make him suspicious."

He dropped his flag. "Copper?"

I said: "No," and let a ten flutter into the seat beside him. My expense account was mounting.

At the end of the first block Vivian peered through her cab's rear window, and I slouched down until my driver's back cut off my view. Apparently her one look satisfied her, because she didn't check again.

Our first stop was the Merchant's National Bank. Vivian's taxi came to a halt in front of the bank and we pulled in a quarter-block behind it. The other cab waited, so I remained in mine until Vivian came out again.

I suspected she wouldn't be long and she would come out mad. If she were trying to get hold of some money, she was going to discover one of the disadvantages of being declared legally incompetent was that you can't cash checks on your own account. It took my signature to get any of her money out of the bank.

In about three minutes she came out, and even from a quarter-block away I could see her face was dark red. When she slammed shut the cab door, it nearly broke the glass.

Her next stop was in front of the Uptown Personal Loan Company. This took ten minutes, but the only result was an even more flushed face and a still harder slam of the cab door.

For the next ten minutes Vivian's taxi wandered aimlessly, while its occupant apparently thought things over. Then it picked up speed and started decisively in the direction of the water front. It stopped a block from the Mississippi in front of an unsafe-looking three-story building.

In this neighborhood of sidewalk fruit stands and dilapidated one-man shops, a taxi was more noticeable than in the uptown section, so I had my driver roll past her taxi and park in the next side street.

When I rounded the corner on foot the other taxi still waited, but Vivian was not in evidence. Unhurriedly I drew abreast of the cab and, without glancing at the driver, turned into the entrance in front of which he was parked.

The building was old and needed airing. A single naked light bulb hanging from the ceiling lit its windowless foyer, disclosing worn stairs ascending on either side and a variety of cigarette stubs and other litter on the floor. On the wall exactly between the two sets of stairs was a faded building directory.

Glancing over the half-dozen directory names, which included a chiropractor, a job printer, a seed company, two novelty whole-salers and a private detective, I settled on the last.

"Joseph Alamado, bonded investigator, room 209," the notice read. I had heard of Joe, and he was no credit to the profession.

Taking the left stairs to the second floor, I passed the print shop and two empty offices before I came to 209. Its plain wooden door repeated the directory's legend. Opening it softly, I pushed into a drab waiting room containing only a black leather sofa, an iron ash stand and a dusty magazine rack. Across the waiting room voices came from behind another plain wooden door on which was painted the single word, "Private."

Leaving the hall door ajar, I crossed to the inner door and leaned one ear against it.

"You know I'll pay you," Vivian Banner was saying in a tone of tight desperation. "I'll bring the money tomorrow."

"You can have the stuff tomorrow," a heavy masculine voice said. After a timed pause, it added: "If you bring the money." There was no sympathy in the voice, and it definitely disapproved of credit transactions.

"Just a shot, then. One shot to carry me over. Against tomor-row's order."

No reply came from the man, but I guessed he had shaken his head. Vivian's voice grew wheedling. "I've always liked you, Joe. I'd be awfully grateful. I'd be so grateful I couldn't refuse you anything at all."

Joe's tone was heavily bored. "I deal in cash, lady. Cold, hard cash. Period."

For so long there was silence, I thought Vivian was turning to leave, and quietly started to leave myself. But her voice, low and vicious, brought me back.

"You rotten, sneaking vulture," she said. "I've poured thou-sands into your filthy hands. Listen to me." Her voice sank till I could barely hear it. "The police would love to know how many thousands—and what it was for!"

A chair scraped back and Joe said sharply: "Just a minute!"

Silence again, until Joe's heavy voice explained reasonably: "You know I don't stock it like a grocery store does apples. I buy when my customers order."

"You've got it right in this office!"

"No, lady. I can get it in an hour, but it takes cash."

"You're lying! You always had it before."

"Sure," Joe agreed. "But I always knew when you were coming. You ain't been around lately."

"All right," Vivian said. "I'll wait an hour while you go for it. I can pay you tomorrow. Honestly."

"Sorry, lady. I ain't got the money to advance. I can't get credit either, you know."

Vivian's voice again sank to a vicious whisper. "Unless I leave here with at least one shot, I'll go straight to the police from here!"

Neither spoke for a long time. Finally Joe said: "You wouldn't want to do that. You'd never get any then."

Vivian's laugh was slightly hysterical. "I'll never get it anyway. At least I can pay you back for some of the torture you've caused me."

For a second time her chair scraped back, and for a second time Joe said: "Just a minute!"

A period of silence ensued before Joe said slowly: "I could fix you up tomorrow, lady, but I couldn't raise you a shot today even if you threatened to phone Edgar Hoover."

"What time tomorrow?" Vivian asked eagerly.

Joe's voice grew persuasive. "Listen, lady. You're well on the way to cure. Why not be smart and stay off the junk?"

"What time tomorrow?" Vivian repeated. Then she said: "How do you know that I've been taking treatment lately?"

"I keep track of my clients."

For a long time neither said anything. Then Vivian asked: "What time tomorrow?"

"Phone me at noon," Joe said resignedly.

"That's too late. Make it earlier."

"Noon." Joe's voice was definite.

"All right," Vivian said crossly. "Noon."

She moved toward the door and I faded back into the hallway, timing the click made by the hall door's closing to coincide with the noise of the other door opening. By the time Vivian reached the hall, I was halfway down the stairs.

But when I reached my taxi and we had swung around the block, Vivian's cab had already pulled away. We caught it two blocks farther on.

As straight as he could go without cutting across vacant lots, Vivian's driver headed for the Rand home. When the cab stopped, Vivian immediately stepped out and ran up the walk to the house. I told my driver to park behind the other vehicle.

"Wait again?" the cabbie asked when I climbed out.

"No."

"That'll be two-thirty then."

I said: "Take it out of the ten I gave you and keep the change."

"Oh," he said. "I thought that was extra."

I gave him the fishy eye and he grinned. "No harm in trying, is there?"

Stopping next to Vivian's cab, I asked the driver: "She tell you to wait?"

"No. Just went in for money to pay me off."

"What's the fare?"

"Two-sixty."

I said: "You guys ought to standardize your rates," gave him three ones and turned toward the house.

At the front door Vivian met me, holding a five-dollar bill in her hand. I flicked it away from her.

"You can't handle money," I said. "You're mentally incompetent."

She looked at me expressionlessly, glanced past me to see that her taxi was gone, and without a word turned and reentered the drawing room. I followed and found the inevitable tea party in session. Mrs. Rand, Claude Banner, Dr. Yoder and Norman Sheridan all sat around holding cups.

I nodded to the group generally and handed Mrs. Rand the five. "I told you not to give Vivian money."

"She said there was a taxi."

"Don't do it again."

Her thick eyeglasses flashed hostility. "You needn't press the point in front of company."

I glanced over the group. "Nobody here who doesn't know what's wrong with Vivian."

Returning to the hall, I phoned the head waiter at the Jefferson and asked him to find Harry and tell him to come on home. While I was phoning, Vivian and Mrs. Rand passed and went on up the stairs. I hung up and returned to the drawing room.

"Where you been?" I asked Claude Banner, none too politely.

He looked startled. "What do you mean?"

"You haven't called to see your step-daughter once."

"Had to fly to Mexico City again," he said in a reasonable tone. "Just got back about an hour ago."

Mrs. Rand came back into the room, minus Vivian.

"Vivian's lying down," she told me. "She doesn't want to be disturbed."

"Lock your door?"

She looked nettled. "Yes."

Deliberately needling her, I asked: "Mind if I look in your room and check?"

She looked even more nettled, but said coldly: "If you wish."

Upstairs I found all three doors to Vivian's room locked. Not caring to rejoin the tea party crowd, I stayed in my room until the guests departed. About five-thirty I heard Mrs. Rand and Vivian talking in Vivian's room, and then a door opened and shut again as Mrs. Rand left. I continued to lie on my back and stare at the ceiling until time for dinner, then I knocked on Vivian's door.

She answered through the panel, but I never saw her alive again. The next morning I found her body . . .

Harry's face was pale and frightened when I slipped into the front seat beside him.

"What's the matter with you?" I asked.

"Nothing."

He started up, killed the engine and had to use the starter again. I decided Mrs. Rand must have told him of Vivian's death.

"Four-hundred block on Second Street," I told him.

"Mrs. Rand wants me to stop by Mr. Sheridan's on the way," Harry said diffidently. "His phone's out of order and she wants him to come over."

"I'm in a hurry."

"It's right on the way."

"Make it snappy, then," I said.

We rolled past Forest Park, made a neat right turn and swung into the driveway of Norman Sheridan's big brick home. The garage doors were open and Harry wheeled the car right through them. Behind us the doors slid shut.

I looked angrily at Harry, started to open my mouth, and closed it again when a voice spoke to me through the side window. "Good morning, Mr. Moon."

# CHAPTER FIVE

### The Bloody Shroud

I glanced sidewise at the round, smiling face of Norman Sheridan. A .45 automatic was half-smothered in one doughy hand, and it was leveled at my ear.

"Move very carefully, Mr. Moon," he said softly. "I understand you can draw and fire a pistol with astonishing rapidity, but you can't possibly do it in the time it takes to press a trigger. If you make any abrupt movements, I won't wait to decide their purpose. I'll simply fire."

I sat still without saying anything.

"Get out slowly, Mr. Moon. Very slowly."

My hand reached for the door handle in slow motion, and I slid from the car at the same rate of speed.

"Turn around and raise your hands, Mr. Moon."

I did as directed, and Harry climbed from his seat and removed the P-.38 from my shoulder holster. Sheridan motioned with his pistol, and I preceded him through a side door into the house's cellar.

Except for the space taken up by a furnace, the entire basement had been converted into a combination office and laboratory. Placed diagonally in one corner was a desk, behind which was a double-width swivel chair. Hanging from the chair's back was Sheridan's heavy cane. Around three sides of the basement ran a wide, waist-high shelf on which were screened cages of buzzing insects, petrie dishes and assorted equipment.

Motioning me to a chair in front of the desk, Sheridan oozed his own vast bulk into the wide chair behind it. He carefully placed the cocked automatic within reach of his hand, leaned forward on his elbows and favored me with a beaming smile. Harry stood in the corner, shuffling from one foot to the other and avoiding my eyes.

"Harry is frightened to death of you, Mr. Moon," Sheridan said. "Your name induces quite some fear among the lesser criminals." He chuckled mildly. "I understand they even carefully address you as 'Mister' when they meet you, a habit you have unimaginatively inculcated by beating them up when they fail to use the title. Now, I call you 'Mister' also, but merely because I prefer to be formal."

I said: "Before you fall asleep at the sound of your own voice, get to the point."

For an instant his eyes frosted over, then he smiled again. "Directness is an admirable trait. I won't keep you in suspense. We're waiting for a phone call."

I thought this over without growing any wiser, and tried again. "Any particular reason you want my company?"

He only smiled, so I kept on. "I suppose you wouldn't have come out in the open like this unless it was urgent to sidetrack me. And since I was headed for a dope peddler, it follows you must not have wanted me to get to him."

The smile continued, bland and friendly.

"So we come to the riddle of how you knew where I was going," I said, smiling just as blandly. "And the only sensible answer is that Harry must have phoned you before we left the house. Then, by the process of logical deduction I learned in my correspondence course in private detecting, a number of interesting things follow." I ticked them off on my fingers for him. "One: Harry is your employee, and his job as chauffeur for Mrs. Rand is only a blind. Two: Joe Alamado is also your employee, or you wouldn't care whether I got to him or not. Three: you're the head of the local dope ring." I stopped and looked at him questioningly.

But all I got was a lot more smile and a deprecating shake of his melon head. "You are wasting your time, Mr. Moon. We are merely waiting for a phone call."

Suddenly his eyes fixed on a fly which had settled to the desk top in front of him. With instant coordination one hand shot out and cupped the whirring insect. Carefully he worked two fingers of his other hand into his clenched fist until he had the fly's legs gripped between the thumb and index finger. Then he calmly stripped its wings and dropped it back on the desk to run in drunken circles.

As though there had been no interruption, he said: "I have no intention of answering any of your provocative questions, Mr. Moon. I'm sure I couldn't think up any explanation for detaining you which would sound more plausible than the one you've deduced, so I won't bother to either affirm or deny your accusations." He raised a thick index finger and shook it at me. "I never underestimate opponents, Mr. Moon. I have studied your history very carefully, and am fully aware of your talents. You have a bulldog tenacity which I consider much more dangerous to my interests than if you were intelligent. The only way to beat a man like you is to catch him unaware and crush him at once. Like this!" He suddenly slapped his fat palm over the wobbling insect on his desk.

I said: "You flatter me."

"No. As I say, I have studied your history. I probably know as much about you as you do yourself."

"For instance?"

Studying me through half-shut eyes, he began to recite: "You were born on the north side in a neighborhood of—ah—lower middle-class families."

"Lower lower-class," I said.

He bent his head courteously. "As you please. Your father was an immigrant laborer, and died when you were three. Your mother died when you were seven, and you and your brother and sister were placed in the state orphanage. Both your brother and sister were adopted, but you stayed until you were eighteen, were turned loose with a high school education and became a dock worker. In a rather rough environment, you soon established yourself as pretty nearly the roughest element, and it was about this time that you received the slight brass knuckle disfigurement your face still bears.

"At twenty you won the Golden Gloves tournament, turned professional, fought three setups which you won by knockouts in the first round; then decided to beat up your manager and, in the ensuing investigation by the boxing commission during which you refused to explain your action, were permanently barred from the ring. Just what was your reason?" he asked curiously.

"He bored me. He talked much too much."

Sheridan smiled benevolently. "Well put, Mr. Moon. I won't bore you much longer. At twenty-one you went to work for the Jones Detective Agency, stayed with them two years and then opened your own business. You've been working alone ever since, with the exception of four years in the Army, and have built an excellent reputation."

I said: "You certainly went to a lot of trouble."

"In the Army you became first sergeant of one of the famous Ranger companies, and succeeded in winning the Legion of Merit, the Silver Star twice, the Bronze Star Medal, the Purple Heart and a theater ribbon with a number of campaign stars on it."

"You forgot the Good Conduct Medal," I said.

"You also succeeded in losing your right leg."

"The left," I said, just to be cantankerous. "Your sources of information must have been lousy."

He frowned, and a tinge of annoyance was in the frown. "Cover him,'' he said to Harry, and watched from the corner of his eye until Harry got my P-.38 leveled at my head.

He heaved himself erect by holding the desk edge in both hands, grasped his cane by the shaft and rounded the desk to bulge over me like an enormous balanced rock. Without speaking, he slammed the heavy crook across my left instep.

If he had not telegraphed the blow, I probably would have shot clear to the ceiling, for the pain was terrific. As it was, even though it felt as though every bone in my foot was broken, I managed a heckling grin.

"You'll bust your cane," I said. "That's aluminum."

Again he raised the cane and brought it down, this time at my right foot. I jerked back my leg and let the cane head crash to the floor.

"Easy," I said, not grinning. "That one bruises."

For a moment he glared down at me, his eyes nearly closed. Then he swung around impatiently and lumbered back to his desk. Leaning back in his oversized swivel chair, he latched hands across his stomach and waited for his color to recede. When it finally did, he revived the benevolent smile.

"A minor point," he said indifferently. "On the whole, my sources of information were excellent."

Since this seemed to call for no answer, I just sat and looked at him. Sheridan looked back, and a conversational pause built up and lengthened. Then the silence was burst apart as the phone on his desk uttered a shrill peal.

Sheridan's body jerked and the gun leaped into his hand, pointed at me.

I laughed aloud. "I make a different noise, fatty. That was the phone."

His smile was a sickly, self-conscious version of the bland original as he laid the automatic back on the desk. Glancing at Harry to make sure I was still covered, he lifted the instrument from its cradle.

"Yes?"

I strained to hear the other voice, but it must have been pitched unusually low, for only a whisper of unintelligible sound trickled past Sheridan's ear.

"He's here and under control," Sheridan said.

A short dribble of sound issued from the receiver, and Sheridan said: "Delay is unnecessarily risky. Suppose he escapes?"

Again he listened. "Of course he's under control. But why delay? What's the point?"

This time the other party talked a long time while Sheridan frowned into space. Then he said: "It will be no harder to dispose of now than when we finally act."

I had an uncomfortable feeling he was referring to my body and silently began to root for the other person to win the argument.

"All right," he said finally. "I'll meet you in thirty minutes. Usual place."

He hung up and glowered at me.

"So I get a reprieve?" I said. "Who was my benefactor?"

His expression relaxed into its habitual smile. "Reprieve? I have no idea what you're talking about."

Again placing both hands on the desk edge, he heaved himself upright. "Do you have any rope in the car, Harry?"

"Moon's got handcuffs in his pocket," Harry said.

"*Mr*. Moon, Harry," I snapped.

Harry wet his lips and shifted his eyes to my feet. Norman Sheridan laughed.

"Harry is being brave, Mr. Moon. Please don't embarrass him." He turned his eyes to Harry. "Take his handcuffs."

Picking up his automatic from the desk top, Sheridan motioned me to rise and turn around. When I complied with his pantomimed directions, Harry reached under my coat and removed the cuffs from my pocket.

I turned back to face Sheridan then, and he swept his gun muzzle toward a stairway and followed behind when I started toward it. In single file, Harry bringing up the rear, we went clear to the second floor and stopped at a closed room.

"Open the door and go in," Sheridan said.

I obeyed his order and we entered a narrow bedroom containing a single bed, a dresser and one chair. The bed had an old-fashioned iron frame.

"Sit on the bed," Sheridan directed.

I swung around until I sat straight-legged in the center of the mattress. Sheridan tossed the handcuffs at me.

"Clip one link to the center bed rung."

I snapped the loop in place.

"Clip the other to your leg."

Automatically I moved my good leg forward and reached for the cuff. Sheridan's soft chuckle made me look up.

"You're a very enterprising man, Mr. Moon. Clamp it to your good leg."

Keeping my face expressionless, I locked the metal band around the ankle of my false right leg.

Satisfied that I was adequately restrained, Sheridan tucked his automatic beneath his arm, informed Harry that he would be back about dark and went off to consult with his associates. Harry leaned the lone chair against the wall and sat with my P-.38 in his hand, watching me steadily.

Every time I shifted position, Harry raised the pistol and pointed it at me. I noticed that it shook slightly in his hand.

"What are you scared of?" I asked.

"I'm not scared of anything."

"You're scared silly," I said. "Relax."

I reached toward my breast pocket for a cigar and the gun came up again. I paused with my fingers touching the cigar.

"Just getting a smoke."

Brooding, he watched me peel the cellophane, search my pockets for a match and light up. "You're crazy if you think I'm afraid of you, Moon," he announced abruptly.

"Mister Moon," I said.

"Mister Moon," he amended quickly.

I finished my cigar, yawned, lay back and went to sleep.

When I awoke, I turned my eyes in Harry's direction and he immediately centered the pistol muzzle between them. I grinned at him, raised myself to a sitting position and glanced at my wrist watch. It was just noon.

"What's for lunch?" I asked.

Harry wet his lips and remained silent.

"Don't I get fed?" I demanded.

"The boss said stay in here with you."

"Oh, sure," I said. "He also said he'd be back about dark. Do we starve?"

"I'm not leaving you out of my sight."

I shrugged. "O.K. I won't get any hungrier than you do. But if you went downstairs to rustle something up, how do you think I'd get out of here? Drag this bed through the window?"

Harry wet his lips again, then came over near the bed to lean forward and examine the locked handcuffs, keeping his pistol trained and carefully staying beyond my reach as he looked. With his left hand he reached out and shook the bed rungs to test their strength. He backed to the door, opened it by reaching behind himself and backed out. The door shut and the key turned quickly in the lock.

Rolling up my trouser, I loosened the harness of my false leg, pulled the stump free and swung my knees over the side of the bed. I pushed myself erect, balanced for a moment and hopped over to the wall next to the door. There I patiently waited for the next fifteen.

Finally a key turned in the lock and the door pushed open. Then Harry was standing with his back to me, one hand on the door knob and the other bearing a tray on which rested a plate of sandwiches, two glasses of milk and my cocked pistol. He just stood there staring stupidly at my manacled leg on the bed.

My left arm went about his throat and my right knee raised to his back.

The crash of the tray was immediately followed by the crash of Harry's body beneath mine as he suddenly went limp, throwing us both off balance. I rolled clear and sat up. Harry had fainted.

It took less time to remove the cuff key from Harry's pocket, unlock my leg and strap it back where it belonged than it did to revive Harry. And when I finally got him awake, he took one look at me and fainted again.

The second time I threw water in his face, he stayed awake, but he was trembling so badly it took ten more minutes to convince him I wasn't intending to kill him on the spot. Finally he was in shape to walk, although he stumbled twice going down the stairs.

I opened the garage doors myself, told Harry to get behind the wheel of the Packard, and slid in beside him.

"Four-hundred block on Second Street," I said.

Harry killed the engine once before he got the car to move, then sideswiped both sides of the driveway in backing out. Normally he was a good driver, but en route to Joe Alamado's office he killed the engine at every light, clashed gears in starting and nearly had me as much a nervous wreck as himself.

In front of the decrepit building where Alamado kept his office, I clamped one cuff to Harry's wrist, the other around the steering column, took the car keys and left him to brood over his sins.

The drab reception room of Joe Alamado's office was empty. I opened the door marked "Private" and found Joe seated behind a cheap desk. He was a squat, narrow-browed man with patent-leather hair slicked back over a nearly flat head. He looked up with a scowl.

I said: "Hello, Joe. We've never met, but you may have heard of me. I'm Manny Moon."

His eyes turned flat and expressionless.

"Get on your feet," I said patiently.

For another moment he remained motionless, then he slowly rose and advanced toward the door, one hand casually slipping into his coat pocket. He started to precede me through the door, suddenly twisting to face me, and his right arm flashed upward.

I let him bring his leather sap even with his ears before starting the eight-inch jab I had been saving for him all day. It connected perfectly, breaking just at the point of impact. He did a backflip and went to sleep.

Harry's eyes bugged out at me and his face turned yellow when I appeared carrying Joe Alamado like a sack of meal. Opening the rear car door, I dumped Joe in, climbed in beside him and leaned over the back seat to loosen the handcuffs. Then I tossed Harry the car keys.

"Back home," I said.

Nellie let us in, examined us sharply and went away muttering to herself. Herding my two captives toward the stairway, I spun Joe around, pushed his chest and let him sit down hard on the steps. "Stick out your left wrist," I said.

Peevishly he held out his arm. I snapped one cuff on it, passed the chain between the railings of the bannister and attached Harry to the other end.

"Don't wander off," I said, and went on into the drawing room.

Most everyone I expected to find was there: Mrs. Rand, Claude Banner, Harry, Alex Carson, Norman Sheridan, Lieutenant Hannegan and, last but not least, Inspector Warren Day.

The moment I walked through the door, Day bellowed: "Where you been, Moon?" and Norman Sheridan's hand snaked toward his chest.

"You'll get a hole in your head," I said coldly, ignoring Day and walking over to Sheridan.

I jerked him to his feet, spun him around until his back was toward me and cramped one fat arm against his spine. With my other hand I removed the .45.

"Cuffs," I said to Hannegan.

Hannegan, surprised but quick on the uptake, moved over and snapped a steel band about the wrist of the arm I held.

Day thundered: "What you think you're doing, Moon!"

Still cramping Sheridan's arm, I dog-trotted him over to Claude Banner's chair, spun him around to face me and pushed him into Banner's lap. Banner let out a large, "Whoosh!" as three-hundred odd pounds smashed down on him, and before either knew what was happening, I snapped the other end of the cuffs to Banner's wrist.

Sheridan struggled from his seat to stand erect.

"That makes four packaged up for you," I said to the now-speechless inspector. "The fifth is a lady."

Crossing to Mrs. Rand, I stood over her, looking down. "Your fat friend was remarkably careful not to implicate you. But no one else knew I was headed after Joe Alamado."

Warren Day shrieked in my ear: "Who's Joe Alamado?" His narrow nose was a pale bull's-eye in a beet-red face.

"I thought Mrs. Rand wouldn't have passed on the message I left for the police," I said. "He's an employee of Sheridan's and hers."

Reaching down, I hooked an index finger around the ribbon of her thick-lensed glasses and jerked them off her nose. The pupils of her weak, watery eyes were contracted to dots.

"We've got two murderers," I told Inspector Day. "Claude Banner killed his wife, Mrs. Rand murdered Vivian . . ."

"I knew the whole setup was phoney when they started pinning the second murder on you," Warren Day told me over rye high-balls at my apartment. "Not that I thought you above murder, but using cyanide was too smart for your lame brain. You'd simply have broken her neck."

Hannegan put in: "How'd the dope racket work?"

I said: "All five helped operate the ring. Mrs. Rand's husband committed suicide when he went broke in 1929, and the narcotic trade has been her source of income ever since. Norman Sheridan and Mrs. Rand directed operations, Claude Banner handled the smuggling through his frequent business trips to Mexico, and Joe Alamado was the distributor. Harry was general flunkey.

"Whether or not Mrs. Banner was part of the ring is unimportant now, but when she discovered her own daugher was an addict, she blew her lid and threatened to expose the whole deal. In an attempt to pacify her, the gang rigged up a quiet cure for

Vivian. But I spilled the beans that the treatment might not work, and wasn't what Dr. Yoder recommended.

"Vivian didn't know that her whole family was involved in narcotic trade but she did know Alamado was the distributor, and she knew her aunt was also a morphine addict. So the gang wanted her where they could watch her in case she broke under the cure and started making accusations. After Mrs. Banner left the Rand home that day, she laid down the law to Sheridan and her husband that Vivian was either going to be committed to a sanitarium, or she was going to the police. So Harry, Sheridan and Banner simply took her for a ride, dumped her body in the river and rigged alibis for each other. Afterward Banner caught his plane."

"I follow all that," Hannegan said. "But how'd you know Banner was the one who pulled the trigger?"

"Simple psychology. Sheridan was too smart to do his own killing, and Harry didn't have the guts."

Warren Day said: "I still don't see why Mrs. Rand killed her niece. She must have been nuts."

"Next thing to it," I said. "She was full of dope, and her thinking wasn't quite sane. After Vivian's unsuccessful attempt to get morphine from Joe Alamado, she went back home, locked herself in her room and began brooding about the next day. Alamado had promised her a supply if she phoned him at noon, remember. Vivian had been off even medicinal doses for two weeks and was bearing up pretty well, but the idea of actually getting a shot worked on her mind until she couldn't stand to wait the night through.

"Vivian knew her aunt had a supply, because she'd swiped a shot during her treatment. I nearly caught her in the act, though I wasn't aware of it at the time. But when Mrs. Rand found Vivian all hopped up, she knew I'd ask embarrassing questions, so she deliberately let Alex Carson in to visit Vivian, hoping he'd get the blame. Her ruse worked, and I ordered Alex to stay away.

"The night Vivian died, she called in her aunt, demanded a shot of morphine and threatened to tell me Mrs. Rand was an addict if she didn't get it. Norman Sheridan had repeatedly warned Mrs. Rand to be careful with me around, and in her drug-punchy mind she thought if I discovered she was an addict, I'd follow through and learn all about the drug ring and the murder of Mrs. Banner. To quiet Vivian, her aunt promised to bring her a shot during the night. But she knew she could never explain to me how Vivian got the shot, so when she brought the needle, it was filled with cyanide instead of morphine.

"After administering Vivian's last shot in the arm, she had Harry lean a ladder against the house, left her connecting door ajar with the key in it, and calmly went to bed.

"Neither Claude Banner nor Norman Sheridan knew she planned to kill Vivian until she phoned them next morning and told them what she had done. Both blew their lids, but there was nothing they could do but try to cover for her. She got hold of Sheridan in time for him to ad lib a quick plan to sidetrack me from getting to Joe Alamado. Once Sheridan showed his hand, he was cautious enough to want to dispose of me quick, but one of his partners phoned and talked him into waiting."

"That was Claude Banner," said Warren Day. "Banner convinced Sheridan they could pin Vivian's murder on you, but only if your subsequent death seemed accidental. He suggested a car accident, as though you smashed up trying to escape. And, of course, if Sheridan had put a bullet in you, it wouldn't have looked very accidental."

"How'd you tumble to Mrs. Rand?"

"I saw her eyes without their thick glasses. At the time I knew there was something strange about them, but it didn't register until I thought about it later. Then I realized her pupils were contracted just as Vivian's had been."

Day said: "They might have gotten away with it if Sheridan had won his phone argument with Banner."

"You sound disappointed," I said.

Mixing himself another drink, Day spread thin lips in a hurt smile. "You misjudge me, Manny. I wouldn't want anything to happen to you." He sampled his drink and nodded. "Not as long as you keep stocking this brand of rye."

# Michael Collins

# EIGHTY MILLION DEAD

WE HAVE KILLED EIGHTY MILLION PEOPLE IN EIGHTY YEARS.
Give or take a few million or a couple of years. Killed; not
lost in hurricanes or famines or epidemics or any of the other
natural disasters we should be trying to wipe out instead of each
other. From 1900 to 1980. The Twentieth Century.

That's a hell of a way to begin a story, except in this case it
could be the whole story. The story of Paul Asher and Constantine
Zareta and me, Dan Fortune, and I want you to think about those
eighty million corpses. Most of those who killed them were fighting for a reason, a cause. A lot of those who died had a reason, a
cause. You have to wonder what cause is worth eighty million
ended lives. You have to wonder what eighty million dead bodies
has done to the living.

I know what those eighty million deaths had done to Paul Asher
and Constantine Zareta. Those were the names they gave me,
anyway. They weren't their real names. I'm not sure they knew
their real names anymore. It was Paul Asher who walked into my
second floor office/apartment that rainy Monday.

"You are Dan Fortune? A private investigator?"

He was tall and dark. A big man who moved like a shadow. I
hadn't seen or even heard him come in. He was just there in front
of my desk—dark-haired, dark-eyed, soft-voiced, in a dark suit.
Colorless. Nothing about him told me anything. Only his eyes,
looking at my missing arm, proved he was alive.

"I'm Fortune."

"I am Paul Asher. I wish to hire you."

"To do what, Mr. Asher?"

"You will deliver a package."

He had an accent. One I couldn't place, and not exactly even an accent. More a kind of toneless and too-precise way of speaking English that told me it wasn't his native language.

"You want a messenger service," I said, "use my telephone book if you want."

"I will pay one thousand dollars," Asher said. "I wish that the package is to be delivered tonight."

No one makes a thousand dollars a day in Chelsea, not even today. Most still don't make it in a month. It was a lot of money for delivering a package. Or maybe it wasn't.

"What's in the package?" I asked.

"I will pay one thousand dollars because you will not ask what is in the package, and because Zareta is a dangerous man."

He said it direct and simple, expressionless.

"Zareta?" I said.

"Constantine Zareta. This he calls himself. It is to him you will take the package."

"Why not take it yourself?"

"He would kill me."

"Why?"

"I possess what he wants."

"Blackmail, Asher?"

"No, I ask no money. You will take the package?"

I shook my head. "Not without knowing what's in it, and why you want to send it to this Constantine Zareta."

Paul Asher thought for a time. He seemed to look again at my empty left sleeve, but his face remained expressionless. He wasn't angry or even frustrated. I had presented him with a problem, and he was thinking about it. As simple as that.

He made his decision. "The package contains documents, nothing more. I am giving them to Zareta. They are of no value except to Zareta. For him they are of great value. The papers are not a danger, simply of value to Zareta. He would kill me to get them, I am tired of danger. When he has the documents I will not be in danger. Until then, I am not safe from him. I cannot take the documents myself, so? You will take them?"

"Let's see the package."

Asher produced a flat package from an inside pocket of his dark suit. It was about as wide as a paperback book, twice as long and thick. I took it. They make bombs smaller and better every day, but the package was much too light for even a plastic bomb. It felt like a package of documents and nothing else. Even a deadly gas has to have a container. I could feel the edges, the folds, the thickness of heavy paper.

"How did you happen to pick me, Mr. Asher?"

"From the telephone book."

For the first time I didn't believe him. Too quick? Something in his voice that wasn't quite toneless this time? I'm in the phone book, but I didn't believe him. Because he wasn't the kind of man who trusted to chance? Maybe and maybe. But if it hadn't been the telephone book, how and why had he picked me out of all the detectives in New York?

"I take the package to Zareta," I said. "What do I bring back?"

"Nothing."

"Who pays me? When?"

"I will pay you," Asher said. "Now."

He took a thin billfold from his inside pocket, counted out ten hundred dollar bills. He wasn't telling me the truth, not the whole truth, but I knew that. Warned, what could happen that I couldn't handle? If anything looked a hair out of line I'd toss the package and walk away. I took the ten bills. Crisp and new, straight from the bank. Maybe I wanted to know why he had picked me for the job. I wanted to know something.

"What's the address?"

"It is on the package."

"How do I contact you later?"

"You do not. You are paid, I will know if you do not do what you have been paid to do."

"Anything else?"

"Yes," Paul Asher said. "You will deliver the package at midnight. Precisely midnight."

He walked out. I tilted back in my chair. I was a thousand dollars richer. Why didn't I feel good?

## 2

The address was on the East Side up in Yorkville far over near the river. Asher's instructions had been definite—midnight—and the slum street was dark and silent in the rain when the taxi dropped me. There was no one on the street. No one in sight anywhere, but I felt the eyes. When you grow up near the docks, start stealing early because you have to eat even if your father ran out long before and your mother drinks too much, you learn to feel when eyes are watching.

I walked slowly along the dark street in the rain and knew that I wasn't alone. I sensed them all around. The address was an old unrenovated brownstone with the high front steps. Two men appeared at the far end of the street. They leaned against a dark building. Two more appeared behind me where the taxi had dropped me. Two stood in the shadows on another stoop across the street. Shadows of shadows all around in the dark and rain. The glint of a gun.

I went up the steps to the front door and into the vestibule. There was only one mailbox and doorbell. I had my finger on the bell when I saw the man outside on the steps. He stood two steps below the vestibule with an automatic rifle. A short, powerful man behind a bandit mustache. There were two more behind him at the foot of the steps. They had guns too. They stood there doing nothing. Too late I knew why, felt the inner vestibule door open behind me.

An arm went around my throat, a hand went over my mouth, another hand held my arm, and I was dragged back into the dark of the entrance hall. I didn't resist. The short one with the bandit mustache and automatic rifle followed us in. They dragged me into a small room, sat me in a chair, came and went in rapid groups. They barely glanced at me. They were busy. Except two I felt close behind me keeping watch.

"What's going on?" I tried.

"Do not talk!" He was the short, powerful man with the automatic rifle. He seemed to be the leader, sent the other men in and out with the precision of a drill sergeant. They spoke some language I didn't even recognize. I didn't have to know the language to know what they were doing. They were all armed, and they were searching the street outside and the neighborhood for anyone who might have come with me. It was half an hour before the mustachioed leader sat down astride a chair in front of me. He still carried his automatic rifle, and the package Paul Asher had sent me to deliver.

"Your name is Fortune. What do you want here?"

"I came to deliver that package."

"Who are you?"

"You've searched my papers."

"You came to deliver this package to who?"

"Constantine Zareta. Is that you?"

"What is in the package?"

"Papers. Documents."

He studied the package a moment, turned it over in his heavy hands. Then he gave it to one of the other men.

"From who does the package come?"

"Paul Asher."

"We know no Paul Asher."

"It's the name he gave me."

"Your papers say you are a private investigator. We know what that means. A man who will sell his weapon to anyone. A hired murderer. An assassin. You came to kill Constantine Zareta!"

"I came to deliver a package," I said. "I don't have a gun. I don't even know who Zareta is or what he looks like."

"Of course not. They would not tell you who you kill or why. They have hired you only to kill. Do not lie!"

"If someone is trying to kill Zareta, go to the police. That's their work."

I had been watching all their faces as I talked. They were grim, unsmiling, and they didn't look like hoodlums. They looked like soldiers, *guerillas*. They were nervous and armed, but they didn't act like gunmen. And as I watched them I saw their faces come alert, respectful. Someone else had come into the room somewhere behind me. A low voice with good English.

"The police could not help me, Mr. Fortune."

I felt him standing close behind me. His voice had that power of command, of absolute confidence in himself and what he did. Constantine Zareta. I started to turn.

"Do not turn, Mr. Fortune."

I looked straight ahead at the mustachioed man. "Maybe the police can't help you because you want to kill Paul Asher."

The mustache reached out and hit me.

"Emil!"

Emil glared down at me. "He's another one, Minister! I can smell them."

"Perhaps," Zareta's slow voice said. "Let us be sure."

"We cannot take the chance, Minister! Kill him now. If they did not send him, what does it matter?"

There was a silence behind me. A chair scraped. I felt hot breath on the back of my neck. Slow breathing. Zareta had sat down close behind me. That was fine. As long as I could feel his breath I was ahead of the game. As long as I could feel anything.

"A man sent you to me at this address."

"Yes."

"Why did he pick you?"

"Out of the telephone book."

"Do you believe that?"

"No."

I could almost hear him nod.

"What was his reason for not coming himself?"

"He said you'd kill him."

"Why would I kill him?"

"Because he had what you wanted. Documents, not dangerous to you, but so important you'd kill to get them."

"And these documents are in the package?"

"Yes. He said he was tired of danger, wanted to give them to you, but was afraid to come himself."

It was strangely unreal to be talking straight ahead into the empty air of the dark room, the silent face of Emil.

"This man's name was Paul Asher."

"Yes."

"I know no Asher, but that does not surprise me. You will describe him."

I described Paul Asher down to the flinty calm of his dark eyes, his silent movement despite his size.

"I do not recognize him, but that does not surprise me either, Mr. Fortune. I do recognize the type of man you have described. It sounds true. You have saved your life, Mr. Fortune. For now."

Emil did not like my reprieve. "The risk, Minister!"

"I think we can take some risk, Emil," Zareta said, his breath still brushing the back of my neck. "Mr. Fortune could be lying, but I think not. This Asher sounds like all the men we have known, yes? Mr. Fortune has acted exactly as he would have if his story is true, and you found no one else who could have been with him. Then, he clearly does not know what was in the package he brought to us, or he would have told a better tale, yes? And he has no weapon of any kind."

That seemed to stop Emil. I've said it before, most of the time a gun does nothing but get you in trouble. Sooner or later you'll use it if you have to or not, and someone else will use theirs. If I'd had a gun this time, I'd probably be dead. I wasn't dead, and I wondered what had been in the package that would have made me tell a different story if I'd known?

"Why?" Zareta said slowly. "I cannot understand what reason

this Asher had to send you to me. That makes me uneasy. Tell me everything once more. Leave nothing out.''

I told him all of it again. I was uneasy too. Why had Paul Asher sent me if the package wasn't the reason? Or was it Zareta who was conning me now? Lulling me to get me to lead him back to Asher? If that was his scheme he wouldn't get far. I couldn't lead anyone to Paul Asher.

''I do not understand,'' Zareta said when I finished the story again, ''but you have done me an important service. I know now what this Paul Asher looks like.'' The chair scraped behind me. ''Take your money, Mr. Fortune, and go home. Forget that you ever heard of Paul Asher or me.''

There was a silence, and then a door closed somewhere in the dark brownstone. The troops began to disperse. The boss had spoken. Emil's heart wasn't in it, but Zareta was boss.

''Tonight you are a very lucky man,'' Emil said.

I looked around. I saw no one that looked like a boss, but I saw the package I'd carried lying on a table. It was torn open to show—a stack of folded papers. Just what Asher had said it was. Only there *was* something wrong, something odd about the package. Not quite right. What? They didn't give me the time to look longer or closer.

They hustled me back out into the dark hall. Then I was out on the street where I'd started. I walked to the nearest corner without looking back. I didn't run, that would have been cowardly. I waited until I was around the corner. Then I ran.

By the time I got down to Chelsea and my one-room office apartment I felt pretty good. I had no more interest in Paul Asher and Zareta and their private feud, whatever it was. I was a thousand dollars richer and still alive. I figured I was home free. I should have known better.

### 3

I awoke in the pitch dark to a violent pounding on my door. My arm was aching. The missing arm. That's always a sign. It's what's missing that hurts when the days become bad.

The pounding went on. Cop pounding. As I got up and pulled on my pants, a gray light began to barely tinge the darkness. Captain Pearce himself led his Homicide men into my office area. The men fanned out and began to look behind the doors and under the beds. Pearce sat down behind my desk.

"What's it about, Captain?" I asked.

"Paul Asher," Pearce said.

"Nice name. Is there more?"

"Asher is enough," Pearce said. "He was a client of yours? Or was there some other connection?"

"Was?" I said.

"Asher's dead," Pearce said. "You should give him his money back."

Pearce doesn't like any private detective much, but especially me. I was too close to old Captain Gazzo. Pearce took Gazzo's place after the Captain was gunned down on a dark city roof. One of the new breed, a college man, and he doesn't like me bringing Gazzo's ghost with me. But he's a good cop, he does his job first.

"We found Asher an hour ago," Pearce said. "Dumped under the George Washington Bridge. Shot up like Swiss cheese. Any ideas?"

The George Washington Bridge is a long way from Yorkville, but that I would expect.

"Constantine Zareta," I said.

I told Pearce about Zareta and Asher, about Emil and all those silent gunmen. Pearce got up, signalled for his forces.

"Let's pick them up."

We went in the Captain's car. He sat silent and edgy as we headed uptown at the head of his platoon of squad cars, drumming his fingers on his knee. He had no more questions. I had questions.

"You said you found Asher an hour ago, Captain. How did you dig up my connection so fast?"

"Your business cards in his pocket."

"Cards?"

Pearce nodded as he watched the dawn city, gray and empty of people but teeming with trucks. "He must have had ten, and your name was in his little black book with a thousand dollars and yesterday's date noted next to it."

Business cards cost money, I don't hand them out without necessity. Asher had found me, there had been no reason to give him a card, not even one. I leave some with uptown contacts in case anyone up there wants a kidnapped poodle rescued, so Asher may have picked up the cards from whoever sent him to me before he came down to my office. Or he could have palmed them off my desk when he walked out. But why? And why ten?

In the dawn the Yorkville street was as deserted as it had been last night. We parked all along the gray morning street. Windows popped open all along the block, but nothing moved in Constantine Zareta's brownstone. The building was as dark and silent as some medieval fortress.

It turned out to be as hard to get into as a medieval fortress. Rings, knocks, shouts and threats failed to open the vestibule door, and the building remained dark.

"Break it down," Pearce said.

His men broke the door down, and Pearce strode into the dim entrance hall. The mustachioed Emil faced him. Emil had his automatic rifle aimed at the Captain's heart. Other gunmen stood in the doorways of the rooms and on the stairs. We were all covered. It took Captain Pearce almost a minute to find his voice.

"Police, damn it! Put those guns down! We're the police!"

Constantine Zareta spoke from somewhere behind Emil, out of sight in the dim hallway. I knew that slow voice by now.

"You will tell me your name, your rank, and your badge number. I will verify that you are police. You will make no moves, my men watch your people in the street also."

The color began to suffuse Pearce's face. The Captain isn't a patient man, and I wondered how long it had been since anyone had asked him to prove who he was. He opened his mouth, looked slowly around the dark hallway at the silent *guerillas* and their guns, and closed his mouth. If Constantine Zareta was as tough as he sounded, we could have a blood bath in the dark hallway and out on the morning street.

"Captain Martin Pearce," the Captain said through thin lips, and explained that a captain's shield does not have a number.

In the silent hallway we all waited.

I imagined the scene down at Police Headquarters when they got the call asking about a Captain Pearce, and would they please describe the Captain! It took some time, but whatever they thought down there they must have gone along with it and given an accurate description. Constantine Zareta appeared in the dim light, and I saw him for the first time—a short, thick man as wide as he was tall, with a shaved bullet head attached to his massive shoulders as if he had no neck. He said something in his unknown language. The guns vanished and the gunmen disappeared.

"Very well, Captain," Zareta said to Pearce. "We will talk in the living room."

Pearce and Zareta faced each other in the same room where I had been interrogated earlier. The Captain stood. Zareta sat on a straight chair, Emil close behind him. Neither Zareta nor Emil had seen me yet.

"Just who and what are you, Zareta?" Pearce said. "Why do you need armed men?" His voice was controlled, but I heard the edge in it. No policeman can tolerate a private army.

"A poor exile, Captain," Zareta said. "My men have permits for their weapons."

"Exile from where?"

"Albania."

That was the language I hadn't recognized—Albanian.

"Was Paul Asher an Albanian too?" Pearce said. "Is that why he was afraid of you? Is that why you killed him?"

For a moment there was a heavy silence in the small living room lit only by a single lamp behind its drawn curtains. Then Emil grunted. Others made other noises. Constantine Zareta leaned forward in his chair.

"This Asher, he is dead? You are sure?"

"We're sure," Pearce said.

Zareta laughed aloud. "Good! He is one *we* will not have to kill! You bring me good news, Captain, I am grateful. But how did you know that this Asher's death would be something I would want to know? How did you know of Asher and myself? How . . . Ah, of course! Mr. Fortune. You have talked with Mr. Fortune. It is the only way." He looked around the small room. "Are you here again, Mr. Fortune?"

I stepped out into the dim light where Zareta could see me, flashed my best smile at the glowering Emil, and missed it. I missed the whole impossible, monstrous plan.

## 4

Sometimes I wonder if there is anyone left who hasn't killed. I know there are millions, but sometimes it seems there can't be a man alive who hasn't killed. I've killed. In my work you kill sooner or later, but I never get used to it. It always shakes me up, killing and death, and maybe that was why I missed what I should have heard in what Constantine Zareta said when I stepped out where he could see me and only smiled at him.

Pearce wasn't smiling. "You're saying you didn't kill Paul Asher?"

"We did not."

"But you would have?"

"If he came here, yes."

"Why?"

"Because he would have killed me."

"Why didn't you ask for protection?"

"The police?" Zareta shook his head. "No, Captain. I am not precisely a friend of your government. I am a Communist. I have no love for your capitalist regime, they have no love for me. In my country the present leaders and I have no love for each other either. They want me dead, *must* have me dead, or someday I will destroy them. Six times they have tried. In four countries. Twice we had police protection. Once the police could not stop the assassin, once they did not want to stop the assassins. Each time I was close to death. I have survived, I have killed four of them, but they will not give up. If I were them I would not give up. One of us must kill the other."

That was when I first thought about the eighty million dead in eighty years. Zareta said the word *kill* the way other men say the word *work*—a fact of life, a necessity. Neither good nor bad, just a tool of life. I remember when we used to say that a man who killed for the fun of it was an animal, inhuman, a monster. Today we kill without even having any fun from it. We just kill. A job, a duty, our assigned role. And it has nothing to do with being a Communist. It isn't only the Communists who have swallowed those eighty million corpses like so many jelly beans.

Pearce said, "So you have your own army, trust no one to come near you, not even the police."

"That is why I still live, Captain," Zareta said. "But we do not kill unless we are sure a man is our enemy."

"You knew Paul Asher was your enemy. Fortune told you."

"Yes, but Asher did not come here."

"Someone else just killed him for you. A lucky accident."

"I ask no questions, Captain," Zareta said.

Pearce seemed to think. He glanced toward me. If Zareta or his men hadn't killed Paul Asher, it didn't leave many known candidates except me. I didn't like that much, but I couldn't think of anyone else to hand the Captain. While I was thinking about it, and Zareta and the glowering Emil had relaxed a hair now that they knew Paul Asher was dead, Pearce nodded sharply to his men. They grabbed Zareta, had their guns out before Zareta's men knew what had happened.

"Maybe you didn't kill Paul Asher," Pearce said. "But I need to know more. We'll go down to headquarters and sort it out there."

"No!" Emil cried. "The Minister does not go with you!"

The police had the edge now, but if Emil and the rest went for their guns it could be nasty. It was a tense moment in the small, dim room. Zareta broke it.

"Very well, Captain," he said. He had little choice. He was an alien, they were the police, and his own chances of surviving a shootout would be slim. "But not alone. I will take Emil and two other men, yes? A precaution of safety in numbers we who do not come from free countries need."

"Okay, but they leave all their guns. My men will stay around here to help protect the rest of your people."

"Agreed," Zareta said.

"Minister!" Emil was uneasy.

"Come, Emil, they are the police," Zareta said.

They laid their weapons on a table, followed Captain Pearce out of the room.

I was uneasy too. Constantine Zareta would kill any enemy, without anger or remorse. He seemed to draw the line at killing without *some* reason, and that had probably saved me the first time around, but it wasn't exactly high morality. Yet, as I watched them go out with Pearce I was suddenly sure that they had *not* killed Paul Asher.

Zareta wouldn't have waited to be caught if he or any of his men had killed Asher. He would have known that the moment Asher turned up dead I would tell the police all about him and his connection to Asher. No, Zareta would have been long gone before the police could connect Asher to me, and I could connect Zareta to Asher and lead the police to him, and the police . . .

And I knew the answer. The whole thing.

I felt colder than I had ever felt in my life.

And I knew what had been wrong about the package I had delivered. It was still there, open on the table next to the guns of Zareta and Emil and the other two men. The sheets of folded paper, the *documents*, were blank. I had been paid a thousand dollars to deliver a package of blank paper to Constantine Zareta.

And all the time I was thinking all this I was out of that room and running along the dark hallway to the gray dawn light of the front door. I thought it all and grabbed Zareta's own automatic from the table and was running out the front door into the morning like a racer coming around the last turn.

They had reached the sidewalk at the foot of the brownstone steps. The door of Pearce's black car was open. The man stood in the dawn not ten feet from the Captain's car. A stocky patrolman with an automatic in his hands. In both hands. A long-barreled automatic that was no part of the equipment of a New York city patrolman. An automatic aimed straight at Constantine Zareta.

I had no time to shout or even aim.

Zareta had seen the man now. And Captain Pearce. Emil had seen him. None of them could have moved in time.

I fired on the run. Three shots.

I never did know where the first went.

The second shot smashed a window of Pearce's black car.

The third hit the fake cop in the arm. Not much, a graze that barely needed a Band-Aid later, but enough. The assassin's arm jerked and he missed Constantine Zareta by inches.

Pearce, Emil and five real patrolmen swarmed the gunman under like an avalanche on the Yorkville street.

<h1 style="text-align:center">5</h1>

I never learned Paul Asher's real name, or who he really was, or where he came from. No one did. No one ever will.

No one will visit his grave in Potter's Field out on Hart Island in the East River. He's buried out there under a marker with only his false name on it. Nameless, even to his partner in the assassination plot, the phony patrolman.

The fake policeman never told us his real name either. No one came forward to identify him or even visit him. No one ever has or ever will where he serves his time up in Auburn. He never told us who sent them to kill Zareta, or what their cause was, their reason, but he didn't mind telling us the unimportant parts, and that it had been Paul Asher's plan all the way. A plan that had very nearly worked.

"Himself," Captain Pearce said as we sat in his office.

It was late evening. Somehow it was hard to think that it was still the same day the police had pounded on my door at dawn. A century ago. The Captain looked out toward the distant East River as if waiting for it to rise up and drown us all.

"Himself," I said. "He had himself killed just to smoke Zareta out into the open where his partner could get a clear shot, to lull Zareta into dropping his guard for an instant. He died so Zareta would die."

"To do his job," Pearce said. "And he almost made it."

"Because I missed it," I said. "Missed that package of blank paper and missed what Zareta really told me. When he asked how you knew about him and Asher, and realized that it had to be through me, I should have seen it all. I was the only one in New York, probably in the world, who could have connected Asher and Zareta, brought the police to Zareta. He said it, and I missed it."

"We all missed it then," Pearce said. "Even Zareta."

Six killers had tried for Constantine Zareta and failed. So Paul Asher made his own plan. The fake patrolman told us all about it. He was proud of the plan, proud of Paul Asher.

"He picked you," Pearce went on in the silent office, "because he heard you were especially close to the police through Gazzo. He sent you to Zareta so you'd know where Zareta was, and so Zareta wouldn't be alarmed when you brought the police. He put your cards in his pocket, wrote your name and the date in his book, and had his partner kill him and dump his body under the bridge. So we would go to you, and you would take us to Zareta, and we'd bring Zareta out into the open."

Paul Asher, dead, had sent the police to me, and I had taken them to Zareta. Asher's plan to kill Constantine Zareta. Even a rat fights to survive, but Paul Asher died just to do his job. His life and death no more than a tool in his own plan.

I said, "Every assassin expects to die if he succeeds, maybe even if he fails, but Asher died without knowing if he would succeed or fail. Anything could go wrong. He died on the *chance* that his plan would work."

"He wasn't human," Pearce said.

There are people all over this world who will say that Paul Asher was a hero. The same people who can live with those eighty million dead, and maybe eight hundred million tomorrow or the next day, and go right on drinking beer and grabbing for a dollar. The Paul Ashers and Constantine Zaretas kill the way other men swat flies, and we let them. We're used to it.

"He was human," I said. "That's the horror."

Paul Asher was human. And it's not the eighty million dead that really worry me, it's what those piled corpses have done to the rest of us in those eighty years.

It's not the dead that scare me, it's the living.

# Fletcher Flora

# THE HEAT IS
# KILLING ME!

THE ROOM, DIM AND COOL, WAS AN AIR-CONDITIONED RETREAT from the white heat outside. The furniture was rich walnut, gleaming like satin. It might have been the office of a bank president, and the man behind the desk might have been the president himself. But his name was Francis Kruger, and he was a hoodlum. No garden variety, of course. Mr. Big himself.

"Danny Clive," he said to me. "Danny Clive, special investigator. How's the grand jury, Danny boy?"

"Like last week," I said. "Like the week before. Still looking for Eric Sands."

Rocking back in his swivel chair, Kruger brought his fingertips together and poutingly contemplated his paunch. His eyes were indifferent slits under lazy lids.

"Funny a guy like Sands disappears," he said.

I shrugged. "He isn't the first guy to disappear when a subpoena was looking for him."

"Do you," Kruger said, "figure Sands had help?"

"Yeah," I said. "Someone either bought him a plane ride to Shangri-La—or gave him a free ride."

Kruger's heavy lips pursed briefly, and his lids flickered momentarily. "A weak guy with too much on his mind," he said. "A guy who'd never get past a grand jury. Time comes when he gets to be a liability."

"You testifying or speculating?" I asked.

He laughed shortly. "That's what I love about you, Danny.

185

Real sense of humor. Here's hoping you never run into someone who doesn't appreciate it. Just speculating, of course. I've already done my testifying for the jury. You know that.''

"Sure. Just like any good citizen.''

He rocked forward in the swivel and reached for a box of cigarettes on the desk. King-sized and gold-tipped. He lit a smoke with a silver lighter and drew deeply. The cigarette had a rich, exotic aroma. He didn't ask me to try one.

"Doing my duty, Danny. Nothing I admire like a man who does his duty. Take you for example. A lot of guys would have welshed on this Sands deal. Lot of guys wouldn't have the guts to play bloodhound with someone they'd called a friend. Not you, though. With you, it's friendship be damned, when you see your duty.''

I took time to find and light a cigarette of my own. Not that I needed the smoke. Just the time. Time for the hard, hurting tension of my anger to soften. Time to tell myself again that rage is impotent against a man like Francis Kruger.

"One guy goes one way, another goes another," I said. "Eric and I parted company a long time ago.''

"Looks to me like you're trying to get together again. Looks to me like you're working overtime at it.''

"I've got a job to do, that's all. The grand jury wants Eric Sands. I get paid to look for him.''

He leaned forward over the wide gleaming surface of his desk and crushed the long butt of his cigarette in a heavy glass tray.

"Tough," he said. "You're a real tough guy, Danny. My kind of guy. You ever get tired of doing leg work for peanuts, come see me.''

"I've come now.''

"Yeah. I'm wondering why. Don't tell me you're looking for a job.''

"Okay. I won't tell you that, but in case you've forgotten, I'm looking for Eric Sands. That's why I'm here. I thought maybe you might have remembered something you forgot to tell the grand jury.''

"I haven't remembered anything. I don't know anything. Not about the murder of that special prosecutor. Not about anything the jury's interested in. Most of all, not about Eric Sands.''

"He was one of your boys.''

"So he was one of the boys. I pay them, but I don't nurse them."

"Eric was always a personable guy. The kind of guy who had a way of getting inside. Rumor has it that he knew too much. Too much to risk before a grand jury investigation."

Kruger's shrug was indifferent:

"Like you say, he was personable. Like I said, he was weak. Sometimes it's a dangerous combination."

"Sure," I said, rising. "I get it. Eric doesn't live here anymore."

His big pale face was smooth and bland. Beneath the thin white hair brushed sleekly over his big skull, the scalp glowed pinkly. He should have been in an album with a baby on his knee. *That's Grandpa with little Alfie. Grandpa loves kids.*

"No idea. None at all. Sorry, Danny."

"Okay," I said. "Thanks for nothing."

He lifted a big, soft-palmed hand. "Wait a minute. I'm a generous guy, Danny. I never like to send anyone away with nothing. So here's something—something to think about. Eric Sands has disappeared. It could be he just slipped away to be alone. Then again, it could be someone decided he knew enough to make him a menace. It could be someone influenced him. There ought to be a lesson in it somewhere. Especially for a special investigator playing bloodhound. You think about it, Danny."

I looked at him across the room, and I thought to myself that death is not a gaunt specter with hollow sockets. Death is a bland man with a pink scalp.

"Thanks again," I said. "Thanks again for nothing."

I walked out of the cool room into the blast of white heat and down to the curb where I'd left my crate. Steering a slow course over the city griddles, I parked again in front of a walk-up on lower Market. In the foyer, I punched a button over the word Sands, and in a few seconds, heard the lock on the lower door click off. I opened the door and went upstairs to Eric Sands's apartment, and when I got there, Gloria was standing at a window, looking down through the half-closed slats of the Venetian blind into a blistered court. From the bedroom came the low drone of a window exhaust fan. The air in the room stirred softly, caressing my skin.

Without turning, Gloria said, "Judas. Judas Clive. Tough guy Clive. Nothing hurts him."

"Listen," I said. "Someone else called me tough today. Francis Kruger. He was wrong, and you're wrong. I'm not tough. I'm just a medium-tough guy with a job."

"You been to see Kruger?"

"Yes. I've been there. He had nothing to offer."

There had been a slight stiffening of her body against the slatted blind, an almost imperceptible sharpening of the overt signs of awareness. Now the brief tension eased, muscles and senses relaxing.

"You expecting donations from Kruger?" she asked.

"No," I said. "A guy just tries."

"Why, Danny?"

I didn't know. "I told you. It's a job," I said.

Gloria's voice came sharp. "How you going to feel?" she said. "How are you going to feel if you run Eric down? You know the grand jury'll crucify him. He won't stand a chance."

"Eric's small fry. The jury's after the one Eric can point to. Francis Kruger."

"I know that. So does Kruger. How long you think Eric'll live if you drag him out of cover?"

"He'll get protection," I said.

Her shoulders stiffened with bitterness. "Like the special prosecutor, I suppose."

"Maybe. That's the risk you take when you tie in with a man like Kruger."

She was silent, looking down into the glaring court where the heat rebounded from concrete in shimmering waves. Her pale blond hair was piled up on her neck and in the soft light, her face was strangely beautiful. She was dressed in a gaily colored bra and white shorts and her long legs were very tan. She would have looked beautiful on a beach.

I stood watching her, wishing I had a cold Collins with plenty of ice in my hand, but no one was offering Danny Clive a drink these days. He wasn't very popular anymore. Not popular, at all—anywhere.

As if reading my thoughts, she turned away from the window, saying, "Once it might have been different. Remember, Danny?"

"Sure," I said. "I remember. I remember lots of things. I remember you and Eric and me growing up together on the streets of Northside. I remember every ache and pain and itch of seeing you change from pigtails and bones to what I see now. I remember as if it were yesterday. It doesn't mean a damned thing, because it *was* yesterday.''

If there'd been a chance for a drink, it was gone now. Two scarlet spots indicating anger burned beneath the golden satin finish of her hollow cheeks. Her voice sank to a menacing gentleness.

"You've never got over it, have you, Danny? You've never got over my choosing Eric instead of you.''

"Don't kid yourself, baby. Plenty of things have happened to me. Some good, some bad. The best that ever happened was running second to Eric in the race for you. I've been thanking the gods. All the time I've been seeing Eric turn from a weak charmer to a rotten one. All the time I've been seeing him reach for the things you're hungry for at the jeopardy of his own soul, or whatever passes for his soul. Now he's on a spot and you put him there because you're a greedy little tramp who'd see a guy in hell for knick-knacks.''

The spots burned hotter in her cheeks. Her bright bra rose and hovered on the peak of a deep breath. Her voice was a whispered whiplash.

"Get the hell out of here, Danny boy. Get out fast.''

I thought I might as well. "Sure. I only came to ask a question. I'll ask it and go. You heard from Eric?''

"Why should I hear from him?''

"You're his wife. You're the only person on earth he'd burn to hear from. The one person he'd try to contact. You know that.''

"There hasn't been any contact,'' she said. "I haven't heard from him, and if I had, you'd never know. . . .''

Downstairs, the heat bounced up around me in a transparent cloud. It was cooking hot. I stood there steaming on the sidewalk and told myself that Gloria was lying. Sometime, somehow, Eric had contacted her.

I thought about driving the blistering thirty miles out to the county seat but wondered if my jalopy could make it without developing vapor lock. Mostly, because I wanted to, I decided I couldn't. I didn't have to be there until tomorrow, anyhow. The note said tomorrow. I'd make the drive after dark, when the mercury might drop as low as eighty. In the meantime, there'd be time to buy the tall gin that no one would give me.

I climbed into my valve-in-head oven and went after it.

*     *     *

Richhill, the county seat, lay prostrate around its square. On the east side, withdrawn behind its defenses of awnings and lowered blinds, the Journeyman Hotel passively bore the full force of the heat. Across the square on the west side, beyond a margin of brown lawn, the buff stone county jail was like an outcropping of the sere earth. In the middle, a country plutocrat with a square block of personal earth and elms, was the county courthouse.

I slowly paced across the courthouse lawn towards the jail. Around me, under the trees, were slatted benches painted green. It seemed as if most of the older citizenry of the town were gasping out the afternoon on those benches. In the northwest corner of the yard, an iron flagpole rose from a huge circular concrete base. Around the circumference of the base, placed to stare toward the compass corners with an iron stoicism that was impervious to heat and cold and all suffering whatever, stood the sculptured figures of four Civil War combatants. Above their heads, the flag hung motionless in the still air.

Crossing the glaring, naked strip of street, I went up the stone steps of the jail into the oppressive disinfected air of a whitewashed hall. Ahead of me, the hall ended in a heavy steel grill. Through an open door to my left, I could see a green file cabinet and part of a flattop desk. On the desk beside a revolving electric fan I saw enormous shoes attached to legs that extended beyond my edge of vision. I stepped through the door and let my eyes continue their course up the legs, over a giant belly, and across a series of chins to a greasy expanse of folds and quivering pendants that did service as a face. Two little eyes twinkled at me with King Cole merriment. As a matter of fact, King Cole was sheriff in Richhill.

"Hello, son," he wheezed. "Come in and sit."

I did. King Cole closed his little eyes and blew a wet sigh through his thick lips. Then he swiped a sodden handkerchief under his chins, beginning with the top one and working down.

"Hot," he said. "Hot as hell."

"Yeah," I said. "Hotter for some than others."

Fanned air lifted the wispy hair on his head. His little eyes closed and opened, brightly bird-like.

"If you're referring to my weight, son, you couldn't be righter. It's hell to be fat in summer."

"I wasn't referring to your weight."

"No? I got an idea you were referring to *something*, but it's too hot to try to figure it."

"It's not hard to figure. I was thinking of a different kind of heat."

"You're still being fancy, son. It's too hot for fancy talk."

"My name's Clive," I said.

This time his eyes stayed closed while the air current crossed and recrossed his face.

He talked with the eyes closed.

"Clive. Special investigator. Now I get you. The Eric Sands business. Heat's on there, all right. Plenty of heat for that boy. If you catch him, that is. You got a lead?" Cole rubbed his nose reflectively.

"Could be," I said. "I figure he's close and been close all the time."

"Close is relative. Mexico instead of Brazil? The next county instead of the next state?" Cole was smiling now.

"Not even the next county," I said. "This county. This town, in fact. Or near it."

Small lids opened slowly over bright wariness. I had a sudden feeling that it made no different whether the lids were raised or lowered. I had a feeling that those sharp little pupils could see right through my pounding guts.

King Cole waved a sweaty hand and laughed. "In my county? Don't be silly, son. You'd better look somewhere else."

With a tremendous gutty sigh, he swung his feet off the desk and let them drop with a crash. Putting a hand on each arm of his chair, he heaved upward mightily. Waddling toward me, he fished papers and tobacco out of his shirt pocket and slowly rolled a cigarette. When he'd plastered it with saliva and stuck it between his lips, he looked at me with one bright eye. The one he wasn't using was screwed so tightly shut in encroaching fat that only the eyebrow suggested there'd ever been an eye there at all.

"You'll have to explain that remark, son. Like I said, fancy talk in this heat just confuses me."

From a pocket, I took a folded sheet of rough paper and tossed it onto the desk.

"Read it," I said.

The perspiration seeping from the coarse pores of his skin glistened on his sagging face and plastered his thin shirt to his bulging torso. A drop ran unheeded down his nose and onto the paper in his hands. His lips pursed, fashioning a silent sequence of vowels and consonants. If I'd wanted to, I could have read every word off his lips. But it wasn't necessary. I knew the brief note by heart.

Dear Danny:

I've got to see you. Just once more, for old times' sake. I know I've got no right to ask, but the heat's on, and there's no one else to turn to. You know the square in Richhill? Be on the bench just across from the hotel next Wednesday afternoon at three o'clock. I'll contact you there.

It was Eric's writing. His name was scrawled at the end. Fat King Cole stood looking down at the paper long after his lips had ceased their laborious pronunciation. He turned the note over and over in his blunt fingers, as if he were searching for esoteric markings. When he finally looked up at me, both eyes were unscrewed and bright with the same contempt I'd seen in the eyes of Francis Kruger and Gloria Sands.

"A mistake," King Cole said.

"Mistake?"

"Sending it to you, I mean. That part about old times' sake."

Anger was rising in me again, as it had risen so often these past few weeks.

"You can forget the sermon. I've told others, and I'll tell you. I've got a job. So have you, incidentally. Part of your job is taking fugitives into custody in this county. The only point is, what the hell do you intend to do about it?"

The little eyes went cold and flat with concentrated deadliness, and I thought to myself that the underestimating of fat men is a common error, and sometimes a fatal one.

"Don't get snotty, son. And don't tell me my job. This letter come from Richhill?"

"It was postmarked here."

"I wonder who mailed it?"

"I don't know. Probably the same person who'll make the contact on the bench."

"You want me to take the contact in?"

"No. That way I'd never get to Sands."

King Cole nodded.

"Maybe I'm slow, son. Just what is it you've got on your mind? Just where do I come in?"

"Wherever I say. Maybe not at all. It depends on how things work out. I just thought you ought to know about this. If I need you, I'll get in touch."

Removing the battered cigarette from his lips, King carefully licked the seam again. The eye he used only part time had once more retired to its socket, and the other had resumed its bright merriment. No evidence of deadly intent remained.

"It's your job, son. You want me, I'll be right here. It's just too damn hot to circulate."

I said thanks and went out. From the door I looked back and saw that he was already under the fan again, his eyes closed, the wisps fluttering on his head, the dead cigarette glued with dry saliva to his lax lips.

It was two-thirty. The note had said three. I went back across the courthouse lawn, past the bench the note had designated, and over to the hotel. From the window of my room upstairs I could look down across the street onto the courthouse lawn. There was a green bench under the spreading branches of a giant elm about ten feet beyond the sidewalk. An old man wearing a wilted Panama hat was sitting on the bench. He leaned forward with his hands folded on a gnarled stick and his white whiskers draped over his hands. He was staring into the glare of the street in front of him, and I wondered if he were reviewing the dead parades of past Memorial Days. At five of three, he hadn't moved, and I decided that maybe, after all, he was only asleep. I left the window and the room and the hotel and went over to join him on the bench. When I sat down, he still didn't move.

Leaning back against the bench, I tipped my Panama hat over my eyes and waited. About five minutes had passed when someone sat down on the bench between me and the old man. I waited a minute longer and opened my eyes, looking down at an angle under the tilted brim of my hat. The someone had smooth brown legs ending in blue socks and white, crepe-soled shoes. Her ankles were crossed, and her calves turned to perfection. I straightened, pushing my Panama way back, and turned for a full view. The legs, stretched straight, kept the promise of the ankles as far as a pair of faded blue denim shorts. The shorts took it capably to a sheer nylon shirt, and the shirt carried it on past valuable contributions to the fulfillment of a red mouth smiling and brown eyes reflecting the smile. Her hair was a shade lighter than the eyes, cut short for the season. A smooth job. The sleek, calculated country job that you buy in city salons for more money than most country girls have to spend. She was holding an unlighted cigarette to her lips. Then she smiled and said, "Light?"

I found a folder of gophers and struck one but its sodden head crumbled with a smear.

"Sorry," I said.

Soft shoulders lifted slightly under nylon. "They've got matches in the hotel tap room. Cold beer, too."

"Tap rooms usually do," I said.

"Sure. Probably a quiet corner as well. A corner where a couple of people could talk."

"With you, talking might seem like a waste of time."

"Maybe. It would depend on what I had to say."

I stood up. "Let's go see," I said.

Dream girl rose with a fluid motion that seemed to have no break, and together we made the long trip across the blistered strip. There was no air-conditioning in the tap room, but several strategic fans maintained the illusion of coolness that comes with air in motion. We found the corner that was quiet, except for the noise of the fans, and the beer that was cold without qualification. We sipped our suds for a while before she spoke: "You don't look like a special investigator," she said. "You look like a bright young guy with a future. Maybe a lawyer."

"I don't feel like an investigator, either. Nor a lawyer. Nor any kind of bright young guy whatever. I feel like I was going on two thousand years."

"It's your conscience," she said. "You should learn to ignore it."

"Sure," I said, "that's what they all say. Look, let's get down to business. What's a dame like you doing here?"

"You were expecting a man?"

"It seemed reasonable to expect."

"Why? Eric's quite a piece of boy. Lots of his friends are women."

"He always had the luck. There's no one nicer for a friend than a woman. If you can trust her, that is."

"You sound like a guy with a sad experience." She licked her lips.

"It's just the heat," I said. "It makes me say things."

"I know. What you need is a long rest in a cool spot like a lodge out on a river, up on a bluff, where a breeze always blows. Like mine, if you're interested. It's ten miles north on 27 State. Turn east on River Road Y. You can't miss it."

"Is this an invitation?"

"It's a suggestion."

I finished my beer and offered to buy her another one. She

accepted, and I stood up to leave her with it. As I turned to go, she said, "It's a hot drive in the sun. Night's better."

I said, "Sure," and went out of the tap room into the torrid lobby and upstairs to my room. The room was like a sweat box. I turned on a fan that didn't do much to change the condition and stripped off my shirt. Lying on the bed under the fan, I tried to make my mind blank, but all I managed was a confused retinal reaction of long legs in shorts that were apparently symbols of some significance. My brain was too seamy to solve the symbolism. The legs in white shorts were named Gloria, but the legs in blue shorts had never been introduced properly. Then Francis Kruger's face swelled upward into an enormous bulbous pink skull. The bulb kept swelling and swelling until finally it exploded and woke me up.

The white glare of the sun was gone from the window. I went over and looked down and across into the courthouse square where darkness was intensified by the spread of elms. A street lamp on the far corner across the square threw weak light against the buff stone of the county jail.

Turning away from the window, I put on my shirt and got my shoulder holster and .45 automatic from the closet shelf where I'd put them. I put on the holster and shoved the automatic into it. Then I covered them with the seersucker coat that matched my pants. That's the trouble with wearing a gun in hot weather. You have to wear a coat to hide it.

By my watch, it was three after nine. I turned off the fan and went out . . .

From where I stood, I could hear the soft undulations of invisible water far below. Ahead of me, the lodge lay sprawling on its bluff, one pale yellow light breaking through its dark mass. Walking quietly under wind-warped trees, I circled the lodge to its rear. Parked there in the gravel drive, near the rear entrance, were two cars. One was a standard sedan, the other a convertible. Neither in itself carried a mark of distinction, except that the convertible was by its character a car that might belong to a sleek-legged looker who cultivated an expensive rusticity. I went on around the lodge and up onto the veranda. The planking under my feet was sound. I made no noise as I tiptoed up to the house.

I stood against the door and listened. At my left, the light fell in a narrow path across the veranda floor from the single window that showed any light at all. The curtains, I could see, were sucked inward away from the window by a draft, and I could hear the remote and familiar drone of an exhaust fan at the rear of the lodge. Other than that sound, there was none. None but the crashing of my own pulse and the small, shrill sighing of my breath in my nostrils. After a long time, I took the .45 out of its holster and put it in the right pocket of my coat. Then I pounded on the door.

When the door opened, my sophisticated rustic stood looking out at me from a yellow frame. She had exchanged the faded blue shorts for faded blue jeans that hugged her hips and long flanks like tights, but otherwise, she was just as I'd seen her a few hours ago over beer suds. The eyes were still friendly and so were her lips.

"We've been waiting for you," she said. "Come on in."

I went. I stepped with my right foot and reached across her shoulder with my right arm. Even a guy who never got more than three stripes and a rocker in the big tussle knows that surprise is an essential element in attack. Before she could fade away, I had a grip on her right wrist. With my free left hand, I took the .45 out of my pocket. Then I guided her right and rearward until her back was against the wall. Her voice was hoarse and ragged with fury.

"What the hell's the idea?"

My laugh was no better than her voice. It cracked with tension.

"You know the idea, honey. You know it too damn well. And don't get the notion you can be a sultry hunk of bait for a death trap one minute and a lady the next. If I have to, I'll blow your pretty little spine to splinters."

Her eyes widened with fear; she stood perfectly still.

"That's right," I said. "And now you can listen. Listen real well, if you want to live to tell Francis Kruger how you fouled up this detail. Across the room there's a door. It's closed. It's the only closed door that opens into this room. Someone's behind it. Shall I tell you who? Eric Sands, or a venomous fat slob who's been Francis Kruger's bought man on Kruger's bought votes for more years than anyone wants to remember. Tell him to get out here. Tell him to get out with his hands raised, or I'll blast him out of his shell."

She spat an epithet and tried to break my grip. I twisted her arm hard, and she stopped. On the other side of the room, the closed door swung inward. Darkness beyond was splashed with flame and shattered by thunder. I felt two cushioned shocks, and the body in my arm seemed to leap upward and outward with a strange, wild violence. Then it sagged again, dead weight, and this time I let it go.

Hitting the floor in a dive, I rolled, scrambling for the wall across the room. Pressed against it, out of range, my shoulder blades maintaining contact with knotty paneling, I inched slowly toward the door. Feet short of it, I stopped. On the floor where she had fallen under King Cole's fire, the beautiful contact was a huddle of nylon and denim. On the nylon was a slowly spreading stain that was as red as the margin of her friendly smile. Around the frame of the door, in the dark room, I heard the faint sound of blubbery breathing, the suggestion of elephantine movement.

"King Cole," I said. "Fat King Cole. Look out and see your handiwork, King. She's on the floor over there. She's on the floor with two of your slugs in her. You know how it is to die with two slugs in you, King? You know how it is to die with blood in your throat? Come out and I'll show you. I've got a .45 for you, King. The biggest gun I've got for the biggest hulk I know."

From the dark room, his windy wheeze was the oral expression of the deadly flat eyes I had seen briefly that afternoon.

"Come after me, son. Just come through the door."

I scraped shoulder blades a little farther along the paneling.

"I'll come. I'll come in my own time. You think I'd walk into this thing blind? You think I'd walk in like a sheep to slaughter? I've known the setup for days, King. I've had the idea for a long time. Ever since the note came. The note I showed you this afternoon, as if you'd never heard of it."

"You're a real brainy boy. Too bad you've got to die."

"Not really brainy. I didn't have to be. It was easy to see you'd run Sands down. It didn't take a genius to figure that he'd written the note under pressure. You've got him in there now, King. Under a gun, just like you had him when he wrote the note. You planned to shoot him to death after you took care of me. A real pretty picture. Very pat. Investigator and fugitive slaughtered by each other in a gun duel. Big headlines for the public. Phony as hell, but not hard to put over with someone like Francis Kruger behind it."

I laughed, and this time, maybe because I'd talked myself into it, there was, above and beyond the strain of tension, a ring of exultation that I really felt.

"There's a joke in it, King. A great big joke on you and Francis Kruger and all your slimy ilk. Shall I tell you why I smelled the trap? Shall I tell you how I knew the note was phony? *Because I hid Eric Sands myself.* That's right, King. I hid him myself in the Northside hole where you finally smoked him out, and in the beginning, I was the only one on earth besides himself who knew where he was. And if he'd had any guts to lie quietly, he'd be there yet. I told him not to contact anyone. Above all, I told him not to contact Gloria. But he couldn't resist it. So behind my back he got in touch with her, and the first thing she did was to sell him out to Kruger for the promise of more gadgets and knick-knacks than her yearning, rotten heart had ever dreamed of.''

I stopped and waited, listening. Listening for the slight sounds of bulk in motion. But in the dark room there was now no sound at all.

"At least, in the end,'' I said, "he used his brains. He shut his teeth on the fact that I was the one who'd cached him. He wrote the note, just as you wanted, and by doing it, *he let you tell me yourselves that you were setting a trap for Danny Clive.* Funny, isn't it, King? Everywhere I went, the scum who wanted Eric's blood looked at me down their snotty noses because I was a guy betraying a one-time pal. And all the time, I was the only person alive willing to lift a hand to save him. Sure. Very funny. I nearly died laughing. I really nearly died laughing.''

Then I heard a sound. The shifting of great weight on boards that gave a little. It seemed to come from back in the room, wide of the blade of light that splashed through the darkness from the open door. Abruptly, I jumped across to the other side of the opening, twisting from the hips and firing blindly back into the room. There was the tremendous clawing sound of a great body moving precipitately, and I wheeled, diving back through the door and out of the light. Now the King and I were in the same dark room fighting for our lives.

The sudden taxing of his fat-cramped lungs had brought the wind whistling through his teeth. I heard the sound and fired at it. There was an answering flash and a glimpse behind the flash. I never even felt the searing burn across my shoulder until the room had stopped rocking and my .45 was empty. Crouching in the darkness, listening for more sound, I realized at last that the most important sound of all, the crashing of his huge bulk, had been lost in the blasting of gun powder. My ears ached and pounded from the noise.

Moving slowly, feeling the shoulder now, I found a switch and made light. He was lying on his face by the opposite wall. His gun lay loose near the clawed fingers of an outstretched hand. Even as I watched, the fingers jerking spasmodically relaxed a little, and the flabby mountain of his prone body seemed to settle softly down into the floor.

In one corner of the room was a studio couch. Lying on the couch, taped at wrists and ankles and across the mouth, was Eric Sands. His pale blue eyes rolled toward me in their sockets, and under the tape, the weak mouth I knew so well tried to fashion a grin.

I went over and jerked off the tape. Not gently. I did it with savage relish, bringing hair and blood and leaving across his face rising and angry welts. He came up on the couch slowly, swinging his feet to the floor. Now he managed a sickly completion of the grin.

"Good old Danny," he said.

My anger required no violence of expression.

"Sure," I said. "There's a dead woman in the next room and a dead man in this one, and all you've got to say is good old Danny. I pawned my good faith to save your worthless skin, and all you've got to say is good old Danny. Good old Danny's dead, brother, and you're dead, too. I hocked the little honor I had for a friend who never was, and now I'm getting it out of hock. You're going back. You're going back to the grand jury, and you're going to point a long finger at Francis Kruger. You'll do it, or I'll blow your brains out."

He stood up, trying his weight on numb legs, and his thin, handsome face settled in lines of tired acceptance.

"Sure, Danny, sure. It's past time I should have gone. Way past time."

I turned out the light on Fat King Cole, and we went out through the other room. On the way, I knelt beside the nylon and denim and put my hand near the spreading stain. She was dead, all right. A dead waste of things that should never have been wasted. I stood up and said, "We'll get the State Patrol on this," and we went on outside, into the river mists.

# John Lutz

# RIDE THE LIGHTNING

A SLANTED SHEET OF RAIN SWEPT LIKE A SCYTHE ACROSS Placid Cove Trailer Park. For an instant, an intricate web of lightning illuminated the park. The rows of mobile homes loomed square and still and pale against the night, reminding Nudger of tombs with awnings and TV antennas. He held his umbrella at a sharp angle to the wind as he walked, putting a hand in his pocket to pull out a scrap of paper and double-check the address he was trying to find in the maze of trailers. Finally, at the end of Tranquility Lane, he found Number 307 and knocked on its metal door.

"I'm Nudger," he said when the door opened.

For several seconds the woman in the doorway stood staring out at him, rain blowing in beneath the metal awning to spot her cornflower-colored dress and ruffle her straw blond hair. She was tall but very thin, fragile-looking, and appeared at first glance to be about twelve years old. Second glance revealed her to be in her mid-twenties. She had slight crow's feet at the corners of her luminous blue eyes when she winced as a raindrop struck her face, a knowing cast to her oversized, girlish, full-lipped mouth, and slightly buck teeth. Her looks were hers alone. There was no one who could look much like her, no middle ground with her; men would consider her scrawny and homely, or they would see her as uniquely sensuous. Nudger liked coltish girl-women; he catalogued her as attractive.

"Whoeee!" she said at last, as if seeing for the first time beyond Nudger. "Ain't it raining something terrible?"

"It is," Nudger agreed. "And on me."

Her entire thin body gave a quick, nervous kind of jerk as she smiled apologetically. "I'm Holly Ann Adams, Mr. Nudger. And you are getting wet, all right. Come on in."

She moved aside and Nudger stepped up into the trailer. He expected it to be surprisingly spacious; he'd once lived in a trailer and remembered them as such. This one was cramped and confining. The furniture was cheap and its upholstery was threadbare; a portable black-and-white TV on a tiny table near the Scotch-plaid sofa was blaring shouts of ecstasy emitted by "The Price Is Right" contestants. The air was thick with the smell of something greasy that had been fried too long.

Holly Ann cleared a stack of *People* magazines from a vinyl chair and motioned for Nudger to sit down. He folded his umbrella, left it by the door, and sat. Holly Ann started to say something, then jerked her body in that peculiar way of hers, almost a twitch, as if she'd just remembered something not only with her mind but with her body and muscle, and walked over and switched off the noisy television. In the abrupt silence, the rain seemed to beat on the metal roof with added fury. "Now we can talk," Holly Ann proclaimed, sitting opposite Nudger on the undersized sofa. "You a sure-enough private investigator?"

"I'm that," Nudger said. "Did someone recommend me to you, Miss Adams?"

"Gotcha out of the Yellow Pages. And if you're gonna work for me, it might as well be Holly Ann without the Adams."

"Except on the check," Nudger said.

She grinned a devilish twelve-year-old's grin. "Oh, sure, don't worry none about that. I wrote you out a check already, just gotta fill in the amount. That is, if you agree to take the job. You might not."

"Why not?"

"It has to do with my fiancé, Curtis Colt."

Nudger listened for a few seconds to the rain crashing on the roof. "The Curtis Colt who's going to be executed next week?"

"That's the one. Only he didn't kill that liquor store woman; I know it for a fact. It ain't right he should have to ride the lightning."

"Ride the lightning?"

"That's what convicts call dying in the electric chair, Mr. Nudger. They call that chair lotsa things: Old Sparky . . . The Lord's Frying Pan. But Curtis don't belong sitting in it wired up, and I can prove it."

"It's a little late for that kind of talk," Nudger said. "Or did you testify for Curtis in court?"

"Nope. Couldn't testify. You'll see why. All them lawyers and the judge and jury don't even know about me. Curtis didn't want them to know, so he never told them." She crossed her legs and swung her right calf jauntily. She was smiling as if trying to flirt him into wanting to know more about the job so he could free Curtis Colt by a governor's reprieve at the last minute, as in an old movie.

Nudger looked at her gauntly pretty, country-girl face and said, "Tell me about Curtis Colt, Holly Ann."

"You mean you didn't read about him in the newspapers or see him on the television?"

"I only scan the media for misinformation. Give me the details."

"Well, they say Curtis was inside the liquor store, sticking it up—him and his partner had done three other places that night, all of 'em gas stations, though—when the old man that owned the place came out of a back room and seen his wife there behind the counter with her hands up and Curtis holding the gun on her. So the old man lost his head and ran at Curtis, and Curtis had to shoot him. Then the woman got mad when she seen that and ran at Curtis, and Curtis shot her. She's the one that died. The old man, he'll live, but he can't talk nor think nor even feed himself."

Nudger remembered more about the case now. Curtis Colt had been found guilty of first-degree murder, and because of a debate in the legislature over the merits of cyanide gas versus electricity, the state was breaking out the electric chair to make him its first killer executed by electricity in over a quarter of a century. Those of the back-to-basics school considered that progress.

"They're gonna shoot Curtis full of electricity next Saturday, Mr. Nudger," Holly Ann said plaintively. She sounded like a little girl complaining that the grade on her report card wasn't fair.

"I know," Nudger said. "But I don't see how I can help you. Or, more specifically, help Curtis."

"You know what they say thoughts really are, Mr. Nudger?" Holly Ann said, ignoring his professed helplessness. Her wide blue eyes were vague as she searched for words. "Thoughts ain't really nothing but tiny electrical impulses in the brain. I read that somewheres or other. What I can't help wondering is, when they shoot all that electricity into Curtis, what's it gonna be like to his thinking? How long will it seem like to him before he finally dies? Will there be a big burst of crazy thoughts along with the pain? I know it sounds loony, but I can't help laying awake nights thinking about that, and I feel I just gotta do whatever's left to try and help Curtis.''

There was a sort of checkout-line tabloid logic in that, Nudger conceded; if thoughts were actually weak electrical impulses, then high-voltage electrical impulses could become exaggerated, horrible thoughts. Anyway, try to disprove it to Holly Ann.

''They never did catch Curtis's buddy, the driver who sped away and left him in that service station, did they?'' Nudger asked.

''Nope. Curtis never told who the driver was, neither, no matter how much he was threatened. Curtis is a stubborn man.''

Nudger was getting the idea.

''But you know who was driving the car.''

''Yep. And he told me him and Curtis was miles away from that liquor store at the time it was robbed. When he seen the police closing in on Curtis in that gas station where Curtis was buying cigarettes, he hit the accelerator and got out of the parking lot before they could catch him. The police didn't even get the car's license plate number.''

Nudger rubbed a hand across his chin, watching Holly Ann swing her leg as if it were a shapely metronome. She was barefoot and wearing no nylon hose. ''The jury thought Curtis not only was at the liquor store, but that he shot the old man and woman in cold blood.''

''That ain't true, though. Not according to—'' she caught herself before uttering the man's name.

''Curtis's friend,'' Nudger finished.

''That's right. And he ought to know,'' Holly Ann said righteously, as if that piece of information were the trump card and the argument was over.

''None of this means anything unless the driver comes forward and substantiates that he was with Curtis somewhere other than at the liquor store when it was robbed.''

Holly Ann nodded and stopped swinging her leg. ''I know. But he won't. He can't. That's where you come in.''

''My profession might enjoy a reputation a notch lower than

dognapper,'' Nudger said, ''but I don't hire out to do anything illegal.''

''What I want you to do is legal,'' Holly Ann said in a hurt little voice. Nudger looked past her into the dollhouse kitchen and saw an empty gin bottle. He wondered if she might be slightly drunk. ''It's the eyewitness accounts that got Curtis convicted,'' she went on. ''And those people are wrong. I want you to figure out some way to convince them it wasn't Curtis they saw that night.''

''Four people, two of them customers in the store, picked Curtis out of a police lineup.''

''So what? Ain't eyewitnesses often mistaken?''

Nudger had to admit that they were, though he didn't see how they could be in this case. There were, after all, four of them. And yet, Holly Ann was right; it was amazing how people could sometimes be so certain that the wrong man had committed a crime just five feet in front of them.

''I want you to talk to them witnesses,'' Holly Ann said. ''Find out *why* they think Curtis was the killer. Then show them how they might be wrong and get them to change what they said. We got the truth on our side, Mr. Nudger. At least one witness will change his story when he's made to think about it, because Curtis wasn't where they said he was.''

''Curtis has exhausted all his appeals,'' Nudger said. ''Even if all the witnesses changed their stories, it wouldn't necessarily mean he'd get a new trial.''

''Maybe not, but I betcha they wouldn't kill him. They couldn't stand the publicity if enough witnesses said they was wrong, it was somebody else killed the old woman. Then, just maybe, eventually, he'd get another trial and get out of prison.''

Nudger was awed. Here was foolish optimism that transcended even his own. He had to admire Holly Ann.

The leg started pumping again beneath the cornflower-colored dress. When Nudger lowered his gaze to stare at it, Holly Ann said, ''So will you help me, Mr. Nudger?''

''Sure. It sounds easy.''

''Why should I worry about it anymore?'' Randy Gantner asked Nudger, leaning on his shovel. He didn't mind talking to Nudger; it meant a break from his construction job on the new Interstate 170 cloverleaf. ''Colt's been found guilty and he's going to the chair, ain't he?''

The afternoon sun was hammering down on Nudger, warming the back of his neck and making his stomach queasy. He thumbed an antacid tablet off the roll he kept in his shirt pocket and popped one of the white disks into his mouth. With his other hand, he was holding up a photograph of Curtis for Gantner to see. It was a snapshot Holly Ann had given him of the wiry, shirtless Colt leaning on a fence past and holidng a beer can high in a mock toast: this one's for Death!

"This is a photograph you never saw in court. I just want you to look at it closely and tell me again if you're sure the man you saw in the liquor store was Colt. Even if it makes no difference in whether he's executed, it will help ease the mind of somebody who loves him."

"I'd be a fool to change my story about what happened now that the trial's over," Gantner said logically.

"You'd be a murderer if you really weren't sure."

Gantner sighed, dragged a dirty red handkerchief from his jeans pocket, and wiped his beefy, perspiring face. He peered at the photo, then shrugged. "It's him, Colt, the guy I seen shoot the man and woman when I was standing in the back aisle of the liquor store. If he'd known me and Sanders was back there, he'd have probably zapped us along with them old folks."

"You're positive it's the same man?"

Gantner spat off to the side and frowned; Nudger was becoming a pest, and the foreman was staring. "I said it to the police and the jury, Nudger; that little twerp Colt did the old lady in. Ask me, he deserves what he's gonna get."

"Did you actually see the shots fired?"

"Nope. Me and Sanders was in the back aisle looking for some reasonable-priced bourbon when we heard the shots, then looked around to see Curtis Colt back away, turn, and run out to the car. Looked like a black or dark green old Ford. Colt fired another shot as it drove away."

"Did you see the driver?"

"Sort of. Skinny dude with curly black hair and a mustache. That's what I told the cops. That's all I seen. That's all I know."

And that was the end of the conversation. The foreman was walking toward them, glaring. *Thunk!* Gantner's shovel sliced deep into the earth, speeding the day when there'd be another place for traffic to get backed up. Nudger thanked him and advised him not to work too hard in the hot sun.

"You wanna help?" Gantner asked, grinning sweatily.

"I'm already doing some digging of my own," Nudger said, walking away before the foreman arrived.

The other witnesses also stood by their identifications. The fourth and last one Nudger talked with, an elderly woman named Iris Langeneckert, who had been walking her dog near the liquor store and had seen Curtis Colt dash out the door and into the getaway car, said something that Gantner had touched on. When she'd described the getaway car driver, like Gantner she said he was a thin man with curly black hair and a beard or mustache, then she had added, "Like Curtis Colt's hair and mustache."

Nudger looked again at the snapshot Holly Ann had given him. Curtis Colt was about five foot nine, skinny, and mean-looking, with a broad bandito mustache and a mop of curly, greasy black hair. Nudger wondered if it was possible that the getaway car driver had been Curtis Colt himself, and his accomplice had killed the shopkeeper. Even Nudger found that one hard to believe.

He drove to his second-floor office in the near suburb of Maplewood and sat behind his desk in the blast of cold air from the window unit, sipping the complimentary paper cup of iced tea he'd brought up from Danny's Donuts directly below. The sweet smell of the doughnuts was heavier than usual in the office; Nudger had never quite gotten used to it and what it did to his sensitive stomach.

When he was cool enough to think clearly again, he decided he needed more information on the holdup, and on Curtis Colt, from a more objective source than Holly Ann Adams. He phoned Lieutenant Jack Hammersmith at home and was told by Hammersmith's son Jed that Hammersmith had just driven away to go to work on the afternoon shift, so it would be awhile before he got to his office.

Nudger checked his answering machine, proving that hope did indeed spring eternal in a fool's breast. There was a terse message from his former wife Eileen demanding last month's alimony payment; a solemn-voiced young man reading an address where Nudger could send a check to help pay to form a watchdog committee that would stop the utilities from continually raising their rates; and a cheerful man informing Nudger that with the labels from ten packages of a brand-name hot dog he could get a Cardinals ballgame ticket at half price. (That meant eating over eighty hot dogs. Nudger calculated that baseball season would be over by the time he did that.) Everyone seemed to want some of Nudger's money. No one wanted to pay Nudger any money. Except for Holly Ann Adams. Nudger decided he'd better step up his efforts on the Curtis Colt case.

He tilted back his head, downed the last dribble of iced tea, then tried to eat what was left of the crushed ice. But the ice clung stubbornly to the bottom of the cup, taunting him. Nudger's life was like that.

He crumpled up the paper cup and tossed it, ice and all, into the wastebasket. Then he went downstairs where his Volkswagen was parked in the shade behind the building and drove east on Manchester, toward downtown and the Third District station house.

Police Lieutenant Jack Hammersmith was in his Third District office, sleek, obese, and cool-looking behind his wide metal desk. He was pounds and years away from the handsome cop who'd been Nudger's partner a decade ago in a two-man patrol car. Nudger could still see traces of a dashing quality in the flesh-upholstered Hammersmith, but he wondered if that was only because he'd known Hammersmith ten years ago.

"Sit down, Nudge," Hammersmith invited, his lips smiling but his slate-gray, cop's eyes unreadable. If eyes were the windows to the soul, his shades were always down.

Nudger sat in one of the straight-backed chairs in front of Hammersmith's desk. "I need some help," he said.

"Sure," Hammersmith said, "you never come see me just to trade recipes or to sit and rock." Hammersmith was partial to irony; it was a good thing, in his line of work.

"I need to know more about Curtis Colt," Nudger said.

Hammersmith got one of his vile greenish cigars out of his shirt pocket and stared intently at it, as if its paper ring label might reveal some secret of life and death. "Colt, eh? The guy who's going to ride the lightning?"

"That's the second time in the past few days I've heard that expression. The first time was from Colt's fiancée. She thinks he's innocent."

"Fiancées think along those lines. Is she our client?"

Nudger nodded but didn't volunteer Holly Ann's name.

"Gullibility makes the world go round," Hammersmith said. "I was in charge of the Homicide investigation on that one. There's not a chance Colt is innocent, Nudge."

"Four eyewitness I.D.'s is compelling evidence," Nudger admitted. "What about the getaway car driver? His description is a lot like Colt's. Maybe he's the one who did the shooting and Colt was the driver."

"Colt's lawyer hit on that. The jury didn't buy it. Neither do I. The man is guilty, Nudge."

"You know how inaccurate eyewitness accounts are," Nudger persisted.

That seemed to get Hammersmith mad. He lit the cigar. The office immediately fogged up.

Nudger made his tone more amicable. "Mind if I look at the file on the Colt case?"

Hammersmith gazed thoughtfully at Nudger through a dense greenish haze. He inhaled, exhaled; the haze became a cloud. "How come this fiancée didn't turn up at the trial to testify for Colt? She could have at least lied and said he was with her that night."

"Colt apparently didn't want her subjected to taking the stand."

"How noble," Hammersmith said. "What makes this fiancée think her prince charming is innocent?"

"She knows he was somewhere else when the shopkeepers were shot."

"But not with her."

"Nope."

"Well, that's refreshing."

Maybe it was refreshing enough to make up Hammersmith's mind. He picked up the phone and asked for the Colt file. Nudger could barely make out what he was saying around the fat cigar, but apparently everyone at the Third was used to Hammersmith and could interpret cigarese.

The file didn't reveal much that Nudger didn't know. Fifteen minutes after the liquor store shooting, officers from a two-man patrol car, acting on the broadcast description of the gunman, approached Curtis Colt inside a service station where he was buying a pack of cigarettes from a vending machine. A car that had been parked near the end of the dimly lighted lot had sped away as they'd entered the station office. The officers had gotten only a glimpse of a dark green old Ford; they hadn't made out the license plate number but thought it might start with the letter "L."

Colt had surrendered without a struggle, and that night at the Third District Station the four eyewitnesses had picked him out of a lineup. Their description of the getaway car matched that of the car the police had seen speeding from the service station. The loot from the holdup, and several gas station holdups committed earlier that night, wasn't on Colt, but probably it was in the car.

"Colt's innocence just jumps out of the file at you, doesn't it, Nudge?" Hammersmith said. He was grinning a fat grin around the fat cigar.

"What about the murder weapon?"

"Colt was unarmed when we picked him up."

"Seems odd."

"Not really," Hammersmith said. "He was planning to pay for the cigarettes. And maybe the gun was still too hot to touch so he left it in the car. Maybe it's still hot; it got a lot of use for one night."

Closing the file folder and laying it on a corner of Hammersmith's desk, Nudger stood up. "Thanks, Jack. I'll keep you tapped in if I learn anything interesting."

"Don't bother keeping me informed on this one, Nudge. It's over. I don't see how even a fiancée can doubt Colt's guilt."

Nudger shrugged, trying not to breathe too deeply in the smoke-hazed office. "Maybe it's an emotional thing. She thinks that because thought waves are tiny electrical impulses, Colt might experience time warp and all sorts of grotesque thoughts when all that voltage shoots through him. She has bad dreams."

"I'll bet she does," Hammersmith said. "I'll bet Colt has bad dreams, too. Only he deserves his. And maybe she's right."

"About what?"

"About all that voltage distorting thought and time. Who's to say?"

"Not Curtis Colt," Nudger said. "Not after they throw the switch."

"It's a nice theory, though," Hammersmith said. "I'll remember it. It might be a comforting thing to tell the murder victim's family."

"Sometimes," Nudger said, "you think just like a cop who's seen too much."

"Any of it's too much, Nudge," Hammersmith said with surprising sadness. He let more greenish smoke drift from his nostrils and the corners of his mouth; he looked like a stone Buddha seated behind the desk, one in which incense burned.

Nudger coughed and said goodbye.

"Only two eyewitnesses are needed to convict," Nudger said to Holly Ann the next day in her trailer, "and in this case there are four. None of them is at all in doubt about their identification of Curtis Colt as the killer. I have to be honest; it's time you should face the fact that Colt is guilty and that you're wasting your money on my services."

"All them witnesses know what's going to happen to Curtis," Holly Ann said. "They'd never want to live with the notion they might have made a mistake, killed an innocent man, so they've got themselves convinced that they're positive it was Curtis they saw that night."

"Your observation on human psychology is sound," Nudger said, "but I don't think it will help us. The witnesses were just as certain three months ago at the trial. I took the time to read the court transcript; the jury had no choice but to find Colt guilty, and the evidence hasn't changed."

Holly Ann drew her legs up and clasped her knees to her chest with both arms. Her little-girl posture matched her little-girl faith in her lover's innocence. She believed the white knight must arrive at any moment and snatch Curtis Colt from the electrical jaws of death. She believed hard. Nudger could almost hear his armor clank when he walked.

She wanted him to believe just as hard. "I see you need to be convinced of Curtis's innocence," she said wistfully. There was no doubt he'd forced her into some kind of corner. "If you come here tonight at eight, Mr. Nudger, I'll convince you."

"How?"

"I can't say. You'll understand why tonight."

"Why do we have to wait till tonight?"

"Oh, you'll see."

Nudger looked at the waiflike creature curled in the corner of the sofa. He felt as if they were playing a childhood guessing game while Curtis Colt waited his turn in the electric chair. Nudger had never seen an execution; he'd heard it took longer than most people thought for the condemned to die. His stomach actually twitched.

"Can't we do this now with twenty questions?" he asked.

Holly Ann shook her head. "No, Mr. Nudger."

Nudger sighed and stood up, feeling as if he were about to bump his head on the trailer's low ceiling even though he was barely six feet tall.

"Make sure you're on time tonight, Mr. Nudger," Holly Ann said as he went out the door. "It's important."

* * *

At eight on the nose that evening Nudger was sitting at the tiny table in Holly Ann's kitchenette. Across from him was a thin, nervous man in his late twenties or early thirties, dressed in a longsleeved shirt despite the heat, and wearing sunglasses with silver mirror lenses. Holly Ann introduced the man as "Len, but that's not his real name," and said he was Curtis Colt's accomplice and the driver of their getaway car on the night of the murder.

"But me and Curtis was nowhere near the liquor store when them folks got shot," Len said vehemently.

Nudger assumed the sunglasses were so he couldn't effectively identify Len if it came to a showdown in court. Len had lank, dark brown hair that fell to below his shoulders, and when he moved his arm Nudger caught sight of something blue and red on his briefly exposed wrist. A tattoo. Which explained the longsleeved shirt.

"You can understand why Len couldn't come forth and testify for Curtis in court," Holly Ann said.

Nudger said he could understand that. Len would have had to incriminate himself.

"We was way on the other side of town," Len said, "casing another service station, when that liquor store killing went down. Heck, we never held up nothing but service stations. They was our specialty."

Which was true, Nudger had to admit. Colt had done time for armed robbery six years ago after sticking up half-a-dozen service stations within a week. And all the other holdups he'd been tied to this time around were of service stations. The liquor store was definitely a departure in his M.O., one not noted in court during Curtis Colt's rush to judgment.

"Your hair is in your favor," Nudger said to Len.

"Huh?"

"Your hair didn't grow that long in the three months since the liquor store killing. The witnesses described the getaway car driver as having shorter, curlier hair, like Colt's, and a mustache."

Len shrugged. "I'll be honest with you—it don't help at all. Me and Curtis was kinda the same type. So to confuse any witnesses, in case we got caught, we made each other look even more alike. I'd tuck up my long hair and wear a wig that looked like Curtis's hair. My mustache was real, like Curtis's. I shaved it off a month ago. We did look alike at a glance; sorta like brothers."

Nudger bought that explanation; it wasn't uncommon for a team of holdup men to play tricks to confuse witnesses and the police. Too many lawyers had gotten in the game; the robbers, like the cops, were taking the advice of their attorneys and thinking about a potential trial even before the crime was committed.

"Is there any way, then, to prove you were across town at the time of the murder?" Nudger asked, looking at the two small Nudgers staring back at him from the mirror lenses.

"There's just my word," Len said, rather haughtily.

Nudger didn't bother telling him what that was worth. Why antagonize him?

"I just want you to believe Curtis is innocent," Len said with desperation. "Because he is! And so am I!"

And Nudger understood why Len was here, taking the risk. If Colt was guilty of murder, Len was guilty of being an accessory to the crime. Once Curtis Colt had ridden the lightning, Len would have hanging over him the possibility of an almost certain life sentence, and perhaps even his own ride on the lightning, if he were ever caught. It wasn't necessary to actually squeeze the trigger to be convicted of murder.

"I need for you to try extra hard to prove Curtis is innocent," Len said. His thin lips quivered; he was near tears.

"Are you giving Holly Ann the money to pay me?" Nudger asked.

"Some of it, yeah. From what Curtis and me stole. And I gave Curtis's share to Holly Ann, too. Me and her are fifty-fifty on this."

Dirty money, Nudger thought. Dirty job. Still, if Curtis Colt happened to be innocent, trying against the clock to prove it was a job that needed to be done.

"Okay. I'll stay on the case."

"Thanks," Len said. His narrow hand moved impulsively across the table and squeezed Nudger's arm in gratitude. Len had the look of an addict; Nudger wondered if the longsleeved shirt was to hide needle tracks as well as the tattoo.

Len stood up. "Stay here with Holly Ann for ten minutes while I make myself scarce. I gotta know I wasn't followed. You understand it ain't that I don't trust you; a man in my position has gotta be sure, is all."

"I understand. Go."

Len gave a spooked smile and went out the door. Nudger heard his running footfalls on the gravel outside the trailer. Nudger was forty-three years old and ten pounds overweight; lean and speedy Len needed a ten-minute head start like Sinatra needed singing lessons.

"Is Len a user?" Nudger asked Holly Ann.

"Sometimes. But my Curtis never touched no dope."

"You know I have to tell the police about this conversation, don't you?"

Holly Ann nodded. "That's why we arranged it this way. They won't be any closer to Len than before."

"They might want to talk to you, Holly Ann."

She shrugged. "It don't matter. I don't know where Len is, or even his real name or how to get in touch with him. He'll find out all he needs to know about Curtis by reading the papers."

"You have a deceptively devious mind," Nudger told her, "considering that you look like Barbie Doll's country kid cousin."

Holly Ann smiled, surprised and pleased. "Do you find me attractive, Mr. Nudger?"

"Yes. And painfully young."

For just a moment Nudger almost thought of Curtis Colt as a lucky man. Then he looked at his watch, saw that his ten minutes were about up, and said goodbye. If Barbie had a kid cousin, Ken probably had one somewhere, too. And time was something you couldn't deny. Ask Curtis Colt.

"It doesn't wash with me," Hammersmith said from behind his desk, puffing angrily on his cigar. Angrily because it did wash a little bit; he didn't like the possibility, however remote, of sending an innocent man to his death. That was every good homicide cop's nightmare. "This Len character is just trying to keep himself in the clear on a murder charge."

"You could read it that way," Nudger admitted.

"It would help if you gave us a better description of Len," Hammersmith said gruffly, as if Nudger were to blame for Curtis Colt's accomplice still walking around free.

"I gave you what I could," Nudger said. "Len didn't give me much to pass on. He's streetwise and scared and knows what's at stake."

Hammersmith nodded, his fit of pique past. But the glint of weary frustration remained in his eyes.

"Are you going to question Holly Ann?" Nudger said.

"Sure, but it won't do any good. She's probably telling the

truth. Len would figure we'd talk to her; he wouldn't tell her how to find him.''

"You could stake out her trailer.''

"Do you think Holly Ann and Len might be lovers?''

"No.''

Hammersmith shook his head. "Then they'll probably never see each other again. Watching her trailer would be a waste of manpower.''

Nudger knew Hammersmith was right. He stood up to go.

"What are you going to do now?'' Hammersmith asked.

"I'll talk to the witnesses again. I'll read the court transcript again. And I'd like to talk with Curtis Colt.''

"They don't allow visitors on Death Row, Nudge, only temporary boarders.''

"This case is an exception,'' Nudger said. "Will you try to arrange it?''

Hammersmith chewed thoughtfully on his cigar. Since he'd been the officer in charge of the murder investigation, he'd been the one who'd nailed Curtis Colt. That carried an obligation.

"I'll phone you soon,'' he said, "let you know.''

Nudger thanked Hammersmith and walked down the hall into the clear, breathable air of the booking area.

That day he managed to talk again to all four eyewitnesses. Two of them got mad at Nudger for badgering them. They all stuck to their stories. Nudger reported this to Holly Ann at the Right-Steer Steakhouse, where she worked as a waitress. Several customers that afternoon got tears with their baked potatoes.

Hammersmith phoned Nudger that evening.

"I managed to get permission for you to talk to Colt,'' he said, "but don't get excited. Colt won't talk to you. He won't talk to anyone, not even a clergyman. He'll change his mind about the clergyman, but not about you.''

"Did you tell him I was working for Holly Ann?''

"I had that information conveyed to him. He wasn't impressed. He's one of the stoic ones on Death Row.''

Nudger's stomach kicked up, growled something that sounded like a hopeless obscenity. If even Curtis Colt wouldn't cooperate, how could he be helped? Absently Nudger peeled back the aluminum foil on a roll of antacid tablets and slipped two chalky white disks into his mouth. Hammersmith knew about his nervous stomach and must have heard him chomping the tablets. "Take it easy, Nudge. This isn't your fault.''

"Then why do I feel like it is?"

"Because you feel too much of everything. That's why you had to quit the department."

"We've got another day before the execution," Nudger said. "I'm going to go through it all again. I'm going to talk to each of those witnesses even if they try to run when they see me coming. Maybe somebody will say something that will let in some light."

"There's no light out there, Nudge. You're wasting your time. Give up on this one and move on."

"Not yet," Nudger said. "There's something elusive here that I can't quite grab."

"And never will," Hammersmith said. "Forget it, Nudge. Live your life and let Curtis Colt lose his."

Hammersmith was right. Nothing Nudger did helped Curtis Colt in the slightest. At eight o'clock Saturday morning, while Nudger was preparing breakfast in his apartment, Colt was put to death in the electric chair. He'd offered no last words before two thousand volts had turned him from something into nothing.

Nudger heard the news of Colt's death on his kitchen radio. He went ahead and ate his eggs, but he skipped the toast.

That afternoon he consoled a numbed and frequently sobbing Holly Ann and apologized for being powerless to stop her true love's execution. She was polite, trying to be brave. She preferred to suffer alone. Her boss at the Right-Steer gave her the rest of the day off, and Nudger drove her home.

Nudger slept a total of four hours during the next two nights. On Monday, he felt compelled to attend Curtis Colt's funeral. There were about a dozen people clustered around the grave, including the state-appointed clergyman and pallbearers. Nudger stood off to one side during the brief service. Holly Ann, looking like a child playing dress-up in black, stood well off to the other side. They didn't exchange words, only glances.

As the coffin was lowered into the earth, Nudger watched Holly Ann walk to where a taxi was waiting by a weathered stone angel. The cab wound its way slowly along the snaking narrow cemetery road to tall iron gates and the busy street. Holly Ann never looked back.

That night Nudger realized what was bothering him, and for the first time since Curtis Colt's death, he slept well.

\*       \*       \*

In the morning he began watching Holly Ann's trailer.

At seven-thirty she emerged, dressed in her yellow waitress uniform, and got into another taxi. Nudger followed in his battered Volkswagen Beetle as the cab drove her the four miles to her job at the Right-Steer Steakhouse. She didn't look around as she paid the driver and walked inside through the molded plastic Old-West-saloon swinging doors.

At six that evening another cab drove her home, making a brief stop at a grocery store.

It went that way for the rest of the week, trailer to work to trailer. Holly Ann had no visitors other than the plain brown paper bag she took home every night.

The temperature got up to around ninety-five and the humidity rose right along with it. It was one of St. Louis's legendary summer heat waves. Sitting melting in the Volkswagen, Nudger wondered if what he was doing was really worthwhile. Curtis Colt was, after all, dead, and had never been his client. Still, there were responsibilities that went beyond the job. Or perhaps they were actually the essence of the job.

The next Monday, after Holly Ann had left for work, Nudger used his Visa card to slip the flimsy lock on her trailer door and let himself in.

It took him over an hour to find what he was searching for. It had been well hidden, in a cardboard box inside the access panel to the bathroom plumbing. After looking at the box's contents—almost seven hundred dollars in loot from Curtis Colt's brief life of crime, and another object Nudger wasn't surprised to see—Nudger resealed the box and replaced the access panel.

He continued to watch and follow Holly Ann, more confident now.

Two weeks after the funeral, when she left work one evening, she didn't go home.

Instead her taxi turned the opposite way and drove east on Watson Road. Nudger followed the cab along a series of side streets in South St. Louis, then part way down a dead-end alley to a large garage, above the door of which was lettered "Clifford's Auto Body."

Nudger backed out quickly onto the street then parked the Volkswagen near the mouth of the alley. A few minutes later the cab drove by without a passenger. Within ten minutes, Holly Ann drove past in a shiny red Ford. Its license plate number began with an L.

When Nudger reached Placid Cove Trailer Park, he saw the Ford nosed in next to Holly Ann's trailer.

On the way to the trailer door, he paused and scratched the Ford's hood with a key. Even in the lowering evening light he could see that beneath the new red paint the car's color was dark green.

Holly Ann answered the door right away when he knocked. She tried to smile when she saw it was him, but she couldn't quite manage her facial muscles, as if they'd become rigid and uncoordinated. She appeared ten years older. The little-girl look had deserted her; now she was an emaciated, grief-eroded woman, a country Barbie doll whose features some evil child had lined with dark crayon. The shaded crescents beneath her eyes completely took away their innocence. She was holding a glass that had once been a jelly jar. In it were two fingers of a clear liquid. Behind her on the table was a crumpled brown paper bag and a half-empty bottle of gin.

"I figured it out," Nudger told her.

Now she did smile, but it was fleeting, a sickly bluish shadow crossing her taut features. "You're like a dog with a rag, Mr. Nudger. You surely don't know when to let go." She stepped back and he followed her into the trailer. It was warm in there; something was wrong with the air conditioner. "Hot as hell, ain't it," Holly Ann commented. Nudger thought that was apropos.

He sat down across from her at the tiny Formica table, just as he and Len had sat facing each other two weeks ago. She offered him a drink. He declined. She downed the contents of the jelly jar glass and poured herself another, clumsily striking the neck of the bottle on the glass. It made a sharp, flinty sound, as if sparks might fly.

"Now, what's this you've got figured out, Mr. Nudger?" She didn't want to, but she had to hear it. Had to share it.

"It's almost four miles to the Right-Steer Steakhouse," Nudger told her. "The waitresses there make little more than minimum wage, so cab fare to and from work has to eat a big hole in your salary. But then you seem to go everywhere by cab."

"My car's been in the shop."

"I figured it might be, after I found the money and the wig." She bowed her head slightly and took a sip of gin. "Wig?"

"In the cardboard box inside the bathroom wall."

"You been snooping, Mr. Nudger." There was more resignation than outrage in her voice.

"You're sort of skinny, but not a short girl," Nudger went on. "With a dark curly wig and a fake mustache, sitting in a car, you'd resemble Curtis Colt enough to fool a dozen eyewitnesses who just caught a glimpse of you. It was a smart precaution for the two of you to take."

Holly Ann looked astounded.

"Are you saying I was driving the getaway car at the liquor store holdup?"

"Maybe. Then maybe you hired someone to play Len and convince me he was Colt's accomplice and that they were far away from the murder scene when the trigger was pulled. After I found the wig, I talked to some of your neighbors, who told me that until recently you'd driven a green Ford sedan."

Holly Ann ran her tongue along the edges of her protruding teeth.

"So Curtis and Len used my car for their holdups."

"I doubt if Len ever met Curtis. He's somebody you paid in stolen money or drugs to sit there where you're sitting now and lie to me."

"If I was driving that getaway car, Mr. Nudger, and *knew* Curtis was guilty, why would I have hired a private investigator to try to find a hole in the eyewitnesses' stories?"

"That's what bothered me at first," Nudger said, "until I realized you weren't interested in clearing Curtis. What you were really worried about was Curtis Colt talking in prison. You didn't want those witnesses' stories changed, you wanted them verified. And you wanted the police to learn about not-his-right-name Len."

Holly Ann raised her head to look directly at him with eyes that begged and dreaded. She asked simply, "Why would I want that?"

"Because you were Curtis Colt's accomplice in all of his robberies. And when you hit the liquor store, he stayed in the car to drive. You fired the shot that killed the old woman. He was the one who fired the wild shot from the speeding car. Colt kept quiet about it because he loved you. He never talked, not to the police, not to his lawyer, not even to a priest. Now that he's dead you can trust him forever, but I have a feeling you could have anyway. He loved you more than you loved him, and you'll have to live knowing he didn't deserve to die."

She looked down into her glass as if for answers and didn't say anything for a long time. Nudger felt a bead of perspiration trickle crazily down the back of his neck. Then she said, "I didn't want to shoot that old man, but he didn't leave me no choice. Then the old woman came at me." She looked up at Nudger and smiled ever so slightly. It was a smile Nudger hadn't seen on her before, one he didn't like. "God help me, Mr. Nudger, I can't quit thinking about shooting that old woman."

"You murdered her," Nudger said, "and you murdered Curtis Colt by keeping silent and letting him die for you."

"You can't prove nothing," Holly Ann said, still with her ancient-eyed, eerie smile that had nothing to do with amusement.

"You're right," Nudger told her, "I can't. But I don't think legally proving it is necessary, Holly Ann. You said it: thoughts are actually tiny electrical impulses in the brain. Curtis Colt rode the lightning all at once. With you, it will take years, but the destination is the same. I think you'll come to agree that his way was easier."

She sat very still. She didn't answer. Wasn't going to.

Nudger stood up and wiped his damp forehead with the back of his hand. He felt sticky, dirty, confined by the low ceiling and near walls of the tiny, stifling trailer. He had to get out of there to escape the sensation of being trapped.

He didn't say goodbye to Holly Ann when he walked out. She didn't say goodbye to him. The last sound Nudger heard as he left the trailer was the clink of the bottle on the glass.

# Robert Twohy

# DOWN THIS
# MEAN STREET

I GOT UP AND HEARD CARMACK'S VOICE. "WE'RE STARTING A big one this morning!"

He's always chipper at the start of a new book. I've heard it before, nearly the same words: "This is the niftiest plot I ever cooked up! It'll win an Edgar! M-G-M'll buy it! It's got all the moves!"

Sure. So did all the others—all the 14 others that we've worked on the past ten years. All of them died a quick death—from public boredom.

I haven't got much older in the ten years—but I've sure got more tired. And I've been punched and shot and stabbed and blown up and betrayed, and I'm no richer now than I was in the first book, and I still work out of the same sleazy office in San Francisco—which is the city where Carmack and I live—and I'm sick of that office and sick of the dumb characters I have to associate with and the hard work I put in, and I know even before I start a new adventure that it's going to turn into a ridiculous mess that even Steve McQueen couldn't make convincing.

Carmack's junk gets published, but he hasn't had a hit yet; he earns about what a good cab driver earns. All he's got from his literary career are a damaged liver and congested lungs, from drinking and smoking too much at his work desk. All *I've* got are lumps from the beatings and scars from the bullets. It's been a great life.

I heard his voice: "Get down to the office."

"Wait till I get my shoes on."

"Hurry up." I knew he was crouched over his typewriter, cigarette hanging from his lips, another burning in the ashtray, a third making a new burn on the edge of the desk. This guy is a smoker. If they paid you for smoking, he'd have no money problems.

He tapped a few irritated sentences on the typewriter. I got off the bed and limped over to the coat-rack and got my checked sports jacket. It's a sports jacket the likes of which nobody wears any more. He gave it to me in the first book, described it in detail, and I've been wearing it ever since. It's frayed at the sleeves and patched here and there where bullets and knives have punctured it. I did the patching myself. I clean it between adventures, clean it with alcohol—there's always alcohol handy. Alcohol seeps through the walls of my cubicle—all I have to do is rub a rag along the wall and the rag is soaked. That's how I clean my clothes—if I didn't clean them I'd be ashamed to walk down the mean streets he's always making me walk down. He likes that phrase, "mean streets"—he lifted it from the same guy he lifts a lot of his plots from.

I put on the jacket and he bellowed again, "Hurry up!"

I growled something and he heard me growl. "What'd you say?"

"Nothing."

"Don't talk smart. Save the wisecracks for the story."

I said, "I need a new jacket."

"What's the matter with the one you got?"

"Apart from the fact it's falling apart, it's out of date. The style is Goodwill vintage '60's."

"Don't bother me with details. The play's the thing. Get on down to your office—somebody just came in."

"I know."

"What do you mean, you know?"

"All the books start with somebody just coming into my office."

"That's my classic introduction. I know what I'm doing."

"Why don't you start this one in a nice restaurant—with me sitting down to a big breakfast?"

I was hungry. I hadn't eaten in a long time—he hadn't given me a bite in the last three books. It would give me a big lift to sit down to a classy breakfast—toasty English muffins with butter melting all over them, baked ham with slices of pineapple, eggs scrambled just right . . . once I'd had a breakfast like that. That was in about the sixth book. I'd got up from it feeling great, and the rest of the story had gone beautifully—I'd never been sharper with the wise-cracks, never taken my beatings with more style, never shot so straight. I reminded him of that.

He said, "Yeah, that was a great breakfast I wrote—but this adventure has to start in your office. I got a reason for that . . . there's a girl waiting there now, and she's getting a little impa-tient."

I had a funny feeling when he said that. There was something lying on the edge of what he was saying. I didn't know what it was. I can read his mind some of the time, but not all the time. He was thinking something that he'd just as soon I didn't know about yet. I had that feeling.

I got my .38 from under the pillow, put it in my jacket, and limped on out of my cubicle. He didn't notice I was limping, hadn't caught on that I'd limped through the last two books, ever since the twelfth book, *The Big Messaround*, which was as stupid as any of the others, most of it written when he was totally drunk. The stupidest part was when he had me jump out the window of the sanitarium to get away from Dr. Mytroba's albino hit man. I was supposed to jump far out and land on top of a chicken delivery truck parked down there. I jumped, and it was a good far jump, but the truck wasn't there—the damn fool forgot that he'd had Dr. Mytroba blow it up six pages previous, the doctor being phobic about chickens among other things. So I landed hard on the pave-ment and my right leg twisted under me.

Later, in a brief period when he was more or less sober, he caught the error and wrote out the truck blowup; but the damage was already done, and my leg's been a little crooked ever since. Being a shlunk he hadn't noticed—and if I was lucky, he'd keep on not noticing.

Because Carmack likes me the way the guy who has the dog act likes the dog that goes through the tricks. If the dog gets old or gets a crooked leg, the guy won't like him so much. And if Carmack gets the idea that I can't handle the goofball routines he hatches up for me, he's going to stop using me. He's going to stop thinking of me. And when he stops thinking of me, then that's the end of me. Because then I'm gone—I turn into nothing.

You see, I live in his mind, and his mind is a muddle and a mess, and reeks of alcohol, and you wouldn't want your worst enemy to live in a dump like his mind, but there's no other place for me. And though my life stinks, being nothing would be worse. I don't know that it *would* be—but for the present I'd just as soon put off knowing. For the present I'll go on trying to hide as well as I can the fact that I've got a crooked leg.

I limped on down the damp gloomy corridor. Some slimy things were moving around there. Slimy things were always finding their way into the corridor. I kicked some of them out of the way, and moved on. I asked, "What's the plot line here?"

"You don't have to know. There's a girl waiting in your office. Take it from there."

"Okay." I couldn't argue about it. His idea is that one thing leads to another—don't lay things out with charts and diagrams. He feels that planning a story takes the life out of it. That wouldn't hurt his stories—they have no life to begin with, except for me. I'm the only character with a breath of reality that he ever created. The characters I work with are people lifted from other, better stories—cut-rate copies made of cardboard. Me, I'm a projection of his daydreams about himself, I'm what he'd like to be if he had any moxie or character. I do the things he wishes he had the guts to do—he endowed me with some of his own hopes, thoughts, feelings. That's why I'm different from the others—why I have a certain reality.

I kept limping along and gradually the walls of that dank corridor faded out and light came in and it was daylight, a nice day, and I was walking down one of the mean streets, 7th Street actually—ahead was the big blue-and-white Greyhound depot. And the usual bunch of people were passing in and out—taxis were parked along the curb, a few drunks and crazies stumbled around in the general crowd. There were street noises, everything seemed authentic, and it *was* authentic. He knows the San Francisco street scene. He fakes and hokes most things, but he can make a picture of the things he knows. Faintly below the street sounds I could hear the steady tap-tap of his typewriter, and knew as I walked toward my office, concentrating on not limping now because he had his eye on me, that this opening shot would be the best part of the book. From here on things would start to go downhill.

I went two blocks and here was where I work, a seedy and despondent-looking building just off Mission Street. My office is on the third floor. There isn't any elevator. I climbed the stairs, wishing I had that big breakfast under my belt, wondering who the girl was in my office. She was in trouble, I knew—the adventures always start with a girl in trouble.

I heard suddenly another sound in the background—the typewriter stopped clacking and there was a splashing sound. I knew that sound: Carmack had got his bottle and glass and started lubricating his brain gears and finger muscles for the task ahead. From now on there'd be a lot of that splashing.

I unlocked my office door, which had lettering on the frosted glass—*FLOGG O'FLANAHAN, PRIVATE INVESTIGATIONS*—and went in. A girl was sitting in the client's chair. She turned and looked at me.

She was about 22. She wore a fuzzy pink sweater that really had shape, and a neat brown skirt. She had dark hair, a pretty mouth, and eyes of deep green that had an intent, anxious look.

She sat stiffly and looked at me with those anxious eyes and said in a soft voice, "Mr. O'Flanahan?"

I said that I was.

She fumbled in her handbag that lay on the desk, took a cigarette from it, put it in her lips, and fired it with a Bic lighter.

Everyone smokes a lot in Carmack's novels—you'd think he had a contract with the Tobacco Institute. But it's because by having the people light up, he can make significant breaks in the dialogue. A character flames up, then pulls a gun and shoots somebody; a girl lights up, says "Goodbye," and jumps out of a window. These significant pauses are Carmack's idea of high drama. He uses them at least a dozen times in every book.

I waited for the girl to say something significant after lighting up, but all she said was "Good morning." And I had the feeling she wasn't saying what Carmack had thought she would say. She was stalling, for some reason. She looked at me with those troubled eyes.

It puzzled me. It wasn't just the usual painted-on look; it had depth.

Which was ridiculous. The depth of her eyes was a trick of the morning sunlight through the venetian blinds—an illusion. Only cardboard people with painted eyes come into my office.

I heard Carmack's irritated voice: "Are you just going to look at her? Say something!" I heard the splash from his bottle again.

I sat down at the desk and said to the girl, "How did you get in here?"

"No!" Carmack yelled. "Forget that! Get on with the dialogue!"

"The door was locked. How'd she get in?"

"That's a detail! I'll clean it up later! Get this thing moving!"

He was right. Being a shlunk, he let people walk through locked doors without giving it a thought. Later he would catch most of the errors, or some of them, and straighten them out, or not. I shouldn't have bothered to mention the locked door. It was because of that look in her eyes, that look of reality—it confused me, took my mind off the job.

I concentrated on myself as Flogg O'Flanahan, Private Eye, and said, "What's your name?"

"Gail Gill."

"That's a nice name."

"I don't feel so nice this morning."

"Don't you?"

"No."

"Why?"

"Last night."

"Tell me about it."

"I don't think I want to."

"Then don't. Tell me instead why you have a look of reality in your eyes."

Carmack banged the typewriter savagely. I knew he was belting out a string of X's. He roared. "That stinks! That goes nowhere! Get on with it, O'Flanahan! Get your mind on this!"

He was right again. What I had said about that look in her eyes had nothing to do with his sap-headed story. I said it because it was what I was really wondering—how could one of Carmack's people have eyes that showed feeling?

I got back on the track, and said to her, "Is it that bad?"

"It's . . . that bad."

I knew what her shiver meant. She might have some inner reality, but that shiver was straight Carmack, 100 proof. It was the signal for me to bring out the bottle.

I reached in the desk. "Can you use a drink?"

She nodded. As far as Carmack is concerned, everybody at any time can use a drink.

I got paper cups and poured drinks. As I was pouring I heard a splash from Carmack's bottle—he was going to have a drink too.

I sipped, and she sipped, and we looked at each other, and my eyes said, "Is something going on that I don't know?" and her eyes said, "Yes." And my eyes asked, "What?" and hers said, "I'm worried and confused."

And Carmack yelled, "What's going on here! Why are you both just goggling at each other! Somebody make a noise, somebody do something!"

I said to the girl, with my mouth, "What happened last night?"

"I . . . need help. Everything's a mess."

"Tell me about it."

"It's about . . . my brother, Jason. I knew that little tramp would be trouble for him. He's a fool, he's always been a fool. A dear fool. I knew she'd ruin him, I didn't know how or why, but . . ."

In the background was the steady tap-tap of the typewriter. Not quite so steady—he was well into his third drink. There were pauses, occasional stutters in the typing. "Go on," I said to Gail Gill. I thought, she's saying what she should say—but under her words there was trouble and doubt, and somehow I knew it had something to do with her brother Jason.

She said, as Carmack tapped away, more and more fumble-fingered on the keys, "I went to her apartment. I went up the stairs. I was going to pay her to go away, to leave Jason alone. I knew she'd accept the money. She was just a cheap little tramp."

"Was?"

"Yes." She shivered—and I filled her cup again, and my own. "I knocked, got no answer. I tried the door. It opened. I went in. The bedroom door was open. I saw her lying there on the bed. She was dead. A knife handle stuck out of her neck."

She lit a cigarette, puffed hard, and gazed at me, and her eyes were full of uncertainty about what was going to happen next. What *was* going to happen next?

She said, "The knife handle had P.G. scratched on it."

"P.G.?"

"Yes. My brother Phineas's initials. It was Phineas's hunting knife, stuck there in her neck."

"I thought you said Jason."

She put her hand to her head. "Jason? Jason who?"

"Your brother."

"Who? Oh. Yes. Of course. Jason. And he shot her with his hunting knife."

She was all up in the air now. She had tried to hold down whatever was disturbing her, but it had taken over. I knew for sure now she wasn't cardboard—the cardboard girls never blew up, unless it was in the story for them to blow up. This girl was really troubled. She sat there at the desk, her hands twisting in her lap, staring at them, chewing her pretty lower lip. I said, "Take it easy. You want another drink?"

She shook her head, still chewing her lip. Carmack's voice came, mushy from what he'd drunk, but trying to be sort of soothing: "S'all right. I can fake out the rest of that story about Jason. It's just padding anyway—just so your next move will be dramatic contrast . . . You did good. Now stand up, and reach into your handbag."

She nodded, got up stiffly, and reached into her handbag on the desk. I sat watching her. I didn't know what was going to happen next.

"Take it out," said Carmack. The typewriter was tap-tapping slowly.

She pulled out a gun.

"Shoot him," said Carmack.

I jumped in my chair—and got both feet hooked in the rung. I struggled but couldn't get clear of the chair—me and the chair went crashing over sideways.

On the way down I'd grabbed the .38 from my jacket, and as I landed on my elbow, the gun flew from my hand, bounced to the floor, and skidded away to the far wall.

"Smooth move, O'Flanahan!" yelled Carmack. "Shows what you've come to!"

I lay there on the floor on my side, my feet still hooked in the rung, staring up at the girl. And she looked down at me and the look of trouble was fading from her green eyes, and coming into them was a look of relief—as if she'd worked out a problem, and now everything was clear.

Carmack shouted at her, "You got him now, he's a plucked duck! Drill him!"

I looked at her and she smiled, laid the gun on the desk, and said in a soft voice, "No."

"No? Whadaya mean, no?" He really sounded wild. The girl sat down in her chair. I reached down and began to unhook my feet from the rung.

Carmack bellowed, "Listen, sister, don't fool around with him! He's got a crooked leg and his reflexes are gone, but he's still Flogg O'Flanahan, and he's got out of worse jams than this! So pick up the gun and nail him while he's klutzing around down there!"

So all the time he had known I had a crooked leg.

"Sure, I knew it." He had read my thoughts. "You've been falling apart for books. You were good once, but you're all washed up now. Nobody wants to read about you any more—your time is past."

Finally I was clear of the chair. I started to get up.

He said, "This is the world of computers, high finance, super-missiles, petro-conspiracies. I've finally faced it—the time for walking down mean streets is over. I need a detective in tune with the new beat, someone who'd be at home in a snazzy disco joint, someone without a gimpy leg. Some of you is me, and I've got to move on from the part of me that's you."

He had lowered his voice, it had taken on the solemn tone that a drunk gets when every word is a pearl of profundity. "Don't look on this as an end—it's a beginning. The beginning of a new career, a bright new detective rising from your ashes. So we all advance. Except you, of course."

I had stood up, and I looked at the girl, who sat there, not stiff now, but easy in her chair; and she looked back at me with those deep and glowing eyes, and smiled.

I said to Carmack, "So you set me up. Who're you going to replace me with?"

"Her."

"A girl? *This* girl?"

"Right. Because this is the age of Liberation—a woman can do all the things you can do. Under those soft curves she's a steel whip—and she's a lot smarter than you. And she doesn't limp . . . She's going to be great. We've talked it over—isn't that so, Magda?"

"Magda? I thought you were Gail Gill."

She said, "No. But I'm not Magda either."

Carmack shouted, "You are too! That's the name I gave you—so that's your name. You're Magda Crajovescu of the C.I.A.—an agent of Rumanian descent."

I asked, "Why Rumanian?"

"I have a hunch that Rumanian will be the thing next year. It's the Olympic year, and that little Comaneci girl will be all over the tube."

He could be right. But this plot line seemed woolier than ever. I said, "Why would a C.I.A. girl of Rumanian ancestry come to a sleazy office and knock off a private detective who doesn't have any high-class international connections?"

There was another splash from his bottle, and a chuckle from him. "Because you're not really Flogg O'Flanahan, private eye. He was disposed of a long time ago—you took over his identity as a cover. You're really Snoutchev."

"Who?"

"Snoutchev. Dmitri Snoutchev of the Leningrad Snoutchevs. Oh, you fooled a lot of people, but finally the C.I.A. got onto you. Too many things about you seemed fishy. Why were pretty girls always hanging around your office? How come you walked down so many mean streets? They caught on to you at last—you weren't the seedy nobody you pretended to be. You've been a leader of the spy apparatus in the U.S. for a long, long time."

"I have?"

"You have if I say you have."

"I don't even speak Russian."

"You do if I say you do. And your dying words, as Magda plugs you will be—Viva Lenin! Can you remember that?"

"That's Spanish."

"So, you had a Spanish grandmother. There are Spanish Communists too. Quit dissembling, Snoutchev, drop the mask. I see through you and so does she. Pick up the gun, Magda."

I looked at the gun. I looked at her. She looked back at me, and smiled. She didn't move for the gun. So I didn't either.

He didn't notice—I heard him pouring another drink. "She's not zapping you just to be mean. It's very important to the C.I.A. plot, and to the plot of the story, that your death seem just a sordid, senseless killing. The security of the nation depends on the artful staging of this murder—which isn't a murder at all, but an authorized and ethical elimination."

His voice was really mushy now, with the booze he'd drunk. "That's right," he said to the girl, "smile at him, look sweet, milk the scene a little—that's good. I like that." There were a few bangs on the typewriter—not much, he was hitting three and four keys at a time, and gave up in a few seconds. "I'll hold it in my mind till later—hey, wait a minute!" His voice was suddenly excited. "Hold it, I'm getting a flash—don't pick up the gun! Leave the gun there—forget the gun! I'm getting a really dynamic gimmick . . . You've been trained at the C.I.A.'s Advanced Institute of the Martial Arts in judo, karate, kung fu—and *bayama gizma!*"

I said, "What's bayama gizma?"

"That's the most secret martial art of all. A Past Master, or in this case Past Mistress, of bayama gizma develops such concentrated power in her gaze that all she has to do is look at a victim, just look at him, and he starts smashing himself with his fists and kicking himself in the groin and jabbing his eyes out. Hey, that opens up terrific complications that the police can fiddle around with, when you're found *self-destructed*! How about it, Magda?''

She said in her soft voice, ''I don't know bayama gizma.''

''Sure you do! You've been thoroughly schooled in it. I say you have, so you have—so start using it on him!''

She looked at me. I waited for something to come over me so I'd start punching myself, kicking myself in the groin, but nothing did. She just looked at me and smiled.

I had to say it. ''You have the most beautiful eyes I've ever seen.''

Carmack yelled. ''Turn on the bayama gizma!''

She murmured, ''No.''

''You have to, because I created you! So you have to do what I say!''

''You didn't create me. You stole me from someone else's story.''

''So what? I ran you through the selector of my mind, gave you different clothes, a different hairdo, different ethnics—I do that with all my characters. I give them something to make them distinctive—a tattoo, a nifty wiggle—''

''I don't have a tattoo or a nifty wiggle.''

''Maybe I'll give you a tattoo.'' He chuckled again—a mean sound. He was a mean drunk. ''I can give you a hundred tattoos. I can give you a nose as long as a cucumber. I can give you elephant ears. I can make your feet flat. I can do anything with you I want! Because I'm a writer—and you're just a character!''

She stood up, and said, ''No. I'm a memory—the memory of a girl who died, and the man who had loved her wrote a story about her. And I live on as a memory in his mind. I live there now—even though I'm here.''

I didn't understand all of what she said. In fact, I didn't understand any of what she said. But that didn't matter. She had life, she had feelings—that was all that mattered. That, and the fact that her eyes were beautiful.

Carmack growled, ''I offer you a chance to be somebody, a big star. If M-G-M buys this, you could play opposite someone like Bronson, Coburn, maybe Travolta. You could have posters, you could be bigger than Wonder Woman—''

"That's what I thought I wanted—to have exciting adventures, go to glamorous places, meet fascinating men. I thought I was tired of being just a memory. And you read the story about me and decided you could use me—"

"I liked your style, your spirit, your inner qualities—and you've got a really great build. I saw the possibilities. That's the artist in me." The booze caught him in the stomach, and he belched.

She said, "Your mind is a dismal place. It's full of dead things and dying things, and slimy things that run in and out the corridor. And there's a room full of cardboard figures."

I said, "That's what he uses in the stories. There's the mobster, the crooked lawyer, the junkie, the evil doctor, the prostitute with heart of gold—he trots them out and paints new faces on them whenever he needs them."

"Bah," said Carmack. I heard another splash. "I can get anyone to play Magda Crajovescu. I can leaf through any collection of stories and find a girl with more talent and as good a build. You had your chance, and lost it—go. Leave my mind."

He said to me, "You're through too, O'Flanahan."

"I thought I was Snoutchev."

"Whoever you are doesn't matter—because you won't be anybody much longer. You're washed up and living in the past, and you got a crooked leg and your jacket's a mess. I've got no further use for you. I move on, unencumbered, to even greater literary triumphs. M-G-M can't wait for this one. I'll be on Johnny Carson, Dick Cavett, Merv Griffin, Mike Douglas." I heard a thump, then a groan, then a louder thump, then a whooshing sigh as he fell forward, smashed his head on the typewriter, rolled out of his chair to the floor, lay there, and started snoring.

The girl got up. I asked, "What's your name? Your real name?"

"Susan."

"That's a good name."

"So is Magda. But it's not *my* name."

She gazed at me and said, "He told me you were only cardboard, and that if I shot you—but I couldn't shoot you. I looked in your eyes and knew you weren't cardboard."

"That's what I knew when I looked in yours."

"I don't want to live in his mind. I'll go back to being just a memory, back to the life I left. There is beauty and harmony there, and pretty streams and sunlight and shade and good places to walk, to lie and dream."

"It sounds nice. Does the guy feed you?"

She smiled. "He remembers wonderful meals we had—before I became a memory."

I listened to Carmack snoring. I said, "He can't forget me till he wakes up and his brain starts functioning again, after its fashion. Then he'll put it to work to forget me. And soon enough he will—and I'll be nothing."

"That's all right." She smiled.

"Is it?"

"Yes. Because you'll come back."

"Will I?"

"Yes. Because after I leave here, I'll remember you. So you'll be a memory too—*my* memory. And then you'll come and we'll walk in a cool place, with dancing water, with sunlight and shade."

It sounded nice—a lot different from mean streets.

I said, "I've got this crooked leg."

"When you come to me you won't have a crooked leg."

"I've got lumps and stuff from being shot and beat up. And this jacket is awful."

"I won't remember the jacket. So you won't have the jacket. But I'll remember the lumps. Because I like the lumps."

"You do? And I'll have a decent jacket?"

"A fine jacket—and you'll come riding to me on a fine brown horse."

"I never rode a horse."

"You'll come riding like a Master of the Hunt. And there will be the sound of trumpets."

"Really? What tune?"

"A lovely tune, a stirring, gallant tune. And we'll have a feast, a marvelous feast."

"That sounds great." I was hungry, all right. "How long from now till this happens?"

"It doesn't matter." And it didn't. When you're nothing, time doesn't matter. And in a little while, when Carmack woke up, I'd start being nothing.

She picked her handbag off the desk and went to the door. She turned and smiled, and then she went out.

I sat there at the desk a while. Then I got up. Her gun still lay on the desk. I left it there. I looked at my own .38, lying against the far wall. I wouldn't be needing it any more.

Then I walked over and picked it up. Because you never know when a gun might come in handy—wherever you go.

I put it in my jacket and went out, locking the door behind me, and limped down the stairs. Halfway down I heard a pistol shot. Somebody was shooting at me. The shot was high. I ducked. Then a bomb went off, making me jump back as half of the stairway in front of me blew up. I ran back up the stairs and to the emergency stairs, and ran down, while somebody ran after me, firing more shots. It was Dr. Mytroba's albino hit man.

I pulled my gun and fired back, and blew his head off. But somebody else started shooting. I got to the ground floor and headed down the hall, limping fast, toward the front door, and a lion was coming in, eyes wild, mouth like a dirty red cave. I fired at him—that made him laugh. He leaped at me and I twisted away just in time, and he sailed on by.

I ran out the door and kept running, because a pack of wild dogs was coming after me. I ran down Mission Street, twisting to snap shots under my arm at the dogs. A bus was coming, I waved at it, and it swerved toward me, and didn't stop, came faster. I was between the bus and the wild dogs. I went flat and the bus rolled over me and piled into the dogs and there was a terrific howling and then a big uproar as the bus piled into a gasoline truck, on which a guy with a submachine gun was sitting, spraying bullets at me—and everyone blew up and disappeared.

And then I heard muttering, and sighing, and Carmack was snoring. His nightmare was over. But he had sure done everything he could in it to finish me. I didn't have any doubts—he didn't like me any more.

I walked down the dank corridor, where slimy things were sleeping, and got to my cubicle that smelled more than ever of alcohol. I took the gun out of my jacket and took off the jacket and my shoes and stretched out on the bed. It had been a tiring trip home and I had a few drinks at the office and thought I could doze off. I knew from the sound of his snores that he was deep in sleep now and I wouldn't start turning into nothing for a while yet. You never know though—he's a drunk who can come to all of a sudden.

I lay there and closed my eyes. I had the .38 under my hand on the bed. I didn't see any reason that I shouldn't try to take it along when I turned into nothing. It sounded fine, what Susan said about that cool place—but you never know. Not when you've walked down as many mean streets as I have.

I lay there with good thoughts. I thought of that big meal she would have for me when I got there. It's been a hell of a long time since I had a good meal. I particularly like roast pork and sweet cabbage. I wish I'd mentioned that to Susan.

I lay there and thought of Susan.

I hope she won't forget me.

I don't think she will.

She sure has beautiful eyes.

I hope she'll remem

# Rob Kantner

# THE FOREVER TRIP

## 1

### Drinking Tom and Jerry

UNCLE DAN STARED DOWN THE LENGTH OF HIS SHEET-COVERED body. "So, Benjy, they're gonna take another piece of me."

I knew what he meant. At the end of him, under the crisp white hospital sheet, his right foot showed and his left foot didn't. Diabetes, controlled for years, had gradually gained on him and caused the circulation in his left foot to fail, resulting in gangrene. Twice in the past year they'd had to amputate, removing the foot first and the leg below the knee second.

"Just your gall bladder this time, Uncle," I answered, seating myself in the chair next to his bed.

"Aah." Uncle Dan stared at me coldly with his crisp blue eyes. His face was lined, pale, and wasted, marked indelibly with the gall-bladder pain that had kept him in a near-fetal position for the past week in his retirement community bed. He looked every one of his eighty-seven years.

"Listen," I said cheerfully, holding up some envelopes, "I picked up your mail. Want to go through it?"

"You go ahead," Dan said dourly. "Let me know if there's any movie role offers in there or anything."

"Sure," I grinned. I inventoried the mail. Mostly ads, which I tossed. The last item was a six-by-nine manila envelope. I ripped it open. A small note fell out, clipped to a Baggie which had another envelope inside it. I opened the note and read it to my uncle. " 'Dan: This just came today. Thought it might be important. Do you believe that crummy post office? Love, Millie.' "

Uncle Dan looked at the Baggie and then at me, eyes narrow. "Millie! My old landlady. What'd she send?"

The Baggie had one of those printed messages from the post office on it, apologizing for the delay in delivery. I ripped the plastic and took out the note-sized envelope. It was faded, wrinkled, addressed in a scrawl to Uncle Dan at his old apartment on Schaefer. I held it up to him. "Looks really old. Want me to open it?"

"Sure, why not."

I opened the envelope and shook out the note. It was small, written on cheap paper, and short. " 'Tuesday morning,' " I read. " 'Dear Dan, I'm in desperate trouble. If you meant what you said, meet me at the bar tonight. I need you. XXXOOO. Lila.' "

I looked at my uncle. He'd raised himself slightly on his thin elbows, staring hard at me, eyes burning, face pale. He whispered hoarsely, "Ben. The date. What's the date on the envelope?"

I checked the cancellation and my heart nearly stopped. "1939," I said. "August 16, 1939, afternoon. Postmarked Detroit."

"Forty-five years," Uncle Dan muttered, lips dry.

"Wow," I stood and read over the note and the envelope again. "This is really something, Uncle. Who's Lila?"

The back of his bald head faced me as he stared out the bright window of the Detroit Metro Hospital at the Jeffries Freeway/Farmington Road interchange far below. After a long silence he said without looking at me, "She was special."

I walked around the bed to where I could get a look at his face. "What happened to her?"

"I don't know. She disappeared. I never heard."

My amusement evaporated as the tone of anguish in his voice sank in. I said, "She really *was* special, huh?" He didn't answer. I asked. "What bar was she talking about?"

"Burly Curly's," he answered. "We met there practically every day for weeks . . . months."

I wanted to press him further, but decided not to. He was going under the knife in the morning to have his gall bladder removed, and he was weak and drained from the pain and in shock from the letter. I went to a grocery sack that sat on the floor next to my chair and took out a red thermos. "Hey. Uncle. I brought some Tom and Jerry."

"Hot?" he asked hopefully, turning to face me.

"Of course." I opened the thermos and poured some into a plastic glass that sat on his tray table. "Egg, milk, sugar, brandy, a tad of salt, just the way you like it."

"Well," Dan said with a wan smile, "just a taste." He took the glass in his thin, veined hand and gulped. I refilled the glass, and he gulped again and set the glass down jerkily. Sighing, he lay back on the bed. "Guess I blew it, Ben. She needed me and I didn't show up."

"Well hell," I said, pacing to the window, "how could *you* know? You didn't get the note."

"Wonder what happened to her?" Uncle Dan whispered. "Wonder where she is?"

"We can find out."

His smile was distant. "You've got cash-paying clients to take care of, Ben, you don't have to do detective work for me. Besides, it's been too many years. I'll never know what happened to her now."

I stepped toward him and fixed him with a stare. "Come on," I said harshly. "You done survived three years in the air over France, and then the union troubles in the thirties, and you're gonna get out of here, too, and by the time you do I'll have the answer about Lila. Believe it."

His smile did not change. "Of course." He looked at me sharply. "You still flying?"

"Sure, every chance I get, Uncle."

"Be careful. I've read some articles. Those ultralight airplanes are dangerous."

"No worse than the bamboo-and-wire crates you flew. And I don't have people shooting at me up there."

He waved a wasted hand at me. "Go, take off. I gotta rest up. And take that crap with you."

I picked up the mail. "I'll be back tomorrow to look in on you after they're done." He waved without looking at me, and as I walked out of the hospital room I saw him drink the last of his Tom and Jerry.

I called the hospital the next morning. The operation, scheduled for eight, had been delayed till ten. They told me I could come by and see him in the afternoon. So, with time to kill, I located an old picture of Uncle Dan and drove through the late fall rain to the Detroit Library main branch on Woodward.

The Detroit telephone directory for 1939 showed a listing for Burly Curly's in the three hundred block of Cass. I drove over there, not expecting much, and wasn't surprised: the block was a devastated shell of burned-out buildings. On the way back to the hospital I stopped at Bullet Realty in Wayne, where Owney Busbee, the owner/broker, was hunched over his cluttered desk; he agreed to run a title search on the Burly Curly's property to try to get a line on the owners.

Back at Greater Detroit Metro Hospital, I found Uncle Dan unconscious in his bed, looking white and shrunken. He sprouted tubes, one conveying, I could tell, oxygen. I sat by the bed watching him for what seemed like the longest time, and he did not move. A doctor, who introduced himself as Ahmed Senatkor, stopped by briefly. He told me that the gall bladder operation had gone as expected, but that the post-operation X-rays had revealed a bowel obstruction. He said that they had Uncle Dan on oxygen and fluids and had inserted an abdominal tube to drain the bile that was collecting in his abdominal cavity.

I found a pay phone in the hall and dialed my sister Libby's number. No answer. I dialed my brother Bill and got him. He said he'd be over to the hospital right away. Instead, about fifteen minutes later, his wife Marybeth arrived.

She gave me a hug and a kiss on the cheek, sat down in a chair facing Uncle Dan's bed, and got out her knitting. Bill, she told me, hadn't felt up to coming. She said she'd stay with me till visiting hours ended. And so we stayed and watched Dan, who did not regain consciousness. Marybeth knitted and occasionally moistened Uncle Dan's mouth with a damp washcloth, and talked to me. I stared at my uncle and took a few trips down to the smoking room and thought about the forty-five-year-old letter and Lila and the long-gone Burly Curly's bar, till visiting hours ended.

## 2

### The Balloon Buster

The morning sunlight drenched Uncle Dan's bed. I stood over him, holding his thin hand. He stared at me through blue eyes that were crystal-clear no more. "Got two of 'em today, huh, Frank?"

"I sure did, Dan," I answered.

Uncle Dan chuckled. "You got *guts,* Frank. Them balloons are *crawling* with D-7's to protect 'em. And you get past 'em and blow the balloons all to hell anyhow."

I said through a dry mouth, "Those observation balloons are just too fat and pretty a target to ignore, Dan. And they're valuable to the Jerries. They keep tabs on movements in the trenches from the balloons."

"C'mon, Frank," Dan said, mouth twisted with sarcasm, "you don't go after the balloons because of their military value. Don't kid me. You go after 'em for the glory. 'Frank Luke, The Balloon Buster,' they're starting to call you. And you love it."

I grinned without feeling. "Got me there, Dan."

"Yeah. Hee-hee. I got you there." His face went pensive and he looked away from me. "I heard something about you the other day, Frank. They tell me you carry a .38 with you to knock yourself off if your plane catches fire."

I squeezed his hand. "Dan."

His thin-lipped mouth went into rictus. "Not gonna catch me doin' that, Frank. I don't think burning up'd be so bad—"

"Dan—"

" 'Dan'? *'Dan'?*" He stared into my face, eyes fierce and blue. "I'm *Uncle* Dan to *you,* youngster!"

"Yes, sir."

"Listen, Ben," he said softly after a long pause. "That'd have been a man's way to die. Burnt into ashes in the skies over France. *That'd* have been a right fine way to go out."

I struggled to keep my voice steady. "Take it easy, Uncle. You're not going to die. Just take it easy."

Back home in my apartment there was a message from Owney Busbee. The owner of Burly Curly's in 1939 was named Earl Eidson. There was no listing of that name in the phonebook, but a check with a contact at the credit bureau gave me an address in Franklin. As I left for my car I remembered the devastated block of Cass where Burly Curly's had stood so long ago and thought that, judging from the address, Earl Eidson had gotten out in one financial piece, indeed.

Earl Eidson offered me a cigar. Margrit Eidson offered me tea. I turned down both offers with thanks. We sat on their patio deck that offered a splendid view of Smithfield Lake beyond a long, smooth, freshly mowed zoysia lawn. It was warm and humid and cloudy, the kind of weather that signals the end of Indian summer.

Earl was short, burly, bald, and tan, dressed for golf. Margrit was tall and lanky in short-shorts and a roomy printed blouse, at the tail end of her years of real beauty. They were childless, wealthy, and, from the welcome they'd given me, anxious for company.

I said to them, "I'm a private detective, trying to track down a woman who used to frequent your bar on Cass back in the late thirties."

"Burly Curly's," Margrit Eidson said affectionately. "I *miss* those days."

Earl Eidson's voice was booming, domineering. "We had lotsa regulars in those days, Perkins. Folks from when my dad ran the place. I inherited it from him, you know."

I didn't know and didn't particularly care. "Woman's name was Lila." I paused. "That ring any bells?"

They looked at each other, shook their heads, and looked back at me expectantly.

I got my old picture of Uncle Dan out and laid it on the glass table in front of them. "She used to meet this man at your bar. Several times a week for months, I'm told."

They squinted at the picture, then reared back and reacted in unison, Margrit with an "Eep!," Earl with a grunt. Margrit looked at me and said in a strained voice, "I *knew* him! Dan! I knew him!"

"You bet she did," Earl said, voice low, glance averted.

"Where is he?" she asked me. "What's he doing?"

"Pushing up daisies, I hope," Earl grunted.

"He's my uncle." They studied me silently. "He's quite ill."

Margrit clasped long-fingered hands in front of her. "I'm sorry to hear that." She looked anxiously at her husband and said, "Please, Earl. It was so long ago." She smiled sweetly. "I don't bring up Lucy, now do I?"

Eidson gave her a dark look, then said with a flat, stiff-lipped voice, "Sorry, Perkins."

Part of me was embarrassed, another part was amused. I'd always known Uncle Dan was a lady-killer in his day. "Do you remember the woman my uncle met there? Anything at all?"

Margrit Eidson straightened her spine, gave her husband a hesitant look, then said to me, "I remember her. I was . . . I was interested in Dan. It was over by the time he began meeting her there. I was jealous, I watched them." She put her hand on her husband's and squeezed it tightly. "Earl," she said urgently, "it was *her*! The mystery woman!"

His face brightened as he looked intently at his wife. "The shooting? The Joe Verdi thing?"

"What shooting? What the hell does old Joe Verdi have to do with this?" I asked faintly.

They looked at me like I'd just arrived from Mars. Earl Eidson barked, "You don't remember the Joe *Verdi* case?"

I raised both hands in a back-off gesture. "Joe Verdi I've heard of. But hell, in '39 I wasn't even *born* yet."

Margrit Eidson fairly bounced with excitement. "Quick, Earl! Get the scrapbook!" Earl scraped his chair back and trotted into the house. Animation made Margrit's face look twenty years younger. "We never knew her name! The police asked us and *asked* us. And the reporters. Oh, we were in the news for *days* after that."

Earl Eidson returned with a string-bound scrapbook as thick as a lengthwise brick and laid it on the table in front of me. He sat back down next to his wife and, as I opened it, they leaned toward me, expecting me to be fascinated.

And I was.


Carlo Infante arrived at the I-75 rest stop near Trenton just after I did. The place was a midafternoon madhouse of truckers and tourists who stared anxiously at the threatening sky and ran ducking against the cool wind into the little buildings to answer the call of nature. As Infante dropped gracefully into the passenger seat of the Mustang and greeted me, I had to make an effort to divorce myself from the scrapbook and its vivid depiction of the Detroit organized mob scene of the late thirties. Carlo Infante, a top finance guy in today's Detroit organization, fit today's image well. Young, cool, smooth, colorless, a businessman.

"Had hell breaking away on such short notice, Perkins," he said as he got a cigarette and a lighter out of his snappy suit jacket. I don't know why he carries smoking equipment around with him; I've never in my life seen him actually light up.

I stared past the restroom buildings at the flat horizon, angry gray clouds roiling above it. "Joe Verdi still alive, Carlo?"

He stared at me, obviously caught off guard. "Well, sure he is, Ben. Retired, though, been for years. Why?"

"I want to see him."

Infante's surprise faded and he became guarded.

"Why?"

"There's an old bit I want to ask him about. Fellow named Henry Porch, gunned down back in '39 at a bar called Burly Curly's on Cass. Word is Verdi knows something about it."

Infante smirked. "You've got me at a disadvantage. I wasn't around then."

"Neither was I." I stared into his thin face. "Porch was an organization finance man. Department of Justice turned him, used him to get an indictment against Verdi for you-name-it. Pre-trial, smuggled him to Detroit, kept him in hiding till testimony time. But the Justice boys ran into a slight snag."

Infante sighed. "Since you mentioned a shooting, and since Verdi's never been convicted, do I have to guess what the snag was?"

"Porch was gunned down late in August. Government lost its witness, Verdi walked. Strutted, more like."

"They prove anything on Verdi?" Infante asked.

"Nope. 'Course not. Had a pretty decent alibi, like about thirty-six thousand people at Briggs Stadium with him watching the Tigers."

"So what's your interest?"

I fired up a short cork-tipped cigar. "I'm not after Verdi," I said firmly. "I should give a damn, after all these years? But there was a woman in the bar. When Porch went down, she ran to him and hugged him and screamed. Then she took off, before the cops got there. Nobody ever got a line on her. 'The mystery woman,' the papers called her. I want her."

Infante toyed with his cigarette and his lighter for a long time, staring distantly out the windshield. "What makes you think Joe knows something about her?"

"Just hoping." I looked at him again through the upward stream of cigar smoke. "This is," I said distinctly, "historical research for an old, extremely important client. Nothing kicks back on nobody, guaranteed."

Infante smiled faintly. "I believe you, Ben. Question is, can I deliver a piece like this for you." He thought. "I'll get the word to Savastano. He's next step up. Best you can hope for is a meet with him. I'll let you know."

As he opened the Mustang door, I put my hand on his shoulder. He looked at me. I said, "It's personal, Carlo. Extremely important to me personally. I got no other angles."

"What you gotta hope," Carlo said as he got out, "is that Savastano believes that as much as I do."

I was just approaching the I-94 interchange on the Southfield Freeway when my car phone rang. It was Marybeth. "Trouble at the hospital," she said.

"You there now?"

"Yes. Hurry, Ben."

"Ten minutes."

I swerved into the left lane of the Southfield and floored the accelerator. The big secondary carburetor ports opened to suck air and the Mustang leaped forward, turning the center lane stripes into a white blur.

Marybeth, dressed office-style in brown skirt and sleeveless white top, stood at Uncle Dan's hospital room and clapped her hands together when she saw me approach. "Ben—"

"Where is he?" I pushed past her into his room. It was a disaster area: furniture askew, paper wrappers strewn around the floor, closet door ajar. My uncle lay on the bed, atop the covers, strips of cloth binding his wrists and ankle to the chrome railings of the bed. His face was frozen solid, lips pursed, and every wasted inch of his body bucked against the bindings as he gasped air convulsively through his mouth.

I felt Marybeth behind me. "What happened?" I asked.

"Cardiac episode," she whispered, taking my hand. "His respiration became irregular. All of a sudden the place was overrun with doctors and nurses, working on him. They shoved me out into the hall. I just got back in here a few minutes ago." She pressed her face against my shoulder. "It's the bowel obstruction. They're taking him into surgery soon. They say they—"

I cut her off with a gesture and approached my uncle. He bucked and wheezed, gasped and panted, eyes glued shut. I touched his forehead. It was burning up. I looked at Marybeth. "You call Bill?"

"Yes." She bit her lip. "He won't come, Ben. He can't handle this kind of thing. You know that."

"Libby?"

"No answer."

A nurse, an orderly, and an older man in a white jacket came into the room, wheeling a gurney. I stepped back around the bed to Marybeth as the nurse and orderly untied my uncle and transferred him to the gurney. The doctor said to me, "We're taking him into surgery now."

He didn't look familiar. "You're Dr.—"

"Levin. Mr. Perkins's attending physician."

"Where's Dr. Senatkor?" I asked.

We stepped back to allow the gurney through the door. Dr. Levin repeated, "I'm the attending physician."

I found strength in my voice. "What *happened* to my uncle, doctor?"

Levin, a moonfaced, kindlylooking man, said, "It's the bowel obstruction. He's collecting too many fluids. Infection could result. And he's weakened, especially his heart. We were hoping to build his strength first, but we have no choice. We have to correct the bowel obstruction now." He looked at Marybeth and back at me. "He's almost in a coma now," he said in a tone he assumed was comforting. "It's distressing to see, but he feels nothing, I assure you." He turned and left.

Marybeth walked aimlessly past Uncle Dan's empty bed to the window. "What are we supposed to do now?"

"Wait, I guess," I answered.

I'd just seated myself when a nurse's aide walked importantly into the room. "Oh, hey," she piped, "you've got to get these things out of here, folks."

"My uncle's in surgery," I said tonelessly.

"Well sure, but after that he'll be in ICU. Intensive care unit. Sixth floor. We need this bed for someone else." She began collecting Uncle Dan's things—suitcase, pillow, shaving kit, and other items—out of the closet. "You can take these to your car if you want," she said hopefully. "He won't need them up in ICU. Okay, folks? Thanks!"

I hijacked a wheelchair and used it to dolly Uncle Dan's things downstairs and out to my car. Back upstairs, on the sixth floor, I met Marybeth in the waiting room of the intensive care unit. We sat and waited, and looked at each other and at the TV, and watched other pinch-faced people waiting for word, throughout the afternoon, into the evening, well past nightfall.

Finally a young curly-haired man in a surgical gown came in the door and said, "Mr. Perkins?"

I bounded to my feet, followed by Marybeth. "That's me."

The doctor was twenty-eight, twenty-nine, tops. Where's Robert Young when you need him? He said, "I'm Dr. Sims. Bowel thing's squared away. Your uncle's in the ICU now. He handled it 'bout as well as we could expect."

Marybeth said, "What are his chances for survival?"

Dr. Sims seemed to suppress an urge to shrug. "A lot better than they'd of been if we hadn't gone in again."

Take it at face value, Perkins, I said to myself. Don't press. But I had to ask, "What happened to Dr. Levin?"

Sims did shrug this time. "I'm the attending physician now, Mr. Perkins. You can see your uncle in the morning. Check the ICU visiting hours schedule on the bulletin board." He turned and left.

The United Airlines 747 had been at the gate for five minutes when the door from the jetway opened. Carlo Infante said to me, "Rick always flies first class. He'll be one of the first off."

"Fine." I watched the passengers start to stream toward us through the door. It was midmorning, but for these passengers on the Los Angeles red-eye, it wasn't even sunrise yet, and they looked it.

I recognized Rick Savastano as he strode into the gate from the jetway. He was tall, well-built, with fighter-pilot good looks, dressed in a pale gray suit and maroon tie and carrying a wallet-thin leather briefcase. He nodded at Infante and his eyes flickered coldly with recognition when he saw me. We fell into step walking up the concourse toward the terminal.

Savastano said, "Carlo filled me in by phone, Perkins. Make your case."

I did so, as briefly as I could, adding information about Lila and her relationship with Uncle Dan, and the note that had taken forty-five years to reach him. Savastano said, "This kind of soppy syrup sentimentality, I didn't expect that of you, Perkins."

"It's important."

Savastano's mouth twisted distastefully. "You're aware, of course, that Mr. Verdi has been retired from the business for years now. Steve Ritchie is running things."

"I know that. I don't want to step on anybody's toes. I want to go through channels."

We entered the terminal and threaded through crowds between the Delta and New York Air desks toward the big glass doors. Savastano looked at me and said, "First it's up to Steve. I don't smell any rats, but he might, and he's the boss. Then, if he goes along, it's up to the old man. That's where it ends, Perkins. We'll be in touch if it's a go."

We went through the automatic swinging doors. The sky was

lead-gray and the wind crisp and chilly as we headed toward the curb where a cream-colored Cadillac stretch purred. "I appreciate it," I answered, feeling bitter at being at this man's mercy. "Let me know either way, okay?"

The chauffeur trotted around the front of the limo and had the back door open just as Savastano reached it. Savastano looked down his long nose at me and said coldly, "We'll be in touch if it's a go, I said."

I thought about Uncle Dan strapped down convulsing in his hospital bed, and as I looked into Savastano's eyes I thought about how much I'd welcome a chance to take a real damaging poke at these bastards. It was a struggle to keep these feelings off my face, but I succeeded. I thanked them, waved, and trotted off for my car as Infante and Savastano boarded the Cadillac stretch and sighed away into the traffic.

Visiting hours in the intensive care unit were strange and rigidly enforced: odd hours only, ten minutes' duration. I showed up for the first, eleven A.M., directly from the airport.

Uncle Dan's room was half again the size of his former one. Much of his extra space was taken up with equipment: an electronic monitor on the wall showed changes in his heartbeat in digits and reflected the same in a scrolling, jagged series of lines; trees of IV bottles stood on each side of the bed, their tubes snaking down and under his sheet; a ventilator loomed on the left side of his bed, its big, plastic accordionlike plunger going up and down with pneumatic sighs, echoed by the rising and falling of my uncle's thin chest.

He lay stiffly on his back, the oxygen tube affixed to his nose, ventilator tube inserted in his mouth, his arms tied down to the rails of the bed. His eyes were closed.

I leaned down to his ear and said, "Uncle?"

His eyes opened. Though cloudy, they showed recognition. He raised a clawlike hand and waved to me. I said, "I know you can't talk. Don't try."

His mouth formed a grisly smile around the mouthpiece of the ventilator.

His wasted face, so unfamiliar, made me feel sick inside. I said heartily, "Thirty-one victories, remember, Uncle? Thirty-one of them bastard Jerries."

He nodded jerkily and his right hand contorted into a thumbs-up. Poor guy. I was trying to hearten him, and all he wanted to do was hearten me.

I said, "You done got through that, and you done made it through this operation, too. You're gonna walk out of here, Uncle. Take a lot more'n this place to kill you, you tough old son of a bitch. Be sure to kiss the nurses as you go. Maybe even pat 'em on the ass, too. They won't mind."

He kept smiling.

"I'll be back here later on today, Uncle. Marybeth's coming for the afternoon visits. Libby'll be by later, too. You'll see."

I looked around the room. Hard to talk when nothing gets said back. I looked back at him. "On Lila. I'm making progress. I know part of the story. I ought to know the rest soon. I'll keep on it, Uncle. You and me'll whip up some Tom and Jerry and I'll fill you in later. Okay?"

He nodded again, eyes fixed on me, filled with spirit and defiance. The ten minutes were over, and I said goodbye and went back to my apartment to wait for Savastano's call.

But Marybeth called first, about three-thirty. She was crying. "He looks so awful, Ben."

"Hey, he's been through two operations—"

"But he was *crying!*" she wailed. "Both times, when I saw him. I tried to cheer him up—told him about the family and old times, and—"

"Steady on, kid," I said, not so steady myself.

"He keeps pointing to his mouth. It's so dry, and—his lips are cracked and—he wants something to drink and—I can't give it to him and—I can't *help* him!"

"Once he's off that damn ventilator, we'll be able to help him, Marybeth."

"Ben," she said, getting control of herself, "do you think he's going to die?"

"Hey," I said loudly, "Dan's been through it all. He survived the fight on the overpass in '36, remember that? When three union-busting goons tried to put him away? He survived that, and he'll survive this."

"Okay. Okay." We stayed silent for a while, then she said, "You coming back later?"

"Yeah, I'll make the seven for sure. And Libby'll probably be out today, too."

"No, she won't," Marybeth said. "She says she'll come but she never does and she never will and you know it."

"I'll be out later," I said, and hung up.

Five minutes later, Rick Savastano called.

Our Lady of Perpetual Mercy Hospital is a small, exclusive, private facility at the lakefront foot of Edgemont in Grosse Pointe Park. A pair of anonymous, suited goons met me at the doors and walked me to another pair, who rode up with me in the elevator and turned me over to yet a third pair on the sixth floor landing. These gentlemen escorted me into a suite that was more like a luxurious hotel than a hospital. Lying in the center of the large bed facing the picture window which looked out over Lake St. Clair was the wizened yet vigorous looking Joe "Gunboats" Verdi.

Flanked by his goons, I stopped at bedside. Verdi, a jowly man with a full head of solid gray hair and dressed in loud red pajamas, smiled at me sardonically. His voice was, totally unexpectedly, weak, wispy, forced. "Ben Perkins?"

"Right, Mr. Verdi."

"The boys said you wanted to talk to me about the old days," Verdi wheezed. I realized that by "boys" Verdi meant Steve Ritchie and Rick Savastano, each of whom was pushing fifty if not past it.

"That's right. I'm wondering about the shooting in Burly Curly's bar back in '39. I told Savastano this is research only, nothing you tell me'll kick back now or ever."

"I should worry about kick-backs?" Verdi squeaked. He patted his bull-like chest. "I've got the Big C, liver. I got maybe a month or two. Nothing that happens now could ever hurt me worse'n I'm about to be hurt." His eyes turned crafty. "But if you're asking me if I ordered the hit on that rat-faced little snitch Porch, I'll be forced with all honesty to say, 'No comment.' "

The last thing I expected to do there was laugh. This was, after all, Gunboats Verdi, Detroit organization boss for fifty years with maybe four times that many murders on his sheet. And though he was dying, he was dying in a place with ten times the luxury of the little room in which Uncle Dan was fighting for his life. But I laughed anyway.

Verdi laughed, too, ending in a sick, rasping cough that turned his lined face purplish-red. He took an empty cup and spit into it, then set the cup down. When he looked back at me, his eyes were cold and dark, the eyes of a dying old man looking at a vigorous younger one. "What do you want to know?" he whispered.

"My uncle was meeting a woman there at the bar," I said. "He was deeply involved with her, but he didn't know much about her. She disappeared right after the shooting. Witnesses have told me that the woman he was meeting seemed to know Porch very well." I paused. "Her first name was Lila. I'm trying to find her. Do you know anything that might help me?"

"Quicksilver," Verdi rasped. He coughed again and repeated the name. "Lila Quicksilver. Porch's fiancée. He brought her to Detroit with him while he waited to testify against me."

Oh boy. I felt my heart pound as I said, "Where'd she go, Mr. Verdi?"

"Chicago," he answered readily. "Still there, in fact." He squinted at my expression and smiled. "How do I know? I kept tabs. I didn't know if she might decide to turn state's evidence the way Porch tried to. And she was an interesting chick. . . . Your uncle has good taste. A lot like me."

I thought, Uncle Dan's like you only in that he's dying, too. It was the first time I'd consciously thought that Uncle Dan was going to die.

Verdi said in what for him was a kindly way, "You're trying to find Lila for your uncle, is that it?"

"That's right."

He waved an imperious hand at one of the goons. "Larry, call Savastano for me. Tell him the notebook in the safe, under the name Lila Quicksilver. Have him call her, give her Mr. Perkins's name, and say he's trying to reach her. Ask her to call him."

"Sure, Mr. Verdi," one of the faceless goons stirred.

Verdi smiled at me. "There. That help you, son?"

One last exercise of power of a dying man. But he could have refused to see me, could have refused to help. I smiled and nodded, "Thanks, Mr. Verdi."

"Maybe," Verdi said with a narrow look, "you'll remember that I did you this service."

"I *will* remember it, Mr. Verdi. Thanks."

Not that he'd be around long enough for it to do him any good.

I met Marybeth in the ICU waiting room just before one the next day. She looked pale and exhausted, and though she held her knitting in her lap, it didn't look as if she'd made any progress since the previous day.

As I sat beside her, she took my hand and said, "He wasn't so good at eleven o'clock. He refused to look at me. Didn't wave, didn't wink, didn't smile."

I breathed deeply. "What'd the doctor say? How's Dan doing?"

"Dr. Bates talked to me. Said Uncle's got serious infections. They're fighting to stabilize him, changing medications."

"Bates? Who's Bates? Didn't you talk to Sims?"

"Sims? But Dr. Bates said he's the attending surgeon now."

I gritted my teeth and said in a low voice loud enough to attract the attention of the other visitors, "Can't a man have a *doctor* of his *own* any more?"

Marybeth shrugged helplessly.

"What about the ventilator?" I asked in a lower tone.

She shook her head. "Doctor said Uncle Dan'll need it at least another week, till he's under control and they've turned the infections around." She gnawed her lip, reached out, and put her hand on mine. "Brace yourself. He's accumulated fluids. He's gained twenty-five pounds in fluids just since yesterday, Ben. He looks just . . . awful."

One o'clock came and we went into Uncle Dan's room. Nothing had changed. Same equipment, same bottles, same tubes, same monitor with its blinking numbers and jagged lines, same ventilator hissing and wheezing, breathing life into Uncle Dan.

The fluid retention was obvious. Uncle Dan looked swollen and shiny, like a newborn baby, skin stretched so tight it looked as if it was about to split. His eyes opened when I spoke to him: "How's things, big fella?"

He stared at me and did not move.

"I'm back again, Uncle Dan," Marybeth smiled as she leaned and kissed him on the cheek.

He looked at us and then raised a hand as far as the cloth restraint would let him and pointed toward the ceiling.

I looked where it pointed. Nothing. "What is it, Uncle? What do you need?"

He lowered his hand, then raised it, pointed his index finger to his temple and dropped his thumb.

I looked away quickly, eyes burning. Marybeth looked at me with frightened eyes and said as cheerfully as she could, "The doctor says you're getting along fine, Uncle Dan. No time at all you'll be out of here. And we'll have a big party for you. Right, Ben?"

We talked like that for the full ten minutes, more to each other than to my uncle, and all the while he pointed to the ceiling again and again and again.

I'd just arrived at my apartment to shower and change clothes when the telephone rang.

"Ben Perkins?" asked the long-distance female voice.

"You got him."

"I'm Lila." Silence. "Lila Quicksilver."

"Oh. Hi." I sat down on the couch, pressing the receiver to my ear. "Glad you called, I—"

"Actually my last name is Brockmann now, I'm married."

"Uh-huh. Okay." Silence. "The, uh—you get told why I wanted to talk to you?"

Her voice was guarded. "Something about the shooting?"

"Really I'm calling about Dan. Dan Perkins. He's my uncle."

This time the silence went on so long I thought she'd hung up. "Dan? How nice. How's he doing?"

"Not so good. But Lila—Ms. Quicksilver—Mrs. Brockmann—let me ask you, you were close to my uncle, right?"

"That was many years ago."

"Forget that! You were real close, I know that. How'd you meet him? What was your connection with Harry Porch?"

"I don't want to talk about that. It's nobody's business. It's past and buried."

Unwillingly, I said, "Fine, tell me or don't tell me, that's not important now. What is important is something that you never knew." I paused. "Dan never got your note. Not till just a few days ago."

A long pause. *"No."*

"It's true. He never got it. He never knew what happened to you. You disappeared and he wondered about you for all these years and *he never knew* and he never forgot about you."

"No," she said definitely. "Even life isn't that cruel."

"Oh, yeah? Well, try this. Right now my uncle is in intensive care at Greater Detroit Metro Hospital. He's strapped down and on a respirator and . . . and he's eighty-seven and alone and drugged and fighting for his life. *Tell* me about cruel, Lila."

"Well, what am I supposed to do about it? All that was my whole life ago. I cared for Dan but he wasn't there when I needed him, and there's nothing I can do for him now!"

"You just do what you want," I said, standing. "But you

should know that you were special to him. And he never got
your note. And if he had, he'd have been there at Burly Curly's
for you. And he never married, Lila, and he never forgot you.
Just do what you want, though. You just do what you damn
well please.''

I slammed the phone down and stomped in several aimless
circuits of my living room. Withholding information from a private detective *just isn't done*, I thought.

Then I went into my kitchen in search of a Stroh's tall boy and
the half-bottle of black Jack I'd been saving.

## 3

### The Forever Trip

The ringing phone brought my eyes open. I focused on the
orange numerals of the bedside clock: one thirty-five A.M. I wres-
tled the receiver to my ear with numb hands. ''Perkins.''

''This is Detroit Metro Hospital,'' came the brisk female voice.
''The doctor has asked me to contact the family of Dan Perkins.
We think you should get here right away.''

''What's wrong?'' I mumbled, raising myself.

She said carefully, ''There's been some cardiac disturbance.
The doctor thought it best that family representatives be present.''

''Okay, all right, I'll be there.'' I hung up the phone, switched
on the nightstand light, picked up the receiver again, and dialed
my brother Bill's number. He answered with a grunt. I said.
''Wake up, bro, there's trouble at the hospital.''

''Oh no.'' He paused. ''You going, Ben?''

''I'm rolling. You?''

Marybeth came on. ''I'll be dressed and on my way in five
minutes, Ben.''

''I'll pick you up.''

''No, it's quicker, I'll meet you there.'' She hung up.

The intensive care unit never closes. The waiting room was
thronged with exhausted people, waiting for word on traffic victims and shooting victims and disease victims; they bore identical
signs of strain mixed with equal measures of hope, fear, and
resignation.

Marybeth, dressed in jeans and a white top, met me at the big
double doors, and we silently pushed through them and went to

the desk. I gave my name to the nurse. "Oh, yes, the Perkins family," she said. "Just step into the office there, the doctor will be right with you."

We went into the closetlike, booklined office. Marybeth took the single chair, I leaned against the door. We said nothing. After a few minutes a short black woman in a white coat that blinked with stethoscope and other hardware came in. "I'm Dr. Johnson," she announced to us generally. "You're the Perkins family?"

"Where's Dr. Bates?" I asked, then repeated with her: "You're the attending physician."

She smiled at us and stepped past Marybeth to seat herself behind the tiny desk. Marybeth asked, "What happened to Uncle Dan?"

She was smooth, practiced, professional. "He had an episode of cardiac arrest. But, happily, we were able to resuscitate him and restore his blood pressure."

For the first time since Uncle Dan had gone into the hospital, my sister-in-law Marybeth let go. Not angrily, but with ultimate despair: "Oh, no. *Why* did you bring him back?"

Dr. Johnson blinked, her composure broken for a moment. "Well, we had to, in order to—"

"He's *dying!*" Marybeth pressed. "He's been dying since he came here. Why, oh *why* didn't you just let him *go?*"

Dr. Johnson sat back and drew herself up. "There are no instructions on file as to the family's wishes in the event of a life-threatening crisis," she said formally.

"You want instructions?" The women looked at me. "*I'll* give you instructions. I don't want my uncle strapped down like a piece of meat any more. I don't want him hooked up to miracle machines and pumped full of drugs and fed through tubes any more. I don't want my uncle reduced to the level of an experiment for ego-tripping doctors. I don't—"

Dr. Johnson cut in sharply, "If we remove medical support, your uncle will die."

"Then so be it." I looked at Marybeth for approval and saw it. "If he can't live without the machines, then he ain't living, and if he understood that, he'd agree with me."

"Very well," Dr. Johnson said, briskly rising. "We'll call you when we're ready."

It took ten minutes, and then we were ushered into Uncle Dan's room and left alone with him there.

Marybeth sat on his left, I sat on his right. She took one of his hands, I sat there and watched him. His eyes were open and dull, his body shrunken, his chest rising and falling in accord with the puffing of the ventilator. I became fixated by the numerals on the monitor that registered his heartbeat. When we came in it was reading in the one hundred thirties.

Long moments went by. A nurse looked in on us. One hundred twelve. I looked at Marybeth. Her face was narrow and pinched and she tried to smile at me and looked back into Uncle Dan's face.

The rate dropped below one hundred.

I stood up and walked around the bed, looking at my uncle from each angle. He was silent, vacant. The machine said sixty-five.

I sat back down. Marybeth looked up at the monitor, then bent and kissed Uncle Dan and whispered something in his ear. Down to forty now.

I tried to say something, thought better of it, then said it anyhow: "I won't forget your stories, Uncle."

"No," Marybeth chimed in. "None of us will." The monitor read into the thirties and, as I watched, dipped to twenty-five. The graph register below showed its jagged peaks much less frequently now, and they weren't as sharp-edged.

Twenty, fifteen, ten, seven, two, zero.

Zero. Zero. Zero.

The graph register made waves like the long swells of a gentle ocean and then went flat.

The ventilator pumped mindlessly on.

Marybeth looked up at me, tears streaming silently, heavily down her thin cheeks. I sighed and wiped my eyes and pressed Uncle Dan's hand one last time. The door to the room opened and Dr. Johnson came in. "Please accept my condolences on the passing of your uncle," she said.

We stood. I said huskily, "Thank you, doctor."

She said, "If you would, I need some information about the arrangements, Mr. Perkins."

I looked at Marybeth. "Would you?"

She nodded, throat bobbing. She walked around the bed and pressed the entire length of her body against me, dampening my shoulder. Then she turned and followed the doctor out of the room.

I looked down at my uncle for a long, long time. Then I stepped out of the room, closed the door, and stood with my back to it in the empty hall.

I thought: No one can touch him any more. I won't let them. I'm the detective, and he's my client, and I fix things and help people and protect them, and I won't let anyone hurt him any more.

Libby said harshly, "I demand an explanation as to *why* my uncle was cremated so quickly."

We sat, the remains of Uncle Dan's family, in the cool, well-furnished silence of the funeral home's parlor: my sister Libby, slimmer than when I'd seen her last a couple of years before, dressed in a white blouse and expensive blue suit; my brother Bill, short, bald, big-shouldered, wearing a tan blazer and tie and dark slacks; and his wife, Marybeth, tall, whip-thin, and elegant in a midnight blue dress with a thin string of pearls around her neck.

Mr. Roski, the baby-faced, pudgy funeral director, adjusted his thick glasses and looked at me. "Those were the instructions we had from Mr. Ben Perkins, Mrs. Gillespie."

Libby shot me a dirty look. I said, "It's what he wanted, Libby."

"Like hell!" she spat. "You had no *right* to make that kind of decision without clearing it with the family, you insensitive ghoul!"

Bill and Marybeth looked uncomfortable, their eyes meeting no one. I said as evenly as I could, "I most certainly knew what he wanted, Libby. I took care of his finances for him for years. I visited him every week. Where the hell were *you* on his birthday and Christmas? Where the hell were *you* when he was dying in the hospital? Who the hell are *you* to swoop in here and start calling people names?"

"I'm his *niece*," she shot back shrilly, "and I *won't* stand by and allow my uncle to—to be *discarded*, like some kind of *refuse*, without a proper funeral!"

Mr. Roski cleared his throat and said carefully, "Of course, our facility stands ready to assist the Perkins family with whatever arrangements you mutually decide to make." He had his eyes on Libby all the while.

She said, ticking fingers as she talked. "We want a *coffin*, and a proper visitation period, and a service in the Baptist church and burial in a nice cemetery. The way it's supposed to be." She looked imperiously at my brother. "What do you say, Bill?"

He sighed, flicked me a look, and nodded to Libby.

"Marybeth?"

Her look my way was regretful, but she had to go along with her husband.

Mr. Roski clapped his hands once and stood. "Then it's decided! Very well. Mrs. Gillespie," he said, taking Libby's arm, "we have a fine selection of coffins and vaults to choose from in the next room. Let me show you . . ."

They left the room, Bill and Marybeth trailing them. I walked out, turned, went through the lobby, and left the building.

As I crossed the parking lot to my car, I looked at the rolling stone-dotted hills of the cemetery and thought, there's no way I'm leaving my uncle in this place.

The visitation at the funeral home the next evening was, thanks to Libby's calls to the newspapers, well-attended. Libby herself held forth in one corner, flanked by Bill and Marybeth and surrounded by old people who knew Dan somewhere or another. I sat alone in the opposite corner, my eyes on the closed bronze coffin which sat on the altar-like stand amid an array of floral arrangements.

Toward the end of the visitation, as the crowd started to thin, I became aware of a woman standing near me. Late sixties, wisp-thin, heavy gray-streaked dark hair cropped close. "Mr. Perkins?" she asked.

She wasn't familiar. "Yes."

Her blue eyes were large in her thin face. She stepped closer to me, looking at me intently. "Mr. *Ben* Perkins?"

"Yes," I said with some impatience. Probably some mortuary ghoul or professional mourner or something.

Her smile made her look younger. "You do look a little like him. He was just about your age when I knew him." She caught my look and added, flustered, "Oh! Excuse me! I'm Lila. Lila Quicksilver."

"Well, jeez." I stood clumsily and shook her thin, firm hand. "You made it, huh? Well, that's something."

"I thought about it," she answered, looking away from me. "It must have been a lot of trouble for you to track me down. And Dan and I were—we were very close." She looked back at me. "And you said he never got my note."

"Never did."

She shook her head. "Such a shame. How different our lives would have been, if. If, if, if."

"Yeah." She took the chair next to me and we sat and looked at the coffin. "So, tell me. How did it happen? Who was Henry Porch? How did you get to know Uncle Dan?"

She sighed. "Henry and I were engaged. Living in Chicago.

He decided to turn state's evidence in an investigation of Joe Verdi. The FBI brought us to Detroit incognito to wait for Henry to testify. We thought the trial would start quickly. But it didn't. We waited and waited. Days. Weeks. Months. Hiding.''

"How'd you meet Dan?"

"I'm getting to that." She paused. "I was afraid. Afraid, and bored. I hadn't known the depth of Henry's involvement with the mob till then. I was afraid of what those men would do to him if they caught him. And I was bored, cooped up in that grimy little motel room day after day. So I began to go out, alone."

"To Burly Curly's."

"Yes. I met Dan there." Her voice softened and I felt her eyes on me. "He was a fine man. Much older than me, of course. But so handsome and dashing, a real wicked twinkle in his eye, yet decent and gentle, too. I became infatuated with him, Mr. Perkins."

"Did you tell him about Porch and the investigation?"

"Of course not! I never even told Dan my last name. I was afraid. And ashamed. I began to think about Dan, about leaving Henry and going to Dan, where I'd be safe."

I closed my eyes and sighed. "So what happened?"

"One day Henry got a phone call. I don't know what was said, but it terrified him. I was convinced that Verdi's people had tracked Henry down and were going to kill him. I dashed off a note to Dan and mailed it, asking him to meet me that evening at Burly Curly's. I was going to tell him the whole story and ask him to take me away. I went to the bar and waited, but Dan never came. Instead, Henry showed up. He'd gotten word of where I went, somehow. As he came in the door, two men with shotguns followed him and shot him."

She touched my arm, and I felt her hand tremble. After a moment she went on, "I . . . I went a little hysterical, I think. But I got out of there and made it to the bus station and grabbed the first bus west. All the way back to Chicago. And I've been there ever since and lived a quiet life and thought all that trouble was behind me." Her voice deepened. "Till the other day, when that horrible man from Verdi's organization called."

"I'm glad you came," I said.

"Just wish I'd come in time to see him."

We stared silently at the coffin a long time. It was late, everyone else had gone, leaving us alone in the room. She said suddenly,

"One thing I know for sure. Dan wouldn't have wanted—" she gestured around the room—"all *this*."

"You're right." I roused myself and stretched and looked at her. "I got some thoughts on that. Want to help?"

"How?"

I told her.

She looked back at the coffin and then at me, eyes misty. "I'm with you," she whispered. "But I want to be in it all the way, Ben."

I snorted. "Come on! It's gonna be dangerous."

She smiled wickedly. "I may look sixty-eight, but I'm as young as you, maybe younger. And I want to do this for Dan."

I shrugged. "Okay." I glanced around, the room was still empty. "Now's as good a time as any. Ready?"

She stood, went to the door of the visitation room, peered out, then nodded to me.

I walked up to the coffin, hoping it was unlocked.

It was.


People drifted across the grass away from the gravesite, hunched in their jackets against the cool, sundrenched breeze. Lila and I were halfway to my car when Libby caught up with us. She certainly was dressed for the role of chief mourner in a black dress, black stockings, black shoes, and a black hat equipped with a veil, for heaven's sake. Ignoring Lila, Libby took my arm.

"I'm sure glad that's all over," she sighed. "These things are so hard on a person, don't you think?"

"True enough."

She swept the veil back from her face. "But don't you agree with me now, Ben? This is the right way, the *proper* way to see to things."

"Anyway, you got it done."

"Listen," she said eagerly. "I'm having everyone over to the house for an early supper. It's important that the *family*—" she gave Lila a meaningful look—"hang together in times like this, don't you think?"

I felt sick. "Thanks anyhow. We've got business." Taking Lila's arm, I turned my back on Libby and made for my car.


The second seat—which I generally used for cargo, never for a passenger—of my modified Maxair Hummer sits directly behind the pilot's seat. I helped Lila into it and strapped her in. She sat nervously, looking tiny in slacks and a warm wool jacket, but she nodded at me with a defiant smile.

I completed the pre-flight inspection of the aircraft by checking the translucent plastic gas tank one last time. Full. Dropping into the bucket seat, I tucked my leather jacket tight around me—despite the full sunlight, it was a chilly day—positioned my feet on the rudder bar, primed the engine with a couple of squeezes of the pressure bulb, set the choke, cracked the throttle, and after yelling "clear!" (even though there was nobody but Lila in sight), I gave the T-handle a good jerk. The 250cc Zenoah engine engaged, barfed, blatted, and caught into a good healthy purr from its mounting ten feet behind us. Killing the choke, I set the throttle at about two thousand rpm and sat back to let her warm up.

It was midday, midweek. There were no golfers using the Norwegian Wood course. Wind was steady at twelve knots out of the southwest—a bit stronger than I'd have preferred, but this wasn't exactly a pleasure flight we were embarking on.

Everything was set. "Here we go!" I hollered over my shoulder. I goosed the throttle and the Hummer began to roll. I swung her around toward the southwest, edged the throttle up a little more, and pressed the stick forward to raise the tail. We passed high taxi, I gave her more gas, the aircraft rolled faster and swayed, the wind began to sing in the flying wires, and just as we reached the eighth green, we left the ground. I did the pattern, tested the wind, checked the trim of the ship, then made a sweeping turn and, gaining altitude all the while, headed almost due west toward Stapfer Lake.

"This is wonderful!" came Lila's reedy voice amid the rush of the wind. Your first time in an ultralight does that to you. You're sitting out in the open, no cockpit, nothing above you but wings and nothing below you but a couple of aluminum frame members and, way, way down, the ground.

We were at a thousand feet by the time we got to the lake. It wandered around jerkily in a wide blue bowl, marred here and there by whitecaps, circled by dense woods. I circled the lake and then, applying maximum stick and throttle, took her up close to five thousand.

The wind was calmer there. The lake looked smaller. Roughly in the center was the small wooded island that Uncle Dan owned. I could see, amid the scrub and trees, the charred ruins of his old cabin, torched a few years ago by a maniac who was trying to kill me and got someone else instead. I put the aircraft on a steady trimmed course traversing the lake, gripped the stick between my knees, reached to the down-tube and unstrapped the medium-sized aluminum canister from it.

The screw-top was hard to get loose but I finally spun it off and tossed it. I reached around the seat and put the canister into Lila's waiting hands. I sideslipped for a moment to correct my course and then, when dead center over the lake, I said, "All right."

Lila leaned down, tipped the canister, and let the ashes stream out.

They fell in a solid gray funnel. Caught by the windstream, they fanned out wider and wider in a descending, ever-lightening V. When the canister was empty, Lila tossed it over the starboard side. I poured power to the Hummer engine, climbed steeply, then leveled, and we looked down silently.

Caught by the lower wind currents and illuminated by the sun, the ashes fell toward the blue water in a just-visible, glinting veil, then disappeared.

I sat up in the bucket seat. Couldn't do France for you, Uncle, but this is the next best thing.

I kicked the wings over, set the throttle a notch higher to maintain lift in the tail wind, and headed for home.

After a moment Lila leaned forward and said, over the engine and wind noise, "You know what Dan called it?"

"What?"

"Death."

"No. I don't remember him ever mentioning it."

"He hated euphemisms like 'everlasting life' and 'eternal rest' and 'the big sleep' and things like that. Said they made assumptions."

"Sounds like him. So what *did* he call it?"

"The forever trip."

# ABOUT THE AUTHORS

MARTIN H. GREENBERG has compiled over two hundred anthologies, including six in Ivy's series of the hottest contemporary crime stories. He is a noted scholar and teaches at the University of Wisconsin in Green Bay.

LOREN D. ESTLEMAN is a veteran police-court journalist and a native Detroiter who now lives in Whitmore Lake, Michigan. He is the author of the popular Amos Walker mysteries, all of which are now published in paperback by Fawcett Crest. SUGARTOWN, the fifth novel in the series, won the Shamus Award given by the Private Eye Writers of America for Best Private Eye Novel of the Year.